Devious Kingpin

KINGPINS OF THE SYNDICATE SERIES COLLECTION

EVA WINNERS

Contents

Kingpins of The Syndicate
Series Collection

Each book in the series can be read alone.

While the book "Corrupted Pleasure" is not officially part of the series, it does have events that lead to the first book in the series.

There are a total of four books planned in this series.
Villainous Kingpin - Basilio
Devious Kingpin - Dante
Ravenous Kingpin - Emory
Scandalous Kingpin - Priest

Furthermore, please note that this book has some dark elements to it and disturbing scenes. Please proceed with caution. It is not for the faint of heart.

Don't forget to sign up to Eva Winners' Newsletter (www.evawinners.com) for news about future releases.

Find Eva Here

Visit www.evawinners.com and subscribe to my newsletter.
FB group: https://bit.ly/3gHEe0e
FB page: https://bit.ly/30DzP8Q
Insta: http://Instagram.com/evawinners
BookBub: https://www.bookbub.com/authors/eva-winners
Amazon: http://amazon.com/author/evawinners
Goodreads: http://goodreads.com/evawinners
Tiktok: https://vm.tiktok.com/ZMeETK7pq/

Playlist

https://spoti.fi/3KpLxL7

Triggers

This e-book contains disturbing scenes and adult language. It may be offensive to some readers and touches on darker themes.

Please proceed with awareness.

Blurb

Dante DiLustro.
Persistent. Stubborn. Deadly.
The devil.
Juliette Brennan.
Tenacious. Beautiful. Formidable.
The minx.
She never expected his persistence, nor the way her body warmed each time the devil came around, which only made her fight the attraction that much harder.
She had vengeance to deliver and now there was blood on her hands. She had her secrets and she intended to keep them. Let the world think she was crazy, out of control. It made her real sins easy to hide.
One visit to Las Vegas sent it all spiraling. There was a reason Dante was considered the Devious Kingpin.
But one thing was certain. This Juliette didn't need a Romeo and she certainly wasn't a damsel in distress.

Prologue

JULIETTE

"'T was the night before Christmas," I rhymed as I swung my bag, back and forth, "when all through the house, not a creature was stirring, not even a mouse."

The words of the poem kept repeating in my head, over and over again.

Christmas was my favorite time of the year. Usually it was about the only time that we resembled a family. I had two bags of gifts, Killian trailing alongside me while handling something on the phone. He was in his first year of college, and suddenly he was very important. At least he thought so.

I rolled my eyes; he was more annoying than anything. At the tender age of thirteen, I thought myself to be the most important girl in the world. After all, I'd be going to high school soon.

"Wait here, Jules," he ordered, stopping in front of Tiffany's.

"Are you buying a gift from Tiffany's for Wynter and me?" I squealed excitedly.

"Stay here," he ordered. In typical brotherly fashion, he ignored me and entered the store. Curious and a bit nosy, I pressed my face against the cold glass, but couldn't see anything apart from Killian's broad shoulders.

The cold wind swept through, sending a chill through my bones.

Winters in New York were frigid. I couldn't wait until Killian, Dad, and I flew back to California.

Warm weather. Palm trees. That was heaven.

Glancing around, I took cover in the alley where I hoped the wind wouldn't whip against my legs as badly. I felt the chill even through my jeans and heavy coat. It was just impossible to warm up, so I started jumping up and down, my ponytail whipping back and forth.

"Hurry up. Hurry up," I muttered impatiently, my teeth chattering.

A kicked can echoed through the alley, startling me. Another kick and I mustered up the courage to turn around, only to come face-to-face with a man. A stranger. His features were obscured by a hoodie but his hands weren't. Glinting in the light of the streetlamp, I could see he was holding a knife.

"What are you doing, little girl?" he drawled in a thick New York accent.

"N-nothing," I stuttered, my eyes darting over his shoulder to the storefront where I should have been waiting for Killian.

He took a step forward, and I instinctively took one back. Except now, it put me even deeper into the dark alley. I knew I'd made a mistake. My little heart pounded against my chest, threatening to crack it open.

Another step toward me. Another mirrored step backward.

My heart continued to drum under my rib cage, but still I tried to be brave. Smart. That was what Dad always said. Be smart. So I attempted to scare him off. "M-my brother's with me."

He chuckled. "Then I'll slice his throat too."

My eyes widened, then darted around in horror. I opened my mouth, readying to scream when another voice interrupted.

"Take another step toward her, and I'll shoot you."

My eyes snapped in the direction of the voice. A tall boy stood there, about Killian's age. Tall. Strong. He flicked a gaze my way before returning his attention to the man with the knife.

"Last warning," he said. "Get lost or I will end you."

"I know you," the old man hissed.

"No, you don't know me," the boy-slash-man with eyes as dark as midnight claimed. "If you did, you'd be running for your life."

The man must have decided to live and that I wasn't worth it, because he scurried away. No, he bolted. I watched him disappear while I held my breath, and it wasn't until he was out of my sight that I was able to release it.

"You okay?" the boy asked softly.

I swallowed, extending my hand with the bags. "H-here, you can take it all," I offered. I felt disoriented, worried that maybe this boy saved me from the other thug, only to rob me himself. It wasn't worth dying over. It would seem shopping right before Christmas was a bad idea, after all.

He smiled, pushing the bags gently back. "You keep the bags."

My eyes darted between him and the bags. "You... you don't want them?"

He chuckled. "What am I going to do with Victoria's Secret bags?" he mused as the smell of rain and damp forest mixed with the crispy winter air and filled my senses.

My cheeks heated when I realized what I was holding in my hands.

"It's for my aunt." Wynter and I wanted her to find someone, and this could be the first step. At least, that was what *Cosmopolitan* magazine had told us. "I'm buying for my dad next, but I have money," I mumbled, embarrassed. "I don't have anything else to give you." I drowned in his dark gaze. I had never seen such dark eyes. They were like obsidian pools of night.

"What makes you think I want something?" he asked curiously.

"Don't all muggers want something?" I retorted.

He smiled, his eyes shining with amusement. They reminded me of the dark nights and beautiful nightmares.

"All right, then," he agreed, amusement sparking his gaze. "How about..." He appeared to think as I held my breath. What could he possibly want? "Your hair scrunchie."

I reached up to touch my ponytail. "My scrunchie?" I repeated, confused.

He grinned this time. "Yes. That way when I find you again and you're older, you'll remember that you owe me."

"And if I don't recognize you?" I wondered.

He smirked confidently. "Don't worry, I'll recognize you."

This time, I smiled too. "So you'll be like my shadow prince, stalker, or something?"

He nodded. "Or something," he confirmed.

I pulled my hair band out, my mahogany strands cascading down my shoulders. He extended his hand and I dropped my hot-pink scrunchie into it, the bright color looking silly in his large palm.

"Thank you," I murmured, offering him a big smile. "For saving me. One day, maybe I'll be the one to save you."

I wanted to return the favor and Dad taught me never to leave a debt unpaid. As he walked away, sadness lingered in my chest when I realized I had no way of knowing whether I'd ever see him again. I could only hold out hope.

CHAPTER 1
Dante

EIGHT YEARS LATER

Royally Lucky Casino.

My brother, Christian, and I came up with the name. It should have been Royally Fucked-Up, but that name wouldn't have attracted the crowds.

While the buzz of the casino was lively out there, here in my office, you couldn't hear a thing. It was convenient for my *business* transactions, and for my sanity. I liked my quiet.

"Please, *please*, it's a misunderstanding." The words filling the room were desperate, the actions of the man speaking them even more so.

Locking eyes with my brother, I raised my drink and we clinked our glasses. "To last rites," I announced.

My casino manager winced at my words. I didn't need to look his way to know he had turned deathly pale. The fucking guy broke our two main rules. *Never lie to us. And never fucking steal from us.*

Both Priest—the nickname my brother had earned—and I downed our drinks in a single swig, then turned our attention to the pathetic man sitting in the chair and shaking from fear.

"Dante..." He swallowed hard, his Adam's apple bobbing in his throat. "Please." My name in his mouth pissed me off. It made me want to shove a whole apple down his throat. Begging wouldn't do him any good. You forgave once, more would get the idea they could do the same shit. Not happening.

I shot a bored glance at my brother. "Do we like begging?"

Priest snickered. "Only from women."

The corner of my lip twitched. Priest fucking loved to be begged. I'd give my life for the guy, but some of his tastes were a tad bit dark. Some might even say *too* dark, even for me.

"Right you are, brother," I agreed. I returned my attention to the fucker just in time to see a bead of sweat roll down his temple.

"I didn't mean to take it," he whined, his chin wobbling.

"Oh, my bad. It just dropped into your bank account, then," I offered calmly. Fucking idiot. "Or better yet, someone set you up?"

He nodded his head so fast, he was bound to get whiplash. Not that it could make him any dumber. It took a real level of stupidity to steal from a DiLustro.

"Don't waste my time," I hissed, a tinge of anger seeping through my cool façade. "You're in enough shit as it is."

He lifted his chin. "I had to do it," he whined. "It was either that or get shipped off to Siberia."

My brows furrowed. Priest must have been confused as well because he said, "I didn't know you were Russian." The fucker reeked of desperation and piss.

"I'm not," he huffed, sweat glistening on his forehead. "I owe a debt to a Russian."

I had to admit his explanation was unexpected. Priest threw me a curious glance, then shrugged his shoulders. It was his "I don't give a shit" expression and he was right. Neither of us gave a shit who this man owed a debt to. He stole from us, so right now, he owed us and that was more important than his fuckup with the Russians.

I set my glass on the table. "Russians are the least of your worries." Locking eyes with him, I added, "Either you pay up the money you stole or you pay another way."

I didn't bother to elaborate. He knew what that meant. My brother and I had pushed the competition out of Chicago, some of it out of Philly, and worked with our cousin Basilio to expand his territory in New York. Our reputation spoke for itself.

And fuck if I would ruin our reputation for anyone, least of all some sleazebag who got involved with the Russians. Did a hundred grand make a difference to our empire? Not really. But would we forgive it?

Fuck no.

My casino manager knew exactly what was coming. His knee started bouncing as though soothing a screaming baby. Panic-stricken terror entered his expression.

"I'll never do it again," he claimed. "Give me a month and I'll pay it back."

Empty promises. If he didn't have a hundred grand today, he wouldn't have it in a month. Even more empty promises followed, but they fell on deaf ears. Priest and I knew better than that.

A beep sounded through the intercom of my office, followed by a muffled, "Mr. DiLustro."

It was my floor manager. "Sorry to bother you, but we might have a problem at one of the tables."

Mildly interested since that rarely ever happened. Curiosity piquing, I decided to answer. "High stakes?"

"No, the lower-stakes tables," he explained. "But she's winning each hand and shows no visible signs of cheating. The girl must be counting cards."

"First floor?"

"Yes."

I rose from my chair, ignoring the incessant begging from my casino manager.

"We'll be right there," I told him, then flickered a bored glance to one of my men. "Take him downstairs and handle him."

They'd teach him a lesson but wouldn't kill him. He was lucky, because I probably would have. Lucky bastard.

My brother stood up. "I'm coming with you. A card-counting girl sounds like a more interesting time than this."

Pulling out my phone, we made our way out of my office and through the hallways that would take us to the first floor. The moment we entered the gaming floor, whispers rippled amongst the patrons.

Despite our reputation, we did a good job of blending in. The people of Chicago knew who we were, but we still managed to lure them in with our eloquence and civility. When we wanted to show it. It was the reason women were always throwing themselves at our feet. Priest and I moved as one, ignoring all the glances thrown our way. I didn't need any more shit today or I'd lose my cool. There was commotion to our left, but my eyes were locked on the table swarming with people.

Gamblers were always attracted to the table that had large winnings. It was a firm tell. More whispers. The sound of a pair of heels ringing out above the chatter.

I spotted her the next second.

The very same girl I'd seen dancing on a bartop last month in New York City was strutting in our direction. She wore an orange minidress then, but tonight, she opted for a midnight-blue dress that hugged her soft curves just right, barely covering her ass.

More than a few men gawked at her, and I had to bite back the words that would tell everyone off. A growl vibrated in my chest but I ignored it, keeping my eyes on the woman.

Mine.

It was the damnedest thing. I wanted to pound my chest like a fucking moron, grab her by the hair, and drag her to my bed. The notion was ridiculous, yet I couldn't shake it off.

Who is she? I wondered.

She wasn't looking at me, but I got the distinct feeling she was coming for me. She moved with confidence, a slight stubborn tilt to her chin telling me she was accustomed to getting what she wanted.

My gaze traveled over the length of her body. Her skin was pale and in stark contrast to her dark shoulder-length hair. She stiffened slightly as if aware of my gaze and kept walking, her strappy heels clicking against the marble. She was just about to pass me when her ankle wobbled and she tripped.

My hand instinctively reached out to steady her. Her long hair brushed against my sleeve and the scent of sugarplums invaded my lungs. *Sugarplums.* I had never met a woman that smelled so fucking good that my mouth actually watered.

Her face was pressed against my chest. It was barely a second, yet it felt like eternity. She felt so fucking right in my arms that it sent a shudder rolling down my spine.

Straightening up, she lifted her face to mine, flushed cheeks and all, then a pair of bright-blue eyes slammed into my fucking chest. The impact was so forceful, it stole my breath away.

They called me the devil, but it was an angel who was the thief.

CHAPTER 2
Juliette

The moment I watched him enter the first floor of the casino, the air shifted. When I spotted him and his blond brother, I gaped with wide eyes. Holy mother of God. There should never be two specimens who looked like that on the same planet, never mind the same room.

They strode through the room like they owned it and everyone in it. The one with dark hair and eyes, the colors of the darkest night, aside from the resemblance to the DiLustros, told me we didn't want him or his blond brother anywhere near the table Wynter was currently sitting at. They moved as one, like two panthers going in for their prey.

Acting on instinct, I rushed toward the two men who gave the impression they'd no doubt killed their fair share of men. I couldn't let them get close to Wynter. It'd be all our heads on the block if they got to her.

So, with a confidence I didn't possess and armed in the dress that revealed more skin than I liked, I rushed in their general direction. The midnight-blue dress hugged my curves just right, and belonged to someone with a much flatter ass. As I got closer to the dark and blond devils, I fought the urge to tug on the hemline.

I kept my eyes on a fictional dot, keeping their movements in my peripheral vision. The moment his dark gaze brushed over my skin, a shiver ran up my spine and my heel caught a crack in the marble, launching me into the air.

I, honest to God, almost face-planted when a pair of strong hands wrapped around me. Instead of the marble floor, my face hit a hard chest. The scent of forest and rain hit my nostrils and for a second my eyes fluttered shut. It reminded me of something, but the memory eluded my grasp.

Then as if burned, I shifted away, almost falling—again—on my ass, before his hand shot out, steadying me by my elbow.

Gosh, this was going gracefully.

"You alright?" he drawled, that obsidian gaze on me. My cheeks burned. It felt like a searing fever boiling me from the inside. Jesus, I hated blushing. Detested it. I took a deep breath, then slowly exhaled. His lips curled into an arrogant smile, probably used to women swooning over him.

I narrowed my gaze at him in distaste. It was at that very moment, I decided. I didn't like him. I didn't like the dark presence that came with him. I didn't like how he watched me as if I were a speck of dirt on his shoe.

"Obviously, I'm fine," I answered, mustering a sweet, seductive smile. I trailed my hand over his chest and felt his heat burning through the material. The man had to be a furnace. "But you won't be, if you don't get that smug smile off your face."

A stifled chuckle came from his blond brother. I shot him a glare, but he quickly raised his hands, ready to retreat. I couldn't let that happen, though, so I blurted out the first thing that came to my mind.

"I'll have sex with both of you. Why don't the three of us take this party... elsewhere?" What the hell did I just say? That was the last thing I'd ever want to do. Just the idea of having sex with either of them had bile rising in my throat. It was a wonder that I kept my own eyes from rolling in my head.

The air stilled then, immediately charged with so much sexual tension, it vibrated through me. It felt like electric shocks running through my veins, buzzing every cell within my body and somehow turning me on.

I know, masochistic. I never thought getting electrocuted would be a turn-on, but here I was.

I waited for a response, any comment, but both men remained staring at me. One pair darker than night and the other lighter than the skies. These two were like night and day. Literally.

"What's the matter?" I purred with a self-confidence I didn't feel, my finger trailing his tie. I must be a glutton for punishment. "Cat got your tongue?"

If only I knew how badly those damn words would haunt me.

My eyes darted between the two men. They *were* both extremely handsome. If I ever felt the need to have a threesome, as unlikely as that would be, physically they seemed the most suitable to have one with.

"You're trouble," the blond one said, his voice slightly annoyed. The fact he labeled me exactly what I detested made him lose some of his appeal. I was misunderstood. Yes, sometimes I tended to get in trouble, but usually it was due to circumstances.

Like now.

Instead of opting to remain quiet, I decided to open my mouth further.

"You mean to tell me you've never had a threesome?" I drawled mockingly, desperate to keep the conversation going and Wynter out of harm's way.

Panic slithered through my veins, mocking me. I immediately locked it away. I didn't need any distractions right now, not with danger so close to the horizon.

The mockingjay's whistle—from *The Hunger Games*—traveled through the air. It was our signal. The dark devil's eyes flickered above my head, and again, I acted on instinct. Raising my palm, I pressed it against his chest—his heartbeat wild and strong—and something flickered across his face.

Time stilled as our eyes locked. His fingers, still holding my elbow, burned on my skin. I had to remind myself I was buying Wynter and my friends time.

"Don't worry, I'm skilled enough in threesomes not to embarrass you," I said, making a further idiot of myself. "All you would have to do is follow my lead."

I smoothed my palms against his hard, muscular chest. My hands trembled and I hated myself for how he affected me.

The blond devil studied us with an amused expression, but something about the way his lips twisted into a sardonic smile didn't sit well with me.

"Can you handle double penetration?" the blond guy asked.

Jesus fucking Christ. DP. Did he really just ask me that?

I needed to clear out of here. Maybe I should punch him in the balls and take off? Did Wynter get her chips yet? She'd better hurry up because I was running out of dumb things to say here.

Double penetration was out of the question. I didn't enjoy *single* penetration. This was like jumping into the ocean and not knowing how to swim.

"What's your name?" the dark devil demanded to know.

A loud whistle traveled through the casino. The next second, alarms pierced the air and both of their attention shifted away from me.

"DP this, you dipshit," I hissed.

In one swift move, I kneed the dark devil where it hurt the most.

In his nuts.

I took off, the scent of lavender oil filling the room. It meant Davina had dumped her scented oil. I didn't even bother glancing behind me, focused on getting the fuck out of there. Those devils suggested DP. That put a whole different kind of urgency to my steps.

I might have been the one to instigate this whole conversation, but it didn't matter. I was not in the business of getting caught up in situations that made me vulnerable.

This Juliette wasn't looking for her Romeo.

CHAPTER 3
Dante

It was still dark in the early morning hours. I was meeting Alessio Russo, the gun dealer from Montréal, in the middle of Lake Ontario. It was cold as fuck, the middle of November already drawing snow and below-freezing temperatures. It was our monthly gun shipment I smuggled through Canada. I regularly bought guns off Illias Konstantin, the Russian Pakhan, and Alessio Russo, this Canadian guy. I sold them all to a cartel as well as different organizations in the Middle East. Business was good.

I watched the rays of the sun flicker across the surface of the lake and my thoughts drifted to the dark-haired wildling that kicked me in the balls nearly six months ago. They still ached, but for a totally different reason.

I couldn't even get it up anymore without thinking about her. Talk about a pitiful case. Maybe I'd been fucked up all along. Or maybe that cursed DiLustro gene had kicked in and spread through me like wildfire, honing in on one woman. It never boded well—not for my crazy uncle, not for my father, and certainly not my cousin Basilio, who hunted for his princess like his life depended on it.

I should do the same for the woman that refused to leave my mind. She'd buried herself into my brain cells and my bone marrow, refusing to leave. Obsession was the curse of the DiLustros.

It was the reason for my father's blindness to what my mother had put my brother and me through growing up. He'd been too wrapped up in his work and the woman he lost—a woman my mother never let us forget.

A breeze swept through and a shudder rolled down my spine. It had nothing to do with the cold.

You're just like him. Lying, cheating sinner.

I could almost hear my mother's voice howling along with the wind that traveled through the upper deck of my yacht.

Crack.

The vivid memory of her whip slicing through the air almost brought me to my knees. It was so fucking hard to escape those ghosts. That dark room. Her sick way of torturing us... especially my little brother.

Alessio's yacht pulled up next to mine and I pushed the memories aside, I focused on the task at hand. Gun smuggling. Our crew piled into my yacht and we made our way over, the spray from the lake hitting my jacket and clearing my head.

A plank was dropped to allow me to step onto his yacht. "DiLustro," Alessio greeted me curtly.

I handed him the suitcase full of money. He took it and passed it on to his right-hand man. Ricardo.

"Next time, I'd rather we do an electronic transfer," I retorted dryly. "Make yourself an offshore account, old man."

I couldn't understand these old fuckers always insisting on cash. They had to keep up with the times. Wire transfers. Bitcoin. Anything was better than moving with so much cash. Yes, I owned a casino and could pull it from there on a moment's notice, but it was a risky move traveling with so much cash.

He tilted his chin toward the steps that led below deck. It would seem his man wouldn't be carrying the cargo himself tonight.

"There won't be a next time," Alessio stated coldly. "Have your guys get the guns off my ship."

I nodded once to my men behind me and they got to work loading the merchandise onto my own boat, walking back and forth across the plank. It made it easier to cross from his boat to mine and vice versa.

"What do you mean there won't be a next time?" I questioned.

15

He and Ricardo shared a look, then he answered, "It means I'm getting out. Or do you need further clarification?"

Smart-ass fucker. "Goddamn it," I spat out. "You tell me only now that you're fucking bailing?"

The shipment he just delivered would fulfill only one month's worth of orders.

"Didn't know." The tone of his voice stated he didn't care either. "Shouldn't make commitments before having a product in hand."

What. A. Fucking. Ass. There was always a fucking wiseass to deal with.

I could shoot him, but that probably wouldn't go over well. Receiving word the guns were secure, I made my way back to my yacht, flipping him the bird as we took off into the night.

I could see the outline of his head tip back as he laughed, the grim fucker actually managing to look happy. For the first time in maybe ever.

CHAPTER 4
Juliette

I studied the file of my parents.

Aiden and Ava Cullen.

The names should be close to my heart, but they weren't. I'd never known them. I didn't remember them. But my brother did.

I had found two birth certificates in my father's desk months back—Killian's and mine. The only problem was that it listed our parents as "Aiden and Ava Cullen." I'd held on to that secret for as long as I could, letting it fester inside me. It wasn't until the girls and I got caught stealing from Priest DiLustro in Philly that I admitted to my father what I had learned. Killian had known it all along. He'd been older when Liam-slash-Dad adopted us and apparently could be trusted with the information, knowing he'd done it to protect us.

Killian and I sat in the library of Dad's—Liam's—home now. It was just the two of us. The flames danced in the fireplace. The scent of pine, pumpkin pie, and sugarplums drifted through the air. A soft song played somewhere in the distance. None of it registered.

Just the beating of my heart and the pain in my brother's eyes.

"Were they like us?" I questioned, shooting a glance at Killian. He'd given me a rundown on everything he remembered and all the facts he had. "Like Dad?" Then, remembering he probably didn't think of Liam as our dad in the same way I did, I corrected, "Like Liam?"

Killian shrugged. "More or less."

I raised my eyebrows. That didn't tell me much. "Don't be stingy with information," I complained.

Killian tilted his head, studying me. I never could tell whether he saw too much or not enough. We both had blue eyes and dark hair, but in terms of personalities, we couldn't be more different. I was rash, he was calculating. I had a temper, he didn't.

"Our father—birth father—was a hitman for the Brennans," he said, his voice cold. "Liam and Dad were best friends, and spent a lot of time together. Mom was—" He paused, searching for the right word. Or maybe he got choked up. Killian was way too good at hiding his emotions. Another thing the two of us didn't have in common, but I was getting better at it. "She was gentle. She had no connection to the mafia. Seeing the brutality of it was hard for her."

I swallowed, a lump in my throat growing. It wasn't because I was mourning what I never knew. It was because I heard pain in my brother's voice.

My hand reached for his and I squeezed it, offering comfort.

"You remember that night, don't you?" I whispered.

Killian nodded, a dark expression passing through his eyes. "I do. And I'm working through my list of accomplices. I'll make every one of them pay, Jules."

There was no sense in scolding him about it or telling him we should take a higher road. Be safe. Fuck taking a higher road and fuck being safe. The bastards who hurt our parents should pay. They'd scarred Killian.

"Can Dad... Liam... help us?" Liam Brennan was the head of the Brennan Irish mafia. He saved both my brother and me, and raised us as his own.

My brother's eyes met mine. "I have a list of names. Behind them all is one person." I held my breath, waiting. "Sofia Volkov."

That night, running through that list of names in my head, I went to my self-defense class with an additional purpose.

CHAPTER 5
Dante

I sat in my office at Royally Lucky Casino.

It had been a few months since I met with Alessio Russo. Life moved on. I found new gun suppliers. Alessio, on the other hand, fucked up. Because now he needed a favor, and I was paying him back with the same courtesy.

What could I say? What goes around comes around.

"It was stupid to get on Alessio's bad side," Byron Ashford stated matter-of-factly. I let the grating voice roll off my back. As if I gave two fucks about it. "You want to make alliances, not enemies, Dante."

He was lucky it was just the two of us in the office and he could get away with talking to me this way. Byron Ashford, a cousin on my father's side, strolled through the door like he didn't have a care in the world and sat on my office couch with an arm resting across the back.

I shrugged, glancing toward him. "He's the one who put an end to our business arrangement, not me. I had to jump through fucking hoops to find a replacement on such short notice."

"He got out because of his woman." He rubbed a hand across his smile, studying me. He was probably searching for my weaknesses. There were so fucking many, but I'd gotten good at hiding them. "Don't you have a woman you want to impress?"

"His woman is not my problem," I deadpanned. Autumn Corbin, Alessio's woman who apparently wanted to save the world, got stuck in Afghanistan in search of a story. Alessio was desperate to find a way into the country so he could save her. Not. My. Problem. "And my woman is none of your business."

I tried to forget the girl with blue eyes and dark mahogany hair. I really fucking did. But it was impossible. Physically, it was fucking impossible. That girl had somehow grafted herself in my bones. Whether she was an obsession of my heart, my soul, or a physical addiction, it didn't matter. There was no moving on.

She was in my dreams and part of my thoughts, every waking moment. Fuck, I couldn't see a woman with dark hair without thinking about her. And her eyes... Jesus H. Christ.

Was this even healthy?

Fuck no. It required a special kind of therapist to cure this obsession. Maybe electric shock or some shit like that.

I shook my head, knowing full well there was no point. It was the curse of the DiLustro gene.

Basilio, my cousin, hunted for the identity of his mysterious blonde princess. I searched for my girl with beautiful eyes, the color of the Ionian Sea. There was something calming about her that spoke to a fundamental part of me, despite all the turmoil that happened over the last few months.

I knew I wouldn't be able to move on. I was fairly certain my cousins and my brother knew it too.

I hadn't seen her since that night in the casino. I didn't know her name, but I'd recognized the girl I saved eight years ago in the alley. The girl that gave me her pink scrunchie. Same eyes—the color of the Ionian Sea. Same auburn hair. Whoever would have thought that girl would end up kicking me in the balls eight years later?

If I remembered correctly, she'd promised to save me, not kick me in the balls. Or it might have been exactly that which had me falling for her.

I returned my attention to my cousin. Byron's connection to the family was layered in politics. His mother was my and Basilio's aunt, who'd been conveniently married off to none other than Senator Ashford, the very connected—and corrupt—affiliate of the Syndicate. Basilio's father saw the opportunity and married her off for his benefit. He had no qualms selling anyone off for his own gain. Even his children. However, there was no denying that this was one of the Syndicate's more lucrative partnerships as it gave the senator access to some much-needed funds while giving us access to the senator and holding political clout over him.

Win-win.

Until Byron's mother was killed.

"I don't know how the fuck you DiLustros are all still alive," he said dryly. "With that impulsiveness and stubbornness. You seem to make enemies everywhere."

I smirked. "From what I hear, we share that quality. Your mother was my father's sister, after all."

A dark expression filled his face. He didn't like the reminder nor the comparison. Tough fucking shit.

I tapped my pen on the desk, leaning back in my chair. "So now what?" I challenged. "I won't help Alessio get into Afghanistan. Not unless he has something of value to offer."

Byron smirked. "Now we're getting somewhere."

"Tell Alessio to get the Corsican mafia out of Philly and I'll get him into Afghanistan." Autumn Corbin's grandfather ran the Corsicans in Philly, and they were in the way of our Syndicate. It was a small world indeed. "My supplier has an uninterrupted way in and out of that clusterfuck."

I didn't think Alessio nor Byron realized exactly how far I'd go to make Philly ours.

"What makes you think Alessio has any way of influencing the Corsicans?"

I let out a sardonic breath. "Well, Autumn has connections to it and she's his woman." He knew that as well as I did. "If Alessio wants to get his woman out of Afghanistan, the Corsicans will have to vacate Philly."

"The Corbin family doesn't keep any connections to the underworld," Byron reasoned. "Autumn doesn't even know her grandparents and her father would sooner lock them up than work with them."

Autumn's father had worked for the agency—an ex-special agent—once upon a time. But he left it for Autumn's mother who was the most lethal assassin for the Corsican mafia—once upon a time. She'd given all that up for her husband.

"You're a tough negotiator." I shrugged at the appraisal. It was simply a way to protect my little brother. Constant ambushes and turf wars in our city were bound to get him killed. Of course, he'd be pissed to know I was doing it to protect him, so I'd just tell him it fell into my lap.

"Tell him to take it or leave it."

"One day you'll need my help," Byron remarked dryly.

"Highly unlikely," I said haughtily, continuing that incessant tap, tap, tap of my pen on the desk. Byron laughed, and I gritted my teeth. The old fucker—okay, maybe a decade wasn't much older—was confident I would indeed need his help one day. Alessio, much like Byron, was older than me too.

"One day you'll be whipped," my cousin stated matter-of-factly. Too fucking late. "And I can't wait to see it."

I gave my head a small shake. My jaw pulsed. So did his. Annoyance unfurled in my chest at the resemblance between our mannerisms. His childhood was all roses while ours was one fucked-up mess.

"Those are my terms, Ashford," I said, letting out a half-laugh. "If you can't pull it off, stop wasting my time."

Truthfully, I couldn't imagine Alessio pulling it off, but it didn't fucking hurt to try. Then if he came back and indicated he could make it happen, I'd give him the name of my contact in Afghanistan. Fuck it! Maybe I was feeling a bit generous today.

"Fine, I'll talk to him."

I tossed my pen on the desk. "Let me know. Time is ticking."

"Women, especially some women, aren't easily persuaded," he said, getting to his feet. Then he added, smirking, "A piece of advice for the future, cousin. For the day you *are* whipped. Fathers usually want to skin you alive before giving you a daughter in marriage."

It almost sounded like Byron Ashford knew something, taunting me.

Jesus Christ. Aren't any secrets sacred anymore?

CHAPTER 6
Juliette

Dante DiLustro. That devil was persistent.

And so was his cousin Basilio DiLustro. Of course, once his cousin learned of Wynter's identity, mine was uncovered too. Small goddamn world.

I'd rather go to my own funeral than attend Basilio DiLustro's wedding. Yet, here I was. Wynter was lucky I loved her. It was the only reason I was here today, preparing to endure Dante DiLustro in the same fucking city as me.

Who in the fuck did he think he was? A goddamn nutjob, just like all the rest of the DiLustros. Asking my father to marry me. I wished I had cut off his balls in his casino nine months ago rather than just kicking them.

Nine months since that incident, and he had the balls—I graciously let him keep—to ask my father for my hand in marriage. Who in their right mind even wanted to marry someone who humiliated you?

DiLustro apparently.

"You should feel flattered he wants to marry you," Dad stated casually, his eyes studying me.

"Fuck flattery. I hope you said no fucking way," I screeched. I could feel panic swelling in my chest. "I'm not marrying that crazy bastard."

The vein in my father's neck pulsed as he clenched his jaw. "You should have thought of that before you and the girls became thieves."

I rolled my eyes. "That's ancient history," I remarked wryly. "You can't hold that against us forever."

"Juliette, I swear to God," he hissed. "Put your bridesmaid dress on and let's get to this fucking wedding."

Wynter was getting married, and truthfully, we should have already been on our way to the church. Instead, I was jerking Dad's chain—his words, not mine.

I shook my head. "I cannot believe you're letting today happen. Wynter shouldn't be marrying that psycho."

"Jules, stop it. Wynter worked it out with your dad," Davina chimed in, cradling her newborn.

It was a shock to all of us to learn Davina and my dad ended up getting married. In secret, nonetheless. Wynter forgave them in the next breath, and while I wasn't exactly mad, the idea of my best friend as my stepmother did rub me the wrong way sometimes. Either way, we all got over it and moved on.

Like I said, it had been a *very* long nine months since The Incident.

And now we had a new catastrophe on our hands. Wynter's wedding to Basilio DiLustro. Our family would forever be connected to the DiLustros. That was wrong on so many levels.

"Wynter's my cousin," I muttered. "I want what's best for her. And this wedding is not it."

Honestly, I couldn't believe that Dad didn't use the baby as an excuse to delay the wedding. It would have bought us more time to get Wynter out of Basilio DiLustro's clutches.

"My niece decided that it is," Dad argued. I started to suspect he might have aged a decade over the last nine months. I, along with Wynter and our best friends, might have been to blame.

The baby cooed in Davina's arms and Dad's features instantly softened.

"What's my little boy up to?" He wrapped his arm around Davina and pressed a kiss to her forehead, then on little Aiden's forehead. Davina was glowing, happiness evident in her smile.

"Sleeping, eating, and pooping," she teased, then wrinkled her nose. "I think pooping has just happened."

"Want me to change his diaper?" he offered. I shook my head at the image those words painted. Then I realized what he was doing. Nobody ever volunteered to change a poopy diaper. He was changing subjects.

"No, no, no," I protested, glaring at my father. "Don't you dare leave me hanging. What did you tell that fucking psychopath?"

Davina gave me a scolding look. She didn't want us cursing around the baby. As if he could talk. I had bigger problems than a baby that might one day utter a curse word. It was called Dante fucking DiLustro.

"I told him that it was enough for one DiLustro to be married into the family, and that there wouldn't be another one."

"Thank fucking God," I muttered.

Wynter's wedding was a lavish affair. A farce about to explode.

Wynter kept glancing Basilio's way. She didn't seem all that unhappy, despite the fact that Basilio kidnapped her and forced this wedding. The guy was seriously obsessed.

If I were Wynter, I'd have told Dad to just shoot him in the church. The fucker dragged her down the aisle to the altar. Literally dragged her.

That would never—fucking ever—be me.

A cold awareness touched my skin and I turned my head to find Dante's eyes on me. His eyes coasted down my body, leaving a trail of ice and something else I couldn't quite pinpoint in their wake.

I gritted my teeth and glared at him, making it clear that I disliked him. It didn't seem to deter him though. His eyes were on me pretty much through the entire dinner. I ignored him, but every single hair on my body stood up in warning. I wished there was a way to get my hands on a gun and shoot him. I'd just feign clumsiness. *Oops, my bad.*

As if he could read my thoughts, he grinned. That smug, arrogant smirk that I wanted to wipe off his face, despite his good looks. I really wished he weren't *that* attractive. The dark three-piece suit fit his tall, muscled frame, making him look more like a sharp businessman than a mobster. He shifted over to say something to his brother and the tip of his gun came to view.

There goes the sharp businessman look, I thought smugly.

Bottom line, he just wasn't my type.

Basilio and Wynter found their way onto the dance floor for their first dance as husband and wife. *Only in the fucking underworld.* Mere hours ago, everyone had guns pointed at each other at the church. All because Ivy and I showed up in the back room to save her. Well, maybe we wanted to kidnap her back from the crazy New York kingpin.

All the DiLustros were nuts. Batty. Looney. Probably a touch of a few psychopathic traits there too.

And here we were. Dancing, eating, bullshitting.

Although, I caught both Dante and Basilio checking their weapons a few times. As if they expected someone to start shooting at any moment.

I stood up and headed for the bar on the opposite side of the lavish backyard. The waitresses seemed to be giving more attention to the men than the women. The freaking reception was full of testosterone.

Basilio went all out for this wedding. It made me wonder whether the fucker had it all on standby before he kidnapped my cousin. The bartender was swift to take my order. *Fireball.* It was only appropriate for this kind of event.

"May I have this dance?" A familiar voice came from behind me and awareness shot through me. It was so stifling I could hardly breathe. It settled in my lungs and filled the room with so much tension, a single wrong word or move could detonate a bomb.

A bomb I wished Dante would lie over and go *boom.* It'd probably be the nicest thing he'd ever do for a human. Saving all our lives.

"I don't dance," I declared, letting his rainforest scent wash over me. Somewhere in the back of my mind, a memory danced along the shadows. One I couldn't quite grasp, but I knew it was triggered by his scent. The intoxicating fragrance taking me over.

"Liar."

I peered up at him, those dark brown eyes appearing almost black. He had the thickest black lashes I'd ever seen on a man. The shadow of stubble ghosted his chin and cheeks, making me wonder how rough it would feel against my palm.

Not that I'd ever touch him.

"Fine," I caved, watching victory flash in his eyes. "I lied. I do dance, just not with you."

He smiled, not letting my rejection deter him. "That's because you haven't danced with me yet."

"Listen, *Dante*," I started, emphasizing his name as though talking to a kid. "I know you think you're godsent and all, but you are not my type." I didn't have a type. The traumatic experience from high school might have scarred me for life. "So do us both a favor, stop gawking at me. Stop talking to my father about me. In fact, erase me from your thoughts. Like we'd never met."

Dante smiled darkly. "But I did meet you. And there's no forgetting you, Wildling."

I really didn't like him. He was annoying and arrogant.

"Name's Juliette." I smiled sweetly. "Unfortunately for you, I have no trouble forgetting you."

My words didn't deter him. If anything, this guy became more persistent. He was definitely stubborn as fuck.

"Is that right?" he drawled lazily. "Did you forget your offer?"

I frowned. "What offer?"

"To give me the night of my life," he said. "To have a threesome." My expression fell. I had hoped he'd forgotten. It wasn't my best moment. "I bet your father would agree to let me marry you tomorrow if I repeated your offer."

I glared at him. Fucking traitor.

"Snitches get stitches." I hissed that tired old phrase at the obsidian-eyed devil, but I realized my mistake the moment his eyes flashed with smugness.

Downing his drink, he dropped it on the bar with a thud.

"But instead of ending in stitches, you'll end up in my bed, sweetheart."

I rolled my eyes. "In your dreams, DiLustro."

Then I flipped him the bird and turned on my heel to go dance with my friends.

Today couldn't end fast enough. I needed to get away from this lunatic.

CHAPTER 7
Dante

Juliette Brennan would be mine if it killed me.

Maybe she didn't understand it, but she was bound to marry someone in the mafia world. And if anyone even attempted to steal her from me, I'd kill them.

After what seemed like a lifetime of being hated and alone, she was the one I needed to fill that empty space. I wanted her so badly. A life with her. A lover. A friend. I wanted to be chosen. I wanted to be wanted. I wanted *her* to want me. The girl that offered me the pink scrunchie. The girl with big blue eyes who promised to save me. I had never dreamt that I'd run into her again, but I was glad that destiny brought her to me. Maybe she was meant to be mine all along; and I was meant to be hers.

My eyes traveled over the guests in attendance at Basilio and Wynter's wedding reception. So many different affiliations of the underworld all in one place. I was surprised that somebody hadn't pulled out a weapon yet. I almost expected it to come from Basilio's father, Uncle Gio. Basilio felt about his father the way I felt about my mother. Nothing spoke more about an unhealthy childhood than our shit.

Soft laughter pulled my gaze to the small group of women across the way. Juliette was close with all four of them, although I had to admit, they were an odd bunch. Their personalities were so vastly different, I couldn't grasp how they even got along.

I searched for Basilio and found him, leaning against the wall with his eyes on his wife. I'd given him a hard time, but I wasn't too far from being in the same boat as he was.

"Don't tell me your wife is ignoring you?" I mocked lightly.

My brother and Emory, his sister who ran Las Vegas, showed up. Priest's gaze followed and locked on Wynter—his baby sister, as we'd all recently discovered. His protective instinct kicked in, just as mine always did with him. I watched Wynter dance with that unhinged Nikolaev.

"They would have made a striking couple," Priest remarked, indicating with the nod of his head towards Sasha Nikolaev, the Russian mafia killer, dancing with Wynter. "Can you imagine how blond their little babies would have been?"

Judging by the dark expression passing through Basilio's eyes, it was the wrong fucking thing to say.

"Too blond," Emory said, punching Priest in his gut. "Their babies would have blinded everyone on this planet. I mean, proof is right there with that kid she's holding." I had to give it to her, she could read the room. I assumed that came with the territory growing up with Gio as a father, that gutless piece of shit.

But Priest wasn't looking at his sister anymore. His eyes darted to Ivy, Juliette's friend with the wild red hair. My father stood with them, all of them smiling like nothing was wrong in this world.

Maybe not for them. Us, all four of us—-Basilio, myself, Dante and Emory—-we were all fucked up. In one way or another.

"Have you heard that Wynter's mother hasn't been back here on the East Coast in over two decades?" I asked Basilio quietly. He met my gaze and nodded. The oddest thing was that Liam Brennan's hard clause for this wedding happening was no Gio at the wedding—not that anyone, especially Basilio, would be missing him.

Basilio apparently had enough of his wife dancing with Sasha and prowled across the dance floor to get to her.

"He's gonna be fun," Emory muttered. "I can't believe one of us is married now."

I flicked her a glance. "Maybe you can be next?"

She scoffed.

"No, thank you." I understood where she was coming from. Anyone who grew up under Gio's thumb would hate the idea of marriage, especially after witnessing his cruelty toward other women. "Why don't *you* get married? It only makes sense that we do it by age."

My eyes found the woman with dark brown hair and a killer kick. She was laughing and dancing with her friends. I liked seeing her smiling and happy, but I couldn't shake off the feeling that there was something she was hiding.

Somewhere deep where nobody could reach. The notion made no logical sense, yet I couldn't shake it off.

Emory's lips twisted. "Yeah, I think you might be next," she remarked. "And you already found your bride."

"Except, she doesn't want him," Priest said, the look in his eyes doubtful. "I'm not sure about how smart that union would be, Dante. She's a ticking bomb."

I shrugged. "So are we."

"Exactly my point," he noted. "Two bombs in the same city could level it to the ground."

When I flipped him off, he shook his head and left me to my thoughts. Emory followed shortly afterward, her gaze longingly on the four girls. She'd always had to be content with us, having a hard time relating to girls that grew up outside our world. But with these women, she felt like she could connect. I hoped she was right.

"Hello, Dante." I raised my eyebrow, surprised to find Liam's new bride, Davina, next to me. "Having a good time?"

"Not as good as your friends," I said, a hint of sarcasm in my voice. Juliette and Ivy were doing some ridiculous version of the macarena or something.

She chuckled. "Juliette knows how to party. Ivy's not far behind."

I nodded, waiting for her to get to the point. It was no coincidence she came to talk to me.

"Ummm, a little birdy told me you want to marry Jules." Ah, there it was. I remained quiet, waiting for her to continue. "I just want to say that... well, the more you chase her, the less likely she'll accept you."

Now that statement did shock me. "How so?"

Davina shrugged. "I'm just offering you what I've noticed over the years. She's all talk and flirting, but try to corner her and she'll fight you tooth and nail."

Despite being surprised that Davina, of all people, would help me, I felt that I should probably take that advice and figure out the best way to lock down my bride.

CHAPTER 8
Juliette

E very time I turned around, someone was getting married. Wynter's nightmare of a wedding a few months ago. Now Autumn's marriage to Alessio Russo. Who in the fuck was next? And why were the DiLustros invited, for fuck's sake?

The venue was beautiful, Japan even more so. Mountains surrounded us. The soft rushing sounds of the river traveled through the air, mixing with the rustle of the leaves and the scent of cherry blossoms blooming. If there was ever a time to visit Japan, it was spring. It was so colorful and vibrant, it would have made a great reception.

If only Dante DiLustro weren't here.

I downed my Fireball shot and sat on the low retaining wall, a cherry blossom tree rustling behind me. The loveliness of the setting was tainted by my foul mood. I took the reception in, the crowds of people mingling and seemingly having a grand ol' time, as I let the liquor warm me. I studied my brother from here, his eyes flickering to Emory every so often. Apart from her looking gorgeous tonight in a soft pink dress, I sensed tension between the two, and I had no idea why.

Well, aside from her being a DiLustro, maybe.

Emory walked by me, headed toward her family, when I stopped her.

"What's happening between you and my brother?" A frown creased between her brows as she looked at me.

Then she shrugged. "He's sensitive to the fact I aimed my gun at him when he came for Wynter in Vegas."

Ahhh. There it was. A man could never handle it when a woman was better than him. Including my own brother.

When Basilio kidnapped Wynter from the hotel room on the last night of the Olympic games, he brought her to Emory's place in Vegas. Of course, Dad and Killian stormed the place, ready to level it to the ground. Obviously, they'd come to an agreement because Wynter ended up marrying Basilio, but it would seem Emory didn't hesitate to stand by her brother.

"I guess my comment about him playing with the big boys didn't help," she added, grinning unapologetically.

The smug grin on her lips reminded me of Dante and instantly my mood soured. It wasn't her fault that she had that arrogant DiLustro attitude.

"Well, your brother kind of asked for it," I remarked wryly. Not that any of that would matter anymore. They were married and they were happy.

Emory shrugged. "I wouldn't have let it happen if Basilio meant her harm. He didn't. He looked for her for months."

Tilting my head, I studied her. She was pretty. Dark hair. Dark eyes. Petite frame. But her strength shone through her eyes. Like she had seen some shit and had come out on top. About our age, maybe a year or two older. Until now, I never really cared to ask her, but it had me wondering what her story was. I knew from what little Wynter shared that Emory's brother, Basilio, trusted her as much as he did anyone else in his circle. She was sharp, smart, and pretty.

"Who taught you how to fight?" I blurted out, her taunting of my brother forgotten.

Her expression softened and she smiled. "My cousins and Basilio, mostly."

"Even though you're a girl?" It felt like a stupid question, but it wasn't. Not in the underworld. Women were usually used for alliances or negotiations, but we were never given the power to be strong.

"Exactly for that reason." When she saw the question in my eyes, she clarified, "They didn't want me vulnerable. They trained me so I could stand up to any man and not let him fuck with me."

Okay, one point for the DiLustros. Our family definitely lacked in that department.

"Did it work?" I asked curiously.

"For the most part." I wanted to know what that meant, but before I could ask, she excused herself. "See you around."

She left me pondering this revelation. For some reason, it was hard to imagine the DiLustro men training a girl and making her strong enough to kick anyone's ass. Even my brother's. Not that I thought she could kick Killian's ass. Unless he let her.

Ivy joined me, taking a seat next to me, her red hair catching rays of sunshine and glimmering like flames. She looked as thrilled as I was about this wedding halfway across the world.

"These weddings are starting to get on my nerves," she muttered under her breath, stealing the words out of my mouth. She seemed agitated. It was uncharacteristic of her. Me, not so much. "I'm half expecting the Yakuza to show up."

Okay, that was going a bit too far.

"What's going on?" I asked her gently. She just shrugged and I narrowed my eyes on her. She was hiding something. "Ivy?"

Her hazel eyes flitted over my head and I followed her gaze to where Priest DiLustro stood.

"Don't tell me you're still hung up on Priest?" I grumbled. A blush crept up her neck, and I shook my head in disbelief. "He couldn't have been that good."

"We didn't go all the way," she hissed in a low voice.

"Did you even get halfway?" I questioned. As much as she swooned over Priest, you'd think he wined and dined her, maybe sent her flowers every day. Yet, as far as I could tell, the two of them barely exchanged a few words. They had a moment back in Philly last year. Ivy might have been reluctant to share with me any more details, but from what little she did share was that Priest gave her the very first orgasm.

Apparently, it left a mark on both of them, because the two were constantly glancing at each other.

She waved her hand. "It doesn't matter because—"

Her voice trailed off, and I waited for her to finish. She didn't.

"Because?" I urged.

Her eyes traveled over the wedding party, pausing again on Priest. The moment he glanced over, she looked away with her jaw clenched. Her cheeks warmed, but something was off. Almost as if she was uncomfortable.

She met my gaze and swallowed hard. Then as if she couldn't hold it in anymore, she leaned closer to me.

"Because that guy is crazy," she whispered.

I scoffed softly. "They're all crazy. Nothing new or unusual there."

She shook her head. "Not like him, Jules. He's totally out there. He'd qualify for a mental institution."

I raised my eyebrows in surprise. "What makes you say that?"

She shook her head. "I can't tell you," she murmured.

My eyes widened. Ivy never—fucking ever—held back. It had to be something bad. The memories of the one secret I'd never shared flickered in my mind and dread pooled in the pit of my stomach.

"Ivy, did he hurt you?"

Her eyes flew my way, an undignified look in them. "No! As if I'd ever let him."

The knot in my stomach loosened and I let out a relieved breath. If he'd hurt her, I'd have to murder him. "You'll tell me if you need help?" She didn't turn to look at me, so I shifted slightly to lock eyes with her. "Ivy, repeat after me. *Juliette, I will tell you if I need your help.*"

"Yes, yes. Of course," she grumbled exasperatedly.

We sat in thick silence, tense yet comfortable as we watched the guests socializing, laughing, and basically making us feel like we might actually be missing out. Some danced. Like Autumn and Alessio. The two couldn't keep their hands off each other.

My gaze darted to my brother who stood with his fiancée, Branka Russo. I frowned. I really liked Branka, but I couldn't seem to picture my brother and her for the rest of their lives. They just seemed too stiff around each other. I wondered what Alessio thought of his sister marrying Killian.

My brother said something and Branka turned toward him. The smile on her face was forced. Almost painful. Maybe I should help Killian.

"I'll be right back," I told Ivy and headed in their direction. Branka's hair was styled in a fancy updo and her makeup was immaculate. She looked breathtaking. Closing the distance with the two of them, I smiled.

"Nice hair," I said. "Will you wear it that way for your wedding?"

She met my eyes and something in their depths reminded me of that exact feeling I got every time I thought about a man on top of me: chest squeezed tight. Panic swelled. My ears buzzed.

My gaze shot to my brother. Could he see it? He didn't see it in me and something told me he didn't see it in Branka.

"Not sure." Branka murmured her answer. Killian excused himself and left us to our conversation. It was clear he didn't have much interest in the wedding either.

"What are we not sure about?" Autumn said as she joined our group. She looked beautiful in her wedding dress, but it was her face that stole the show. She fucking glowed.

"Wedding hair," Branka replied, forcing another smile.

"Ah." Autumn smiled in understanding and reached over to give her best friend's hand a squeeze. "We have a little time to decide."

I kept my expression blank. Killian and Branka's wedding was fast approaching and we were down to weeks, but I didn't point it out.

Instead, I just said, "Congratulations. It seems as though it's the season of weddings. Davina, Wynter, Autumn, next is Killian. I don't know if I can take much more of it."

Wynter and Ivy joined in.

"You'll take more of it and like it," Ivy said wryly. My eyes shot her way. Didn't she just complain about the weddings herself? Talk about whiplash. "Stop being a wedding grinch."

My eyebrows jumped up to my hairline.

"I'm not a wedding grinch," I insisted. "But you have to admit. It's all a bunch of fuss for nothing."

Wynter being Wynter had an answer for that. "It's not for nothing. Two human beings pledge their love and devotion to one another for the rest of their lives."

I rolled my eyes. "And when life is cut short? For either husband or wife. How do you move on?"

"Well, you continue with the knowledge that he or she would want you to be happy."

What a bunch of bollocks. She didn't actually believe her husband would want her to carry on without him. Did she? All you had to do was look at Basilio to know that fucker would come back to life just to chase any man away from Wynter.

"I wouldn't." Branka's voice cut my train of thought and my attention shifted to her.

"What do you mean?" Ivy asked what we were all thinking.

"I wouldn't want him to move on. Fuck that shit." God, I loved it when she cursed. "I'd demand he get in the fucking casket with me. Together forever, life or death."

I didn't know whether to be worried for my brother or laugh. The images of a dead person ordering anyone to get in their casket had me bursting into laughter.

"I like that," I mused, holding my stomach and tears in my eyes. "Get in the fucking casket. My brother is fucking doomed."

I could picture it already, Branka ordering him to do just that. Except, I didn't think she loved him enough to share her casket. In fact, I couldn't picture them together at all.

Autumn rolled her eyes. "Somehow I think Juliette and Branka shouldn't be left alone together."

"Juliette alone with anyone is a dangerous thing," Davina chimed in as she approached our group. I shot her a glare, only to notice Dante was joining us too.

"Excuse me," I muttered and headed in the opposite direction. I'd give Davina, my evil stepmother, a piece of my mind later.

Without another look back, I headed in search of the restroom. I could hear footsteps behind me, but I ignored them. I weaved through the guests, nodding my greeting every so often. I was almost there when that now familiar and aggravating voice came from behind me.

"Running, Wildling?"

My feet stopped of their own accord. My brain screamed for them to get a move on and get me behind the bathroom door. But no such luck. I remained glued to the spot.

I glanced over my shoulder. Just like every time I saw him, he was wearing his three-piece suit. It was perfectly molded to his broad shoulders and toned body. Crisp black lines matched his dark hair and eyes.

"I'm saving myself the trouble of putting up with annoying company," I remarked dryly.

He plastered a grin on his handsome face. *Handsome, but still definitely annoying*, I added silently.

"Perfect, then we can do that together."

I knew he wasn't that dense. He just liked to agitate the living daylights out of me. Impatience flared within me, and it took all my self-restraint not to turn around and just punch him. Maybe kick him in the balls again. It seemed he needed a reminder of what I was capable of.

Instead, I took a deep breath in and then exhaled slowly, letting my temper somewhat cool. I couldn't ruin Autumn's wedding. I turned around and faced him, craning my neck to meet his gaze.

"Dante, let me make one thing clear," I said, as sweetly as I could muster it. "I don't want to do anything 'together' with you. I don't want to talk to you. I don't want to see you. Honestly, I'm not even fond of knowing you." His dark eyes flickered with something dangerous. I ignored it. "But I can be reasonable. So I'll tell you what"—I tapped my fingers against my chin pensively—"we'll be acquaintances. *Casual* acquaintances like the kind that nod to each other as we pass on our way to talk to someone who actually matters. Okay?"

He didn't comment. I went to turn around when his question stopped me. "Why?"

He stood there in the hall, his gaze heavy and full of something— nerves? I didn't care to know. He slid his hands into his pockets as that same gaze fell down my body. It wasn't leering, more so observant. But under his dark, thick lashes, there was something that set me on edge. A warning. A flare of self-preservation. It was exactly the reason I'd never let this man get near me.

"Why what?"

"Why do you want to stop at acquaintances?" he demanded. Why couldn't he just let it go?

"You're not my type," I snapped harshly. Truthfully, I didn't have a type, but that was beside the point.

His gaze returned to my face and he pulled a hand out of his pocket to run a thumb across his bottom lip. As if he were considering my words. Maybe he'd finally give up. He gave his head a small shake, then took a step forward. I took one back.

An odd thumping began in my chest. I didn't like it. I didn't like *him*.

He was a DiLustro. His cousin kidnapped my cousin and Dante helped. Then, the devil went behind my back to my dad to ask for my hand in marriage. As-fucking-if. But I was a reasonable woman. I got over all that and forgave him. For the most part.

But the part that got me freaked out the most when it came to Dante was my body. He made me feel things I couldn't face. The way my body responded to Dante DiLustro brought back the memories that I worked so hard to forget. *Longing. The need to be consumed.* Except, it could never happen. Not with the panic attacks that plagued me when any man even attempted to touch me.

Therefore, it was best to avoid him—make Dante hate me—so I couldn't get hurt. He wouldn't want me anyhow. Not if he knew how broken I was.

Dante took a step forward, and again, I took another one back. My instincts warned me to get the hell out of here. Away from him.

His eyes locked with mine, burning me from the inside. I detested the feeling. I detested being around him. Period.

"I am your type, Juliette," he drawled lazily. Softly. His hand wrapped around my wrist. Calloused, rough, and firm. Something hot leaked into my bloodstream and shot through my veins like a drug. "You just don't know it yet."

It was like time had stopped as we stood there, his thumb brushing my knuckles. My pulse raced in a combination of fear and something else. Maybe panic? I tugged my wrist free and his grip slipped down my wrist, palm, fingers. As if he couldn't bear to end the touch, the same one I couldn't wait to escape.

I rushed out of there, leaving him to stare after me. I pushed the door to the bathroom open and it wasn't until I was inside one of the stalls that

I felt like I could breathe again. I leaned against the door and shut my eyes. My heart raced, although I didn't know why.

I used the bathroom next, and when I exited the stall, Autumn stood at the sink, washing her hands.

"Hey," she said, her smiling eyes meeting mine in the mirror.

We stood side by side at the sink when, for no good reason, I asked, "How did you survive those months in Afghanistan?" She raised a brow, probably not expecting a question like that. "Sorry," I added. "Not even sure where that came from."

She smiled softly. I didn't really know her and I think our invite came only thanks to our connection to the DiLustros.

"Kian."

I frowned. "Huh?"

"There was a guy there with his men, he protected me. His name was Kian. He has a security agency, I think it's pretty 'exclusive,' if you know what I mean. He could track anyone and anything. People out there know him, he has a really good track record for keeping people safe."

"Hmm."

She tilted her head, studying me. "Please tell me you're not thinking about going to Afghanistan."

I scoffed lightly. "No."

"Look, I'll give you his contact information. Whatever you're planning, at least he'll keep you safe."

And that was how my *relationship* with Kian started.

CHAPTER 9
Dante

I t had been months since Alessio's wedding to his woman. Months since my cousin's wedding to Wynter.

Months since that spitfire cousin of hers, my future bride, destroyed my grandfather's priceless antique car. My jaw clenched at the memory. I loved that car. Unfortunately for me, I loved the woman who took a bat to it and then drew a penis on it with her lipstick even more.

Healthy? Fuck, no. I seriously considered seeing a goddamn therapist.

Especially now as I watched her across the street sitting at the tiny table—why did the fucking cafe have such small tables—for their guests. It was a cafe, not speed dating. Although I wouldn't mind this dude rotating right along. Ten minutes were up, asshole. It took all of my control not to storm in there and drag her ass out of it.

My chest twisted and aversion slithered through my veins. Instead of dragging her ass, maybe I should just kill him. That would be a more permanent solution. *Then* I'd drag her ass out of there. I didn't care about witnesses. I didn't care about the consequences.

The only thing that was louder than my need for her was the need to kill this fucker who was now smiling at her. It wasn't even a sweet smile. It was condescending. Like he knew something about her that I didn't.

Zooming in from my spot across the street, I snapped a picture and sent it to Nico Morrelli. He ran Maryland, D.C., and Virginia. The guy was a tech whiz and could dig just about anything up. Usually I would just send it to Priest, but he'd jerk my chain for months afterward.

Need a name. Price is not an issue.

It had been exactly one hundred sixty-four days, twelve hours, and—I glanced at the clock—thirty-eight minutes since Juliette and I crossed paths. At Alessio Russo's wedding. It was the last time I touched her soft skin. And fuck, I had never met a woman with such smooth and soft skin. I could ask her father for her hand in marriage again but being rejected twice was my limit.

Besides, she might take her anger out on another one of my vehicles. My grandfather's car was still suffering the damages of her outburst when I asked Liam the last time. That girl was hotheaded.

Bottom line, Juliette had been avoiding me for months now. Considering Davina's words of advice, I attempted to give her space, so I wouldn't push her away. But my patience was waning. I couldn't wait anymore—I missed her the way the desert missed the rain. The way the moon missed the sun. All I had been doing was thinking about her. It was absurd, the girl had hardly given me the time of day.

Talk about the ironies of life. But I was a persistent man unfamiliar with the concept of giving up.

When Basilio said Juliette was in New York—declaring his annoyance —I rushed to the Big Apple. I'd been tailing her since my plane landed, following closely as she walked the streets aimlessly, right before she stopped in front of this coffee shop. She'd just stood facing the "Welcome" sign for a few moments, as if crossing the threshold of that cafe would change her life forever.

It actually reminded me of that evening right before Christmas so many years ago. The little girl, aged twelve, maybe thirteen, pressing her face against the Tiffany store window. She was all grown up now. It was impossible to forget those eyes. They weren't a normal blue. More like the shimmering surface of the Ionian Sea. The one I swam in during my one amazing trip to Greece. I hadn't seen eyes that color since.

I wondered if she knew that the boy who'd saved her that day was me.

Would it make a difference if she did? Seemed like fate had been throwing us together for a long time, if you asked me.

We must have come full circle because now it was me with my face pressed up against a window on the streets of New York City, trying to catch a glimpse of those blue eyes once more.

My brows furrowed and my hand froze midair, my phone still in my hand. Something flickered in the back of my mind. Something important. Something that had been bugging me from the moment I'd met Juliette.

My phone buzzed, vibrating through my palm. I shook my head and checked my phone.

Brandon Dole.

The name Nico sent meant nothing. And I hated it simply because he was sitting at the table in a romantic cafe with her.

I glared across the street to where the fucker smiled at and chatted with *my* girl. Their table was right at the window, giving them a view of Central Park. So fucking romantic, I couldn't stand it. I wanted to pull my gun out, aim, and end him. Right here and now in the street heaving with tourists.

My anger simmered. Jealousy burned. Something inexplicably dark rose in my chest and refused to ease. No matter Juliette's refusal. No matter her stubbornness. She was *mine*.

My phone buzzed. Another message from Nico. ***Rest of the information is pro bono. Can't wait to see her cut your balls off.***

"Fucking bastard," I muttered. "I hope his daughters fall for heathens."

Nico sent the guy's entire background. A tattoo artist. A lousy one by the number of lawsuits pending against him. My eyes skimmed over the page and then I saw it. He and Juliette went to high school together.

Taking a deep breath, I prepared for a long evening. My car parked illegally, I found a spot across the street from the cafe and leaned against the wall where I had the best view of the two of them. Pedestrians threw me glances as they rushed to their destinations, but I ignored them all. My eyes were zeroed in on my woman.

Juliette would bolt if she heard me say that out loud.

As if she could sense my thoughts, her eyes darted out the window. Glossy. Darker than ever. And it was then that it hit me.

The little girl I rescued almost a decade ago didn't have that look in her eyes. Even in the face of the thug, her eyes were bright. No burden or secrets in them. But now, there was a darkness in those depths that she was desperate to hide. How had I not seen it before?

Before I could ponder further on it, a hand came to my shoulder.

"I see you're in full-blown stalker mode," my brother muttered as he leaned against the wall next to me.

A groan vibrated in my chest. "Aren't you supposed to be in Philly?"

Priest just shrugged. "With the Corsican mafia gone, I'm the king there. So not much happening lately," he noted.

My own father had started dating Wynter's mother. We learned Priest was in fact my half brother and shared a mother with Wynter, explaining why my mother was always harsher with him growing up. *Not that she was ever gentle with me.*

It was quickly becoming difficult for even me to keep track of the ties that bound my fucked-up family.

Mother had hated both of us and used her belt to show just how much. The skin on my back tightened and I resisted the urge to scratch it. I hated her; Priest hated her even more, even now eight years after her death. It was the reason my brother couldn't move past the revelation that he shared a mother with Wynter. She could have saved him and she didn't. But then, neither did our father.

"Maybe we should invite them back?" I said. "You know, just to keep you busy."

Priest chuckled. A rough sound since he rarely laughed. "My big brother ensured they left the city. Even the East Coast."

I shook my head. It didn't surprise me he'd learned of my deal with Byron Ashford. Alessio came through. He didn't even take long... nobody could claim that man wasn't efficient. I guess he just wanted his woman back and would have given up his entire empire—and hers—for it.

My eyes found Juliette again and realization sunk in. I would give it all up for her, too. If only she'd let me. Instead, she held her walls firmly, keeping me at bay.

"Shouldn't you thank me and go enjoy your peace?" I asked with sardonic amusement.

"Nah, it leaves me nobody to kill," he deadpanned.

I gave my head a shake. Sometimes I wondered whether his need to punish was the result of my bitch mother or whether it was just part of his DNA.

"Well, don't kill anyone in this city. Basilio won't be happy."

Priest just shrugged. "He'll deal."

"Or your sister will save you if he refuses to deal."

Wynter was just as protective of her brother as I was. It was still hard to believe that Wynter and I shared a sibling. It had been a year since that revelation, and it was just as incredible now as it was back then.

Priest's blue eyes turned my way. "Jealous?"

I snickered, my chest tightening slightly. I wasn't exactly jealous, but I did worry. I didn't want to see my brother hurt if word of what he did on a regular basis got out. I accepted that part of him. Would others?

"No, I'm not jealous," I said. "Just cautious."

Silence followed. Ghosts stood in the shadows right along with us, taunting us. I wished I could murder them, make them dissipate into the atmosphere. Although I suspected it wouldn't work. They'd stay with us for the remainder of our days.

"Are you sure she's the one?" Priest questioned.

I nodded. She was the *only* one.

Buses passed, the loud honks startling passersby. Neither Priest nor I flinched. It took a lot more to startle us. The buzz of the city was all around us. A baseball game. The constant sound of an air-conditioning unit whirring. The smell of hot dogs, drifting from a nearby food truck.

"We should grab something to eat after you're done stalking her," Priest said, breaking the silence.

I had planned on heading to my favorite joint for my favorite burger. Right after Juliette left this dude. My appetite was the only thing that remained intact since meeting Juliette.

My dick suffered. It wanted the mahogany-haired woman with porcelain skin and blue eyes. My thoughts also suffered, because they all revolved around her.

If our fleeting interaction at the last wedding was any indication, Juliette would fight our attraction. It was at Alessio's wedding that I made the decision to be more devious moving forward and make that woman mine through any means necessary.

So I devised a plan. She wouldn't be able to escape me once I trapped her.

And she'd never see me coming.

CHAPTER 10
Juliette

Brandon Dole.

He was the only reason I'd come to New York after Kian passed on his whereabouts, and I couldn't believe the fucker was in my father's city all along. Kian was godsent. The best recommendation I had ever gotten. The fact that I could hire him incognito worked perfectly.

After I had a mediocre late lunch with Brandon—my soon-to-be victim—I took a cab and went home.

Supposedly.

Brandon had no way of knowing that my phone synced up his information, allowing me to track him from that moment forward. When I showed up at his building, it was dark. He lived in the shitty part of the city, the one you never saw on postcards.

I'd already checked the cameras on this block. There were none—aside from traffic cameras. I kept my face down and stuck to the shadows as I made my way down the alley, then up the fire escape.

Clank. Clank.

Each step made a clunking noise, but every apartment window I passed looked empty. Everyone was used to city racket and didn't spare me a single glance. It was fine by me.

Once I made it to the top floor, I peered through the window into a shitty apartment. Old, worn-out furniture. Yellowing walls. Broken chairs. It was dirty and disgusting.

I checked my knife holster. My gun tucked in the back of my pants. My taser. All there.

With that I slid through the open window, landing softly on my feet and shutting it behind me. It was risky. I could be shutting my way out.

My eyes drifted around the living room. This guy was a pig. There were dirty dishes everywhere. Open cans. The stench of rotten food.

I'd need a long, hot scrub in my own shower—with bleach—to clean off after this.

Speaking of showers, the sound of running water registered. *I could kill him in the shower.* It'd be cleaner than waiting for him to come out... but I didn't want to be cornered in a small space.

I decided to wait.

Reluctant to sit down on any of the surfaces in this pigsty, I opted to lean against the wall so he wouldn't see me until he was well into the living room.

My heart thundered. There wasn't any fear drifting through my veins, but there was no shortage of adrenaline. It might have been wrong, but the idea of punishing him had been the only thing on my mind for such a long time.

And it was finally here.

The shower cut off. I tensed slightly, reaching for my taser in my pocket. Just in time. He walked through the door with a towel around his waist. My taser at the highest setting, I pushed it to the back of his neck and a yelp pierced my ears.

He fell to the floor, his body jerking against the filthy linoleum. The towel flopped off his body, exposing his disgusting naked skin. He looked like a stiff, scaly cockroach trying to move. Comical.

My lips curved into a sadistic smile.

"Hello, Brandon."

He opened his mouth but no sound came out. I guessed the taser worked on the tongue too. Good to know.

"What's the matter?" I taunted quietly, eerily. "Lost your voice?" I squatted down, pulling the knife out of the holster strapped to my ankle. "Don't worry. You'll be screaming by the time I'm done with you."

I glanced around. If he screamed, somebody could call the cops. It was the last thing I needed. Ah, there it was. A stereo. I headed for it, turned to the first music station. Opera. How fucking appropriate. I pushed the volume button to its highest number.

Pavarotti's aria "Nessun dorma" came on. "Thank fuck it's not Andrea Bocelli," I muttered. I actually liked Bocelli and didn't want to associate him with this asshole, rolling all over the ground. I returned to the fucker on the ground, my blade fisted in my palm.

I put the end of the blade to his naked back and sliced him. Slowly. Painfully. From the back of his neck, down his spine and all the way down to his tailbone.

This time, a sound did leave his lips. Piercing. Pained. And so fucking delicious, it had me feeling high.

I smiled darkly, pushing the tip of the blade against his tailbone. I should really shove it up his ass. There was time for that.

"I'll give you a hint," I said, watching his fear with delight. "That four-teen-year-old girl survived. But you won't."

His death didn't come swiftly. His pain and sins would paint these walls crimson.

And there'd be no mercy coming from me.

I learned two things by the end of the night. It was way too easy to kill. And there was something so fucking sweet about the revenge I dished out.

Brandon Dole robbed me of my innocence. I robbed him of his life. He became my first kill.

CHAPTER 11

Juliette

ONE YEAR LATER

Wearing a blue evening dress that fell softly around my body, I headed toward the booked room where everyone agreed to meet. My heels clicked against the marble floor, drawing glances my way.

I ignored them all, entering the room, decorated with lights and glittering balloons floating against the ceiling. It was a kickoff party to Emory's birthday celebration tomorrow at her home outside Las Vegas. It made no sense to me to have a party at the Bellagio hotel the day before her actual birthday party, but a party was a party. So, here I was.

Spotting Ivy's signature red hair and Wynter standing beside her, I walked over to them. Ivy's eyes landed on me and a wide smile spread over her face, her hazel eyes instantly lighting up.

"Finally!" Wynter muttered. My dear cousin had become less and less inclined to attend any of the events taking place this weekend. "I thought you weren't going to show up until tomorrow for Christ's sake. How long does it take you to get ready?"

I ignored her comment. Her meek personality was replaced by a cranky one when she got knocked up.

"Where is your husband?" I asked instead. It was rare to see one without the other. Like they were joined at the fucking hip. It was annoying as fuck.

"He's talking to Dante."

"They look to be in deep discussion," Ivy said, rolling her eyes. "All the DiLustros."

I followed Ivy's gaze and found all four of them—Dante, Basilio, Emory, and Priest—discussing something, their faces serious and their heads close together. Well, except for Emory. She looked like a little kid playing with the big boys. I still couldn't get over the fact she ran the Las Vegas crime world for the Syndicate. The girl was barely five foot four, yet I knew her looks were deceiving. She was just as lethal as her brother and cousins.

"They're probably up to no good," I noted. "None of the DiLustros are ever up to any good. Especially Dante."

Then as if he heard me mention his name, his gaze drifted over the large room and makeshift dance floor and caught mine. His eyes sparked and burned as if igniting a fire. They slid down my body and goose bumps rose over my skin.

It was exactly for this reason I couldn't bear to be around this man. I fucking hated this damn reaction my body had to him. No matter how hard I tried to steel my response to him, it always failed.

"God, I can't stand him," I murmured.

"Then stop staring at him," Wynter deadpanned. "I swear, this game of cat and mouse is getting old."

"Not if I'm the cat," I said, amused, turning my back to Dante. Yet, it did nothing to ease the burn of his stare. He might as well have been right in front of me.

I noted my father approaching with Davina, both of them smiling softly.

"You look beautiful, Juliette." He pulled me into a tight hug. "Your mom would be so proud. You're the spitting image of her."

It was only since I learned of my birth parents that he dropped comments like this. I appreciated it, but it was also a reminder to myself. That I'd make those responsible pay. My body count kept growing, but I wasn't finished yet. It started with Brandon Dole. After him, I'd moved on to Sam Dallas, the second boy who did nothing. Travis fucking Xander was untouchable—hiding behind his parents' walls—so I'd moved on to my parents' killers. I didn't have all their names. Only six. Killian had put four into early graves. I had done the same with two, unbeknownst to him.

Four more were left, and they would pay for their sins. Sofia Volkov included. But she'd get hers, I would make sure of it.

What goes around comes around, and all that.

Liam had hidden us from the world. Juliette Ava Cullen was my birth name, and he'd changed it to Juliette Brennan. He couldn't bear to erase all traces of me. But I'd be damned if I stayed silent. They'd learn you never fucked with a Cullen.

"Thanks, Dad."

I still loved Liam. He raised me and he was a good dad. I sighed happily as I soaked up his strength and love.

"You know, your mom gave your dad a hard time too," he said casually. "Although *they* settled their differences a lot sooner." His insinuation didn't escape me, but I chose to ignore it.

"You're a lot like her," Killian added, showing up out of nowhere.

Guilt pierced through my chest because what little I knew about her, I was nothing like her. She never killed. She never tortured. And she certainly wouldn't have enjoyed either one. In the deepest corner of myself, I actually liked making these men pay for what they'd done—to me, to my parents, to our family.

"Except you're wilder," Dad said. "You must have taken after Aiden in that regard."

Pulling away from Dad, I gave Killian a playful scowl. "Let's not ruin the night."

He shook his head, but thankfully he let it go. I turned to my big brother and wrapped my arms around his waist.

"Where have you been hiding, stranger?" I scolded him softly.

The whole fiasco with Branka Russo didn't seem to affect him, but for some reason he seemed to be around even less. Shortly after Alessio's wedding to Autumn, my brother and Branka's wedding took place. Much to everyone's shock, she was kidnapped as she made her way down the aisle to marry Killian. Long story short, she'd loved her kidnapper way before she ever liked my brother and had never stopped.

"I've been in New York," Killian said, pushing a strand of hair from my forehead. "It's you who's been distant. And hiding. What trouble have you been up to?"

My stomach dropped like lead, fearing that maybe he had found out about my extracurricular activities. But he wouldn't be smiling the way he was if he did. He'd tear me a new one.

"Moi?" I asked brightly, batting my lashes innocently. "My life is boooring."

Killian quietly observed me, probably seeing more than I wanted him to.

"I'd dare say, your life is more exciting than mine," Ivy remarked, cutting in. "Try living with my family and you'll love boring."

Edward Murphy, the head of the Murphy Irish mafia, and his brothers were anything but boring. And I'd stake my life that living with them wasn't boring either. They probably sheltered Ivy and that alone drove her nuts.

"At least your brothers are hot," Wynter chimed teasingly. "I'd have fun living with them."

Her husband showed up out of thin air and promptly growled. "Jesus, how did you get here so fast?" I muttered.

Wynter immediately blushed and added sweetly, "But not as good looking as my husband. Nobody compares to him."

Basilio watched Wynter with a volatile yet vulnerable look in his eyes. I couldn't understand their relationship. That intense longing.

"We'll come and visit," Davina told Ivy. "Liam's dad invited us over again."

"You mean he invited my son," Dad corrected her. "He's okay with us not coming."

Davina shrugged. "He's crazy. Good man, but crazy. So to Ireland we'll all go."

I wouldn't be going. I loved Grandpa Brennan, but there was no mistake that he'd only considered his grandchild part of his bloodline. Being adopted, Killian and I didn't count. I couldn't blame him, but I'd be lying if I said it didn't hurt a little bit.

"What time do you want to leave?" Davina asked my dad. "I'm tired already." Then she yawned as if to emphasize her fatigue. I really hoped she wasn't knocked up again. It'd make hanging out with her and Wynter unbearable. It seemed sixty percent of our conversation revolved around babies and diapers already.

"Are you pregnant?" Ivy blurted out, obviously having a similar line of thought.

"Well, I am," Wynter answered, grinning while rubbing her belly at the same time. It didn't escape me how she diverted the attention from Davina. I narrowed my eyes on my stepmom and noted she wasn't drinking alcohol.

"Motherfuck—"

"Juliette!"

"You are knocked up!" I hissed. "Again? I mean, don't they say to wait at least two years or some shit like that. We are too young for brats."

"*You* are a brat," a voice came from behind me and I whirled around, coming face-to-face with the man who made the tiny hairs on the back of my neck rise.

"This is an A and B conversation. See yourself out of it," I muttered. When he didn't move, I continued, "Why are you always where you're not wanted?"

He didn't seem fazed. His hands slid into his pockets and he leaned against the wall, his posture casual and self-confident.

"This is *my* cousin's birthday party," he pointed out, his tone self-righteous. I gritted my teeth at his insolence, but I kept my cool and feigned indifference as I returned my attention to my friends whose eyes were darting back and forth between Dante and me.

Dante leaned forward, his scent invading my lungs and tingles exploded over my skin. The man hadn't even touched me and my body reacted.

Breathe, Juliette.

I inhaled deeply and that cologne of rain and forest overwhelmed all my senses. His aftershave wrapped around me. Confidence rolled off of him in waves, his magnetism intoxicating. It was what pissed me off the most. My body reacted, fooling me into thinking I could overcome my phobia of having sex. It was a lie. I'd attempted it enough. The moment the man's body pressed on top of mine, cold panic settled in and suffocated me. Every time. Just thinking about it, an invisible hand wrapped around my throat and almost cut off my oxygen supply.

I released a shuddering breath. Choosing not to tempt my body further, I took a step back to put some distance between us.

"Let's dance," I said to my friends.

Basilio was already all over Wynter, his hand rubbing her growing belly, and it took all my self-control not to roll my eyes. Those two had to stop or they'd end up with a whole soccer team before they were both forty.

Ivy tugged on my hand and we headed onto the dance floor, leaving all my troubles behind. Mainly the DiLustros. But it didn't take a long time for them to catch up to us. Music blared through the speakers. Disco lights cast a glow against our skin as our bodies moved together, limbs jiving and hips rolling.

I moved my hips sensually to the beat of the music. Sexy. Slow. And all along, I was aware of Dante's gaze on me, burning on my skin.

It took only five songs for Wynter to finally give up on us. She and Basilio made their way out and Davina followed not long after.

"Gosh, everybody is heading out," I yelled into Ivy's ear.

She shrugged. "I might too."

"What?" I squealed. "The night has barely started."

"I have a headache," she complained. "Or jet lag."

"God, it's barely nine p.m."

She sighed. "I'm sorry, Jules. I'm just not feeling it tonight."

And she left me too. My eyes skimmed over the room, looking for my brother. I spotted him. Maybe I could catch up with Killian. I walked toward him. He stood with another man, the two of them discussing something serious by the looks of it.

"Hey, brother," I greeted him, my eyes flicking curiously to the hot daddy. Silver-gray beard. Dark eyes. Hot dad body. Jesus, it should be forbidden to be so attractive at that age.

"Ah, Jules, this is a friend of mine. Kian Cortes." I stiffened. "He's a friend of the Ashfords too."

Was that my Kian? The guy that tracked down the fuckers I was killing? No, it couldn't be, that would be far too serendipitous. Yet, that name wasn't exactly one you heard every day. And he's a friend of the

Ashfords. The Kian I worked with protected Autumn, Branka's friend, as a favor to the Ashfords.

I swallowed, deciding to clear out of here as soon as possible.

"More like an acquaintance," Kian added. His gaze came to me and he smiled. My heart skipped a beat at hearing his rich, deep voice. And his smile was beautiful, although it didn't exactly reach his eyes. There was something dark in them. "Nice to meet you, Jules."

I squirmed like a fish on the hook.

"Likewise," I said, suddenly feeling parched. "I'm gonna head to the bar," I said with a forced smile. Kian and I had been communicating for over a year now—I used initials to be safe—but I didn't want to risk this man connecting the dots. The intelligence behind his demeanor was easy to spot. "Come join me, brother, when you're free."

I left without waiting for their response and headed for the bar. Once there, I took a seat.

"Fireball," I ordered. "Make it two. Or three." I barely had time to blink and three shot glasses were placed in front of me. I downed the first shot and was just about to sip the second when a hot sensation trailed down my spine.

I turned my head and my gaze collided with Dante's. My heart slowed, each beat racing as heat licked beneath my skin. It had to be the Fireball.

Dante stared into my eyes. Something about the way he watched me had my insides quivering with so many damn feelings that it terrified me. Except now, I had a few shots swimming through my veins, feeding this infatuation I had for this man.

He sat on the barstool next to me. "Is this seat taken?"

"It is now," I joked, my mood kind of mellow now that I had an infusion of liquor in my system. Any other time, I'd have a snarky comment and an even sharper attitude. To my surprise, tonight it was nowhere to be found. "Where is the birthday girl?" I asked curiously, my gaze traveling over his shoulder. Emory should be around here somewhere. After all, all this was in her honor. But I only saw Priest standing there, his arms folded over his chest.

"She went somewhere with Killian," Dante answered.

My eyebrows shot up. "My brother, Killian?" I questioned in surprise.

"One and only."

"I guess nobody is in a party mood tonight," I remarked. "Wynter and her annoying husband *retired* for the night." I used air quotes for added theatrics. We all knew what they were doing. Pregnancy wasn't putting a stop to their bedroom activities. A shudder rolled through me at that image. Just gross. "Ivy has a migraine. Davina is probably fussing over her baby and my father." That image was even worse.

"They all left you, huh?" Dante mused. "It's a good thing I'm here to keep an eye on you."

I rolled my eyes. "Somehow I think you'll land me in more trouble. Priest is here to keep an eye on both of us," I remarked, tilting my chin in his direction.

Dante chuckled but didn't say anything else. My fingers curled around my glass and I stared at my drink, the amberish liquid of the Fireball made some girls go crazy. Not me. My alcohol tolerance was pretty high, either thanks to our college years or my Irish heritage.

I glanced around again, marveling that I was sitting here with Dante and not my girlfriends. Things had been different since Davina and Wynter married their men. Or maybe it was the fact that I had this secret thing going on. Hunting down anyone connected to my birth parents.

"Why is my brother with Emory?" I asked again, not willing to go down my double-life path.

Dante shrugged. "No fucking idea, but it's odd as fuck."

"Right!" I agreed. "I didn't even know they knew each other well enough to go somewhere together. In fact, I thought they couldn't stand each other."

Dante let out an amused breath. "Well, considering he came with your father to collect Wynter in Emory's home, I'd say they've crossed paths in not-so-friendly circumstances a few times."

"Hmmm." It still seemed odd to me.

"Want to dance?" Dante offered and I shot him a look.

"What makes you think I'm into dancing?" I said. Every other time, we were ready to kill each other and here we were having a half-decent conversation.

"I've seen you dancing on more than one occasion, Juliette. Once even on top of a bar."

My eyebrows shot up to my hairline. "Stalk much?"

"Come on," he encouraged. "It's better than sitting here and staring at our drinks. We must be the two most depressing people in this joint."

I glanced around and back to the spot where Priest stood, but he was no longer there. "I was going to say, your brother takes the cake for the most depressed person, but he's no longer here. So I guess you're right."

Dante grinned. "So...? Yes to dancing?"

He extended his hand gallantly.

"Fine," I agreed, putting my hand into his. His fingers wrapped around it, the warmth instantaneous. "You're being so damn nice."

He chuckled. "I'm always nice to you."

I blew raspberries. "You're always agitating me," I said in a semi-playful tone.

"That's not my intent." His scent prickled my senses and seeped into my system, getting me drunk. My eyes were leveled with his square jaw, stubble darkening it.

"What's your intent?" I asked, tilting my head and putting some space between us. Contrary to everyone's belief, I didn't particularly care about being too close to men. Especially the ones that I considered to be a threat to my self-preservation. "Your ulterior motive. You must have one."

Something flashed in his eyes, but it was gone before I could hone in on it.

"I don't always have an ulterior motive," he said, that smug smile curving his lips.

Our bodies moved together as if we had danced a million times before. We didn't. It was actually our first dance. I scoffed softly thinking of it as that.

"What?" he challenged.

I shook my head. "It's probably the first time that we haven't been at each other's throats," I said.

"We are not at each other's throats," he replied. "You are at my throat."

The song ended and I took a step away from him. Our eyes remained locked, his darkness tugging on me and threading invisible strings.

"I need a drink," I muttered, turning on my heel.

When we returned to the bar, Priest was there waiting for us. He held both of our drinks, leaning against the bar counter casually and looking sharp. Ivy had the hots for him. Like, major hots. She pretended she didn't, but it was plain as day. Ever since she had that moment with him in Philly and it ended in her experiencing her first orgasm—something I still needed more details about, come to think of it.

Dante tilted his head up, swallowing his drink in one swig. Almost as if he were nervous. The only reason it jumped out at me was because he was usually so calm and nonchalant about things.

I returned my attention to Priest who watched both of us with an unreadable expression. Maybe he felt odd being here alone too. Everyone had kind of made themselves scarce around us.

"Thank you for guarding our drinks," I murmured. He didn't answer. No surprise there. There was something about Priest that set you on edge. I couldn't quite pinpoint what but it was definitely there. I brought my glass to my lips, then paused. "So what's the deal with you and Ivy?" I questioned.

He raised one eyebrow. "Deal?" he said in an amused voice. "I didn't realize we had a deal."

I let out an annoyed breath. "Seriously, you men are such jerks," I mumbled. I downed my drink, alcohol burning down my throat. Instantly, warmth followed. Placing my drink down on the bartop, I added, "You don't see what's in front of your nose."

"Please elaborate," Priest demanded, his blue eyes so damn different from Dante's, zeroing in on me.

I blinked, the alcohol creating a haziness in my brain. He wanted me to elaborate. On what? Then I remembered. Ivy. I waved my hand, smiling.

"Girls' secrets," I replied, a soft giggle escaping me. My brows furrowed. Did I giggle? What for?

"I promise never to repeat it," Priest said, his voice softly urging me on.

The music was slightly less loud here compared to the dance floor, but something in his tone pulled my attention to him. His eyes were so similar to my father's that it freaked even Davina out at times.

Except, there was something in the depths of Priest's eyes that he hid. A storm. Maybe pain. I couldn't quite distinguish it.

"Elaborate, *please*," Priest added.

"You give Ivy her first orgasm and then you just ignore her," I said, and his eyes lit up like fireworks in the night sky. "That's what. You men are fucking idiots." Another giggle escaped me on a hiccup. "You don't see what's right in front of your eyes."

"It's not just limited to men, you know," Priest deadpanned. "I know women who don't see what's right in front of them either."

My chest shook, giggles overtaking me.

After that, Dante and I danced. And laughed. Everything was a blur. Distorted images of us walking while he held me. His jacket on my shoulders.

CHAPTER 12
Dante

I was nothing if not persistent.

And this long weekend in Vegas for Emory's birthday celebration was my opportunity. It'd give me a chance to be alone with her. I'd ensure that.

"Basilio, you take your wife and do whatever the fuck you do with her," I told him as we got ready to head out. "Make more babies," I deadpanned.

"She's pregnant," Priest called out from his room on the other side of my suite. "And I don't like that fucking image."

I shrugged. Ever since he learned Wynter was his half-sibling, his protective instinct with that girl skyrocketed. It was fucking annoying as shit.

"Fine, don't make more babies," I said. "Just fuck her so hard she pops this one out. Isn't she due any day now?"

"What the fuck, man!" Basilio and Priest spat at the same time.

"Bottom line is to distract your wife," I hissed, annoyed at my family. "I want Juliette alone."

Basilio shook his head. "Man, maybe that's not the best plan. It sounds like it's headed for a disaster."

"There is no maybe about it," Priest answered, his voice clearly indicating he didn't agree with my plan. "Liam will freak the fuck out."

"We'll worry about Brennan some other time," I told him. "Stop raining on my parade."

"Cuz, you don't have to worry about us. Juliette will be the one raining on your parade. She'll cut your balls off. Your 1934 Hudson Convertible Coupe's damage will be mild compared to her fury if you lock her up."

My brother and cousin were the only ones who truly knew about my obsession for Juliette. But at this moment, their support sucked balls.

"I'm not locking her up," I snapped. "I'm marrying her. If she stops fighting me, she'll see we're perfect for each other. Without her entourage, she'll be forced to spend time with me."

"Well, you're both delusional, so maybe you're right," Priest agreed.

I just flipped him off, ignoring his snarky comments.

Emory strode into the room right on time. "Ah, birthday girl."

"Not yet," she snapped. She didn't want the birthday party. "And don't think I can't see through your devious plan. You started this fucking idea for my birthday party so you could seize a chance with Juliette Brennan."

I glared at her. "Stop saying it so fucking loud."

Emory narrowed her eyes on me. "You know you're on the top floor of the Bellagio. The Presidential Suite, no less. No other guests are here."

I was so fucking paranoid that I forgot.

"Maybe someone is visiting," I offered.

"Yeah, like the unknown bride," Basilio snickered.

I growled at him. "Listen, fucker. You kidnapped your wife from the goddamn Olympics. Did I object? No, I helped you. Now, shut the fuck up. All of you. And follow the plan."

That got their attention. Good. I was sick and tired of waiting for Juliette to come to her senses. She belonged to me. I belonged to her. Cities sizzled and sparked every time we were in the same location.

So help me God. She'd be mine.

"Emory, you distract Killian. Basilio, you bribe the babysitter and have her call Davina for an emergency."

"And the lamb will be left unguarded," Emory finished dryly.

My family fucking sucked sometimes.

Fuck.

Juliette looked breathtaking. Two years of pining after a girl who couldn't stand you were too goddamn long. She was stubborn as fuck and even more proud. But I was even more so.

So far everything was going according to plan. My father and Juliette's aunt didn't plan on attending tonight's nightclub gathering. Basilio already dragged Wynter upstairs. Davina and Liam had the so-called emergency with the sitter. Ivy had a headache.

And Emory dragged Killian out.

Taking another sip of whisky, Juliette and I made it back onto the dance floor. My gaze settled on her. Her cheeks were flushed. Her eyes were shining but her pupils were slightly dilated.

The plan was working.

My lips curved into a smile. I inhaled deeply, my eyes burning over Juliette's creamy skin, the elegant curve of her neck, her stunning-as-fuck body, and her dark hair.

Juliette's eyes locked with mine and she smiled freely. It had to be her first free smile in the two years I'd known her.

"Regretting the dance?"

A smirk curved my lips. "Not even a bit."

Her tongue darted out, swiping over her bottom lip. I had no fucking idea whether she did it on purpose or not, but the gesture made my dick harden in my pants. All she had to do was smile at me and she looked like a goddess of seduction.

I knew I had it bad when I couldn't get it up or get off with another woman after my first encounter with Juliette in my casino. It would turn out that the DiLustro curse finally caught up to me too. We pined and wanted what we couldn't have.

Except, this felt different. Deeper. Stronger.

I remembered the little girl with eyes shining like sapphires under the sun staring at me, offering me her pink scrunchie. The little girl that promised she'd save me one day. Nobody ever saved me and this little girl didn't even know me. And she was willing to save me.

My fucking brother and cousin would die laughing if they knew. I ensured they didn't. I was close with them but not that fucking close.

Juliette's lips curved up, drawing my eyes to them. "Well, I'll give you one thing, DiLustro. You are a smooth dancer."

Things couldn't be going any better. I had Juliette all to myself. She reached for a waiter who offered drinks and downed another shot glass of Fireball. She seemed to love those way too much. Her eyes sparkled and her cheeks stained with a permanent blush.

Without warning, she stopped dancing and closed the distance between us. She rose on her tiptoes, bringing her face close to mine. Well, she attempted to. She was so much shorter, I had to bend my head down.

"Let's go barhopping," she suggested, her words slightly slurred. "And then chapel-hopping."

Taking her chin between my fingers gently, her skin soft under my fingertips, I forced her to focus her eyes on me.

"Just how drunk are you right now?"

She rolled her eyes, but a lazy smile spread across her face. It told me she was drunk as fuck. The substance was well past kicking in and she was feeling the effects of it.

She leaned closer to me and bumped her forehead against my chest, leaving it to rest there.

"Yes, let's do it. Chapel-hopping. I've never even seen a chapel and I've been here for two days."

The evening was looking up.

Then she lifted her face, and before I could even say anything, she slammed her mouth against mine. I stilled for a moment, surprised at her move, but before I could think rationally, my hands cupped her cheeks and I thrust my tongue into her welcoming mouth.

Every muscle in my body tightened. A groan vibrated in my chest, adrenaline rushed through my veins, and a pulse buzzed in my ears.

One word seared into my mind and echoed in my chest.

Mine. Forever mine.

She tasted so good. I sucked on her tongue, hungry to taste her. Her hands wrapped around my neck, her blunt nails scraping along my nape.

Her breasts pushed against me, burning me even through the three-piece suit I was wearing.

Reluctantly, I pulled back, and my eyes searched her face. She was breathless, blinking with a dazed look in her eyes. Her cheeks were flushed, her lips swollen and parted... she looked downright fuckable.

So damn tempting.

But that wasn't part of my plan. Not when she was drunk and drugged.

"Let's go bar and chapel-hopping," she announced again, then before I could even answer, she grabbed my hand and dragged me off the dance floor. The moment we stepped outside, goosebumps broke out over her skin.

Vegas was warm during the day, but nights could be chilly. So I slid my jacket off and put it on her shoulders.

"Thank you, Dante." She glanced my way and offered a dazzling smile. Jesus Christ. Where was this side of Juliette hiding all this time? I didn't even know she could knock a man off his feet with just a smile.

Then it hit me. It was the first time she uttered my name. It sounded so fucking hot coming from her lips. Soft. Like a lover's whisper.

She slid her arms into the sleeves and I wrapped my arms around her, almost expecting her to push me away. Instead, she leaned her slender body further into me.

Fucking shit. I was whipped.

"Let's walk," she suggested. "We don't need to drive down the strip."

"Okay," I agreed. *Fuck, did I do the right thing?* I wanted to ask for forgiveness but I wanted her even more. So we walked. It'd help with clearing her head. Mine too. Although I feared her kiss might have gotten *me* drunk. I had definitely fallen under her spell.

I kept my eyes alert, flicking my gaze her way every so often. My hand around her shoulder, and her hands wrapped around my waist, we looked like two lovers taking a stroll. We passed a few bars, but thankfully, she didn't bring them up.

After a few blocks, she stopped in front of a building and shouted out, "A drive-through wedding chapel." This was where I'd always wanted to end up with her, but now, I wasn't so sure. The marriage license burned a hole in my pocket. I should drag her out of here. This plan was so damn wrong, yet my feet remained still.

Two years. It was to give us a chance. Yet deep down, I knew I was taking it too far.

My lips brushed over the soft skin on her neck, then traced my mouth up her jawline and ended the trail with a kiss on her forehead.

Her eyes were closed and a small smile curved her lips. Then she slowly opened them, the depths of them shining like stars trapped in the blue seas.

"Do you think we need a car?" she asked softly. "I really, really want to do it."

Fuck it.

"We don't need a car."

And that was how I sealed our future.

CHAPTER 13
Juliette

A pulsing ache pounded in my temples.

I felt like I had been run over. By a tractor trailer. I shifted to my side and let out a groan as a wave of nausea hit. It felt like a hot flash, building and building until I could feel it in my throat.

Throwing the covers off me, I stumbled out of the bed and face-planted.

"Dear God," I mumbled, crawling on my hands and knees toward the bathroom, squinting. What did I drink last night? Did someone drug me? I couldn't remember much of anything aside from going out to dance with the girls.

I barely made it to the toilet, retching shit I didn't remember eating into the toilet. Disgusting noises vibrated through the bathroom, bouncing off the tile and I swore at that very moment I'd never drink alcohol again.

Never. I retched. *Never again.*

Alcohol was banned forever. No longer part of my vocabulary.

Leaning my forehead on my forearm, I inhaled a deep breath, then exhaled. I repeated it again. Feeling somewhat better, I rose to my feet and padded to the sink, the tile cool against my feet. I brushed my teeth, erasing the horrific taste from my mouth.

Once done, I decided to take a shower. Maybe it'd wash off some of this hangover. Keeping the temperature on the cool side, I tilted my face up at the showerhead and let the water fall down my body.

Once I lathered my hair with the lilac shampoo and finished washing off, I stepped out of the shower already feeling better. I dried myself, then wrapped a towel around me.

The corner of my eye caught a sparkle in the mirror. What the—

My eyes lowered to the hand where a large solitaire diamond sat. In a daze, I brought my hand up to my face, almost expecting the ring to disappear.

Nope, still there.

The enormous diamond stared back at me, refusing to budge. I blinked, faster and faster. Maybe I was seeing things. I touched it. It felt real. Oh. My. God.

My breathing picked up. My pulse raced into marathon mode. My knees weakened.

What happened last night, I thought again.

I braced myself on the counter with my free hand. I had to find Wynter. Or Davina. Actually, it might be wiser to search for Ivy. There'd be no judgment there.

God, please don't let me be married. Anything, literally anything but that. I couldn't be married. *Please, please, please.*

Frustration clawed at my chest. At myself. At my stupidity. I'd always been on the wilder side compared to Wynter, but never reckless. Okay, maybe occasionally reckless. But not like this. I couldn't remember jack shit.

Attempting to recall what happened last night, the pulsing ache against my temples increased tenfold. I'd ask my friends. They wouldn't have left me. They'd know for sure.

I rushed into the bedroom to find something to wear when I came to a sudden stop. A man sat at the edge of my bed with a cup of coffee.

Dante DiLustro.

Of all the men in the world, he was the last one I wanted to see right now. I needed a special kind of pill to deal with him.

"Hello, my wildling," he greeted me. My eyes narrowed on him suspiciously. I fucking hated that nickname, but there was one thing I'd learned about Dante. The more you fought him on something, the more insistent he was on doing exactly that which irritated. "Cappuccino for you. I figured you'd need it."

Dante DiLustro was the biggest pain in my ass to ever walk this earth. Expensive Italian suit. Sharp lines. Charisma. And that grin. That fucking grin that got on my fucking nerves because it got me so damn wet.

"What are you doing in my room?" I snapped, glaring at him. "I don't have time for you and your bullshit today! Get the fuck out!"

His free hand came to his heart. "What? No time for your husband?"

I froze. His left hand tapped against his muscled thigh. *Tap. Tap. Tap.* My eyes lowered to his and my lungs tightened. I swore something or someone gripped them, taking all the air from them so I'd suffocate. Dante had a wedding ring on.

The. Fucking. Wedding. Ring.

Opening my mouth, I couldn't find my voice. For the first time in my life, I couldn't find words for this pain-in-the-ass man.

"Cat got your tongue, wife?" he asked, amused.

He threw back at me the same words I gave him when I first met him. This was the reason Dante and I were like fire and gasoline. Somehow he always knew how to pour just the right amount and create a raging inferno.

"There is no way I'd ever be drunk enough to marry you," I hissed. "I refuse to believe it."

He was on his feet the next second and stalked toward me, ignoring the mess and discarded clothes all over the hotel room. Instinctively, I took a step back and my back pressed against the cold wall. He took another step forward, his three-piece suit brushing lightly against my chest, and rested his hands on the wall above my head.

The look in his eyes changed from amusement to pleasure-soaked intensity and satisfaction. Pure, unadulterated heat. My pulse whooshed in my ears and a tremor rolled across my skin. Inhaling his scent had been doing things to me since the moment I fell into his arms. Literally.

The closeness of his body had the most peculiar impact on me every damn time. I fought it for two years. At every turn. Instead of easing, the reaction became worse. Like a fucking rash refused to go away.

"We were both drunk enough to marry each other," he drawled with a dangerous note in his voice. "And we'll bear the consequences. Together."

I couldn't find enough air to breathe. His voice resonated warmth, a thoughtful rumble so close to my mouth I could taste it. What was wrong with me for Christ's sake? He was practically threatening me and my body melted.

A sanity check was needed.

"I told you two years ago, I don't want to marry you," I breathed, while heat pulsed in my core.

"And I have told you I'd never give up." Then his lips touched mine, softly, only a whisper.

"I'll run," I rasped, but my stupid body worked against me. It arched off the wall and pushed against his hard, lean body. I needed more. So much more. Yet I knew it wouldn't end well. At a certain point, my panic would kick in. Except, in this very moment, it was nowhere to be found.

Only desire. Only need.

"If you run, Juliette, I'll chase you."

It was a vow. A promise.

Just as he had vowed he'd never give up on me. Not until we were married.

His lips pressed against mine, then nipped my bottom lip. The graze of his teeth moved a desperate noise up my throat. My breathing was erratic, and instead of pushing him away, my fingers gripped his suit and pulled him closer. He drew on my lips softly, first the top lip, and then the bottom. Need vibrated through me, humming and buzzing, burning everywhere we touched.

I arched against him, feeling an incredible heat beyond his expensive black suit. He licked inside of my mouth, then sucked on my tongue. Heat, tiny pricks of heat, consumed me from the inside out.

He pulled back and said in a rough voice, "Promise you won't run."

It was one goddamn weakness I had. I always, fucking always, kept my promises. He was using this burning desire between us against me because like a weak woman, I uttered those two words that would bind me to him.

"I promise."

The pressure of his mouth on mine was rougher. More possessive. Wetter than before. His kisses must have been some kind of dirty, carnal sin once upon a time. A blaze seared through me as I drew my blunt nails down the length of his back. He growled low in his throat, and the slow glide of his mouth roughened. Dante pressed his hard-on against my lower stomach and that was when I froze.

The blaze was extinguished and turned into a frozen tundra.

Fear was a paralyzing bitch.

CHAPTER 14
Dante

Juliette's body froze. Her breathing sped up. Panic entered her expression.

I took a step backward, giving her space. This reaction was the last thing I expected from this woman. Trouble. Fight. Argument. Passion. All of it, yes.

Panic, never.

"Breathe, Juliette," I ordered, locking gazes with her blue eyes. "Breathe." She inhaled deeply, then slowly exhaled. "Good. Again."

I watched her as she did it again. And again. Slowly the panic faded, replaced with her customary feistiness. Or maybe it was a façade she kept firmly in place to hide something dark underneath all that stubbornness.

"What?" she snapped. "Why are you staring at me?"

I studied her, taking note of her breathing. The redness of her chest. There were still traces of a blush staining her pale skin, evidence of her arousal before she panicked. Just as my balls ached painfully and my dick was hard as marble. But there was no chance in hell we'd go any further until I learned what triggered it.

Last night, under the influence, I had a hard time keeping her hands off my body. She groped me and insisted on stripping our clothes off. Not that I minded. She even insisted on helping to disarm me, stating my gun holster looked so sexy on me.

I'd wear that fucking gun holster to bed if she found it sexy. Maybe then she'd find me irresistible like I did her.

I made my way back to the bed and sat down. She was still naked, wrapped up only in a fluffy white towel, hiding her body from my view.

"Do you want to talk about it?" I asked her.

She rolled her eyes. "I don't know what you mean. Talk about what?"

She knew exactly what I meant. She seemed to forget who I was. I was used to seeing fear on people's faces. They feared me because of my name, Syndicate skull tattoo, and who I represented. The Syndicate. The underworld.

Juliette shifted on her feet uncomfortably when I refused to play her game.

I raised my hand, pointing to the ring on my finger. "I'm your husband. Remember your vows from last night. Thou shall not lie, cheat, and steal."

"Aren't those part of the Ten Commandments?"

"You insisted on making up your own vows," I told her dryly. Juliette under the influence was a force to be reckoned with. "Something about if I must steal, then I should steal away your sorrows. So here I am, stealing away your sorrows."

An unreadable expression passed her face, but then she quickly gathered herself together and rolled her eyes.

"Whatever, there's nothing to talk about." Although this time, her voice wasn't as sure as all the times before.

I'd break through her walls. We'd been playing this game for two years now, but that road had come to an end. She was my wife now. My ring was on her finger, and whether she liked it or not, I'd get to the bottom of her fear.

It was my job to protect her.

CHAPTER 15
Juliette

O f all the scenarios, this had to be the worst one. My eyes kept darting between his finger and mine. The wedding rings. A simple black band on his finger and a platinum band with black diamonds on mine. The diamond, on what was presumably my engagement ring, was beautiful. Except, I couldn't remember a single damn thing that happened to get it on my finger.

Shocked prickles spread over every inch of my skin. I returned my attention to the well-dressed Italian, his eyes resting cautiously on me. Suddenly, I felt parched. My tongue darted out to wet my lips.

"What happened last night?" I asked cautiously. Dante reached to the bedside table where a fresh cup of Starbucks coffee sat in the paper cup holder, then held it out to me and I took it, our fingers brushing together. "Did we—" I couldn't even finish the statement. God, we might have had sex and I couldn't even remember. Fuck! There was one thing that was certain to be a glorious memory and that was sex with this man. Or maybe I panicked and embarrassed myself, just as I had a few minutes ago. "Did we have sex?"

Dante shrugged. I took it as a yes and pushed my hand through my dark hair.

"Oh my God," I rasped. "I can't even remember it." I gripped my hair as if that would pull memories from some dark corner of my mind. Maybe I should look at the bright side of things. If I slept with him and he was still alive, apparently, it must have gone okay. I didn't punch him. Or bite him, as far as I could see.

He'd remember that. Right?

"I can't remember anything," I repeated in a whisper.

Then horror shot through me and my eyes widened. If I opened my mouth, sex with Dante would be the last thing to worry about. I watched him cautiously, studying his masked expression. That was the thing with Dante. You could never tell what he was thinking. Either to fuck you or kill you.

"Did I say anything?" I questioned, swallowing the lump in my throat. What if I had admitted my secret to him? I steeled my spine, already working out some ludicrous explanation in the back of my mind. "Last night," I clarified.

Dante stood up, his tall frame making me crane my neck. God, the man was tall. Too fucking tall. I preferred a man that didn't tower over me. That didn't make me feel smaller. This guy made me feel vulnerable and that was the feeling I hated the most.

"Well?" I asked, my tone slightly insolent. I couldn't help it, he brought out the worst in me.

"Like what?" he questioned, his tone curious.

"Anything," I gritted. "Why do you make everything so difficult?"

He raised one eyebrow nonchalantly. "I'm simply asking a question, Juliette," he elaborated. "I'm not your enemy here."

Jesus Christ, this fucker. Always irritating me. Nobody ever made my temper flare as much as Dante DiLustro. It was the reason for destroying his precious car. When he first approached my father with his ultimatum for destroying his casino—a marriage ultimatum—I'd lost my shit. Truthfully, my girlfriends and I didn't destroy his casino. We just made it smell a bit better, more... lavender-y.

"What do you think you said last night?" Dante questioned again.

I let out an exasperated breath. "What do you remember?" I asked instead. It wasn't as if I'd tell him what I hoped I *didn't* say. He was probably working that reverse psychology on me.

He pushed his hand, with the black band, through his thick dark hair.

"The last thing I remember was having drinks with you, and then heading onto the dance floor," he stated matter-of-factly. I nodded. I remembered that too. "Then we headed out to hit another bar. You insisted on barhopping and seeing at least one chapel in Vegas."

Wonderful. So it was my idea! What. The. Actual. Fuck.

"Well, that is more than I remember," I grumbled. "Dancing with you must have been the worst idea I ever had. Clearly it led to a string of bad decisions."

That smug smile reappeared on his face. "Clearly you find me irresistible."

I rolled my eyes, annoyed at his self-confidence. My gaze darted to the rumpled sheets, then back to Dante.

"God, I don't know which is worse," I muttered. "The idea that we slept together or the idea that we got married." My eyes lowered down to my finger. "Maybe we played pretend or some shit," I added hopefully.

Reaching into his breast pocket, Dante removed a piece of paper and held it out to me. I watched it wearily. "Take it," he demanded.

I shook my head. If I saw an official document with what we'd done, I wouldn't be able to pretend it was a nightmare. That it didn't happen.

"I didn't take you for a coward, Juliette," he drawled, studying me with a dark expression.

My eyes jumped between Dante and the document, then slowly I reached for it. For a second, I studied it, not wanting to open it but finally, straightening my shoulders, I set the coffee cup down, tightened the towel wrapped around my body, then unfolded the document.

Oh. My. God.

It was a marriage certificate with both of our names on it. My lungs squeezed and I shook my head.

"No, no, no," I murmured over and over again, as if that would make it all better. I squeezed my eyes shut, then opened them hoping I'd find different information on the certificate. Still the same names.

Dante DiLustro and Juliette Brennan—now DiLustro.

"Oh my God." I gulped as I moved over to sit on the side of the bed. "Oh my fucking God." My brain cells must have still been drunk because it took a while for the knowledge to sink in and for any ideas to come. There had to be a way to rectify the situation.

In a numb state, I watched my sparkling blue toes press against the wooden floor of the hotel.

"How much did we drink, exactly?" I asked.

"Apparently a lot," he replied, his voice slightly hoarse.

Closing my eyes, I tried to recall a single detail of last night. Yet, nothing came forward. Not a single image. It made no sense. I could hold my liquor. The girls and I drank bottles and bottles of vodka and other hard liquor. I had never blacked out.

"Are you okay?" Dante asked, concern in his voice evident.

"Okay? No, I'm not okay"—I waved the marriage certificate in front of his nose—"I got married. This is the most unoriginal thing I have ever done. Getting married in Vegas."

He took the certificate from my hands and tucked it back into his pocket. "It could be worse. You could have robbed a casino in Vegas," he remarked wryly, referring to our robbery of his casino in Chicago.

"Why can't you let that go?" I mumbled under my breath. "I've never met a man that holds a grudge like you."

It seemed like decades ago when it was only two years ago. Gosh, how things have changed. When I first met him, I wasn't a killer. Yet as it stood, I had blood on my hands.

My eyes darted to Dante. Now both of our hands were drenched in blood. Two years ago, mine were at least innocent.

I should have never gone down this path. Who knew the road would lead us here that day in his casino? Two years of circling each other. Two years of bickering. Two years of... foreplay?

"Drink the coffee," Dante urged. "The cappuccino is just the way you like it." The fact he knew the way I like my coffee combined with his deep, warm voice had my insides shuddering. "You need it." I didn't move. I didn't say anything. "It seems the cat indeed got your tongue," he said, a light sarcasm in his voice sending an alert through me. "I don't think I've ever seen you speechless before."

In hindsight, it wasn't the best thing to say that night in his casino, but fuck it. I wasn't good at thinking on my feet. I reacted. Maybe I reacted last night too.

He pushed the cup closer to my face and I took a sip, letting the warm liquid rush down my throat. It tasted good, and apparently it was exactly what I needed to come up with a brilliant plan.

"We can get an annulment," I exclaimed. "It happens all the time."

"No."

My spine stiffened. I slowly turned my head and narrowed my eyes on him.

"No?" I repeated, ending it on a question.

His dark eyes burned, locked on me. If he'd pulled on my towel, I'd be left standing here naked next to him fully dressed in his signature three-piece suit.

"Check your phone." My eyes lifted to him.

"Why?" I questioned, furrowing my brows. "It's hardly the time to be phoning anyone."

He shook his head. "It seems you sent a mass text announcing our marriage."

My mouth dropped and my eyes popped out of my head.

"What?" I rasped in disbelief. "I—I did what?"

At that very moment, the hotel room door burst open and I jumped to my feet with a squeal. My girlfriends had shown up at the door, their wide eyes darting between Dante and me. My gaze traveled over Wynter, Ivy, then ended at Davina.

"Oh my gosh, it's true," one of them whispered. Their attention ping-ponged between the two of us and the rumpled sheets behind us that clearly indicated something happened last night.

Before I could say anything, Dad showed up behind Davina. He looked from me to Dante, then behind us. Disappointment flashed across his expression and he shook his head.

"It's done, then," he remarked, his voice tight. "You could have saved me the grief over the years and just done it when he asked to marry you."

"Dad, it's not like that," I started to say but he put his hand up.

"It's exactly as it looks, Juliette," he answered.

"No, it's fucking worse," my brother spat, showing up out of nowhere. He was furious, glaring at Dante. "He's been stalking Juliette, unwilling to let go. I'm willing to bet he just waited for her to get drunk, then dragged her to the nearest chapel."

I swallowed hard. It wasn't right to put all the blame on Dante. "We were both drunk," I murmured. "He doesn't remember anything either."

Besides, I didn't want to be the cause for the war between my family and Dante's. If I let my brother lay all the blame on Dante, I could get out of the marriage but at what cost? The image of dead Dante flashed in my mind and something about it unsettled me. Upset me even.

"You're actually defending him?" Killian growled, pulling out his gun and aiming it at Dante. The latter wouldn't have it and responded the same, jumping to his feet. "As much as you hate him, you're defending him?"

"Whoa, hold on," Wynter chimed in. "You can't shoot him, Killian."

"Why the fuck not?" He kept his weapon trained on Dante. I rushed to them and put myself between my brother and my... ugh, my husband.

"Get behind me, Juliette," Dante growled. "Before your fucking brother makes a mistake and shoots you."

I rolled my eyes. What a stupid thing to say!

"Juliette, listen to your one-minute husband," Killian snickered. "I'll end him before we leave and you can be a widow."

It sounded tempting, but not at the cost of Dante's life. I couldn't let my fear dictate what happens to him. I swallowed hard, fear trembling in my chest. It felt cold, icing over my lungs.

"Killian, lower your weapon," Dad chimed in calmly. My brother ignored him. According to the expression on Dad's face, he was close to losing his shit. "Dante, lower your weapon, then; since my son has turned into a stubborn ass."

Dante ignored him too.

"Liam, let's take Killian and go check on the baby," Davina said, attempting to ease the tense situation. "I don't like to leave him with the sitter."

I forced a smile. "You will leave my hotel room too," I said, locking eyes with my brother. "Now."

"This isn't over, DiLustro," Killian warned as he turned on his heel and left us. At least he listened. Usually he did whatever the hell he wanted. Although, he'd been different lately. More pensive. Less aggressive. I didn't know if it had something to do with his broken engagement or something else.

Once he was gone, the girls all started to leave. I could see by the look in their eyes, this wouldn't be the end of it either.

"Can we get the juicy details?" Wynter mused. "After all, it's payback time."

"Get out," I snapped. "Everyone, get out."

"Well, that seems unfair," Davina mockingly sneered. "We shared all the juicy details with you."

I narrowed my eyes on her. She knew very well I never wanted to know the juicy details of her with my dad. Yuck! No, thank you.

"No, you didn't." I padded across the floor, Dante right at my back. God, if this was how things would go, he'd be dead by my own hand before the week was over. "Now, get out."

I pushed them out of the room, ignoring their snickering remarks.

With the door shut, I leaned against it with a heavy sigh. "This is a clusterfuck," I grumbled, searching Dante's eyes. "We need an annulment. Right away."

Dante's phone beeped and he reached for it. Something resembling satisfaction passed his expression before he masked it.

He gestured between us. "Get dressed. Your father wants us at Emory's birthday party."

I groaned. I forgot about the birthday party being hosted at her place tonight. It was the only reason we'd come to Vegas.

"I'll go with my family," I reasoned. "You go with yours. No need to act like we're married."

"But we *are* married." He gestured to my hand as if to bring his point home. As if I could forget. I'd only held the stupid marriage certificate minutes ago. "And your father expects us to go together. So do I."

I gaped at him.

"So what? Just because you two insist, I have to follow?" I snapped. We stood chest to chest, the scent of a forest after rain and leather seeping into my lungs. An involuntary shudder traveled through me. "I won't go with you," I protested. "We are not together."

"We're married," he gritted.

"I don't know what happened last night but mistakes happen. Everyone knows we'd never have gotten married if we were sober."

He maintained his composure, his gaze cold on me but his jaw ticked, betraying him. "Never say never."

I let out a frustrated breath. "I *am* saying never, Dante." When he remained silent, I continued, my tone higher in pitch. "I'm not sleeping with you. I'm not going to be married to you. I'm not doing anything with you. I'd sooner cut your dick off than have sex with you."

"Get dressed, Juliette," he ordered. Placing both his hands on my arms, he lifted me up like a stiff doll and shifted me to the left.

Then he left the room as I stared after him and the closed door.

I fucked up royally this time.

CHAPTER 16
Dante

I left the bedroom and headed downstairs. I found my brother and cousin already dressed in their tailored suits and sitting at the Bellagio bar by the lobby.

"Ah, there's the groom," Priest announced. "I'm surprised you came out of it alive."

Basilio, deciding to play a jerk too and reminding me that I needed to find a new family, asked, "Your dick still intact?"

My expression hardened and strain entered my body.

"I assume you two will hold back your comments until you're dead," I said as I took a seat between them.

"Don't worry," Priest replied dryly. "I know when to shut up."

"That's debatable," I muttered.

Basilio felt the need to chime in. "What's debatable is your fucking plan to tie Juliette Brennan to you. The girl hates your guts."

"Give it to me softly, why don't you?"

"You realize that Brennan will put a bullet in your head if he ever finds out what happened last night," Priest said.

I shrugged as I flagged a bartender over. Priest usually had a good handle on his emotions, but for some reason, he was being a dick today.

"Don't worry, he won't risk war with us," Basilio remarked. "Sofia

Volkov is a bigger problem than Juliette." My cousin's gaze locked on me. "Although for the fucking life of me I don't understand why you are so fixated on that girl."

My brother smirked. "He hasn't been able to get his cock up for any other girl ever since Juliette bumped into him not-so-accidentally back in Chicago."

He wasn't far off. Juliette was the definition of my obsession, had been ever since fate had brought her back into my life. Nothing else had ever come close. The more she fought our attraction, the more fixated I became. Until it was part of me and there was no way out.

I waited. I really did. I tried. I really did.

But instead of her caving to our attraction, she slipped further away from me. So I devised a plan, and it worked. She was now mine.

"I just hope she's worth it," Basilio said dryly. "Personally, I think she's more of a headache than she's worth."

"You're wrong," I snapped.

Basilio sighed, touching his temple. "I hope my kids are nothing like us."

I agreed with him; although I was in no rush to bring children into this world. First, I needed my new wife to fall to my charms, then I'd enjoy our time together, and I fucking refused to share her with snotty little kids.

Priest's eyes darted to something behind me. I looked over my shoulder and spotted Juliette. Her expression darkened as she sent a snide glance my way. She was wearing a red minidress and sky-high heels. I gritted my teeth. Was she trying to have every fucking man from here to Emory's house drool after her?

A few passersby already stared at her openly, not even trying to hide the desire lurking in their eyes. I wanted to shoot them all, then make her go get dressed in a nun's outfit.

"Don't," Priest warned in a low tone and his eyes locked on mine in that annoying, brooding way. I returned my attention to Juliette. It was a much better view. She was tapping her foot impatiently.

"I don't have all day," she snapped. "Are we going or not?"

I didn't have to look at my brother and cousin to know their mouths twitched. They were such assholes.

"You wanted her, Dante," Basilio said under his breath as he slapped my shoulder playfully. "Have fun with her."

I stood up, flipping him the bird. "I hope you have tons of kids that are like their aunt," I muttered as I walked away.

"Let's hope you survive to see it," Priest yelled after me.

Their chuckles followed behind me.

"What in the fuck are you wearing?" I hissed under my breath. "Every man is staring at you, stripping you with their minds."

She shrugged a slim shoulder. "I can't control what men do."

I took a deep breath in and let it out slowly. "Juliette, I'd rather not kill anyone today for gawking at you."

She started walking, heading for the exit.

"Nobody's asking you to kill anyone," she answered, staring straight ahead.

I took her elbow and pulled her to a stop. "Juliette, go change," I gritted out.

"No."

"Now!"

She jerked her arm out of my grip. "Give me an annulment," she countered.

"No."

Her feistiness would end up driving me insane, if I wasn't there already.

She lowered her eyes to her little shoulder bag that matched her dress, then started rummaging through it. She pulled out a car key.

"There you have it." The smile she gave me could freeze an active fucking volcano over. "I don't get my way and you don't get yours. Now, let's go or I'll skip this damn birthday party altogether."

My jaw clenched so fucking hard it hurt my eardrums. "Put the fucking key away. I'm driving."

We resumed walking, my car already waiting for us. When the valet's eyes landed on Juliette, he ran to open her door but my glare stopped him short. I opened the passenger door to my Bugatti and she slid into the leather seat angrily. The hem of her dress hiked up and she quickly tugged it down.

My lip curved. It reminded me of our first meeting and that midnight-blue dress she wore. As she ran away from me after kicking me in the balls, I caught her tugging on the dress. Even back then I somehow didn't think she liked to wear minidresses but insisted on it for whatever ridiculous reason.

The drive to Emory's place passed in silence. It didn't bother me, but the constant sighs coming from the passenger's side told me something bothered my wife.

My muscles tensed when I pulled up my car in front of Emory's massive stone-and-stucco villa.

I parked at the front entrance and came around the car to open the door for Juliette. She hadn't said a single goddamn word the entire way here. I'd attempted conversation, even tried to get a rise out of her but gave up pretty quickly.

Nothing.

The woman refused to react.

I held out my hand, a silent order, and her eyes flashed with that defiance I'd come to know since I met her. *Good*, I thought silently. I'd been starting to worry.

She put her fingers into my palm and I wrapped my hand around them. She stood up, barely reaching to my chin. It always surprised me to realize how short Juliette was. Her personality was so damn big, I'd expected her to reach my six foot three.

I regarded her. She was angry. Of course, she had every right to be, even more than she realized. She narrowed her eyes, then took a deep breath in, only to slowly release it.

Thud-thud. Thud.

Her pulse raced in an erratic rhythm. It was a novelty. Juliette Brennan was always the wild one. Fearless. Yet, ever since she woke up with my ring on her fingers, a switch had been flipped.

She had been acting like she had been given a death sentence.

"Let's go," she gritted, her voice trembling.

Without another word, I led Juliette inside where the party was already in full swing. The guests mingled, but the moment we appeared,

85

the voices lowered a few notches. I'd wager the two of us were a topic of quite a few circles tonight.

The Ashfords. The Kings. The Russos. The Nikolaevs. And of course, the DiLustros and Brennans.

Everyone who was someone was here.

"Ah, my cousin and his new bride." Emory rushed toward us with a tight smile. "Thanks for coming."

Juliette gave her a tight smile. "Happy birthday, Emory." My wife handed her a gift bag. "Open it when you're alone," she suggested.

Emory's cheeks blushed. "God, I never know what I'm getting with you."

"You and me both," Juliette replied, her tone more than a little dry.

"Oh my gosh, show me the ring," Emory exclaimed, clapping her hands and smiling widely but guilt passed her expression. She hid it well, accustomed to hiding her emotions as well as Priest. We spent a lot of time together growing up, so it was easy to recognize her nervous signs. To anyone else, she looked to be in her element.

Strong. Badass. And fearless.

I scoffed in my head. I couldn't believe I hadn't recognized it until now. Emory was just like Juliette.

Juliette reluctantly offered up her hand, the diamond sparkling under the lights of the chandeliers in the large hosting room. I considered my wife as she kept a forced smile on her lips. Her face was heart shaped, and her dark hair was in stark contrast to her pale skin and those sapphire-blue eyes.

"Do you like it?" Emory asked softly. "It belonged to Dante's grandma. She was a sweetheart."

It was the only piece of jewelry my mother couldn't get her hands on. Thank fuck. Or it would have all been gone.

"It's lovely," Juliette answered but enthusiasm couldn't be found on her face. My cousin flicked a fleeting glance at me, exasperation in her eyes. She hated that she was a part of my plan.

Then Juliette's brows furrowed in thought. "How did you happen to have it here? In Vegas?"

Emory's smile faltered, but before she could say anything, I jumped in. "Emory held them for safekeeping."

Pulling my wife away from my cousin, we made our way past the rest of the guests and stopped in front of her father, brother, and her stepmother-slash-friend. While Liam and Killian carried grim expressions, Davina smiled and hugged her friend.

As they hugged, Killian shot a glare my way. If looks could kill, I'd be dead. Not even twenty-four hours after I had finally gotten an "I do" from Juliette Brennan.

Liam kept his eyes on me, keeping his expression unreadable. When Juliette pulled away from Davina, he turned his attention to her and his expression softened.

"Jules, I'm glad you came," he said, pulling her into a hug. "I was sharp with you this morning, but I am happy for you." My wife pressed her cheek against his chest. "I just wish you hadn't gone about marrying without the family present." Juliette paled slightly, but she didn't comment. "I talked to the hotel and some guests here," he continued, his tone softer. "We'll have a wedding ceremony tomorrow and a small reception. No daughter of mine will have a Vegas drive-through wedding."

"Drive-through?" she asked, her brows furrowed, and this time Liam glared at me too.

"Yes," Killian hissed. "You sent us the pictures of your drive-through wedding."

I wished I had confiscated her phone that night. Unfortunately, Juliette reacted unexpectedly to the drug Priest slipped into her drink. She loosened up, raved about how handsome I was and how she wanted to memorize my face. She even smiled at me affectionately, patting my abs and trying to take my clothes off.

Of course, I wouldn't let her. She was too high. I wanted her to remember every time I touched her. I wanted her sober and conscious.

"Jesus," my wife muttered. "I'm swearing off alcohol for good."

"About time," Liam grumbled.

Juliette inhaled a deep breath. "About the wedding, I'd rather not."

Liam waved his hand. "Nonsense. We're doing it."

"Liam, if they don't want to—" Killian started to argue before being interrupted.

"Her mother is probably turning in her grave. I remember when Juliette was born. My best friend and his wife vowed they'd throw her a big Irish wedding."

"They did?" she questioned, surprised. Liam nodded. "They aren't here, Dad," Juliette reasoned. She kept herself together but I noted her hands trembling. What in the fuck was going on? "So let's leave the Irish wedding for some other time and all just move on."

"I agree," I chimed in. "We'll do what Juliette's most comfortable with." Ironic considering how I trapped my wife.

Liam sighed. "Okay, we'll leave off the Irish wedding, but we'll do the proper wedding. Tomorrow."

Juliette let out a frustrated breath, her eyes flashing with annoyance. "It isn't like this was a dream match or anything. The two of us got drunk and had an unoriginal idea to get hitched. A mistake. Nothing more; nothing less."

I gritted my teeth while bitter amusement filled me. This dark-haired woman was all I'd been thinking about and she was calling this a mistake. I let out a sardonic breath. She was put on this earth for me and only me, so I'd show her how perfect of a match we were.

And with that, I wrapped my arm around her waist and pulled her closer to me, tightening my grip around her.

"Tomorrow. Formal. Wedding." Liam's tone made it clear it was non-negotiable. Then, just in case he didn't get his point across, he added, "That's final. We already finalized the idea with the guests."

"So good to know it's about what I want," Juliette said. "Aye, aye, Captain, we'll be there." Her eyes held something dark when she turned to me. "Right, husband?"

"Correct, wife."

Something was off about her, I just couldn't put my finger on it.

CHAPTER 17
Juliette

This was what they called shit backfiring in your face.

Wynter, Davina, and Ivy gushed over the wedding preparations while I stood there, barely keeping it together. My fingernails dug into my palms while I desperately held on to my composure.

For everyone, it was where Dante and I were always meant to end up. For me, it brought a different kind of worry.

The wedding night.

I survived it last night, but then I couldn't remember much of it. Maybe it had been as horrific as that night all those years ago, only I had no real way of knowing. A cold shiver rolled down my spine each time I thought about it. My breathing hitched and terror spread through my veins. Some would say it served me right. I taunted and mocked, acting tough, and now I wanted to crawl into a hole and hide.

"What's going on?" Ivy asked under her breath. "You're walking around like a zombie. It's Emory's party and you're acting like it's a funeral."

I met her gaze, but nothing but mild curiosity met me. Even she didn't know of my demons. She didn't know me back then. Wynter and I met Davina and Ivy in college, but Wynter also had no idea about that night.

My ears buzzed, fear pushing adrenaline through my bloodstream and making it hard to breathe.

"She's probably upset that Dante finally got her," Wynter attempted, easing pliable tension with a joke. She was wrong. It was so much worse than just that. There was a reason I never went past a certain point with a boy. It brought ghosts and terror back with a vengeance.

Davina gripped my hand hard. "I know you're upset," she murmured. "Liam insisted on a more formal wedding tomorrow. I tried to dissuade him, but you know how stubborn he gets." I nodded. I knew my father's stubbornness very well, even though we didn't share any genetics. There was nothing anyone could say to stop him when that man made up his mind.

I swallowed while my heart thundered in an erratic rhythm in my chest. My stomach revolted at what was to come, and I pressed my palm against it. At this rate, I'd stroke out before tomorrow. I had to calm down.

I could get through this. Many had gone through much worse and survived. My eyes flickered to Alexei Nikolaev who stood alongside his wife. He'd survived unspeakable horrors.

His arctic-blue eyes met mine for the briefest moment. It was hard not to feel fear when that man focused on you. You never knew whether he was planning on killing you or just extracting all your secrets out.

I forced a smile, then returned my attention to my girlfriends.

"So who's getting me a wedding dress?" I asked, my voice slightly higher pitched.

My best friends weren't fooled but they decided to play along. The next thirty minutes were spent talking about readily available designer dresses to choose from in Nevada.

All the while my mind worked on the next man I'd hunt down and torture. I had another name—Jovanov Plotnick. He was present the night my birth parents were murdered.

A girl had to have an outlet. Right?

Two hours later, we left the party.

My stomach was in knots. A good part of the underworld now knew I was a DiLustro.

Juliette DiLustro.

It sounded foreign. Not exactly wrong, but definitely strange.

Dante opened the door of his car for me, and I slid into the passenger seat as he walked around the car and got behind the wheel. Without a word, he drove out of Emory's driveway, the tires screeching against the pavement.

"Don't rush back to the hotel on my account," I said, cutting through the silence. Was he trying to kill us?

"Maybe I want to get back to the hotel and fuck my wife."

My head snapped in his direction, my mask slipping, but I quickly reined my emotions back in. I was determined not to let anyone see past my mask. It was my shame. My burden to carry. I had survived fine so far. I was sure to survive whatever came my way next.

"Since we're getting married tomorrow, you'll have to wait until then," I said quietly. His eyes darted my way and something about the way he watched me made me feel self-conscious. So I turned my head and stared out the window.

I wasn't sure what to expect from Dante. I knew he was eager for my body. He never hid that fact, but I couldn't gauge his cruelty. Would he relish in suffocating me and taking what he thought he was entitled to? I didn't think I'd be able to hold myself back and not kill him. And that would cause a full-blown war.

No doubt about it.

"Always taunting," he muttered. "Always a fucking tease."

On a normal day, I'd tell him off but I was too tired for that. It didn't matter. We both knew there'd be no sex tonight. So I just shook my head and returned to staring out the window at what I could make out from the landscape. I couldn't see much of anything. Not that there was anything to see. Just cacti and desert for miles and miles.

The ride to Emory's house had been tense, but that paled in comparison to the tension that danced through the air now. I turned my head to find my unexpected husband keeping his eyes on the road, his jaw tight. His profile was all hard lines and dark expressions.

The constant buzz of the engine had my eyelids growing heavier and heavier. As I was about to doze off, I was yanked down, my face flattening against my knees, just as glass shattered.

I pinched my eyes shut as glass flew all around me.

Dante's voice was tense. "Keep your head down."

Bullets sprayed all around us and I turned my face to Dante. "You're going to get hit," I screamed.

He ignored my comment, pulling out his phone. My heart hammered in my chest, adrenaline surging through my veins. The chase and gunfire gained momentum and the shots sounded closer and closer.

Dante pressed on the brakes, letting the lights of the chasing cars pass us. Suddenly, the roles were reversed—from being chased to being the chasers. Three SUVs were in front of us. Expertly shifting the gears, Dante pressed the gas pedal to the floor and his Bugatti sped up toward whoever had hit us. He pulled out his gun and aimed at the first car's tires.

Bang. Bang.

The first SUV lost control of the vehicle and smashed against the second SUV, then swerved to the side. It went tumbling, over and over, while the other SUV ended up in the ditch on the side of the road. The third SUV was on my side and Dante couldn't make a clean shot.

"Give me the gun," I hissed, extending my hand.

His dark eyes connected with me for just a second, yet it felt like a lifetime. I held my breath, wondering if he'd trust me enough to hand me the gun. When he extended it, I took it firmly while the sign of his trust washed over me like warm honey.

"Aim at the tires, then shoot when I say," he instructed.

I nodded, reloaded the magazine, lowered the window, then cocked the gun and aimed at the dark SUV. The back window rolled down and a face appeared. A woman's face.

With a fur coat and hat? Jesus fucking Christ. Didn't she know we were in Vegas and there was no snow forecasted, despite it being February? Her dark brown eyes met mine and a peculiar feeling slithered up my spine. Something was off about that woman. Creepy.

"That fucking psycho bitch," Dante hissed. "Forget the tires. Shoot at her face."

Without questioning him, I aimed and pulled the trigger. *Bang. Bang. Bang.*

Screeeech.

The SUV mirrored Dante's maneuver and their driver slammed on the brakes. Except when it slowed behind us, he suddenly turned the wheel one hundred and eighty degrees and sped up heading the opposite way.

Adrenaline still pumping hard through our veins, the silence that followed fell like a dead weight around us. My ears buzzed and each heartbeat felt like a hammer against my ribs as I put the safety on the gun on autopilot and dropped it to the floor.

"You okay?" Dante's voice penetrated through the buzzing in my ears and drumming of my heartbeat. He reached over and took my hand into his. My eyes lowered to our hands, his fingers interlocking with mine. "Juliette, answer me."

Peeling my gaze from his hand holding mine, I answered in one breath. "Yes, I'm fine."

Our gazes met and chaotic emotions ran through me.

"When I get my hands on that woman—" Rage coated Dante's words.

"You know her?" I asked, my gaze flicking back to the rearview mirror.

"Yes."

"Who is she?" I kept glancing through the shattered glass that used to be the back window, worried the SUV would come back. I couldn't help my paranoia.

"Sofia Volkov."

I froze, disbelief washing over me.

The woman I'd been searching for had slipped through my fingers.

The next few hours passed in a blur.

The DiLustros and my family crowded in the Bellagio suite. Mine, of course. Killian and Dad kept throwing somber-looking glances my way. I kept my expression calm and answered all of their questions.

"Why would she attack us?" Dante growled. "Unless she's declaring an all-out war."

"The bitch is crazy enough to do exactly that," Basilio hissed, remembering the events from two years ago. Sofia Volkov attacked him and Wynter, landing him in the hospital. He was lucky Wynter saved him. If she hadn't thrown herself on top of his unconscious body, Sofia would have ended Basilio's life.

"We need to tighten the security. This is probably not the last of Sofia Volkov." Everyone turned to look at my father. Killian's expression was unreadable, but something in his gaze warned me. I knew my brother well enough to know he'd try something.

"Killian, everyone's safe and sound." My voice must have startled everyone because their eyes darted my way. I was the only woman in the room. Davina and Wynter preferred to get their information from their husbands and stay out of the meetings like this. Ignoring them all, I tilted my head and studied my brother. "Promise me you won't do anything."

Killian's jaw tightened, but he remained silent. Stoic.

"Your brother can take care of himself." Of course Dad would defend him. Killian wanted to kill someone? Dad would hand him a weapon. The support aspect of it was great, but I'd be damned if I lost my brother over it.

"So can I," I answered readily. "But you wouldn't be okay with me chasing anyone for a vendetta. And I know Killian will try to go after her."

Priest whistled and I narrowed my eyes on him, challenging him to say something. But all I found on his face was... approval? In fact, I could have sworn all the DiLustros looked slightly impressed. Why? It couldn't be because I worried about my brother.

My brother slipped his hands into his pockets and smiled. "Don't worry, Jules. I won't do anything you wouldn't."

I blinked. *How do I take that?* It almost sounded like he knew—or suspected—of my extracurricular activities.

"Everything will be okay." Dad placed a tentative hand on my arm. "Don't worry. I'll never let anything happen to you or Killian." I gave him a flat smile. I loved my dad, but sometimes he was too blind. Despite his calm demeanor, I could detect a hint of fury in his eyes. There was no sense adding fuel to his worry, so I just accepted his explanation. "Go to bed and get some rest, Jules. We'll work out security details and be right behind you. Tomorrow is a big day for everyone, but mostly for you."

A shudder rippled down my spine. It was all I needed to hear to be reminded of my impending doom.

My eyes strayed toward Dante, who looked remarkably composed. If he was worried about what had just happened, you couldn't tell by his expression.

"Okay," I said. My voice sounded strange to my ears. Almost resigned. Low and tired. "Good night."

I headed to my room. Tomorrow would require the patience of a saint.

And God knew, I wasn't a saint.

CHAPTER 18
Juliette

"**R**ise and shine, blushing bride!"

Wynter's cheery voice woke me up and I let out a frustrated groan. Not even bothering to answer her or even open my eyelids, I turned onto my stomach and buried my head under the pillow.

"Come on," Davina urged. "We don't have all day. Your father threatened to come here and dress you himself if we don't get you ready on time. So get your ass out of bed."

"That'd be awkward as fuck," I mumbled, my voice muffled against the pillow.

"I don't think he was joking, Jules," Ivy chimed in.

Someone snatched the pillow off my head and threw it across the hotel floor. I turned to my side and popped open an eyelid to find my girlfriends standing there all dressed up as bridesmaids.

"You look like you're getting ready to go to the circus," I hissed.

"Tell me about it," Emory grumbled. "You're married already. Why in the fuck do I need to wear a dress now?"

My lips curved despite this fucked-up situation. Truthfully, they didn't look bad. All four of them wore blue minidresses. Wynter's front looked like she stuck a balloon into it, but other than that, she looked fabulous too.

A knocked-up bridesmaid, I snickered silently. There had to be bad luck in that. Right?

"Here, have a drink." Ivy shoved a champagne flute in my face with a grin. "It helps with nerves."

Ugh, I wanted to roll over and hide. Under the bed. In the bathroom. Anywhere, but here.

Pushing the glass of champagne out of my face, I said, "No, thank you. Alcohol got me into this fucking mess. So no more of that shit for me."

Silence followed. Glances were shared.

They didn't believe me. It didn't matter. I would never touch alcohol again. Things could have ended badly that night. Really, really badly.

I rolled out of bed, grinding my molars and keeping my temper in check. Rage blistered through my veins, demanding I explode. But I'd be a "good" daughter for once and not cause a scene. Maybe my father would finally be proud of me.

Passing all the girls on my way to the bathroom, I ignored their glances and their enthusiasm. Their heels clicked against the hardwood, following me to the bathroom and I quickly locked the door. I would at least shower on my own.

"Hey, let us help you," Wynter protested through the keyhole.

"I can shower myself," I retorted back, turning the shower on. "I've been doing it for years in case you didn't know."

I stepped in the cold shower and let the water cool my rage, until it turned too hot which ended up scalding my skin. I winced but didn't adjust the temperature. Maybe this would wash off my filth. My sins.

A shudder rolled through me, along with the panic that was suffocating me.

If Dante forced himself on me tonight, I didn't think I would be able to handle it. Images flashed through my mind.

Ugly. Dirty. Painful. Shameful.

I cranked the heat of the water by a few more degrees and closed my eyes, letting it burn my skin. This had to be what hell felt like.

By the time I was done and dry, my skin was red and my face flushed. I fully expected to see blisters on my skin, but my expression in the mirror reflected the same old me. Clear skin, slightly pink from the hot shower. Auburn hair soaking wet, droplets of water at the tips. High cheekbones. And the same blue eyes with dark circles under them, evidence of my fatigue.

As I stepped out of the bathroom, I fully expected my bridesmaids to be gone. They weren't. They sat on the bed, quietly, their eyes locked on me and frozen smiles on their faces.

"We have to be ready in thirty minutes," Wynter announced calmly. "Or Uncle Liam is taking over."

No reply.

I walked past them and toward the wedding dress someone else had picked out that hung over the door by the tall standing mirror.

"Jules—" Wynter attempted softly, but I was quick to react.

"Please don't," I warned, my tone sharp. "Let's not throw cheer-leading bullcrap into the mix and pretend this is what I want." My cousin flinched and a flicker of regret passed through me. Being the bitch that I was, I didn't stop there. "You're fine with being manhandled. I'm not. Dante is not what I wanted."

"That's not fair," Davina chimed in, her gaze narrowed on me. "You got married all on your own. Liam wants it formalized and we're here to help. So don't you fucking dare act like this is because of any of us."

We stared at each other in thick silence. Resentful silence. Bottom line was that Davina was right. I knew it; they knew it. Alas, it didn't make this situation better. If anything, it made it worse because it made me hate myself even more.

And there was plenty of self-hate going around.

Davina's brows shot up, challenging me to contradict her. "Fine, tell me where you want me."

A terse nod by my stepmother. *Stepmother. This really has to be what hell feels like*, I thought for the second time that morning.

Today for the first time, though, she was actually acting like a step-mother. Up until now, she was always just my friend.

"Good," she said calmly, offering me a smile. As if she knew this was hard for me, but promised it'd be better. It wouldn't be. Nobody knew how deep my issues ran. "Now, let's do your hair and makeup first."

A few beats passed. Another nod as I swallowed the thickening lump in my throat. I sucked in a lungful of air, then padded across the floor to the dresser. Davina quickly typed on her phone and the knock sounded on the door the next second.

Emory jumped up and rushed to open the door. "Here is the makeup artist and stylist," she announced. "Ummm, I don't think you need me. I'm gonna just—" Wynter, Davina, and Ivy gave her curious looks, but I just shrugged. It didn't matter whether she was here or out there. I'd still be forced to be in the same position. "Yeah, okay. I'll see you later," she murmured, then disappeared.

The door shut behind her with a soft click, and I watched in tense silence as the makeup artist, hairstylist, and seamstress set themselves up. Next thing I knew, there was poking, prodding, and preparing. I felt like an animal being readied for the slaughter.

My scalp protested at the tugs. My skin stung as makeup was applied. The room was uncomfortably quiet, which was a novelty. For me and my friends at least. Next I was shoved into a corset, then the wedding dress full of silk, lace, and shit that I would have never regularly worn. The seamstress slid a lace garter up my thigh and I clenched my jaw, swallowing the words that burned at the tip of my tongue.

The seamstress bolted upright and clapped her hands, making me jump out of my skin.

"All finished!" she exclaimed, like it was the biggest achievement of her life. "Magnifique!"

A string of French words followed, though by the look on all our faces, it was clear, none of us understood a single word after *magnifique* and stared at her blankly. I couldn't stop an eye roll. Nobody here was French, so I wasn't sure why she switched languages.

She paused for a moment, as if expecting a response. "Thanks," I mumbled as my chest tightened. It was getting harder to breathe. So I focused on the dressmaker. She was younger than I'd initially thought. Her eyes were brown and light freckles covered her nose and cheeks. Her golden hair was pulled up in a slick, fashionable ponytail. "Are you really French?"

She kneeled, busying herself with this fancy dress. She was efficient and seemed to know what she was doing. "Yes, I am."

Her English was perfect. No accent at all.

"What's your name?"

"Billie Swan."

I frowned. Maybe she was pulling my leg. "That name doesn't sound French. And when you speak English, there's no accent."

She shrugged as she busied herself fixing the hem of my wedding dress. A needle and thread in her hand, I watched her fingers expertly push into the material, disappear and then reappear. With each stitch, the tightness in my chest loosened. "My mother was American. After she died, mon père"—I assumed that meant father... my French was virtually non-existent—"he packed us up and moved us back to France."

She stood up, eyeing me critically as if searching for faults. There were so many; I wondered if she could see them. Then she beamed. "You're ready and the dress fits you perfectly."

Her brown eyes met mine, shining with self-satisfaction. "*Je te souhaite tout le meilleur pour ton mariage.*" When I gave her a blank look, she added, "Best wishes for your wedding."

I sighed. I'd need all the good luck I could get.

"You look beautiful," Davina cooed, clasping her hands together. I had forgotten about my friends.

"Very beautiful," Wynter agreed, padding over to me and giving me a small smile. I was always the bad-tempered troublemaker. Wynter was always the peacemaker. My cousin lost herself in her sports. Whatever she lacked in affection from family, she got it from ice-skating. And me... I was left somewhere in between missing Dad, Killian, and Aunt Aisling's affection while trying to find myself.

Whenever I acted out, Dad and Killian came to deal with me. It was exactly the result I needed and wanted. But then, Travis, Brandon, and Sam happened. That had left me alone. The shame was too great. The blame was a self-inflicted wound that kept festering.

"Look." My cousin's voice interrupted my trip down memory lane.

With gentle hands on my shoulders, Wynter spun me around to face the full-length mirror before I could protest. My eyes met my reflection and a small gasp tore from my lips. I didn't recognize myself. I looked beautiful and innocent.

Except, I was neither.

My hair was fashioned into a long French braid with diamonds woven into it. The white dress mocked my virginal status that was stolen from me. It was an off-the-shoulder corset dress with crystal trim around the top and lace and flowers adorning the bottom part that stretched to the ground.

Heat prickled my skin. Panic spread through my veins. My breaths came out harsher.

"Breathe, Jules," Wynter murmured softly.

"We can always kill him," Ivy suggested. Unhelpfully. "Although that might make Wynter's relationship with her husband awkward."

Wynter rolled her eyes. "We're not killing Dante. They are already married. This is just Uncle Liam giving his approval."

I stopped listening to them. It didn't matter what this was, I knew where it led. Tonight. In the same bed.

Don't think about that, I scolded myself.

Dante was hot as sin. Attraction was definitely there. I didn't panic when we had sex the other night. Of course, I couldn't remember that night at all. In fact, Dante hadn't exactly said we had sex, so maybe we never went that far.

Fuck!

My gaze shifted from my reflection to the window. Clear blue skies. The sun was shining. Even birds chirped. Calmness engulfed me. I'd make it through this. I'd made it through worse and survived.

If only I knew whether I believed myself.

Feigning a smile, I smoothed down the dress and stepped off the box. My heart thundered wildly. I'd killed men, yet this terrified me more. Committing to Dante. Trusting him with my life and my secrets.

Because I knew one thing for sure, they were bound to come out.

The door swung open and Emory was back. The smile on her face resembled my own. It was fake as shit, but there was something else there. Deep in her eyes so similar to her brothers.

It almost looked like... guilt.

"It's time. The priest is waiting downstairs," she announced, her voice trembling.

I mustered a smile. "Let's get married, then."

CHAPTER 19

Dante

Juliette was a fucking sight to behold.

I couldn't look away from her as she walked down the makeshift aisle. Toward me. The dress hugged her curves that I couldn't wait to explore. I couldn't wait to lay claim to every inch of her body and hear her moans. I wanted to own them all and make her forget everything and everyone before me.

Juliette's gaze met mine. She chewed on her bottom lip, and with each step, her complexion seemed to pale further. If I were a decent man, I'd put a stop to this. But I wasn't. And I'd waited too long for this.

For her.

Juliette stopped beside me and I took her hand into mine. It trembled. It was cold as I gripped it gently, hoping to reassure her. For all her sassiness and bravery, this woman sometimes reminded me of a scared little girl hiding under her tough bravado.

I'd seen it enough to recognize it.

The priest spoke wedding vows while she avoided my eyes for the duration of the ceremony. Her bottom lip was raw from her chewing on it, and when it was her turn to say "I do," I half expected her to say "no." Not that it would make much difference since we were married already.

Thank God she didn't and a relieved breath left my lungs.

It was time to slip on the wedding ring and I held her trembling hand firmly, noting her shivers. I wanted to assure her she was safe. Maybe the knowledge of the DiLustros and the fear of the Syndicate was ingrained so deep inside her that she was terrified of us.

Though it made no sense. Her cousin was married to my cousin. They'd had a few hiccups along the road, but they were happy. Couldn't she see that we could be happy too?

"You may kiss the bride," the priest announced, interrupting my internal monologue that pretty much resembled rambling. It was what this woman did to me every-fucking-time.

I didn't hesitate. I cupped Juliette's face and pressed my lips against hers.

She stiffened but didn't pull back.

And I... I was done the second her lips touched mine. My fingers gripped her nape, pulling her closer to me. I swept my tongue along the seam of her mouth and her lips parted with a gasp. It made me groan. She tasted better than anything on this fucking planet.

Sugarplums. Christmas. Home.

All fucking wrapped in one. Too sweet. Too perfect.

My heart thundered so hard, it cracked my soul and clung to this woman. I'd lock her inside me and throw away the key. I bit her lower lip, then eased the sting by sweeping my tongue over it.

Then she pulled back. Abruptly.

Her lips were swollen. Her face was pale. My wife met my gaze head-on. It was full of defiance and something else.

Something dark.

The ballroom of the hotel hosted the reception.

I had no idea who pulled this off or how in such a short time, but they'd done it. Maybe it helped that a lot of the visitors were already here for Emory's birthday party.

Like the Morrellis. Or Cassio King and his family. The Nikolaevs. And then there were the Ashfords. There were a few that weren't here.

Not that they mattered. The only woman I cared about and the only family I needed were here.

After we'd accepted congratulations from our guests, the buffet opened up. Juliette and I sat down together at the table. Her father, aunt, and my own father sat along with us. Everyone chatted, trying to keep the atmosphere light, but Juliette was tense throughout the meal. She hardly ate anything, her eyes darting longingly to the exit.

"No more running, Juliette," I said softly into her ear so only she could hear it.

The look she gave me resembled that of a deer in the headlights. She looked terrified. It was the last thing I expected from someone like her.

She stood up, excused herself, and walked over to her friends. My father's eyes followed her, then returned to me.

"This was rushed," he said, sounding less than impressed.

"This was two years in the making," Liam shot back. "Didn't your son tell you he asked for her hand?"

I didn't tell my father I'd asked to marry Juliette. It had hardly been the time since Basilio lay in the hospital and Priest was still coming to grips with learning who his real mother was. Besides, Juliette's message on my antique car was received loud and clear. She'd refused me, therefore there was nothing to talk about.

Killian rolled his eyes. "You Italians," he hissed. "Always looking for trouble."

My eyes tightened, but I decided to ignore him. It was my wedding day. No sense in starting my union with bloodshed. With my brother-in-law, nonetheless.

"Very much like the Irish," I drawled. I got up and buttoned my suit before another smart-ass comment came my way and this wedding turned bloody. "Excuse me."

I grabbed my scotch, moving toward my cousin and brother standing close to the buffet.

"Is it all that you imagined and more?" Priest asked dryly. I narrowed my eyes on him. He was being as annoying as Killian. Maybe he should find himself a spot at my table and the two of them could be cranky together.

"What's up your ass lately?" I hissed.

Priest shrugged but didn't answer. His eyes darted to the red-haired woman who he'd claimed as his a long time ago. I pondered what held him back.

My eyes found my wife, talking to her friends, Ivy included.

"You two look like lovestruck puppies," Basilio muttered, taking a swig of his drink.

"You fit right in during those crazed months you hunted Wynter," I muttered under my breath. He just about killed every Russian in New York's vicinity. As if remembering that feeling, he headed toward his wife who was standing with my own and wrapped his arms around her growing belly.

The look Wynter gave him, full of love, had something twisting inside my chest. I didn't care about any of that. What the hell would I even do with all those damn emotions? They were messy; they complicated things.

Yet, the idea of never getting that was physically abhorrent.

I'd make her love me. Need me. Adore me.

Just wait and see.

"There's the groom." My head turned in the direction of the voice, and it was only then I realized my brother had left too. My gaze traveled the room, but he was nowhere to be found.

"So, you and Juliette, huh?" Sasha Nikolaev asked sarcastically, his wife on his arm. I groaned, wishing they'd say congratulations and get moving. No such luck. He remained glued to his spot. "Good luck with her. Hopefully she doesn't rob you and then leave you stranded on an island."

I gritted my teeth. Sasha was the fucking worst. Of all the people in this world, I could have done without him at my wedding.

"I'm surprised your wife tolerates your annoying old ass," I remarked, bringing the glass of scotch to my mouth and swallowing it in one gulp.

Branka chuckled. "Barely said 'I do' and already so cranky," she teased, her eyes sparkling.

Jesus, it would seem Sasha was a bad influence on his wife. The chick was reserved from what I had heard and yet here she was fucking with me. I should have made a better deal with her brother, Alessio, and had him hand over Philly, all Canadian business, as well as a clause to stay away from us DiLustros. That would at least give me a break from this shit.

Too fucking late.

"Well, thank you for coming," I said, grabbing another drink from the tray as the waiter passed us by.

"Ah, so eager to get rid of us," Sasha remarked. "The pressure of marriage has barely begun, you young stud."

"Jesus, don't you have someone else to harass?" I grumbled. "Go nag Wynter or Cassio. Anyone. Just move on."

Branka chuckled, while Sasha slapped me on the back, causing my drink to almost spill over. Fucker.

"She looks beautiful, Dante," he finally said. "Congratulations."

"Yes, congratulations," Branka chimed in. "You're a lucky man and Juliette's a lucky woman."

"Not as lucky as me," Sasha said with vehemence. His wife's gaze darted to Sasha and something about the way she looked at him made my chest squeeze.

This fucker kidnapped his bride and she was all goo-goo eyes, swooning over the unhinged bastard.

You did worse, my mind whispered, but I promptly told it to fuck off. I didn't need my conscience kicking in now.

The two of them finally made themselves scarce—thank fuck—and I searched around, finding Juliette standing with her friends and her family. I watched from where I stood as they all chatted and laughed while she kept a feigned smile on her lips. Killian didn't even attempt a smile, feigned or not. He stood next to his sister, shooting glares my way.

"That fucker wants you dead," my brother remarked, showing up out of thin air.

Of course, Basilio was right behind him. "Of course he does. He's losing another woman in his family to the DiLustros. The fucker can't stand it that we are irresistible."

First Wynter and her mother and now his sister.

Priest followed my gaze toward the girls. "So you plan on having your wedding night once you get back to the hotel room or back in Chicago?"

I didn't answer him.

The chemistry was there, there was no denying it, but my wife wouldn't make it easy for me and give in to it. I didn't know how I knew it but I'd stake my life on it. That look after our kiss haunted me, and each time I thought about our wedding night, that image flashed in my mind.

My hands curled into fists and frustration bubbled inside me.

"You think she'll fight you?" Basilio asked, his eyes x-raying me and probably cataloging all my thoughts. I shrugged. His eyes took in my balled fists, then returned to my face. "You insisted on having her."

Priest snickered. "Got us all in on his scheme. If Dad finds out, there'll be hell to pay."

I glared at him. "Shut up," I muttered. "Don't ever mention it again."

Priest didn't even miss a beat. "Emory's already regretting her role in it all."

All our eyes flicked to her. She stood in the far corner talking to the Nikolaev psycho, of all people.

"She shouldn't be talking to that devil," I hissed. I didn't trust Sasha as far as I could throw him.

Just as those words left my mouth, Royce and Byron Ashford joined them, almost as if they thought the same thing. Royce had a beer in his hand, rolling his eyes at whatever Sasha was saying, while Byron kept his face a blank mask.

"It seems the Ashfords agree," Priest remarked. "I'm surprised they showed."

"Well, Kingston and Winston didn't come," Basilio said. "We'll probably never see Kingston, and Winston... well, who in the fuck knows what he's doing? Probably making some poor woman miserable."

Priest chuckled. "Kind of like our Dante here."

I shot him a glare, my first instinct was to punch him. I counted slowly in my mind, and by the time I got to four, a voice came from my left. Right between Priest and I.

"Juliette's ready to cut the cake," Ivy uttered, her eyes focused on me and Basilio. It was way too obvious she was trying not to look my brother's way. If I weren't feeling so frustrated, I'd fuck with him, but be that as it may, I didn't have it in me. "Are you ready?"

I noticed Priest's body angled toward Ivy, crowding her. She took a small step away and he took one in. Almost as if he were protecting her, his eyes shooting around the room, looking for possible threats.

Interesting.

I'd hate to burst his bubble, but I didn't think Ivy was the type of woman with a rough-sex kink. She seemed more of a romantic type and my brother didn't do romance.

"Well, are you ready or what?" she said, her voice too soft, too meek. The girl should grow some balls if she had plans to handle my brother. Otherwise, he'd smother her.

"I was born ready," I answered confidently. Ivy must have found it unoriginal, because she rolled her eyes right along with my brother and cousin.

"Yeah, you and Juliette," she muttered. "We see how that worked out for both of you."

My cousin snickered, and rather than punching him, I stepped hard on his foot. "Cake time it is."

His hiss and curses sounded behind me, and I couldn't help but feel slightly better. At least there wouldn't be a fight at my wedding.

CHAPTER 20
Juliette

Dante had a strange look on his face every time he glanced my way.

I started to fear that he could read my thoughts, or even worse, what I was about to do. It made me nervous, but I pretended to be unaffected.

Dante took my hand and held it firmly as we rode the elevator up to the hotel suite. When we'd stepped in, a group of rowdy teenagers piled in and I pressed my back against the wall, leaving space between us.

They kept laughing, throwing glances my way, leering at me.

"Look at my wife one more time, and you'll lose your eyeballs by the time the elevator door opens."

Dante's warning slithered through the air. The chatter suddenly stilled, and it was so quiet that I could hear my own heartbeat.

Ding.

The elevator stopped with a beep and the doors slid open. Like the devil was at their heels, the teenagers rushed out and disappeared from our view.

"What was that about?" I hissed under my breath.

He didn't answer. He just leaned back against the elevator wall with a smile, but his eyes remained sharp. Dark and possessive. It sent shivers down my body.

The elevator door closed as it started gliding up again.

We had another two floors to go. To the penthouse suite.

Only the best for the groom and bride.

Apprehension shuddered through me. I wished now that I hadn't been so brave with Dante the first time I ran into him. I played the part of an experienced seductress instead of a woman with invisible scars. The ones that wouldn't heal, festering in my mind while I hid it all under my obnoxious persona. But it had all caught up to me.

My breaths came short and heavy as I felt my thoughts begin to spiral. My heart thundered against my ribs. The urge to flee was strong, but I remained still, my eyes locked on a single spot on the elevator door.

Ding.

The door opened too quickly.

"You ready?" Dante asked as he pushed off the interior wall, then took my hand. He tugged me forward, my feet practically dragging across the floor. They felt heavy, like each foot weighed a ton and it was an effort to move them.

"I don't have a choice, do I?" I bit back icily, hiding the fear that was quickly overtaking me.

He said nothing else. The next thing I knew, he was swiping the keycard and we were inside. It was only when the door clicked behind us that he released my hand.

Dropping his keys and wallet onto the table by the door, he strode through the room and into the closet. Jesus, was he going to strip right away?

"Change out of the wedding dress, Juliette. Sleeping with that dress on will smother us both and I have no intention of dying just yet," he stated softly as he disappeared into the closet.

No, no, no. It was mid-afternoon. Barely. I wasn't ready to start the wedding night.

I remained standing, glued to the spot. My eyes darted to the table and my heart fluttered. It couldn't be that easy. Could it?

Dante's car keys sat right there in front of me. I held my breath for five seconds, then snatched them up, and without a second thought, I burst out the door and stumbled blindly down the hallway.

I didn't bother with the elevator. It would give him a chance to catch me while I was waiting for it and I couldn't risk that. Instead, I took the emergency staircase. The stupid heels slowed me down, so I kicked them off and started running down the stairs. I gripped the fabric of my dress, rushing down each step and expecting to hear him call out at any moment.

Yet... nothing. Only the sound of my breathing and the soft padding of my steps. Once on the garage level, I lifted my dress up further and broke into a run. The concrete felt cool under my feet. Blood pounded in my temples. I ignored it all.

The tiny bit of reason I had left deserted me the moment I said those vows and the desperation to escape had been building ever since. I frantically clicked the button on the key fob, searching for Dante's car. *There!*

The headlights to a blue vintage 1962 Chevrolet Corvette convertible flashed in welcome. Thank God he decided to upgrade that feature on this car, or I would have been screwed.

This is happening. It's really happening.

My run was cut short when I spotted a familiar head of blond hair. I froze and bit back the panicked gasp. It was Priest, leaning against the column separating two sections of the garage. He looked sharp in his tux. A lit cigarette was halfway up to his lips, but he wasn't smoking. He simply twisted it between his fingers, his eyes flicking my way.

Without pausing to think, I closed the ten feet of distance to Dante's car and slid into the driver's seat. My hands were shaking, and it took me a few tries to finally push the key into the ignition. My eyes kept reaching for the rearview mirror, but oddly enough, Priest didn't appear to be coming after me.

Adrenaline sped up through my veins, leaving me panting like I had run a marathon. As my bare foot slammed against the accelerator, the engine roared in protest, and I sped up through the garage and out onto the busy Las Vegas street.

When we first arrived, I heard Emory mention the cliffs thirty-five miles northwest of the strip. It was where I'd race to. I had no idea what I'd do when I got there, but I needed peace and quiet. There was no way anyone would find me there and I needed time. Time to think. Time to figure my way out of this. My shoulders ached from the tension. It'd been there all along, only increasing as the day went on. As I turned onto the highway, I let myself spare one last glance at the rearview mirror.

Still nobody was following me. I could hardly believe my luck.

I kept driving, my mind in a state of turmoil. I had no idea how I got there, but the next thing I knew, I was pulling up at my destination. The lookout that would have usually been busy with tourists was empty this time of day. Stepping out of the car, my legs were shaking as I ignored the stones that bit into my bare feet. Each step closer to the edge of the cliff almost brought me to my knees, yet I stood. I probably looked tall and proud, but in truth, I felt broken.

It didn't matter because as I stood on the edge, pebbles digging into my feet, I finally felt free.

Free for the first time since I was raped.

Free for the first time since I learned who I was.

Free for the first time since I started to make those accountable for my pain pay.

I stared at the ledge of the steep mountain, the breeze pushing against my dress. Almost as if it demanded I take a step back. Instead, I tempted fate and took another step closer.

For some stupid reason "Hush Little Baby" played in my mind. Not the children's version, but the one sung by Ashley Ryan. I never had a mama who protected me. Aunt Aisling couldn't protect herself, never mind me. She'd been too focused on Wynter's career to see the signs. Besides, the same was too great to admit it to anyone else. It was my cross to carry. My burden.

So I'd taken matters into my own hands. By now, they were drenched with blood. It only took learning about my birth parents' brutal death to push me into a murderous rage. I lowered my eyes, almost expecting to see my palms stained red.

They weren't. The French manicure and white dress mocked my lost innocence. It almost made me laugh at the irony.

Balling my fists around the lace, I closed my eyes. Maybe it all had become too much. The sins. The lies. The pretense.

Even now, it led me into a forced marriage.

Dante wouldn't want me if he knew the true me. The damaged me. I hid it all underneath my rebellion and not even my cousin, who had known me my entire life, could spot it.

A scream bubbled in my throat. I was that lost girl again. Terrified and alone. I didn't scream that night all those years ago. I only cried and begged.

But today, I couldn't hold it back anymore. I let out a scream so loud that it scratched my throat. The breeze carried it down the canyon, right along with my pain and memories. I had tried so hard to keep them locked away. I had tried so hard to convince myself it didn't happen. That it had happened to someone else.

Yet, here I was. It would seem ghosts did have a way of catching up to you.

I lifted one foot and inched further to the edge. Was this the end of the road for me? There was no more earth to step on. Only thin air.

Adrenaline twisted with fear shot through my bones and warned me to take a step back.

I should end it all, my mind whispered. But could I do that? Wasn't I stronger than that? I was scared, but maybe also just brave enough to try and push through it. Maybe I could just let Dante fuck me and—

My breath cut short. Goosebumps rose on my skin and cold sweat beaded over my forehead. A shiver of terror zapped down my spine. It was irrational. I'd tried for so long to get rid of that fear of being suffocated. A body heavy on top of mine.

My lungs tightened. My head swam. Despite the fresh air and the wind, it felt like oxygen was in short supply.

One minute I was standing still, wind in my hair and horror in my heart. The next, a set of strong and warm arms wrapped around my waist and tugged me backward.

"What—"

"If you jump, Juliette, so do I," Dante said, his voice muffled against the back of my head. "You want to fly, my wildling? We'll fly together."

Panic punched through me, but oddly enough, it was quickly replaced by a relief so strong, I felt tears burning in my eyes. My body started to tremble. My hands covered his strong forearms, nails digging into his skin.

Then to my horror, tears came. Sobs shook my body. Salt stained my lips, bruised from chewing on them nervously over the last twenty-four hours. The buttons of his shirt pressed against the skin of my back, his breaths hot against the nape of my neck.

"Come on, Juliette. Let's go home."

I shook my head, sobs wracking my body. But when he tugged me another foot backward, I let him. Then he gripped my hips and pulled me further back and away from the edge. My head fell back against his chest, the familiar scent of him filling my lungs and exhaustion settling into my bones.

"What are you doing here?" I gasped, my voice raspy.

Once we were a distance away from the edge, he turned me around, bringing me face-to-face with him.

"Saving you," he growled in my ear. My eyes locked on his handsome face filled with fury. Stormy and dark. "I had a tracker installed on the car when I bought it in case someone was stupid enough to steal it," he said derisively, but underneath his tone there was something else. Something resembling concern. "How could you even think about jumping?" The accusation felt like a whip. Then his gaze softened. "Fuck, Juliette. Do you hate me so much that you'll choose death over me?"

The venom rolled off his tongue, but there was also a hint of pain. Disappointment. His gaze fell to my lips, soft and hungry. He squeezed the back of my neck as his nose brushed against mine.

"I can't have sex with you," I rasped, my body trembling at the images in my mind.

"Can't or won't?" he asked.

The mind was such a peculiar thing. I couldn't remember a few nights ago, but that night from long ago slithered through it so easily. Something so dark and ugly, I just couldn't forget. I wished I could, yet it remained entrenched in my memories.

"Both," I admitted, my voice betraying me with a slight tremor.

His expression changed, became pensive, his dark eyes penetrating my soul and digging out all my secrets. All my fears. All my nightmares. Then, as if he'd seen all those horrible scenes from my past, he turned rigid.

"Who hurt you?" Three little words and they changed everything.

I swallowed, scared to hear myself admit it. I had yet to say it out loud to anyone. There were four of us, with me included, that knew what happened that night. Today, there was only one of those other three left, because I'd killed the other two. It took me years to realize that I could only move on with their deaths.

When they hurt me, I heard all their snickering comments. Felt all their slaps, the pain, the humiliation. I felt it all. My voice wasn't the only thing I lost that night. I lost me. But I made *them* scream. I didn't drug them like they had me to make them compliant. I made them feel it. All of it. Every damn slice.

My only regret was that I couldn't kill the senator's son. I couldn't get through his family's intricate protection detail. And the weaselly fucker was hiding in his family's home. Never left it.

Dante cupped my face. His touch was warm, but I couldn't stifle the slight wince. I hated being touched. I knew he wanted me, and I didn't trust him not to take me whether I wanted him to or not. Of course, if he did, he'd better learn to sleep with one eye open because I'd make it my mission to end him.

Fuck war. Fuck everything.

Nobody would ever make me feel that way again. I wouldn't be a helpless girl ever again.

"I promise, no sex," he vowed quietly but with conviction. "Not until you're ready." I'd never be ready. It had been eight years, and I was still stuck in that dark room with those boys suffocating me. My breathing sped up thinking about it. I couldn't go there. "But I will need the name. Who. Hurt. You?"

He assumed there was only one. I'd let him believe it. There was only one left alive.

"Travis Xander." The name left my lips and the pressure in my chest eased just a tiny bit.

Dante's eyes flickered in recognition. "Senator of California?" he asked.

I shook my head.

"His son?" he demanded, his dark eyes studying my face. I had no doubt he studied my every muscle twitch.

I nodded, swallowing the lump in my throat. I despised even hearing his name. It made my skin crawl. My lip trembled and I hated this feeling of vulnerability. It made me want to take a baseball bat and start smashing everything until I beat this vulnerability and memory away.

Silence followed. Dante raked his teeth over his bottom lip, then his expression hardened. If I didn't know it before, I knew it now. Dante DiLustro was a formidable enemy. I'd have to keep that in mind.

"He'll be dead by the end of the week," he vowed.

"Really?" I breathed, a sadistic pleasure washing over me. Maybe it was always in my blood. The mafia. The thirst for revenge. Or maybe I was evil. Either way, I relished in the knowledge that the last boy who dared to touch me would be dead soon.

Despite Dante's fury, dark amusement tugged at his lips. He gave a small shake of his head.

"You like that," he stated matter-of-factly.

I tilted my chin upward. "He deserves whatever's coming to him."

He let out a sardonic breath, his gaze clashing with mine. A vicious smile flashed across his face and his smile made a shark's grin appear like a welcome home sign. I didn't care. I hoped Travis's last sight on this earth would be Dante's cruel smile.

"Damn fucking straight." He was still grinning in that feral way. "Nobody touches what's mine."

"Well, I wasn't yours back then." Truthfully, I wasn't his now either, but that was beside the point.

A smug grin spread across his face. "You've been mine a lot longer than you think, little wildling."

Before I could ask him what he meant by that, he scooped me up and threw me over his shoulder. His hands, warm and possessive, found their way under my dress. I stiffened but his fingers stopped at the garter, pulling it down my leg.

"We're going to save this for when you're ready," he growled. "Now let's go home." Then, as if he needed to clarify, he added, "Chicago."

Home. Chicago.

The world suddenly didn't seem so terrifying.

CHAPTER 21
Dante

For the first time since I'd seen Juliette shaking her ass on top of her father's bar, I understood her recklessness. I saw it in my brother during his teenage years. Even in Emory. It was their way of coping.

She didn't say much about it. She didn't have to. All I knew was that I'd make Travis fucking Xander pay. And it wouldn't be a quick kill.

The vulnerability in my wife's eyes gutted me from the inside. Every time I thought of the fucker who'd hurt her, rage rose inside me.

Juliette had always been too impulsive. Act first, think later. It'd get her killed. I was fucking surprised it hadn't gotten her killed already. Like when she trashed my car in front of the hospital, with police and guards all around.

"Juliette is destroying your car," Priest announced casually, like he was reciting the weather. "Keying it."

"What?" I barked, striding toward my brother who was leaning against the wall. His eyes studied the landscape of the hospital outside. Bas and Wynter had been attacked by the psycho bitch, Sofia Catalano Volkov, and we got there right on time to save them. Bas was injured badly, but thankfully Wynter was okay. She'd protected him with her body.

Lucky cousin. If I had found myself in a similar situation, Juliette would gladly step aside and probably offer them money to end my life. Fucking maddening woman!

Priest chuckled, then returned his attention back to the window. I followed his gaze. Juliette was indeed destroying my car. She dragged keys along the side of it, scratching the fucking hell out of it.

And what did my eye focus on? The sun reflecting against her thick dark hair, colors of mahogany under the bright sky. Jesus Christ, I couldn't wait to wrap my hand around that mane of hers and have her submit to me.

She reached for a crowbar—where in the fuck did she get that—and lifted it high above her head before smashing it against the window.

"Are you sure you want to marry her?" Priest asked. "She's a bit on the psycho side."

I rolled my eyes. "So is your great-grandmother," I remarked dryly. "Jules will fit right in."

Priest folded his arms. "Sofia Volkov will be dead the moment I get my hands on her. And don't ever call her my great-grandmother—or whatever-the-fuck she is—again."

I shook my head. I still couldn't believe it. Truthfully, I'd always known we were half brothers. His blond hair. The way my mother hated him even more than me. A sliver of hate sawed through me remembering that bitch. The shit she'd done to us.

Instead, I focused on the wild woman outside. Oh, lovely, now she was drawing on my car window.

Leaving my brother behind, I ran down the stairs, ignoring the weird glances thrown my way. My steps echoed through the hospital hallway, my blood pumping wildly through my veins. Every car was a hunk of metal but that one... fuck, that one was special. It was my grandfather's 1934 Hudson Convertible Coupe. It was the only thing I had left from him.

I stormed out the emergency exit into the parking lot to see Juliette speed past me, almost fucking running me over, and flipping me the bird through the window.

My ears buzzed.

I ground my teeth as I approached my car. My windshield was smashed. So was the passenger's side window. The drawing on the only unshattered window pulled my attention.

"Motherfucker," I hissed.

Juliette had drawn a dick in red lipstick and then an arrow pointing to a stick figure with my name underneath it. At least she didn't draw a small dick. It was the words underneath that captured my interest.

I'd kill you before I'd marry you.

Fucking shit.

My brother was right. The girl was a psycho. Yet, there was nothing I could do to forget her. Trust me, I had tried. It was as if she'd cast a spell on me binding me to her. From that first fucking moment I'd seen her.

"Ahh, that kind of resembles your dick." My brother's voice came from beside me and I narrowed my eyes at him, silently telling him to shut the fuck up. Priest loved agitating me. It used to be the only pastime we had during those days at the goddamn convent when my mother ensured we got preferential treatment. I couldn't even fucking go there. "Are you sure she hasn't seen it?"

I shrugged. "If she had, she'd be coming to me willingly."

"You wish," he retorted dryly. "I don't think that girl wants to touch you with a ten-foot pole."

Without another word, he left me standing there, staring at my destroyed car. He learned not to get attached to things. I never quite succeeded. While our dad wasn't looking, our narcissistic mother ensured everything we loved was destroyed. First, the blanket we preferred. Then the toy, and it slowly progressed from there.

As I drove down the highway bound for Harry Reid International Airport, Juliette dozing quietly in the seat next to me, I pulled myself from the thoughts I rarely let myself cycle through. The mid-afternoon sun reflected against her hair, colors of mahogany dancing under it. Just like that day she destroyed my car. I finally understood her—at least some of her. The way we'd grown up had always affected Priest differently than me. He'd learned to get attached to nothing and nobody. I, on the other hand, had a hard time letting go. Most of the time, I didn't care for things, but every so often I got attached. To my grandfather's car. To Juliette.

My brother was probably right. Juliette didn't want me, might never want me. So why, oh why, couldn't I let her go?

Today I finally got my answer. Because she needed me.

CHAPTER 22
Juliette

Less than sixty minutes later we were in the air and on our way to Chicago.

Help had come from the most unlikely place. Dante DiLustro.

The man I had been resisting from the moment I'd met him. That clean, earthy scent had been tickling my nostrils ever since the priest had pronounced us husband and wife and he kissed me.

Our first kiss.

At least, the first kiss with him that I could remember. His lips claimed mine, and strangely enough, it was pleasant. Even as I felt his lips curve into a satisfied smile, I enjoyed it. But that was a far cry from sex.

Then there was Dante's scent. It was soothing. Clean and manly. He always smelled like a damp forest, rain on hot pavement.

After the whole incident on the cliff, he helped me into his car before driving toward the airport. Priest had driven him here, apparently more than happy to blow my cover. For some reason though, I couldn't find it in me to be mad at him. Dante hadn't said a word, not that much conversation was possible in the convertible. Once at the airport, a private jet was waiting for us, ready for takeoff.

Since I didn't have shoes on my feet, Dante scooped me up into his arms and carried me up the steps and into the cabin, set me in one of the luxurious seats, buckled me in, then took his own spot on the other side of the cabin.

I was surprised he didn't take a spot next to me, but I certainly wasn't complaining. I reveled in the space.

"What about all our stuff?" I asked. I had left everything in the hotel. My purse. My phone. Everything.

Dante didn't look up from his phone. "It's already in the baggage compartment."

"Efficient," I muttered, since I had nothing else to say, sufficiently drained. He didn't comment, so I turned my face to stare out the window where all I could see were fluffy, white clouds, reminding me of pillows.

Exhaustion pulled on my bones, but I didn't feel comfortable enough to fall asleep. It wasn't that I thought Dante would attempt anything. Not after what had just happened on the cliff. My mind refused to calm down—especially after that little catnap in the car. I snuck a peek at him through my lashes, but he seemed oblivious to my presence.

The silence stretched, Dante vigorously typing on his phone. Probably planning world domination. *Or Travis's ending*, I thought smugly. The latter was so fucking satisfying. There was raw elation in knowing that he wouldn't be alive for much longer.

A good person would feel remorse. I didn't. Not even an ounce. I wasn't a good person. I was so hungry for revenge and blood that it suffocated me. I would have preferred to kill Travis myself, but I'd settle for this. For years, I had lived in fear—an irrational one—but I couldn't shake it off. The terror that that fucker would slip to the world what they had done to me plagued me. It was bad enough I knew my shame. I didn't want anyone else knowing. Strangely enough, my small admission to Dante didn't shatter me. In fact, it almost felt like a weight lifted from my chest.

Maybe I'd let it all fester inside me for far too long and I ended up consumed by it.

I let out a heavy sigh. There was no point in pondering about it. Regrets brought you nothing. I had to move forward, deal with it my own way.

"I'm assuming you have at least two bedrooms in your place in Chicago," I said, breaking the silence that suffocated the cabin.

His eyes darted my way. "More than two," he replied.

I offered a small smile. "Does it matter which bedroom I take?" I asked.

Dante's dark eyes watched me, a flicker of hunger gleaming in their depths. I was a mess. My hair that started the day in a French braid with diamonds weaved into it was now a frizzy disaster and my white dress had dirt smeared all over it. And then there were the black soles of my feet. Yeah, like I said... I was a damn mess.

Though you wouldn't think it by the look in my husband's eyes.

My husband.

The words felt foreign in my head. I couldn't fathom how they'd taste on my tongue.

"We'll share a bedroom," he stated calmly, returning his attention to his phone.

I stiffened, all my good thoughts about Dante instantly turning darker. "I thought you said—"

"I won't force myself on you, but we'll sleep in the same bed."

His tone was calm and measured. Soft and vehement. But there was something raw in his obsidian gaze that had me shuddering. It slowed the blood in my veins. It made the world turn just a bit slower. And the buzz of the engine just a bit duller.

"But—"

"That's final, Juliette," he said, a dark edge to his voice. I shivered. "Besides, there are no other beds in the house."

His tone was dry and amused. I had a feeling he'd played me, but I couldn't be sure.

"I could sleep on the couch," I grumbled under my breath.

He said nothing, so I returned the favor. For the remainder of our flight, I chose to ignore his presence.

CHAPTER 23
Dante

Traffic was nearly at a standstill on the Eisenhower Expressway in Chicago.

I was weaving in and out of both lanes, eager to get home while Juliette sat in the passenger seat, quietly staring out the window. Her jaw was pressed tightly and she was definitely brooding. She was adamant about looking anywhere but at me.

My phone rang and I answered it without looking at the caller ID. "DiLustro."

"You left without a word. Aisling wanted to have a word with Juliette." My father's voice was sharp on the phone.

Exhaling a hard breath, I kept my temper under control. As far as I was concerned, Aisling could go fuck herself. Both her and Liam Brennan. I had been researching Travis Xander, and it would seem he attended high school with Juliette. He must have assaulted her under her aunt's watch and the dumb bitch didn't even know it.

No girl should suffer through that. But then to suffer through it alone, it made me murderous.

"We're on our honeymoon," I gritted. "She can talk to her later."

I sensed more than saw Juliette stiffening next to me. I flicked a gaze her way and mouthed, "Want to talk to your aunt?"

She shook her head and returned to stare out the window.

"Well, I'm going to get back to my honeymoon, Father."

"Listen, son. I know you and Christian are upset," he said, matter-of-factly, as though almost two years ago we hadn't learned that our life could have been normal. Different. Not full of pain and torture leveled on us by his first wife. The narcissistic mother.

It was thanks to my mother that Christian was known as Priest.

"What makes you think we're upset?" I asked coolly.

He had no fucking idea what I had been through. What Christian had been through! He was too blind being the kingpin and mourning his mistress to be involved with our lives. To see the signs.

"Anything else?" I said when he didn't reply.

He let out a sigh. "No, nothing else."

I ended the call and the rest of the drive to my Chicago home passed in silence. I didn't mind, because in my mind I was going over all the creative ways I'd make Travis Xander suffer.

It was almost six in the evening when we finally pulled into the driveway. A three-story brownstone building with white columns on the front porch welcomed us from behind the surrounding fence.

I clicked the gate opener on my dashboard and the wrought-iron gates swung open, slowly gliding to the left.

"Nice crib," Juliette said, her first words in over three hours. "You bought it or did your dad?"

My eyebrow shot up. "Why would my father buy me a place to live?"

She rolled her eyes. "Okay, Mr. Big Shot. We get it," she muttered. "You bought it with your own dirty money."

Amusement filled me. "Dirty money?" I asked. "Didn't you and your friends cheat at my casino only a few years ago?"

I knew from Basilio that the four friends wanted to start a school for up-and-coming criminals together. The idea was interesting. In fact, I was surprised nobody thought of it before. Either way, I'd help her with it—if she'd let me.

She shrugged. "Forced by circumstances."

I pulled into the garage and parked next to a Mercedes SUV, and then I got out. Of course, Juliette was already grabbing the door handle but I was faster. Opening the door for her, I helped her out.

"Welcome home."

The air smelled crisp and fresh. Like upcoming snow. Which meant that the ground was too cold for her bare feet.

Without warning, I scooped her up and carried her across the threshold of our home.

"What are you doing?" she squealed.

"You're barefoot and winters are cold in Chicago," I reasoned.

Somehow, my gut feeling warned that Juliette wasn't ready for any signs of a real marriage. But we'd get there. Even if I had to hammer through her walls and burn every piece of furniture in the house. I anticipated her wanting her own room and her own bed.

The moment we left Vegas, I sent instructions to my staff to get rid of all the beds in the house. Burn them. Donate them. I didn't give a shit, as long as they were all out. All but one—the one in my bedroom.

"I'll have a tray brought up to the bedroom for us," I told her as I carried her up the stairs. Her eyes darted left and right, studying her new home. "I have a cook and a maid."

"Hmmm."

Her arms wrapped around my neck and I didn't think she realized her fingers played with the hair on my nape.

I headed straight for the staircases, her tension evident by the way she gripped my hair.

"You can take a bath and soak. You've had a rough day."

Juliette's huge blue eyes met mine, but she didn't say anything. Fuck, she didn't even know how easily my dick responded to her. It was all it needed, one simple look and I was hard. Ignoring it, I kept walking toward the master bedroom.

Once I entered our bedroom, I let her slide down my body and onto the soft rug. She was observant, studying every piece of furniture.

"How come none of the guest bedrooms have beds?" she asked, her finger trailing over the dresser.

"I never have guests," I lied.

She flicked me a disbelieving look. "Not even your brother and cousin?"

"They prefer to stay in a hotel," I said. At least it was a half-truth. They preferred to stay in the hotel but never did.

"Hmmm, that's weird."

She padded across the room, peeking into the walk-in closet.

"There are some things for you already here," I told her. "More of your stuff is downstairs. I'll bring it up tomorrow morning and you can buy whatever else you need. Take any side of the closet you want."

"Thanks," she said absent-mindedly as she walked toward the window, peering outside. She didn't seem that interested in fashion.

Honestly, I had yet to figure Juliette out. She seemed to be all over the place with her interests. Ballet. Robbery. Recently even self-defense classes and shooting.

"Long winters here, huh?" she remarked.

They were long and extremely cold. February was one of the coldest months in the year. And darkest. It was way too dark for her to see anything out there, except for the outline of the gardens under the moon.

"I prefer a warm climate," she mumbled. "I've spent most of my time in California."

I knew that. It's where she went to high school and where that asshole Travis lived. But he'd pay. Very soon. I already had it all lined up. The thought of that fucker had my vision filling with a red mist. I had to take a deep breath and focus on Juliette, instead of frightening her with my rage.

She looked small next to the large master bed and massive mahogany furniture. Even standing in front of that huge floor-to-ceiling window. This decor didn't seem to be her style but then she didn't strike me as a girl overly concerned with the decor of a home.

"Shower or a bath?" I called out as I strode into the bathroom.

Juliette jumped and whirled around. Lovely. She forgot I was here and all I could focus on was her. Her eyes as blue as the sky on the clearest day met mine.

"Excuse me?"

"Shower or a bath?" I questioned again, gritting my teeth. "Which do you prefer?"

Ever since the scheme I rolled out the night Juliette married me, I had been on edge, wound tightly with no way of releasing the tension. As soon as Juliette fell asleep tonight, I'd make my way down into the gym and release some of my pent-up energy.

The last thing I wanted was to take it out on my new, young wife.

Not that I was old by any means. At twenty-eight, I was only a few years older than her. Despite that, I felt ancient sometimes.

"I guess a bath," she replied. "It doesn't really matter."

I turned on the faucet and reached out for the toiletries that were brought in for her. I stared at the five different variations of the bath bubbles. They all looked the same, just different colors.

The sound of the water splashing filled the bathroom, echoing against the tile. Dumping one bottle into it, I watched bubbles fill the tub as I held the empty container in my hand.

"You dumped that whole thing into it?" Juliette's voice came from behind and I sent a glance over my shoulder. She stood before me in the short robe I'd had them put in the closet for her. Her legs appeared awfully long for the tiny thing that she was.

"Yes."

"We might have a bubble disaster on our hands," she said with a teasing smile. My heart skipped a fucking beat. It thundered in my chest with longing. Was Juliette making a joke?

Dark hair covered her neckline begging to break free from the edge of her robe, brushing against her shoulders. Fuck, her skin looked soft and there was nothing I wanted more than to touch her. I wanted to feel every inch of her. Hear her moans. Feel her writhe underneath me in pleasure.

My gaze flickered behind her where the wedding dress lay in a pile on the floor.

"I'm gonna burn it," she remarked, following my line of sight.

"It's your dress," I noted dryly.

She narrowed her eyes at me, but she said nothing else. I stood up and pointed to the right. "Towels are in that cabinet."

Leaving her, I walked out of the bathroom. I needed an intense workout to kill this desire for her. At least for tonight.

She didn't move until I left, shutting me out with a soft click.

CHAPTER 24
Juliette

I quickly closed the door of the bathroom and turned the lock.
It wouldn't stop Dante from entering his own bathroom, but it made me feel better.

Catching my reflection in the mirror, I scrutinized my face. My eyes were bloodshot, but not from tears. Those rare drops from earlier on the cliff were long gone. It was from exhaustion. My bottom lip was red, bite marks from my nervous habit all over it.

While the water still filled the tub and bubbles grew, I washed the makeup off my face and brushed my teeth with a new toothbrush. Then I slid into the tub and sighed with relief. The warm water felt good on my muscles. The tension slowly seeped out of me with each minute that passed. I even submerged my head underwater, letting the sensation wash over me.

For the first time in a very long time, I felt at peace.

I didn't know what this marriage meant for me, but I knew one thing, he wouldn't force himself on me. And that alone made up for all the stress of the last few days.

An hour later, I padded down the corridor, wrapped up in a fluffy, black robe that reached down to my toes and smelled like Dante. It was much warmer than the one I wore earlier and covered up a lot more of my assets. The clothes that Dante mentioned were all fancy lingerie and designer clothes, and I certainly wasn't going to parade around wearing just lingerie. I wasn't an idiot and there was only so much restraint a man could have. I was too tired to sort through the other clothes.

So here I was parading around in the fluffy, unattractive robe. I stopped by one window and the same view greeted me as it did back in Dante's bedroom. Well, our bedroom. The large lake in the middle of the property. Dark woods in the background.

Peeling myself away from the darkness outside, I looked down the long corridor. I opened the first door. It was a guest room, and sure as shit, Dante wasn't lying. The bedroom was decorated, but the mattress and box spring were missing.

"So fucking odd," I whispered under my breath.

I moved down the staircase, leaving the exploring for another day. I knew where our bedroom was and the exit. Other than that, it was all unfamiliar territory. Just as I reached the bottom step, Dante's dark hair appeared in the doorway and my steps faltered.

"You went out?" I asked, shocked.

It was obvious he did. It had started snowing and the soft veil of snowflakes on his hair made for a stark contrast. White on black. My eyes traveled over him. He was dressed in black sweats, black sweatshirt, and a pair of white running shoes.

His breathing was hard, but he wasn't panting. Not like I would be if I went for a jog.

"Yeah, for a run, but it started snowing." I glanced behind him as he shut the door. It barely looked like flurries. "There's a snowstorm coming. I can smell it in the air," he continued.

"Really?" I smelled the air. "The only thing I smell is our dinner. Dessert to be exact."

"Trust me," he remarked. "Tomorrow, we'll wake up to everything covered in white."

"Well, I hope we have plenty of food. Bread, eggs, and milk," I said and then because I was nervous, I added, "And toilet paper."

He chuckled, shaking the snow out of his dark hair. Then he kicked off his tennis shoes and left them by the door as he strode through the large foyer.

"Don't worry, we have plenty of toilet paper," he mused, then his eyes took me in and they'd darkened. Something possessive entered his expression.

"I hope you don't mind," I breathed. "There were no comfy pjs, so I settled for"—I lowered my eyes and tugged on the ropes of the robe— "this."

He shook his head as if trying to shake off an image. He walked past me and headed for the stairs.

"I'm going to take a shower," he remarked.

I nodded. "I'll wait for you and we can eat together." It was the least I could do. I couldn't fight him at every turn. Even though not having my own private bedroom did annoy me. "I'll go back upstairs with you. One of the people you gave off must have brought it up."

He nodded in agreement and we made our way back up the stairs where the two dinner trays still sat, waiting to be devoured. Dante was quick to disappear into the bathroom and I held my breath, waiting for the click of the lock.

It never came.

I sat on the bed, my legs crossed and staring at the door. The shower kept running and running, while I chewed on my lip. I glanced around the room. There wasn't even a television in here to keep me busy. My bags, along with my phone, were somewhere downstairs.

I was left with me, myself, and I, not very good company to be honest, to keep myself busy while Dante was taking a ridiculously long shower. I chewed on my lip. Then on my fingers. I stood up, walked in a circle around the room, peeked inside the dinner trays to find sandwiches, salad, and a freshly baked cake. My stomach growled in reply but I ignored it. I told Dante I'd wait, so I'd wait. I walked back to the massive bed and sat down.

My gaze kept darting to the bathroom door, then to the clock. Back to the door. After ten minutes, I'd had enough. That had to be the longest damn shower. The sound of running water continued, so I jumped out of the bed and padded across the plush rug and hardwood to the door.

I raised my hand to knock and ask Dante whether he was alright when I froze.

Was that—

No, it couldn't be. But then I heard it again. A faint groan. So I did what any self-respecting woman would do, I pressed my ear to the door.

Another groan. Oh. My. Gosh.

My cheeks caught fire. My body burned. Yes, I had panic attacks when I even thought about a man lying on top of me and having sex, but it didn't mean I had zero sex drive. And something about hearing Dante jerking off was just so damn sexy. Images played in my mind how he'd look in the throes of passion.

So another brilliant idea hit me. I could watch him through the keyhole located below the doorknob.

Holy fuck, I was such a voyeur. It was wrong. I shouldn't do it.

Another groan sounded from the closed door.

It's your wedding night, my twisted mind justified, and I lost the fight with myself. Next thing I knew, I was peeping through the keyhole.

My breathing hitched. Dante DiLustro might be many things, but nobody could take his sex appeal away from him. He was so fucking beautiful. The sculpted, lean muscles. Slick, glistening skin.

And that ass. Oh my fucking shit, was it right for a man to have such a beautifully muscular ass?

My thighs clenched as I watched Dante's head bowed, his bicep flexing with each pump, his movements jerky. Back and forward. Faster and harder. The muscles in his neck strained as he pumped himself.

Suddenly, I wished the stupid door was open. The view was too obstructed. I wanted to admire him in full view. His hips rocked faster, his fist pumped harder. Wetness pooled between my thighs and my breathing hitched. My heart raced in my chest, and I couldn't hear anything but the buzzing in my ears.

Another soft groan vibrated against the tile, my husband's head tilting back and his moans raspy. He came with a guttural sound, setting me aflame, and I had to bite into my lip to stop my own whimpering moan from slipping out.

My cheeks heated. My body burned. Then the shower stopped running and I bolted back to the bed like the devil was on my heels. I jumped on the bed, breaking a sweat. I slipped Dante's robe off but then I remembered I was in only a pair of sexy shorts and a silky top.

"Shit," I hissed, jumping out of bed again.

I was burning up. Like I had an honest-to-God fever. I rushed over and grabbed it, but instead of putting it back on, I started waving it through the air, hoping to cool off my body. If anyone would have seen me, they'd think me mental.

I probably was.

I waved the robe up and down, letting the air cool my skin and the whole time keeping my eyes locked on the door. The door handle moved and I froze. A towel wrapped around his waist, Dante came into full view. I remained staring at him, my hands still frozen midair with the robe hanging off the fingers.

Dante's dark eyes met mine and I jumped into motion, wrapping the robe around me. Upside down. Perfect.

He cocked an eyebrow, waiting for me to explain what I was doing. There was no sane explanation on this earth that could work. So, I settled for the insane one.

"Chasing a fly." Jesus fucking Christ. Of all the stupid things to say, I said this. *Someone kill me now,* I thought silently.

"Okay," he muttered in an unsure voice. He probably thought I was crazy. He was looking at me like I had lost my mind.

He disappeared into the walk-in closet and I debated whether to die of embarrassment or just pretend this didn't happen. I went for the latter.

I still had some people to kill.

CHAPTER 25
Dante

O ur wedding night.

I wore a pair of black pajama pants and a plain white T-shirt. For my wife's sake.

My wife.

It sounded so fucking right. Years of chasing her and she was finally where she belonged. Right here with me. In my city. In my home. In my room. On my fucking bed.

Although she'd avoided locking eyes with me ever since I'd finished in the shower. That was a first. That girl was never shy to stare anyone down or blurt out something inappropriate. Yet, here she was sitting on our bed, her legs folded and staring at her sandwich like it was godsent, chewing it slowly as if that would stop her from talking.

The only thing that should stop her from talking was my cock in her mouth.

Fuck!

All the heat rushed to my groin and I silently cursed myself. The last thing I needed were images of Juliette on her knees. She'd sooner bite my dick off than suck it. Although the aversion had nothing to do with me.

That alone sent a cold fury running through my veins.

I couldn't wait to spend some quality time with that fucker Travis. He'd regret the day he was born.

"Do you want to talk about it?" I asked her softly.

She had put the robe back on, the right way this time, but she must have still been hot. The robe slipped off her shoulder and she didn't bother pulling it back up, giving me a glimpse of her beautiful skin. Unlike my tan skin, hers was fair. Too fair. Almost like a porcelain doll.

Juliette's eyes flared and her cheeks turned a deep shade of red. Red blotches marred her chest and she quickly tightened the robe, hiding her body.

The moment I lowered myself on the bed, she tensed and panic entered her expression. Goosebumps broke out over her skin and her hands trembled as she gripped the robe against her body.

"I'm not going to touch you," I promised quietly. I'd rather cut my dick off than hurt her. Yes, I'd obsessed over her for two years—even longer if we considered NYC. But I hadn't sought out any other women since she'd reappeared in my life. I was saving myself for her. And I'd continue that. But it didn't mean I'd lose control. That wasn't me.

She peered at me through her thick, dark lashes, vulnerability shining in their depths.

"I'm sorry," she muttered, red blotches still marking her flawless skin. She hated her own vulnerability. "I bet you never thought you'd get a defective bride."

I took her chin between my fingers and forced her to face me. "You. Are. Not. Defective." Our gazes clashed. My darkness. Hers. My ghosts. Hers. "And don't you ever fucking apologize for the actions of others. It's not your fault." My hold on her chin tightened. "Not. Your. Fault."

"I know it's not," she spat, though her usual spitefulness wasn't in her words. Tears glimmered in her eyes and one made its escape. I refused to let her hide in the dark and combat her ghosts alone, so I stayed silent and let her speak her truth. "Sometimes I just can't help thinking about what I did wrong. Why me?" Her tongue darted out, sweeping over her bottom lip. I tried to stay focused on her words. I wanted to be a good husband to her. "Did I smile too much? Maybe it was perceived as flirtation. My clothes were too revealing, so I must have been asking for it. Right?"

"No," I growled. "I don't care if you parade naked; it doesn't give any man the right to take something from you. Understood?"

Guilt pierced through my chest but I ignored it. I fucked up, because I took her free will when I slipped her the drug but this was neither the time nor place. Maybe when we are old and gray, madly in love, I'd admit it to her. But first, I'd worship her for decades to come.

"I feel silly in your robe," she remarked after a beat, changing subjects.

"You don't have to feel silly," I said, thinking she was embarrassed that I'd caught her waving the robe in the air like it was a flag on Independence Day. It looked ludicrous but I'd come to expect that from Juliette.

Her mouth parted and she turned an even deeper shade of red. "W-what?"

I chuckled. "You're adorable in my robe," I told her softly and her cheeks blushed attractively. "Do you want to tell me what happened?"

Her brows scrunched but the flush didn't leave her skin. "You want me to tell you why I was waving the robe like a maniac?" she asked carefully, her blush deepening.

Why did I feel like I was missing something here?

"No, I was asking whether you want to tell me what happened with Travis," I said softly, my tone careful. "I had a—" My voice trailed off thinking back to those days and instantly my mood turned gloomy. "A friend. It helps to talk."

Although my brother never talked about it. Fucking ever. Neither did I. We locked those demons deep inside and pretended they didn't exist. But they reared their ugly heads every so often. For Priest, more than me, and it gutted me that I couldn't save him.

So I focused all my attention on Juliette. Her blush paled and her eyes lost their sparkle. Her bottom lip quivered and my chest squeezed. Jesus, at this rate, I'd have a heart attack.

"Nobody knows," she murmured, her voice trembling. "I never told anyone."

"What about your aunt?" She shook her head, chewing on her bottom lip. "Wynter?"

Another shake of her head. She fucking dealt with it all on her own. It sent another shot of anger through me. I had to remain still or risk raging and that was the last thing I wanted to do. Scare Juliette off. On our wedding night, nonetheless.

"Your aunt should have been there for you," I hissed, but Juliette's eyes darted away from me and locked on the dark window. The flurries had turned into snowflakes and brightened the night.

"I promise I'll make him pay," I vowed softly. She didn't need to know how he'd beg for mercy and never get it.

A shudder rolled over her, making her look so vulnerable. It was hard to come to grips with this Juliette, so different from the reckless one I'd gotten to know over the years.

She nodded, her eyes darting past me and looking out the large window, staring at snowflakes, falling harder by the minute. I didn't think she'd say anything else on the matter when her small voice broke the silence.

"It was my first year of high school," she whispered in a rough voice. Her fingers trembled and she interlocked them as if she wanted to lock down any sign of her weakness. "There were parties and older boys seemed to make prey out of us younger girls." She swallowed hard, her pale neck bobbing. "A friend of ours from school was hosting this party. Usually Wynter and I tag-teamed and went everywhere together. That night, I went alone." She let out a rough sound. "I didn't drink alcohol—I was too young. So nobody could blame that on my bad choices. I did everything right. Kept my soda with me. I didn't flirt. I stuck to people I knew. And I avoided drunks."

She took a deep breath in and reached for her glass of water. She had to grip it with two hands to stop it from spilling. After taking a sip, she lowered it back onto the tray that sat between us.

"I don't know," she muttered. "One second I was dancing, the next I was in the room. And Travis was—"

She was drugged!

Fuck, fuck, fuck. It was at that exact moment I realized how badly I'd fucked up. I slipped her a drug to get her compliant. So I could marry her without her permission. Revealing the truth was off the table now. Goddamn it, I had never miscalculated so badly before. Why did I feel like I had already lost her?

Her breathing was labored and shudders rolled down her body. Her eyes met mine, anguish and pain so fucking raw that it stole my breath. The fierce, reckless woman reduced to feeling such pain. I couldn't stand it.

She shrugged and the robe slipped off her slim shoulder. "Anyhow, it didn't end well. Just the idea of someone on top of me now—" She swallowed, wrapping her arms around herself. "It takes me back to that night. Even just the thought of it makes me claustrophobic."

An idea came to my mind but it wasn't the right time to discuss it. I'd table it for another day. I wanted Juliette for my wife from the moment I saw her. Now she was and we'd get through her trauma together. As long as she never found out what I did to get her to marry me.

But first, I'd make the fucker suffer.

"He will pay," I assured her in a cold voice.

There was a flash of satisfaction in her eyes, then it was gone. Her eyes flickered around us. "Now what about the sleeping arrangements?"

My lips twitched. "What about them? It's the only bed in the entire home."

"Well, there are couches," she suggested. Fuck, I should have made them burn all the furniture in this place before we arrived.

"No," I stated, calmly. "You'll sleep here, next to me. See this," I said, pointing to the middle of the bed. She nodded. "This is Switzerland. The neutral zone."

"A neutral zone?" she repeated in disbelief.

I nodded. "Yes. I'm not saying we'll never have sex, but we have the rest of our lives to get there."

Juliette narrowed her eyes. "You seem confident."

I smiled. "You'll learn one thing about me, Juliette. I always keep my word, and I always get what I want."

I wasn't sure if it registered or not, but I knew there was no dissolving this marriage. Not when she learned how I'd trapped her. And not when her brother and father got wind of it. I was a fucked-up person with fucked-up morals. My miscalculation when I drugged her might backfire. I'd repent. I'd grovel. I'd crawl. And it would all lead me back to her.

Because I'd be a good husband. I'd be a good father—eventually.

Better than our parents were to us.

CHAPTER 26
Juliette

When I woke, warmth and a clean, fresh scent surrounded me. Light poured through the windows. I blinked my eyes, the soft white landscape greeting me. Then slowly, events of the last few days came rushing in and I remembered where I was. Who I was!

Juliette DiLustro.

My pulse quickened, registering a heavy arm around my waist and a hard, warm chest pressed against my back.

I took a deep breath, then slowly exhaled.

"You're awake." Dante's warm breath brushed against the back of my neck, sending shivers down my spine.

"What happened with the two of us sticking to our sides of the bed?" I asked, not turning around. I didn't want to risk coming face-to-face with him and tempting fate. The thought of his body suffocating mine had my pulse racing and blood rushing. "You said the middle was Switzerland. A neutral zone."

"Sorry." He didn't sound sorry at all. "I didn't grope you or anything. I'm just holding my wife."

I rolled my eyes but he didn't see it. Not that he'd care. He'd seen me roll my eyes at him plenty of times.

"Guess you were right," I muttered. "Blizzard came. We're buried in snow."

A light shiver rolled down my spine. I wasn't overly fond of the cold. His hold tightened, but it didn't suffocate.

"This is far from being buried," he rasped behind me. "We can go for a ride, if you want?"

This time I did risk looking over my shoulder and my breath caught in my throat. Dante's ruffled dark locks and the sleepy look on his face made him seem less arrogant. Less formidable.

My heart rate picked up. I didn't like how my pulse kept speeding up around him. It was as if it were influenced by his closeness. I'd rather be aloof and resist his charms, but my body seemed to have a mind of its own.

It wouldn't be such a bad revelation, if only my brain could process those fears that cowered in the corners of my mind and always came forward at the worst time.

"Are you serious?" I asked him, my tone slightly breathless. "Or are you trying to get me killed?"

He let out an amused breath. "My dear wildling wife, that's the last thing on this earth I want to do."

"Can you stop calling me that?" I spat out, slightly agitated. "Have you seen the damn movie? It's a horror flick. Nothing cute about it at all."

He chuckled. "Let's get dressed and I'll show you the house."

Pulling out of his arms, he reluctantly let me go and I rushed into the bathroom, then closed the door behind me. I hurried through my shower, then headed into the walk-in closet through the door that connected the bathroom directly to it.

Dante must have heard me because he called out, "You all done with the bathroom?"

"Yes." There was little that escaped that man. "You know if we had separate rooms, we wouldn't have to worry about sharing a bathroom."

Ignoring my comment, I heard him shuffle out of bed, and shortly after, the shower restarted. In awe, I stared at one side of the walk-in closet, *my* side. It was fully stocked with designer clothes. Anything and everything a woman desired was here—jewelry, dresses, bathing suits, ski suits, shoes. But no signs of any old-fashioned pajamas. Did he have that stuff ready for me the entire time? Creepy! *And convenient,* my heart justi-fied him.

Whatever. My eyes roamed over all the clothing. Well, he had every-thing except combat boots and weapons.

My eyes flicked to Dante's side and I caught sight of the section where he had stored his weapons. I could see them through the glass. Glocks, sniper rifles, knives. I wondered if he kept them all locked up.

My steps silent against the plush rug, I rushed to his side of the walk-in closet and reached for the door. It refused to open. So I tried again to no avail. It was then that I noticed it. A digital thumbprint. That was his lock.

Oh well. I needed to find some place to store my weapons securely. Or convince Dante to have my thumbprint added to the file so I could open the weapons drawer.

For now, I simply returned to my side of the closet and picked out clothes to wear. Something appropriate for this cold. I started with a matching bra and panties in soft pink. Once I put them on, I prowled through a selection of jeans and then a thick, yellow pullover followed.

I spotted a shelf with women's shoes and made my way there, noting they were all new. I reached for a pair of Uggs, when the door from the bathroom opened.

His eyes traveled over me, a dark triumphant gleam in his eyes. "Do they fit right?" he asked.

I nodded and something sparkled in his eyes. Satisfaction maybe? Emotions that I couldn't pinpoint. He could be hard to read sometimes.

"I bought them for you," he stated matter-of-factly as he headed to his own side of the closet and started pulling out his own outfit. Jeans. A light gray sweater. Combat boots.

Then his words registered. "When did you buy them?" I asked carefully.

His shoulders tensed for a fraction of a second before they relaxed. "The morning after our first wedding."

I eyed him suspiciously. That was just three days ago. There was no way all this shit arrived in two days. "Really?"

Fully dressed, he turned around and extended his hand. "Let's give you the tour and then let's go grab something to eat."

The first room he took me to was a library. A massive two stories high with shelves that reached to the top and were fully stocked. There was a ladder on small wheels that leaned against each row to allow a person to reach for the books at the very top.

"Wow," I murmured, my eyes traveling over the room. I wasn't even the reading type. My literature started and ended with romances. Some sweeter than the others, but mostly filthy. Of course, I'd never admit that to Dante.

I walked through the nearest aisle of books, my eyes gliding over the fancy spines. History. Science. Warfare. Classics. Not surprising, no romance.

"You look disappointed?" Dante remarked. I turned away from the books and caught Dante watching me with a small frown. "If there is a particular author you like, we can get it. Just say the word."

I flushed. There was no fucking way I'd tell him to get me dirty romance novels.

"Maybe some romance novels?" he suggested and my cheeks burned. Dante was annoying as fuck.

I cleared my throat, keeping my composure. "I read mostly on my Kindle. But thank you. The library's impressive." Then I walked to him. "Okay, next room."

So the tour continued. Pool room and cigar lounge. I crinkled my nose. I hated the smell of cigars. Then we moved on to a few more guest rooms. All without beds or mattresses.

"So what happened to the beds and mattresses?" I asked curiously.

Dante shrugged. "Bedbugs."

My head whipped around to look at him. "I hope yours didn't have bedbugs," I hissed, suddenly feeling every inch of me crawling. I scratched my neck, then my back. Shit, my whole body suddenly itched.

"It was a false alarm," he said, rolling his eyes. "Stop scratching yourself."

I glared at him. "You're an ass."

He laughed all the way down the stairs. Dante's mansion was bigger than I thought. It had several wings, although most were unused.

We made our way through the game room when I realized something. "So you live here by yourself?" I questioned, frowning. "No guards. Nothing? Just a cook or a maid?"

He flicked me a curious look. "From what I understand, you grew up without guards."

He was right. Dad and Aunt Aisling tried to give us a semblance of normalcy growing up. So much normalcy that we were blindsided when having to deal with Davina's ex. We really attempted our best at criminal activities but somehow none of them went well.

"Yes, I did," I agreed. "I don't need guards. I was just surprised."

He gave me a pensive look. "I don't usually need them. I can defend myself. When Priest and I lived together, it was the same way. But that might need to change. You're not capable of defending yourself."

I narrowed my eyes on him. "How presumptuous."

His one eyebrow rose and he watched me curiously. "Are you saying you can defend yourself?"

I shrugged. "Maybe."

"Okay," he went along with me. "Later today or tomorrow, we can test your defense skills. If you prove to me that you can, then we'll keep our place free of guards."

It took all I had not to snicker. Dante was in for a big surprise.

Chicago was cold.

And somewhat dreary. To my surprise, the city remained open, not missing a beat, with the blizzard that swept through last night. When I expressed my shock at stores being open, people just laughed. It wasn't a blizzard until cars were unable to drive on the streets.

We ended up having lunch at one of the local pizzerias. Curious glances were thrown our way the moment we arrived.

It was clear by the way the manager rushed to us that Dante was known. He greeted us personally, shaking Dante's hand and then bowed his head slightly to me.

"The married couple," he said, taking my extended hand and kissing the back of it. The gesture was so old-fashioned that for a moment I stared at him, floored. "Your wife is stunning, Mr. DiLustro."

"She is," Dante drawled, his dark shimmering eyes locking on me.

As we were led to the table, the looks turned to gawking. I glanced down a few times to ensure I didn't have a hole in my pants or an open zipper.

Dante took my hand into his, pulling me closer. "Are you okay?"

My cheeks felt hot. It only ever happened around this man. I didn't know whether it was his hand or his concern. I met his eyes, letting them pull me in. It was the oddest thing. My mind wanted me to fight him, but my body was the exact opposite. It encouraged me to let myself go. The conflict was driving me nuts.

"Why is everyone staring?" I asked as we were seated down.

It was the manager who answered. "Mr. DiLustro keeps peace in our city," he announced. "Naturally, his wife would attract interest."

Dante shrugged. "We all do our part," he said, discounting it. "They're just being nosy."

The manager chuckled. "Mr. DiLustro refuses to take credit, but before he took over, we had Russians attacking us. Corsican mafia. The Irish. Our city was a battlefield."

I stiffened at the callout of the Irish. My eyes flashed with annoyance. "Well, if something happens to me, you can count on the Irish to come back," I snapped slightly annoyed.

The manager's eyes flashed with surprise and his gaze darted to Dante with uncertainty. My husband lowered the menu, a hard look on his face and I straightened my shoulders, ready for battle.

But as always, Dante managed to surprise me.

"My wife has the Irish backing and I would support them if anything were to happen to her." The waiter brought us a bottle of sparkling water, but Dante didn't bother stopping. It would seem he wanted everyone to know whose wrath they'd earn if anything happened to me. "Anyone touches my wife, they can be certain that the Irish will be the least of their concerns."

The manager cleared his throat, then excused himself. The waiter was right behind him. And all the while I stared at my husband dumbfounded.

Why did it feel like there was more to Dante than met the eye?

CHAPTER 27
Dante

A strange sensation coasted through my chest.

Pride.

It was clear by Juliette's expression that she was surprised by my words and reaction. She had never tried to be meek. Unless she attempted to distract you, but that was beside the point. It was what I loved about her. Her strength. After learning what happened to her, I admired her even more.

I wanted her to know that I'd always be behind her if someone wronged her. And I'd damn well be in front of her if someone tried to hurt her. I'd shred them to pieces.

Her blue eyes that reminded me of the Ionian Sea stared back at me. When Priest and I were kids, our father took us on a vacation. It was one of the best ones since Mother didn't tag along. The fact that it was Greece made it even better. We stayed at a little cottage overlooking the sea, and it was the bluest water I'd ever seen.

Staring at my wife now, she reminded me of that time. The happiness with my father and younger brother. The warmth against our skin. The sounds of the waves against the shoreline. Neither my brother nor I ever wanted to leave.

With the manager and waiter cleared, I picked up the menu. "So what are you in the mood for?"

Juliette got herself together, glancing down to her own menu. "Considering it's a pizzeria, maybe a pizza?"

I nodded. "Good choice."

As if watching us, the waiter showed up and we placed our order, then he made himself scarce again.

"You mean that?" Juliette questioned, her eyes studying me for any signs that I'd be lying.

"Mean what? That I'll rip anyone to shreds if they hurt you?" She held her breath, keeping her eyes on me. "I do."

She let out an incredulous breath. "But you don't even know me."

A sardonic breath left me. "I've known you for two years at least, Juliette. You're the longest relationship I've had with a woman."

Not to mention that I'd met her first when she was thirteen. Of course, I never thought that I'd fall for that same girl once she grew into this stunning woman. I wanted her to want *me* like I wanted her. To need *me* like I needed her.

She rolled her eyes and my lips twisted into a smile.

"We didn't have a relationship," she breathed, though her cheeks were slightly flushed. "We know nothing about each other."

I could have laughed, though I wasn't amused at all. She was right. For the past two years, our interactions had been limited. Most of the time, it ended with the two of us bickering. But I made it my mission during that time to learn everything about this girl.

Everything.

Her favorite color. Her favorite foods. Her reading selection. Her favorite flowers. Her bucket list.

Yes, she had a damn bucket list on Pinterest and I stalked it. I hadn't touched another woman since this wildling bumped into me and proceeded to seduce me. All the years between us and she practically had me wrapped around her finger.

But Juliette's favorite activity—and by default mine—was the St. Jean d'Arc School project. A school for our future generations. She and her friends started stealing to fund their idea. Their goal was to establish a school for children, including girls, of the underworld families.

Heat crawled beneath my skin, and suddenly, I wished I'd worn a T-shirt despite the freezing temperatures. I reached for my spare cigarette I always kept on me for emergencies and put it between my lips.

Bottom line was that my wife, Juliette Brennan, newly DiLustro, unsettled me. We'd shared barely a kiss, the groping she subjected me to while under the influence of drugs didn't count—hardly even qualified for a grade-school relationship and she fucking unsettled me.

I leaned against the chair, locking gazes with her shining blue eyes. She thought she got me, but in the end, I'd get her. Under me. On top of me. Beside me.

All the fucking positions. Doggy style. Spooning. Rocking horse. Missionary.

I couldn't fucking wait.

"Ask me anything," I offered.

She snickered. "If you think I'll offer the same, you're delusional."

I smiled confidently. "I already know everything about you."

Her eyes narrowed to slits. "No, you don't."

"Then test me, Wildling." Her eyes flashed in annoyance at the nickname. She hated it; I fucking loved it. Juliette was wild, through and through. "Unless you're worried."

She blew a frustrated breath. "Fine. What's my favorite color?"

"Yellow." Surprise crossed her expression. "Because it reminds you of sunshine and you believe it looks best on you, but you're wrong." She narrowed her eyes, and before she could say anything, I added, "Every color looks great on you."

It was the truth. She always looked breathtaking. Her eyes always sparkled, but when she wore yellow, somehow her eyes turned even brighter. Like the sun against the blue sea.

"Flirt," she muttered.

"What is my favorite color?" I asked her though I was certain she didn't know.

A heartbeat passed. "Black?"

I rolled my eyes. "Why black?"

She blinked her eyes innocently. "Like a DiLustro's soul," she answered, keeping her tone soft but having a hard time keeping her face straight. It was best I didn't comment on it.

I shook my head. "Wrong. Want to try again?"

146

She waved her hand in exasperation. "Just tell me."

"Blue. Specifically, the blue of the Ionian Sea."

Her brows knitted. "Why?" she questioned.

"Why what?"

"That color seems so specific," she explained. "Why that specific shade of blue?"

"It reminds me of your eyes," I admitted. "And it was one of the best vacations my brother and I ever had."

I waited for some comment to come, but Juliette remained pensively quiet. Sometimes she managed to surprise me with her reactions. I never knew what to expect from her. She'd certainly keep me on my toes for the rest of our lives.

"My favorite food?" she asked after a few minutes of tense silence.

"Dessert. Specifically parfait."

She widened her eyes but quickly schooled her features. "You must have seen me devour that shit at Wynter's wedding." I tilted my head, watching her. We both knew she didn't eat that shit at her cousin's wedding. "Fine! My favorite drink?"

"Whisky," I answered. "Although now that you've sworn off alcohol, maybe we'll switch to lemonade in the future?"

"Hahaha," she retorted dryly. "Stalker."

"Damn straight." Then I brought the glass of sparkling water to my lips. I'd prefer beer with my pizza but if Juliette decided no more alcohol, I'd support her. "Giving up already?"

"Geez, you're exhausting," she muttered. "My favorite book?"

My grin widened and smugness swelled in my chest. "*Fifty Shades of Grey.*" Her face turned so pink, I worried her skin would permanently stain. And still I didn't ease off. "Is it the sex or the story that you like?"

She reached for her own glass and gulped it down in one swig. Her sapphire gaze met mine head-on.

"You tell me," she grumbled. "You seem to know it all."

Heat raced to my groin. There was nothing more I wanted than to grab the nape of her neck, pull her closer, and press my lips against hers. I wanted the taste of her mouth thoroughly on my tongue.

It was a *need,* no longer just a want.

CHAPTER 28
Juliette

S omething pulsed in my chest.

It reminded me of a beat on a heart-rate monitor. Almost like when Wynter listened to the baby's heartbeat during her sonogram.

A constant flutter. *Swish. Swish. Swish.*

Maybe it was just a thrum in my chest. Or maybe it was the beginning of something new.

We left the little pizzeria as the urban lights twinkled. The cold temperatures didn't stop women from wearing heels or short dresses. Night had barely started but the casino that Dante owned was already in full swing when he pulled up around the back. The private entrance I assumed.

Wynter, Ivy, Davina, and I came to this casino two years ago. Naturally, we used the front door. We made quite a stir. Wynter played poker and cleared three hundred thousand counting cards.

It was that very same night that I ran into Dante and Priest, pretending to be a seductress. It was probably the same night that I crossed the line with this man.

He gave chase. I ran. Until he caught me.

Although, I should be proud I managed to elude him for this long. I made him wait after all. Well, he probably didn't wait. He had women throwing themselves on him, I could be sure of that. He'd just been biding his time until I finally stumbled onto the dance floor with him. Literally.

As we made it into Dante's casino, I noticed the way money, sex, and alcohol hung in the air. As well as the memory of our first meeting. An electric beat pulsed through me, remembering the moment we locked eyes for the first time.

It seemed like a different lifetime. I hadn't thought at that moment we'd ever become connected. Not by Wynter's marriage, and not by my own.

The two of us walked down the dark hallway, bypassing the open floor where people drank and gambled. A certain thickness permeated the space. The deeper into the building we went, the more the atmosphere smelled of money. The men in expensive suits played exclusively back here. Higher stakes. Higher debt.

Dante's hand was on the small of my back, and even through the thick pullover, I could feel the warmth of his touch. He guided us left, then right until we came to stop at a heavy metal door.

He knocked five times. *Thump-thump. Thump-thump. Thump.*

The door swung open and a man stood across from us. The moment he spotted Dante, he moved to the side, letting us pass.

Dante guided me down a red-carpeted hall as my first visit to this place flipped through my head.

It didn't take long to arrive at his office, a perfectly spaced square room with a simple blue couch and carpet, a mahogany desk, a few leather chairs, and a minibar. There was a single piece of art on the wall and it reminded me of the Mediterranean. The sapphire-blue water sparkling behind an old town.

"It's the little village where my father took us," Dante explained, noticing me looking at the painting. "The Ionian stretching behind it."

I glanced at him, but his attention wasn't on me. He was already seated behind the desk and his attention was on the computer.

Then something registered. Both times he mentioned the vacation, he only mentioned his father and brother. Never mother.

"Did your mother not vacation with you?" I questioned him.

A bitter chuckle vibrated through the room, but he quickly stifled it. I studied my husband as if seeing him for the first time. Maybe there was more to Dante than he let on.

His shoulders tensed and his strokes fell on the keyboard harder. Louder.

Finally his gaze lifted, burning into mine. I knew Dante wouldn't be an easy man to get to know. Very much like his cousin Basilio. Except with Basilio—or Bas, as Wynter affectionately called him—I never had the interest of getting to know him.

Until now, I thought the same was true with Dante. Yet now, I found myself wanting to know him. Needing to know him.

Because for better or for worse, I knew there was only one way out of this marriage.

Death.

"Dante?" I breathed, then waited. He wasn't one to hide, but I knew firsthand how hard certain things were to share. I had one single night that had been festering inside the dark corners of my mind, torturing me. Haunting me. I understood the reluctance to open that part of yourself up, but I could now see how much it helped. "You can trust me," I murmured softly. "I trust you."

Dante let out a harsh breath and my stomach tightened with the need to assure him. He was the only person I ever admitted to that I was raped. No matter what, I'd never betray him. He stood up abruptly and walked across the floor of his office.

My eyes followed his tall frame, watched as the broad shoulders under his gray sweater tensed and his ass filled those jeans. He opened the door, his hand on the doorknob paused, then glanced back at me.

"You shouldn't trust me, my wildling wife. I've already lied to you once since we've been married."

I swallowed. "About what?"

"I'll be right back," he said instead. "Stay here."

Then he left without another word.

I fell asleep on the couch in Dante's office while he handled business.

What felt like a catnap ended up being three hours of restless tossing and turning. Dante's revelation, things that I didn't care to think about, men I was still hunting—it all came knocking on the door.

My husband woke me up with a light nudge on my shoulder. I was slightly disoriented, worried I had drool running down my mouth. Although by the way Dante looked at me, you'd think I just came off the runway.

I blinked, finger-combing my hair in a daze, then slipped my shoes back on.

"You look beautiful," he murmured. "Come on. My car is waiting."

He pulled me up and held my hand all the way to his car.

Dante drove the same way he walked and talked. Sure of himself and everyone around him. It wasn't as if I were insecure or doubting myself, but it was irritating to see him so confident at times.

Ever since he left me with that cryptic answer about a lie he'd told me, he'd been quiet. A part of him shut down, and I didn't think I'd be able to get through to him.

Finally, I couldn't take it anymore. An hour of utter silence was too much for anyone.

"I'm sorry if I upset you, Dante."

His eyes darted my way, a dark edge lingering in their depths. My hand reached to his arm resting on the wheel and I squeezed softly. Although his gaze returned to the road, there was no doubt where his focus was. On me.

Cool confidence seemed to brew under his skin but also something darker. A secret he didn't want to share. Perhaps it hurt him as much as mine hurt me. His mood was electric and affected me like a contagion. I had been fighting my attraction to Dante for years, fearing the darkness that crept into my mind every time a man tried to take a physical relationship a step too far.

Yet now, I felt the need to help him. Just as he'd come to my swift rescue, I wanted to come to his swift rescue.

"You do for me, I do for you," I whispered softly.

"What are you talking about?" he said. There was a sharp note to his voice. "I didn't do anything for you. You almost jumped to your death to escape being near me."

I sucked in a breath. It had been a moment of weakness. I regretted it now. I thought he'd force himself on me. He didn't. Instead, he'd vowed to avenge me. Kill Travis. My most elusive rapist.

"That was stupid," I admitted. "I wouldn't have jumped. I'm too stubborn and I like agitating you too much. I just needed to get away. The thought of you—" A shuddering breath filled the space. Every time I even thought about someone on top of me, I started to suffocate and images of that night so long ago returned with a vengeance. "I should have just talked to you instead of running off. How did you know I took your car anyway?"

"Priest," he answered. "He saw you drive away in it and called me."

"Of course he did," I retorted dryly.

"And then there was the tracker too," he added.

My hand was still on his forearm, so I peeled my fingers off him. But before I could put my hand back on my lap, he took it and interlocked our fingers.

His big hand to my small one. He killed people. So did I. He thought I was innocent. I wasn't.

It turned out maybe the two of us weren't so different after all.

"My mother was a vindictive and narcissistic bitch." His words slashed through the silence. "She liked to torture Priest and me." My gasp filled the inside of the car. What kind of mother would torture her own sons? "She hated me because I reminded her of our father. I couldn't understand why she hated Priest until we learned he's actually Wynter's brother. Or half brother, I guess."

Something about the tone of his voice told me he had more ghosts in his closet too.

"Jesus, I'm sorry." I squeezed his hand gently. "Didn't you tell your father?"

He shook his head. "We tried once. Mother was a very good liar. It did us no good. Especially Priest. After that, we relied only on each other." I wanted to know exactly what happened to them, but then, on the other hand, I was terrified of the answer. It was hard for me to talk about my experience, and it seemed Dante and his brother endured *years* of torture. "Our vacation to Greece was one of the rare times she wasn't around. That's why it's a happy memory."

I nodded, and for the next five minutes we sat in silence, while he drove through snow-filled Chicago. It was incredible how one day could change everything.

My life. My perception of life. My perception of this man.

He parked the car on the side of a dark street and my eyes darted around. "Aren't we going home?"

Home.

Did I really just call his house home?

His intense gaze met mine, the pressure of it touching my skin. "We'll go home after this. I want to take you out for dinner."

My eyes lowered to my casual outfit, then flickered to his. "We're not exactly dressed for it. We'll stand out."

His dark chuckle followed. "You and I are meant to stand out, Wildling."

I rolled my eyes, but a smile curved my lips. "Okay, where are we going, then? This street looks deserted."

He exited the car, then came around and opened my door. Reaching behind me, he grabbed a jacket and helped me slip it on.

"Chicago has a long history with gangsters," he started as I pushed my right hand into the sleeve. "Prohibition was their busy time. They ran Chicago and opened secret spots throughout the city to keep the party going."

I chuckled. "So we're going to a Prohibition-era speakeasy? Isn't that what they called them?"

He nodded. "I own a few of them. It's a popular theme to the nightlife here."

I threw my head back and laughed. "Do we need a password to get in?"

He gave me that boyish grin that used to drive me crazy because I hated the way it did things to my body. Made my heart flutter. My thighs quiver. Now it just drove me crazy.

"We certainly do, but not to worry. I can guarantee our entrance."

We made our way inside what looked to be a very elegant restaurant.

"Welcome to The Library at Gilt Bar," Dante announced.

We were seated right away, and it didn't take long for a train of food assortments to be brought over. Apparently, Dante was a regular here.

"Take your pick," Dante offered. He met my gaze, a playful glint in his eyes. "Whatever your heart wants, you'll get."

"In that case, how about we start with a dessert?"

He flashed me a grin. "If that's what you want."

It was exactly what happened. I had a dessert first, then a salad, while Dante had his favorite burger. It was one more thing I learned about my husband. He loved eating burgers.

After a meal in the elegant bar, we headed downstairs. "An evening nightcap?" Dante offered.

I chuckled. "I gave up drinking in Vegas," I pointed out.

"Then keep me company, my wildling wife."

Hand in hand we headed down the hallway lined with photos until we stopped in front of an unmarked door on the right. When we reached the basement, a gasp tore from my lips. "Oh my gosh," I said, my voice filled with awe.

The place was not what I expected. Instead of some hole-in-the-wall, a romantic space lined with books and flickering candles welcomed us with open arms, setting the mood. Cushy red velvet booths invited us to sink into them and get comfortable.

"So a nightcap and *Fifty Shades* feel?" I mused, my eyes darting left and right, trying to commit the room to memory. Dante's carefree laughter caught me by surprise, and I whirled around to look at him.

God, he was handsome. Dark expressions and an overwhelming arrogance seemed to be permanently part of his face but there was more. Craving. Possession. Obsession. Protection.

"You're handsome when you laugh," I remarked.

He pulled me closer into him and I let him, inhaling the deep scent of him into my lungs. Clean. Rain and forest. It'd forever make me think of him.

We took the booth that was furthest away, set apart from the others, and sunk into the plush seats. The drinks came instantly, but I was still determined not to drink alcohol. Instead I asked for sparkling water.

"You mind if I have a beer?" Dante asked when the waiter disappeared to go fetch my San Pellegrino.

"Of course not," I murmured distractedly, unable to keep from soaking it all in. "I can read you *Fifty Shades* while you drink beer."

He laughed. "Better not, I wouldn't want to embarrass myself in front of my wife and come in my pants."

I sucked in a breath as warmth rushed to my cheeks and spread throughout my entire body. Dante's eyes sparkled with amusement. His unique scent surrounded me like a protective bubble, and I let it seep through my pores.

He leaned back, resting his elbows against the top of the armrests.

"You blush easily," he stated.

I rolled my eyes. "Actually I don't," I grumbled. "Just around you, it seems. Why you have that effect on me is something I haven't quite figured out yet," I admitted.

A dark smile pulled on his lips. "I like that," he admitted. "I like that a lot."

"Don't get yourself all worked up, Mr. DiLustro," I said quickly, my face burning with my admission. "Eventually I'll become immune to your words." And sex appeal, I added silently.

"I hope you don't," he said in an amused drawl. "I want to see your blush when we're eighty. I want you to want me when I'm wrinkly and old. I'll go with you. Like that *Notebook* movie."

A choked laugh escaped me. "Well, that's... romantic," I said softly, my cheeks warm from his stare. "I didn't take you for such a romance buff."

His words were so quiet I barely heard them. "I wasn't until I fell for you."

My heart raced from the shock of hearing them. He didn't touch me, but my skin tingled as if he had. He was so big and warm and hard that I had to fight my body's need to lean into him. The pull tugged on me, like he was my center of gravity. My fingers pulsed with the need to run my hand along his strong jawline and then bury them in his hair so I could pull him closer and meet my lips with his.

Maybe I had been fighting Dante DiLustro for the past two years for naught.

CHAPTER 29
Juliette

I loved the way Dante drove. It was infinitely him.

His hand wrapped around the wheel while he sat in the seat with confidence, taking us home.

Home.

Twice in the short span of twenty-four hours I let that word come to the surface. Maybe Dante felt like home because it was just the two of us. Dad had made a home with Davina and their child. I still had a room in his home and Aunt Aisling's but they were both mostly empty. Aunt Aisling lived with Dante's father, mostly in New York, Wynter lived with her husband, and Davina spent most of her time with Dad in their penthouse.

Probably getting freaky, I thought wryly.

And then there was my brother, Killian. I loved him, but I honestly had no fucking idea where his head was or what he was up to. His engagement to Branka Russo had been surprising and short-lived. He didn't seem heartbroken when she'd been kidnapped—in the middle of his wedding I might add—by Sasha Nikolaev.

Since then, he seemed to spend increasingly more time in Ireland.

Regardless, it left me alone for most of the time over the last year and a half. Which was fine when I went after the men who killed our parents. Or my rapists. But it was incredibly lonely in between.

I heard a buzz and I glanced at my husband behind the wheel.

"I think your phone's ringing," I remarked.

He shook his head. "It's probably your phone." He leaned over, reaching across my lap and opening the glove box. "I forgot to give it to you back in Vegas. Sorry."

Handing it to me, I saw a list of missed calls and messages. "Jesus, has it been a week or just a day?"

Dante chuckled. "You're a popular girl."

He remained silent as he drove and I scrolled through all the messages. Quickly typing back responses to my family, I assured them all I was good. In fact, I typed GREAT.

"Hey, you still have that photo we took?" I asked Dante. On the way out of the Prohibition bar, there was a booth and we took a selfie. One to leave on the wall behind and one for us. Except, I didn't remember either one of us grabbing it.

He reached between us and pulled out the photo from the console. I took it and smiled. It was a goofy photo. My eyes crossed and his smile crooked, like we were both drunk as hell. I snapped a photo of it and sent it off to all of them.

Went to a Prohibition bar. No, I didn't drink but it was totally gangster cool.

First reply came from Dad and Davina.

Dad: *Don't let him turn you into a gangster. I'll break his bones.*

I chuckled, then read Dad's message to Dante.

"He'd have to catch us first," Dante joked. "We'll be like Bonnie and Clyde. Unstoppable."

Leaning forward, I reached for the stereo. "Maybe Beyoncé and Jay-Z playing while we run out of town with sirens blasting behind us," I said, egging him on.

A deep, full-blown laugh vibrated through the space as I watched Dante, mesmerized. In the two years that I had known him, I had never heard him laugh like that. Fucking ever. And now he'd done it twice in one day, and I was addicted to the sound.

"I own most of the cops in Chicago, Wildling," he uttered in an amused tone. "There'll be no need to go flying out of town with cops chasing us, but if it'll make you happy, I can arrange it."

My phone buzzed and I lowered my eyes, smiling. "Nah, let's just stay and light up this town."

Ivy: *Yeah, learn some gangsta shit so we can be the best.*

Davina: *No. More. Criminal. Activities.*

I typed back my reply. ***Okay, Stepmom.***

Grinning, I raised my eyes to find Dante eyeing me. "You look like you've done something bad," he remarked.

"I called Davina 'Stepmom,'" I explained, still grinning. "She hates that."

Dante smiled, his expression unreadable as he watched me. For the rest of the ride, he hardly said another word and I focused on clearing out my text messages.

The next message was from Kian—it was short and to the point. As always. I stiffened, my brows furrowing. ***Another killer found.***

A shudder rolled through me. Somewhere deep down, I loved making every single one of the bastards pay. From what I'd learned, my biological father had been a good killer in his day. It seemed I inherited that quality.

"Is it weird for you, now that you know Liam's not your biological father?" Dante inquired.

"Weird how?" I rasped.

His head tilted to the side, holding my gaze for a moment before returning it to the road.

"Not really," I said quietly. "He raised me and Killian. He made sure we were all safe. He saved us from a burning house."

"But?"

It didn't surprise me that he sensed there was more to it.

"I wonder who they were," I admitted softly. "Not the names. I know those now. But *who* they were."

I knew about my father's reputation, the violence. I knew my mother loved to play piano and sing. But Liam wasn't the one to reveal that information.

"I can get that information for you," Dante offered.

I pulled my bottom lip between my teeth, trying to think of how to respond. I had all the information on my birth parents now. I gathered some of it via torture and learned the rest of it all on my own by digging through Liam's stuff.

"No." He raised a brow, surprised at my response. "No, thank you," I added.

Curiosity and something else washed over his features as I took in his side profile. But there was definitely amusement there. Whether at my manners or what, I didn't know.

"I thought you wanted to know more information," he said, the ghost of a smile on his lips.

"I do," I breathed in a quiet voice. "I did. But not anymore. I've learned it all already." The glance he cast my way was dark. Knowing. And I realized, he knew all there was about my birth parents. "But then so did you, isn't that right?"

He nodded.

I swallowed. "It doesn't worry you?"

After all, our parents' sins became ours. Their enemies became ours. The people who had it out for my family could come after him too. A sliver of fear breathed into my lungs. I didn't want anything happening to him—not because of me.

He caught my gaze, studying me for a moment, then turned back to the road. "Juliette, I don't give a shit who your parents are or were. I married *you*. I've wanted you from the moment I saw you dancing on top of that bar at The Eastside dressed in those ridiculous Irish flag colors with your friends."

My eyes widened. "Not in the casino?" I rasped, unable to form a full sentence.

"No. You were shaking your ass on top of your father's bar wearing a sparkly orange minidress. When I saw you again in my casino, the deal was sealed. You were mine."

His answer was a silent admission. There was one thing I couldn't take away from my husband. He was honest, despite him telling me he'd already lied to me once. I was no angel in that scenario either. He didn't bother with feigned emotions or niceties.

He pulled into the driveway of his mansion ten minutes later and something about it felt *right*. Something about *him* felt right. Nerves danced in the atmosphere. Heavy tension had settled in the space between us.

He leaned over, his minty breath like a breeze against my skin. "Am I scaring you, Juliette?"

My pulse fluttered. The pressure built. I swallowed, battling all these emotions and cravings within me. I was starting to realize that maybe the last two years with him had been a sort of foreplay, and we were always meant to get to this point.

My body wanted this man. My mind resisted him.

But I was quickly losing this battle. Each breath I took pulled me in the opposite direction.

Confusion grew. My breaths were labored. My heart thundered. It scared me that I wanted to experience it all with Dante knowing where it all led. To him on top of me. It'd find me cornered and my ugly fear would rear its head.

"Juliette?"

Something pounded in my chest. I couldn't distinguish whether it was fear or something else.

"How many women have you had?" I breathed out, adrenaline buzzing in my ears. His eyebrows rose and I swallowed, averting my eyes. His thumb brushed across my lips and down my chin, until it followed the vein in my throat.

"Look at me." My eyes immediately obeyed. Satisfaction washed over his expression. "Your pulse is racing," he remarked. "Are you scared of me, Wildling?"

I scoffed softly. "No."

His full lips curved into a smile. "Good," he drawled. "That means you're excited."

His thumb swept over my fluttering pulse. My lips parted and our gazes locked. A heavy weight settled between my legs and another one in my chest, pounding. I pressed my thighs together and Dante's eyes flickered to the movement.

"I can smell your arousal," he rasped in a deep voice.

A breath escaped me and I leaned into his touch. He applied pressure against my pulse—not hard, but just gentle enough to feel him. None of this made sense.

"Do you want me, my wildling?" he purred. I swallowed hard, then nodded. "Because I want you so fucking much that the thought of living without you makes me want to end it all." A sharp intake of air into my lungs filled the small space between us. Letting myself drown in his darkness, I stared at him. My husband. The man who I'd avoided for the past two years. "You and I, Wildling, we were meant to be together."

Then slowly, painfully slowly, he closed the distance between us. He captured my top lip between his, kissing me with the sweetest pull. Then he pulled back. His face was barely an inch from mine, yet it was too far away.

My heart fluttered like it had wings and my pulse skidded to a stop.

Time stilled. My mouth tingled. And he waited.

He wanted me to decide what the next step should be.

My heartbeat danced lightly for the first time in such a long time. I wanted to see it through. It was scary. It was thrilling.

A tremor ran through me and I leaned forward, our breaths intermingling. My eyelids fluttered and a strong need pulsed through my veins again, never stopping. My lips brushed against his softly.

A single word vibrated through my bloodstream. *Mine.*

He parted his lips and I slid my tongue inside. A groan came from deep in his chest and his hand came around my nape, gripping it tightly. I moaned, my fingers finding themselves around his neck. He sucked on my tongue. I licked every inch of his mouth.

His hand cupped the back of my head while his kiss turned rougher. More possessive. My blood drummed in my ears, but it wasn't in fear. It was in pure desire, fueling something deep inside me.

I felt complete. *Consumed.* So much so that it terrified me.

CHAPTER 30
Dante

Juliette tensed and I pulled back, searching her face.

She blinked, then looked away. Her fingers slid down to my front, and I noticed them trembling slightly.

"Juliette, look at me." She raised her chin, her Ionian-blue eyes meeting my gaze, shimmering like the sun's rays against the surface of the sea. "Are you okay?"

Her lips were swollen, tempting me. But I wouldn't cave into my desire. She was more important than my hard dick.

"Yes," she rasped, her fingers gripping my sweater. Her tongue darted out, wetting her full bottom lip that I wanted to bite. Fuck, I had to get my thoughts in order. She needed space, not my impulsiveness. Not my love. "I don't want to stop."

My cock swelled, on board with her plan, but my mind cautioned.

"We should take it slow." I encouraged hoarsely while my dick protested, calling me all kinds of idiot in every fucking language. "There's no rush," I added, ignoring the hard bulge in my pants that threatened to spill in my pants and embarrass me in front of my young wife.

Two years without a woman was a long fucking time. I wasn't a saint. Before my wildling ran into me, seducing me with her filthy words and her incredible eyes, I went through women like they were a commodity. But since then, I couldn't get my fucking dick up for anyone. It zeroed in on her promise and her mouth, refusing to get hard for anyone else.

Juliette's hand trailed down my chest and down to my pelvic area. She cupped my dick through my jeans, her small hand unsure of her movements.

"Are you sure?" she asked, tightening her grip slightly until a groan spilled from my mouth. Even with invisible scars, my wife was a formidable woman.

"I have an idea," I gritted out, my hips pushing into the palm of her small hand. Thank fuck we were in the car or I'd have lost all my control. "You said panic comes when someone's on top."

A flicker of pain passed across her expression and her grip loosened, but before she could pull away, I continued. "You could tie me to the bed and you would be on top of me."

A sharp gasp passed through those lush, red lips. I searched her face for any signs of repulsion at my plan. There was none. Her blue eyes were hazed and her cheeks flushed. Fuck, she was sexy as sin.

"You'd let me tie you up?" she murmured. I nodded. "Aren't you scared I'd hurt you?"

"You can do anything you want to me, my wildling," I rasped, like the damn lovestruck fool that I was. "Pain, pleasure... anything from you, it's heaven."

She blinked, her dark lashes casting shadows against her pale skin. I wished she were an open book. There were so many layers to her that she always managed to surprise me with.

"Then take me to bed, Dante."

I didn't waste any time. I jumped out of the car, opening her door, then rushed into the house, practically dragging us both up the stairs. Like the end of the world was upon us, and it was about to be the first and last time I'd taste my wife.

Once in our bedroom, I let her go and prowled through the room, kicking my shoes off. In one swift move, I took off my sweater and discarded it on the floor. Then I unbuttoned my jeans and took them off. I lay on the bed and found my wife watching me, smiling.

"You seem very eager," she teased softly, walking slowly toward the bed.

"Two years is a long time," I grumbled.

"Two years? Seriously?" At my nod, she agreed. "It is." Tilting her head slightly at my still-covered dick, she said, "You going to keep your boxers on?"

I lowered my eyes. I left them on for her so she'd feel safer. "Probably better since it's our first time."

I knew it was the right choice when relief skirted over her expression. She wanted this but there was anxiety there too. After the way I tricked her into this marriage, I owed it to her to do right by her. I *wanted* to do right by her.

"Okay," she said.

Reaching to the nightstand, I pulled out a pair of handcuffs. Her eyebrows rose to her hairline and curiosity entered her blue eyes.

"Don't tell me you've used those before?" she asked, a hint of jealousy lacing her voice.

"I haven't," I assured her, smiling smugly. I'd be lying if I said I didn't like her jealousy. It meant she wasn't as indifferent toward me as she let me believe for the past two years. "Trust me, I'd never been cuffed or used cuffs before. Priest left these." She raised a surprised brow while curiosity flared in her eyes. "They're brand new," I added. "I'll get better ones from the sex store." I winked. Her face turned crimson, but she couldn't hide her lingering curiosity. *Ah*, it would seem she liked the idea of going to the sex store. "But you'll have to go with me," I added. "Do we have a deal?"

She blew out a breath with less gusto than usual. "I guess, if I must."

"You must," I confirmed. "Now, come and cuff me, wife. I know you've been dreaming of this your whole life."

She rolled her eyes, but there was no bite to it. Her smile was too soft and her blush told me she was eager to try this.

She kicked off her Uggs, then she drew her yellow pullover over her head. Her breathing was heavy, but there was an eagerness in her gaze she couldn't hide. Her hips swayed as she made her way toward our bed, but she kept her eyes on me.

My cock twitched with each step she took closer to me. The pushup bra she wore hid her breasts from me, but I could still see how full and gorgeous they were. I couldn't wait to taste them. To hear more of her moans as I sucked on her nipples.

Fuck.

We'd have to hurry up or I'd truly come in my boxers.

The mattress dipped as she crawled onto the bed, then came to rest between my spread legs. She reached for the cuffs, her body above me and her boobs hovering right by my face. I couldn't resist lifting my head and licking her right nipple over the thin material.

She shuddered, and before I could wonder whether it was in pleasure, a tiny moan slipped from her lips. It was heaven. It was fucking hell.

Click.

"You're cuffed," she announced softly and she fell back down my body, straddling my hips. "Now what?"

Her eyes darted to my lips and she licked her own. The sight had my cock straining for her pussy. But she was still wearing jeans.

"Maybe you can lose the jeans and your panties," I suggested. "If you feel comfortable."

It wasn't as if I was experienced in fooling around while being cuffed. But this was for her. For our future. She nodded before standing and shimmying her jeans and panties down her gorgeous legs. Her bra followed, joining the pool of clothes on the floor. My cock jumped eagerly. She was breathtaking, but it was so much more than that. Her eyes sparkled cobalt blue, the lightest shade I'd ever seen them turn. Her auburn hair spilled down her back, following the graceful curve of her shoulders. Her fair skin tempted to be marked. Ruined. The sight of those full breasts and pebbled nipples was almost enough to set me off.

I couldn't wait until she was ready for me to touch her. If I could tattoo myself onto her skin, I totally would. She was already buried in my heart and etched into my soul; I wanted to return the favor.

"You have a beautiful body," I rasped and her eyes snapped to me. Vulnerable. Fierce. Stubborn. Juliette had layers for it all.

"So do you," she murmured.

Her gaze traveled over me, from my calves, up my muscular legs, then lingered at the tent in my boxers. She darted a look my way, then let it fall back to my cock as it strained, eager for her touch.

She sat next to me, and to my shock, her hand wrapped around my cock through my boxers. A tortured groan left my lips and my hips bucked into her palm.

"Touch me later," I growled. "Straddle me and sit on my face."

I watched in fascination as she obeyed me, her generous breasts rising up and down with each breath. The dim lights of our bedroom reflected against her glossy dark strands. It reflected colors of auburn and dark brown. One day, I'd wrap my fist around her long hair and fuck her mouth. But not now. Tonight was for her.

Her legs parted and she scooted up my body. Her inner thighs were slick from her arousal and left smears over my chest. I closed my eyes and inhaled deeply. Her scent was intoxicating.

Juliette's hands came to my shoulders, holding on for balance.

"This is gonna be awkward," she grumbled, shifting up and trying to figure out how to do this gracefully. I didn't want grace. I wanted her pussy. On my face. Now.

"Juliette," I rasped, my control rattling the bars of its cage. "Fuck awkward. Sit on my face. I want your pussy to suffocate me. Now!"

My wife gasped in shock. If my hands were free, I'd slap her ass to get her going.

"But you won't be able to breathe," she protested on a whimper.

"If there is a way to die, it's with your pussy on my face," I growled. "Sit. On. My. Face."

With a shocked and excited expression, she scooted further up my body, her hands reaching for the headboard to steady herself. I tilted my head upward and inhaled deeply, then licked a slow path over her entrance. She smelled like heaven.

Mine.

The word was like a growl in my chest, threatening to spill, but I didn't think she was ready.

I nipped her clit in gentle punishment for making me wait so long, then licked it.

"Oh my God," she whimpered, her thighs quivering. Fuck! She was dripping wet.

Her arousal perfumed the air, and it was the best kind of scent. I scraped the scruff of my beard against the delicate skin of her inner thighs. I tilted my face and she lowered her hips down until her pussy came to settle over my face.

"Fuck," she breathed, and finally sat all the way down. Her eyes locked on me as my mouth went to work. Her blue eyes became hazy, like she was drunk. Our eyes locked as I ate her pussy like it was the last fucking meal I'd ever get. She was my heaven and hell. My yin and yang.

I licked and sucked, her hips rocking against my mouth. Her moans were the sweetest fucking sounds I had ever heard. Her hips rolled each time I flattened my tongue against her pussy.

"My wildling wife, this pussy is mine," I hissed as I nipped her clit and a loud whimper vibrated through the air.

"Oh my God," she groaned, the desperation in her voice spurring me on. She was wet and slippery, the flesh around her sensitive nub swollen. My wife was needy and greedy.

This was the best fucking idea I'd had in my entire life. Leave me cuffed, chained, I didn't give a shit. As long as my wife's pussy was on my face.

I lapped at her, drinking my fill, thrusting my tongue inside her entrance.

"Dante," she exclaimed on a moan, rocking back and forth, fucking herself on my tongue and my face. "O-ohhh…"

"You are fucking beautiful," I purred against her. "Smother me with that pussy, Wildling. This is how I want to die."

She stilled, her eyes locked on me. Her cheeks were flushed, but so was her entire body.

"Don't die," she breathed, inching away slightly. "I—I like you eating my pussy. I want it every day."

Fuck!

My cock twitched and throbbed. "Give me back my pussy," I demanded in a growl. "I won't die. Now let me finish what I started."

Her little moan filled the air. She watched me through her heavy eyelids and she shifted her body down and I slammed my face against her pussy. A groan left me at the same time she moaned, her thighs shuddering with the impact. I drew her clit between my lips, her hips rocking back and forth.

Relentless and eager to see her come, I pushed my tongue inside her entrance and her thighs tensed around my head. I hummed my approval as her hips rocked hard against my face. I sucked hard like my life depended on this. Her fingers left the board and threaded through my hair.

Her head fell back and her eyelids fluttered shut. The most magnificent blissful expression passed her face, and I knew she was coming. Her fingers gripped my hair. My scalp burned. It didn't fucking matter. It was the best feeling in the world.

Her body jerked and trembled as her thighs squeezed around my head. She came with a whimper, her body shuddering in climax. It was the most gorgeous sight I had ever seen. She rocked her hips and I lapped her sensitive sex as shudders rolled down her naked body.

Breathless, she slumped over, sliding her body down over mine, her bare breasts in my face. I pressed my face between them and chuckled. "Woman, you're tempting the devil," I said, taking her nipple between my teeth and tugging it gently.

Another shudder rolled down her spine and a soft moan sounded from her lips. I let go of her nipple and searched her face.

"Take my mouth," I ordered her. "I want you to taste yourself on my lips."

"Holy shit," she rasped, but she obeyed. It turned out Juliette was more than obedient in the bedroom; she was eager. I fucking loved it.

Our lips met and I thrust my tongue into her mouth. My cock was painfully rock hard in my boxers. It throbbed to be inside her. My balls ached, but I didn't give a shit. My wife let me eat her pussy and she orgasmed. On my face. And soon, hopefully on my dick. I didn't give a shit when. I was just fucking happy.

Bottom line, she was in my bed. My home. My heart.

CHAPTER 31
Juliette

My pulse raced. My heart danced. My desire craved him.

If I'd known Dante would be such a generous lover, I might have given in to him a lot sooner. He always seemed so cold, so demanding, and yet, he was the opposite.

After our kiss, I buried my face in the crook of his neck. He was still cuffed. I should uncuff him, and truthfully, it surprised me he didn't ask me to do so.

My pulse raced at what I contemplated doing. For that, he'd have to remain cuffed.

I shifted around, my entrance brushing against his hard length accidentally. He stiffened and so did I.

"Sorry, I can't help my body's reaction to you," he grumbled under his breath.

My heart warmed. It couldn't be comfortable for him to be hard and cuffed. Yet, not a single complaint left his lips. I raised my head and met his dark eyes. I used to think of them as the devil's eyes. Not anymore. Yes, they were dark. But they were beautiful. Like the night sky with stars shimmering in them.

Leaning closer, my mouth brushed against his.

"I—I can make you feel good too," I murmured against his lips. Of course, I never stammered but it'd seemed all my firsts happened around this man. My blushing. My stammering. The most amazing orgasm. The first orgasm at a man's hand—well, technically at his mouth. The best part, it wasn't just any man. It was Dante. My husband.

The lazy, possessive look in his eyes alone had my body buzzing with excitement. I wet my lips, dying to taste him now. He might have been possessive, but so was I. He owned my orgasm, but I'd own his too. This went both ways—two-way street.

"You do for me, I do for you," I murmured, reminding him of my promise.

"You don't have to." His protest had no heart in it. "Really, Juliette."

Ignoring his halfhearted protest, I moved down his body. He watched me with a tension that radiated from his gaze but not another protest left his lips. Keeping his stare, I hooked my fingers over the hem and pulled his black boxers down his muscular legs. He shifted on the bed, attempting to assist me. But all the while, his eyes set me on fire.

Our breathing felt like a seductive echo through the room. He was cuffed, but it didn't fool me into thinking he was weak. There wasn't a single weak thing about this man.

My fingers trembled as they wrapped around his smooth length. His hips bucked and my eyes flickered to his face. His jaw clenched. His gaze burned.

"Are you okay?" I asked.

His cock felt so smooth and warm. Hard and thick. I couldn't resist pumping him in my fist once. He hissed, his pelvis pushing into my palm. Precum glistened at the top of his shaft, and suddenly, my mouth watered. I leaned in and drew my tongue out, licking the tip of him.

He tasted good, different. Salty.

So I licked him again, all the way from the base to the tip. A soft groan escaped Dante and his muscles tensed. My eyes flickered up to his face and found his expression dark and demanding.

"Suck," he said simply, his voice raspy.

A warm wave rushed through me and pulsed between my legs. I hated being bossed around but something about Dante doing just that had a hum of satisfaction traveling up my throat. So I obeyed, running my tongue around the head as if he were a lollipop before I sucked him into my mouth.

"Fuck," he groaned, his head falling back against the pillows.

Suddenly, I knew this would be my addiction. Seeing Dante DiLustro tethered on the edge of his control and falling to his knees for me. My mouth. My pussy.

My hands came to his muscular thighs and I clawed my nails into him. My nipples brushed against his thighs and sparks of pleasure fluttered through me. This man had just given me the best orgasm of my life and my pussy already clenched for more. I sucked him harder, wanting to reciprocate the same pleasure he gave me. I took more of him in my mouth, letting his cock glide in and out, hitting the back of my throat.

He controlled his hips, thrusting them into my mouth, and if my mind had been clear, I'd marvel at the way he'd taken control of my body without even touching me. Heat bloomed in my stomach, moving lower. I had to squeeze my thighs together to ease the dull ache.

Breathy noises vibrated in my throat. My body hummed in approval at his intrusion, wishing he were deep inside me. But I didn't think I was ready to go there yet.

"Look at me, Wildling," he ordered roughly and my gaze instantly flicked to him.

"You look so fucking good with my cock deep in your throat," he praised, pushing himself deeper inside my mouth. Deep enough to hit the back of my throat. I gagged but refused to let go, relaxing my throat and letting him fuck my mouth.

His lust-filled gaze burned hot. It had grown darker and hazier than even the midnight sky.

"Fuck, I can't wait until you let me touch you," he rasped, watching me like I was precious to him. Like I was his whole world.

Dark whispers of devotion and something else settled deep inside me.

"Can I come in your mouth?" he asked and I hummed my agreement.

The next second, his groan rumbled from low in his throat and he finished in my mouth. I swallowed every drop of him, some of his cum trickling down my chin.

His cock slid out of my mouth with a soft *pop*. His hands were still handcuffed to the headboard. I reached for the cuffs and unlocked them, then sat back on my knees, licking my lips. My eyes on him, our gazes clashed, and he reached out his hand, wiping his cum off my chin and bringing it to my lips. My skin burned under the intensity of his stare. I darted my tongue out, licking his finger, then closing my mouth around, sucking it clean.

He'd given me all the control, yet I felt he had it the entire time. Dante was exactly what I'd needed all along and I'd never even known it.

CHAPTER 32
Dante

Juliette slept in my arms wearing nothing but her thong and my white button-down dress shirt that she dug out of my side of the closet.

I ran my hands down her back, loving the feel of her soft skin against my rough palms. Her even breathing filled the space and the cracks in my chest. Her scent lingered everywhere—on our sheets, on my hands, in my lungs.

There was something peaceful about this moment and I feared something would come along and break it. More than likely my betrayal. I should admit to her what I had done. I should admit to her my devious plan with which I entrapped her. But the fucking admission refused to leave my lips.

A hollow ache vibrated through my chest. I couldn't risk her hatred. Not now. Not ever. We were making progress and that was what mattered. We were moving forward.

A soft sigh brushed against my chest, and I lowered my eyes to my wife. Her breaths fanned my skin. Her cheek was pressed against my chest, her mouth slightly parted and those long, dark lashes casting shadows against her cheeks, becoming a sight I could not get enough of.

My fingers tangled in her soft strands. I marveled at the softness of her

173

dark hair sprawled all over my chest. She was so small and breakable, although sometimes it was easy to forget it. Her personality made up for her lack of height.

My chest tightened at the thought of anyone hurting my wife. My obsession. My blood and my oxygen.

It wasn't healthy to feel this obsessive about anyone, but then that never stopped the DiLustro men before.

Just look at Basilio's father. My own father. Basilio and I weren't any better. God help Priest and any woman he zeroed in on, though it seemed maybe he'd already found one.

My phone buzzed and I reached for it. Surprised to see a message from Illias Konstantin, I slid it open.

Why is your man lurking in my territory?

I sighed. Why did the Russian fucker have to know everything. It wasn't that I had any shipments routed through his territory. I had my guy scouting Travis so he could kidnap him and bring him to me.

I typed a quick reply. ***He's picking up a guy.***

At the ex-senator's house? I could practically hear Konstantin's snicker through the text. Fucking old man. He should really consider retiring or something.

His kid hurt my wife. He needs to pay.

If he had the senator or his family under his protection, I'd just have to fight him, because letting Travis Xander get away with what he had done to Juliette, wasn't an option.

My phone buzzed again and an unexpected message came through.

Let me know if you need help.

Today was an absolute clusterfuck.

I wanted to be in Chicago with my wife, stuck in the house during a blizzard and handcuffed to the bed while she explored my body. Not in fucking California.

Irritation ignited in my chest. Couldn't I at least have a peaceful honeymoon?

The morning after my text exchange with Konstantin, I received a message from my own guy. He was unable to get into the ex-senator's house. I flew in and out of countries under the radar and this fucker couldn't enter an ex-senator's house. A dead ex-senator.

Hearing my guy wasn't able to retrieve Travis fucking Xander out of his mansion irked me to no end. Either my guy was incompetent or Travis knew someone was coming for him. If I found out Konstantin gave a heads-up to the son of a bitch, there'd be hell to pay.

That's why I left my bride, warm in my bed, so I could hop on my goddamned private jet and come here myself. If you wanted shit done right, you had to do it yourself.

It was close to midnight when I entered the former senator's home. Travis's old man was the senator who was found in his office almost a decade ago, his pants down and his dick cut off and shoved in his mouth. It had caused quite a stir amongst politicians in power back then. Turned out the fucker had a thing for young girls. There was speculation that one of his victims' relatives had killed him. The killer was never found, but it made his widow paranoid.

She should have been more paranoid about keeping her son on a leash.
Like father, like son.

The background check showed that the widow remarried but her paranoia remained. Hence the excessive amount of security.

I pulled out my phone and sent a text to Konstantin. ***Cut the security.***

It took ten seconds and the reply was back. ***Security down.***

Not bad for an old man, I thought wryly. I made my way through the gate and across the expansive lawn, sticking to the shadows. I entered the home through a side entrance, the door unlocked. Disadvantages of iHome and having it depend on electronic security.

It was quiet, as was to be expected. Light streamed into the foyer from the living room, and I followed it, my combat boots silent against the marble.

I stopped at the arched doorway, my lips curving into a cruel smile. *Talk about luck*, I thought smugly.

The prick with blond, matted hair sat sprawled on the couch, his feet on the coffee table as he shoved popcorn into his mouth. His cheap beer sat next to his feet, disregarding the coaster that sat beside it.

A sardonic breath left me. The fucker was almost thirty and he couldn't even use his mother's coaster.

"Yes," he shouted at the television. "To the left. Damn you, to the left." A college football game played on television. An old one. This fucker barely graduated college and still lived as if he were the proverbial big man on campus. What a dick.

"Florida wins," I remarked coldly. He whipped his head around, his eyes meeting mine. "Just in case you're wondering, since you're going to miss the second half."

He scrambled to his feet, the popcorn falling silently all over the rug. Fucking slob.

Before he could run, I pulled out my gun, the silencer already on and pulled the trigger. The bullet tore through his palm, blowing it apart. Blood and flesh splattered everywhere. He roared in agony, but before he could hit a higher note, I had my hand over his mouth.

His screamed muffled, I clicked my tongue.

"Now, now," I drawled. "You don't want to wake up your mommy and step-daddy. Do you?"

His eyeballs popped out of their sockets, staring at me. What a miserable excuse for a human.

"Do you know who I am?" I purred in a low voice, keeping my rage at bay. At least until I got this fucker into a basement where I'd relish in his screams. He shook his head frantically, his eyes full of terror.

I grinned menacingly. "I'm your worst fucking nightmare, Travis."

Then I knocked him out cold.

An hour later, I was in the basement of one of Illias Konstantin's buildings in downtown Los Angeles. When I pulled up out front, he was there waiting for me.

His hands in his pockets, he casually leaned against the frame of the door, his sharp eyes on me.

I jumped out of the car and strode to him. "You didn't have to welcome me," was my greeting to him. "Don't you have a pregnant wife to tend to? Or have the babies already come?"

His expression filled with amusement. "It takes nine months for babies to cook," he replied coolly. "We have a few more months to go."

I shrugged. I hadn't put much thought into having babies. I was only in my late twenties. Too young for diapers and milk.

"Whatever."

Konstantin's mouth curved into a smile. "Not to worry, you'll learn soon enough. I heard you got married. Drive-through wedding in Vegas nonetheless. Congratulations."

Of course, he'd heard. The underworld was like a gossip column.

"And you got married in the mile high club," I remarked dryly. "You should add that to your resume."

It wasn't too long ago, four months ago to be exact, when Illias Konstantin kidnapped his bride and had a priest perform their ceremony while on their way out of the country. The old man had nothing to preach to me about.

He chuckled. "That I did," he replied. "Best fucking day of my life."

I rolled my eyes. I didn't want to hear about his happy ending and shit like that. Guilt gnawed at me and my methods already. I didn't kidnap Juliette. I'd done something worse, and I knew if it ever came out, heads would roll. Probably starting with mine.

"So you gonna get your cargo or what?" Illias asked, tilting his chin toward the trunk of my car.

"Are you gonna hang around for the torture or what?" I retorted with my own question.

Konstantin shrugged. "I might," he said, his tone bored. "But not for long. Tatiana's cooking dinner."

I shook my head, then jogged back to the trunk of my car and popped it open. The preppy senator's son was still unconscious, so I lifted him like a sack of potatoes and threw him over my shoulder.

Making my way back to the building, Konstantin opened the door and motioned with his hand for me to enter.

"I still can't believe you'd marry one of those crazy Nikolaevs," I muttered as I passed him.

He chuckled. "I'll bet you a million bucks your wife is crazier than they are."

I flipped him off, then stopped. "Lead the way, old man."

"Freaking know-it-all kids," Konstantin muttered as he passed me, then made his way down the long hallway and down the stairs into the darkness. Basements weren't where nightmares happened for most people. For a brief moment, I thought about where Priest's and my nightmares happened, but I refused to go there. Now wasn't the time. I pushed those thoughts into a dark corner. There was no room for them and I had a world of pain to dish out at the moment.

"So the ex-senator's son, huh?" Konstantin asked as we reached our destination. The last door at the end of the basement.

"Yep."

"What did he do?" Konstantin asked as I dumped Travis's unconscious body into the only chair in here. He slumped to the side, but didn't fall over. I kind of wished he had so he'd crack his skull.

"He drugged my wife and then he touched her," I hissed.

"Apparently, I should have ended the son along with the father," Konstantin said matter-of-factly, his eyes narrowing on the unconscious man. The fucker who raped my wife.

My eyes darted to Illias. "You killed the fucker?"

He nodded. "Yes, he groped my little sister. Nobody gets away with that shit."

A groan sounded behind me and we both turned our attention to Travis who was coming to. Dazed, he studied the basement until his eyes reached me. He tried to get up at the same time as I shot his foot, feeling sick satisfaction at his cry of agony.

"What the fuck, man!" he screamed as he fell back into the chair, sweat breaking out over his forehead.

I stalked toward him, closing the distance between us and I grabbed his throat.

"What did you do to my wife?"

His eyes rolled back, before they focused on me. "Man, I don't even know who the fuck your wife is."

"Juliette DiLustro," I roared. "It will be the last name on your mind as I tear you to pieces."

He slumped forward and I shook him, forcing him back. He'd lost a lot of blood, was losing more with every passing second. He wouldn't leave this basement alive.

"I don't know Juliette DiLustro," he cried as piss trickled down his leg and onto the hard floor. "There was only one Juliette I ever knew." Then his eyes widened while rage boiled up in me like an unstoppable wave. "The i-ice-skater's cousin," he stuttered.

I grinned savagely. "You fucked up, Travis."

He shook his head, back and forth, probably giving himself whiplash. "It wasn't my idea."

I stilled. "What?" I asked, my voice dangerously cold.

"It was Brandon's idea. The rest of us just came along for the ride."

My hands balled into fists. Suddenly the entire room was coated in red. Red walls. Red floors. The fucker stained with red in front of me. Static rushed in my ears. I threw myself at him, raining punches down on his face, his chest, his stomach. I beat every inch of him I could reach.

The DiLustros were known for their tempers and mine just flared to its worst. It was what made us good at killing. It was what made us good at being the kingpins.

"Dante, stop!" Illias Konstantin's hand came to my shoulder, holding me back but I shoved him away with a roar. My fist flew through the air, ready to connect with Travis's face again but he caught it.

"Their. Names." His voice penetrated the murderous rage. "Get their names, then beat him to death for all I care."

He was right. I needed their names. Why did Juliette give me only one name? Maybe she was ashamed. Jesus fucking Christ! Anger blazed through my veins. My fists burned, ready for another round of punching this fucker.

I swallowed the rage, its ball searing my airway. My vision cleared and I uttered one word through my teeth. "Names," I demanded.

"What names?" Travis spurted. He stunk like piss, beer, and bad blood.

"The names of the boys that were in that room," I ground out. "All of them."

The fucker had the nerve to start crying. I kept still, not trusting myself to keep from lunging at him and beating him until the light left his eyes.

"Names! Now!" Konstantin barked, probably sensing I was ready to snap.

"Brandon Dole. Sam Dallas."

My knuckles throbbed. My rib cage burned from the need to tear him to pieces. The first name sounded familiar. The second didn't. But I was too pumped up to think clearly.

"No others?" Konstantin asked.

"No, that's it. I swear."

"What did you do to her?" I growled. By the look on the fucker's face, I wasn't sure he'd answer me.

He gulped. "We were at a party. We saw her come in by herself and we thought we'd have some fun, you know? We slipped something into her drink, then took her upstairs. She seemed willing. Just needed something to relax her."

"That's it," I repeated icily as red slowly seeped into my vision again. "That's it."

"Yes, yes. I swear," he cried, shaking like a leaf.

Then I let the rage take me. I lunged on the fucker. I punched him, over and over again. My fists burned with each hit. I hit flesh and bone, even the floor beneath us in my blinding rage. I punched him until I couldn't breathe anymore and my ribs felt broken. My chest heaved, my knuckles split.

I gasped for breath as my eyes met the empty stare of Travis fucking Xander. There was no need to check his pulse. He was dead. My chest heaved, my ears still buzzed with adrenaline. My rage felt unsatisfied. I wanted to kill more. Two more men, specifically.

"You okay?" Konstantin watched me with a guarded expression. Like I was an unhinged beast ready to attack unprovoked. He wasn't far off. He regarded me with a penetrating intensity that set my teeth on edge.

Falling back on my ass, I sat on the floor, blood all around me. I lowered my eyes to find my clothes drenched, my arms covered in blood. My fingers ached and my knuckles were bruised, crimson covering them.

I leaned back against the wall, my knees raised and my forehead resting against them. My chest constricted until every breath was a struggle. My head fell back, images my mind conjured mixed with another torture I'd witnessed. I hadn't realized how badly I had truly fucked up until now. This exact moment.

"What are you going to do now?" Konstantin asked. I lifted my head, meeting his cautious gaze. So many different emotions slammed through me. Guilt. Rage. Pain.

It was all fucking wrong. A wave of despair rose in me.

"Dante." Konstantin's calm voice penetrated through the fog of despair. "Why don't we get you cleaned up? Then come to my place for dinner."

I didn't move. I couldn't.

"I fucked up," I rasped. I drugged my wife. I was no better than this fucker and his friends. No, I didn't touch her, but I made her marry me in her condition. "Jesus, I fucked up."

Konstantin's arm came to my shoulder and he squeezed it. "Every one of us has fucked up in one way or another. Let's get you changed and then I'm taking you to my place."

I shook my head. "I have a hotel."

"And I have a spare bedroom," he said in a cool tone. "Now, let's go. I don't like to keep my wife waiting."

CHAPTER 33
Juliette

"So, how's married life?" Wynter asked.

It was our weekly four-way FaceTime call. Wynter's idea of staying in touch. It worked most of the time except that today, I had better things to do. Like torture the man who set my birth parents' home on fire.

Kian, the man that Autumn Ashford recommended, had come through again. He helped her get out of Afghanistan. The guy was stellar. He searched for my parents' killers, passed on the names after he dug them up and tracking them down. My body count was about to increase.

~~Brandon Dole~~
~~Sam Dallas~~

Travis Xander. I didn't physically kill him, but I'd take credit for it anyhow. Dante promised he'd end him and I believed him.

The above were personal to me. The below were personal to both Killian and I.

. . .

~~Petar Soroko~~
~~Raslan Rugoff~~
~~Igor Bogomolov~~
~~Yan Yablochkov~~

All four were killed by Killian. The next ones were mine.

~~Vlad Ketrov~~
~~Nikola Chekov~~
Jovanov Plotnick—not yet dead, but he'd be very soon.
Sofia Volkov would be the icing on the cake.

I stared at the Russian names on the list. Killian handled four; I was about to take care of my third one from our parents' murder. Between us, we killed seven of their murderers. I wouldn't be satisfied until we were given all the names to scratch off.

"Hello," Wynter called out again, interrupting my thinking. "Earth to Jules."

I tried to remember her question, then recalled it.

"It's fine," I answered curtly.

Two days ago, Dante had to fly out. Some emergency in California that he had to handle. Much to my dismay, I missed him. We had barely begun working on the physical aspect of our relationship and then he flew out. It agitated me.

The impatient part of me wanted to test the theory of how far we could go before my panic kicked in. I wanted to expunge the ghosts that plagued my mind and stopped me from having meaningful relationships with the opposite sex.

Not that I'd have any going forward, other than Dante.

My husband.

It still seemed surreal. Maybe I was dreaming and I'd woken up. Alone.

"Jules? Snap out of it." It was Ivy's voice. I blinked my eyes, then shook my head. I had to focus on this call or we'd never get off it.

"Yes, I'm listening," I said, mildly agitated. I really wasn't, but it didn't matter.

"So did you know that?" Ivy asked.

My brows furrowed. "Know what?"

"Dante's 1934 Hudson Convertible Coupe you destroyed," Ivy started, but I didn't understand why she was bringing up the ancient past. "It belonged to his grandfather. Apparently, Dante's very attached to it."

"Was very attached to it," Wynter added wryly. "I don't think it's drivable anymore. So how is the sex? Rough? Kinky?" Wynter teased. She was the reserved one in our group, so this was definitely her way of payback for all my questions.

My cheeks warmed remembering Dante cuffed to the bed. The way he watched me with burning heat in his dark eyes as I came against his face. That image would be forever ingrained into my memory.

"Ohh, definitely kinky," Davina chimed in with a devious smile. "Just look at that blush on her cheeks."

"Don't tell me your sex lives are so boring you have to get details on mine," I drawled in a dull tone. "Maybe you should have thought twice before jumping into the marriage bed."

Snickers came over the line. "Oh, look who's talking," Davina snorted loudly. "The girl who jumped into a marriage with the same man she's been avoiding for two years."

I rolled my eyes. "Well, the alcohol was strong and my friends abandoned me for the night. What was I to do?"

"Not get married," Ivy grumbled. "Now I'm the last single lady in our group and my family's nagging me with prospects."

"Tell them you're too busy with our school project," I offered. "It's a true statement. They broke ground and have started building."

"Jules, I'd have to be the one digging the ground with my own hands and building brick by brick for that to be a valid excuse. Trust me, I've offered the contractor my feeble skills." Ivy sounded seriously desperate. "I got rejected when my qualifications had nothing to do with construction."

St. Jean d'Arc School was well on its way to becoming a real thing. It had started with the blackmail and robbing my dad's safe, then counting cards in Chicago, and ended with robbing an armored money truck from Priest's club.

Bottom line, when Davina's ex-boyfriend blackmailed us, it showed us how unequipped we were to deal in the underworld. So we decided to start a school that would prepare both boys *and* girls for their life in the underworld.

Nobody should be as unprepared as we were.

"Are the prospects at least decent?" Wynter asked compassionately. "I just don't get it. Why do they demand you marry? You're barely twenty-three."

It made no sense to me either.

"Marry Priest," I offered jokingly. "Then every one of us will be married to a DiLustro. Well, except for my stepmom."

Davina glared at me through the small screen. "Shut up, Jules."

I grinned mischievously. "Yes, Stepmom."

Twenty minutes later, distractions started happening. My little half brother wailed and that distracted Davina. Basilio must have gotten home because suddenly giggles and blushes started, next thing I knew, Wynter excused herself. It left Ivy and me alone at the end.

"Are you okay?" I asked her. Davina and Wynter were always the reasonable ones in our group. Ivy and I were more on the reckless side. "If you need me, I can visit Grandfather and then rescue you from your family home."

She chuckled. "Only if you come dressed as a boy, ready to marry me."

This time I chuckled too. "I'm afraid it'd be considered bigamy."

She locked her eyes on me through the screen.

"What the fuck happened in Vegas, Jules?" Nobody had bothered to ask me. Not that I had much to tell them. I woke up married. I didn't remember anything aside from dancing with Dante, then doing shots. "We've gotten plenty drunk in the past," she continued softly. "We've drunk hardcore stuff, and you never blacked out. We're Irish for Christ's sake. We can hold our liquor."

I sighed. It made no sense to me either.

"We danced. We had shots. After that, everything's a blur," I told her. "I woke up married."

Ivy shook her head. "The video you sent out was wild. Like you were on steroids or something."

I let out a small laugh. I couldn't remember a thing from that night, but it wasn't exactly something I was proud of. Although in the grand scheme of things, it worked out. So all was well that ended well.

"Forget me and the idiotic stuff I did," I told her. "Tell me what I can do to help *you*."

She rolled her eyes. "Find women for my Irish prick brothers so they can be busy with their own shit and forget me."

Another few words and our call ended.

Glancing at the clock, I hurried upstairs into our bedroom and changed into the clothes I preferred to torture men in. It was a small world, because the man who lit the fire to my parents' home was actually in Chicago.

During a blizzard.

My lips curved into a cruel smile. "Nowhere to run, old man," I whispered as I pushed the key into the ignition of Dante's Land Rover. Seemed the best choice of vehicles out of all his collection.

My phone dictated the directions past the city and into the industrial part of Chicago. I parked in front of the shabby three-story building close to the tracks. I blew out a harsh breath, then waited for my racing pulse to calm. I put my gloves on and switched my flats for snow boots. Well, it was the next best thing to combat boots. My dear husband didn't think I'd need a pair of my own, but I'd correct that immediately.

I strapped the backpack on my shoulders. It held guns, ropes, and knives. A tranquilizer. I wished I could take the credit for the tranquilizer. I'd never used one before but I happened to see the needle in Dante's safe and decided it wouldn't hurt to have one on hand. Breaking into Dante's safe wasn't a small effort but I succeeded. Of course, he'd have to replace the entire thing.

Opening the door of the car, I stealthily walked toward the house. I picked the lock and slipped in, silently moving through the house. I noted the door to the basement and was careful not to make noise as I made my way downstairs. My lips curved into a harsh smile. It was perfect—all stone.

Lowering my backpack onto the floor behind the steps, I pulled out a single knife and the tranquilizer. The information on my target was that he was an older and not-so-bulky man. That told me nothing. I didn't want to have to fight him and drag him down the stairs. It'd be fatal to both of us.

Next, I headed back up the stairs. I couldn't believe how shitty this place was, but according to Kian's intel, this guy had a gambling problem. He probably pissed it all away. Not that it mattered to me. It made it easier to break into this shitty place than a fancy manor.

Careful to ensure no creaks woke up my prey, I made my way up, ignoring my racing heartbeat.

When I reached the bedroom door, my eyes darted to the bed. A man slept soundly, soft snores breaking the night air. Anger simmered through my blood. He slept like a baby, enjoying his time on this earth while my parents and who knew how many others had lost their lives.

Because of him. Because of Sofia Volkov.

Sitting on the concrete step, I took deep breaths, then slowly exhaled. Repeat.

Thank fuck for the tranquilizer.

The damn information on my target was way off. Yes, he was old but he was thick and broad-shouldered. My muscles still shook from his weight. I had to drag him down the stairs. I might have dropped him a few times.

Okay, so I pushed him. But fuck if I was going to break my back carrying that fucker down two flights of stairs and then further into the basement.

I'd taken self-defense classes over the last two years. Mixed martial arts. I even earned myself a black belt, but it didn't mean I was a fucking weight lifter.

I was dressed in all black: black jeans, black T-shirt, black combat boots—okay, snow boots, but whatever—and I was fully prepared to get dirty. With my strength and my breathing back to normal, I shot to my feet and made my way toward the slumped, unconscious form. I had bound his wrists and feet. Just to be safe.

I studied the man. Gray hair. A scar slashed across his face. He was in his sixties. He fit the description of one of the Russians that had set my birth parents' house on fire. There were ten men responsible for our parents' death who attacked their home. Killian had hunted down and killed four of those men. I had killed only two so far. After tonight, it'd be three, taking my number of hits to a grand total of five, including the pieces of shit from high school.

It was strange how easily the killing came. The first one had been the hardest to stomach. The piercing screams. The begging. But then I'd remind myself what they did to me. To my parents. To my brother.

Killian told me how it all went down. The screams. The cries. The torture. He blamed himself because he'd remained hidden, holding me. I was just a baby at the time, but Killian wasn't. Some nights, in his sleep, he was still that eight-year-old boy witnessing our parents' torture.

The anger buzzed under my skin. They took—-actually stole—-our parents from us. They had given Killian years of nightmares, of trauma. That spurred me into action.

I kicked his foot. "Wakey, wakey."

A soft groan vibrated against cellar walls and I kicked his foot again. He slowly roused from his unconsciousness. I watched with rapt fascination as his eyes darted around and locked on me before a myriad of emotions passed his face.

Confusion.

I'd imagine I didn't look scary at all at my barely five foot five.

Surprise.

He probably couldn't believe that I'd managed to capture him. But it was the last one that intrigued me.

Recognition.

"What are you doing?" he hissed.

"Chasing old ghosts," I drawled lazily. "Do you know which ones?"

He just stared at me blankly. Bruises had formed on his forehead and the side of his cheek. I'd wager he had some on his body too.

Just as I was beginning to think he wouldn't answer me, he uttered, "Aiden and Ava Cullen."

A smile curved my lips in a cruel way. So he did remember and he did recognize me. I was told I look a lot like my mother, but it would seem I have my father's temperament.

"Time to get what you gave," I taunted, watching as realization settled in his gaze. "There's no way out."

Maybe it was sadistic but I quite enjoyed seeing the panic on his face. I imagined it was how my parents felt as their home burned with all of us trapped inside.

He attempted to struggle against the ropes, but it was pointless. Even if he managed to free one hand, he'd be dead by the time he went for his other hand. And fuck, I'd enjoy filling him with bullets. But even more, I was going to enjoy cutting him with a dull knife and listening to his screams. He might not be burning in a fire, but he'd scream just the same.

By now, I was an expert and had learned what worked and what didn't. Fucking with their head seemed to break them the easiest. Physical torture—not so much. I turned on the stereo and Lana Del Rey's song "Season of the Witch" came on.

"It's my song," I remarked, smiling savagely. "Do you know why?"

He shook his head, so I said, "Because I'm hunting. Except it isn't the season of the witch. It's the season for bad Russians. Specifically the ones that killed my parents."

God, I loved fucking with their heads.

"You fucking bitch," he shouted, struggling against the ropes more vigorously. "Unbind my hands and see how brave you are. Psycho, like your father."

I should have injected the entire tranquilizer into the bastard. Maybe he'd shut the fuck up with his own taunting.

"Now, now, you don't want to hurt my feelings," I purred sweetly as I grabbed the overhead circular light and shone it into his face. "Tell me where Sofia Volkov is and I'll make this quick. If not, I'll make it more fun for me. But it won't be so fun for you."

"I'm not telling you anything, you crazy bitch," he spat.

The light illuminated him, and I grabbed his hair, then slammed his head against the wall in the back.

"Good thing the ropes are secured and long enough," I said in a taunting tone. "It makes it so much easier to smash your skull against the wall."

The fucker had a hard skull. More bruises formed around his eyes and forehead. "I have to say, you have a thick skull. Every other guy I've done this to was knocked out cold after I smashed their skull the first time."

"You fucking psycho," he spat again.

"And you don't even have a concussion," I continued pensively, ignoring his outburst. "You can still form words. In English, nonetheless."

He jerked his arms, but the bindings were too strong. It was another little handy thing I'd learned. How to tie knots, just like the military guys. He jerked his arm again and an ugly pop filled the air and I shook my head.

"Now you've gone and dislocated your shoulder."

He didn't heed the warning nor the pain. He kept struggling against the ropes, kicking and screaming and warning of retribution. The sounds were an unrelenting warning. The kind that my parents never got.

"Where the fuck did you come from?" he barked, glaring at me, but it was all in vain. He'd never get away from me. "How did you get into my home?"

He jerked his head from side to side when I put the lamp closer to his face. He kept squinting his eyes, his eyeballs probably burning.

"Where I came from is irrelevant," I noted. The four stone walls in a small cellar were the setting of every creepy nightmare. It was perfect for torture. "The only relevant location is Sofia Volkov's." Pulling a knife out of my boot, I pushed the sharp blade between his ribs. "Where is she?"

His scream pierced the air, shattering my eardrums. "I don't know," he roared. "Nobody knows. She shares her location with nobody."

"Impossible. Someone has to know where she is," I snickered, twisting the blade in his flesh.

The warm liquid soaked my hands, reminding me of the sins I was collecting. I didn't fucking care. I wanted revenge. For my parents. For my brother who had to watch our mother and father tortured. He hunted. Well, so did I.

The music switched from Lana Del Rey to "Crazy Train" by Ozzy Osbourne just in time for this asshole's screams to increase in pitch. Ozzy's heavy metal drowned out all the screams coming from this Russian. Blood seeped onto the floor, painting the gray stone red. The musty scent of the basement mixed with copper.

"It's Jovanov, right?" I asked as I sliced at the skin between his ribs. He continued to scream, but Ozzy drowned out most of his pleas. By the time I was done with him, he'd pissed himself, shit himself, and passed out.

A smile curved my lips. I wasn't ready to let him go into oblivion yet, so I reached for the first aid kit and patched him up. I even made him take some Advil and forced water down his throat. His one eyelid opened and terror filled his expression seeing me instead of death.

"Yeah, it's not a dream," I said. "I'm not done with you, not until you tell me why you killed my parents and walk me through every single thing you did to them. You will tell me, or I'll kill your family like you killed mine."

He must have read the truth on my face because he broke down, sobbing fiercely.

"Why are you doing this?" he hissed, his brows pinching in confusion. "She'll never let you get away if she learns you're alive. You and your brother should hide."

I gritted my teeth.

"I'm going to be her worst fucking nightmare." I cut another piece of flesh from him. "Now start talking or I'll get your pretty grandson. Slice him and dice him in front of you until you start talking. I know they live just two blocks over."

He didn't need to know I'd never hurt his family. I wasn't of the same caliber as these assholes.

My threat worked, although Jovanov glared at me, but he didn't dare say anything else.

"It was an order by Sofia Volkov," he started, wheezing. "Kill the entire family and burn the house down with the bodies inside." I stilled, a rage burning through my veins. It wasn't the first time I'd heard about this order, but it still hit me the same way every fucking time. The pure fury and hate. "Th-the woman, some men raped her while her husband watched." He swallowed while my own stomach twisted and bile rose in my throat. "She screamed and screamed. The husband fought but he was tied up and each move he made to save her earned him another beating."

"Why did she want my family dead?" I asked, my voice deadly calm.

"Your grandfather on your father's side—Cullen—helped kidnap Sofia Volkov's daughter." And there it was. The single detail I didn't know. "Sofia's men killed your grandfather, but that wasn't enough. She wanted the entire bloodline extinguished. Burning the house with everyone in it was a way to erase you all."

Images painted my mind and I lost it. I screamed and screamed like a madwoman. Then I slashed the blade over his thigh. Over and over again.

Jovanov shook with fear, his eyes wide and his body trembling. The color started to drain from his face. He turned as white as the ghosts I was chasing.

I wanted to make him pay. I wanted him to feel the pain that my father felt as he watched my mother raped. I wanted him to feel the pain that my mother felt when they hurt her over and over again.

The blade dug into his yielding flesh, splitting it into two. Then I started at his ear, left, then right. He screamed and cried, but I heard nothing aside from the angry buzzing of adrenaline.

Until he was finally dead.

CHAPTER 34
Dante

Konstantin's home was as expected.

White. Luxurious. Guards everywhere.

None of it registered as those fuckers' names played in my mind on repeat. A dull ache had been throbbing at my temples for the past hour. We stopped on our way to his home where I could shower and change into clean clothes. Thank fuck I always carried a bag with me. You never knew when you'd get lost in a butcher session.

"*Moya luna*, I'm home," Konstantin announced as soon as we entered the foyer. "And I brought a guest, so make sure you're decent."

I groaned inwardly, regretting accepting Illias's invitation.

Tatiana showed up at the far left door, rubbing her belly and wearing a long pink dress with golden shoulder straps. She looked like a pregnant Greek goddess, ready to pop any minute.

"It's a good thing you warned me," Tatiana answered, her hand at her hip, "I was about to drop my clothes and parade around naked for dinner."

Illias chuckled, then pulled her into a hug. "Then I'd have to dig DiLustro's eyeballs out."

"Truthfully, he doesn't need them," his wife claimed mischievously as

193

she pecked him on the cheek. "Nice to see you, Dante DiLustro. Heard you snagged yourself a wife recently. In Vegas, nonetheless."

"You know what they say," Konstantin remarked. "What happens in Vegas, stays in Vegas."

I couldn't help rolling my eyes, but my insides twisted watching them interact so affectionately. Would my wife and I ever be like this? If only they knew what actually happened in Vegas, they wouldn't exactly joke about it.

Tatiana didn't cook dinner, but she did set the table. She ordered a five-course Italian meal in my honor. Very thoughtful. But for some reason I couldn't comprehend, she insisted on proper plate settings and utensils. Way too many utensils.

She even drew a diagram, then ensured both her husband and I understood it. I wanted food, not a fucking lesson on place settings.

"Why are you doing this again?" I asked, my temples throbbing harder.

"Well, I'm going to have royalty coming into the world soon," she announced. My eyebrows popped in surprise. I didn't realize Tatiana knew royalty. "They have to learn those things from an early age."

I blinked, staring at her dumbly. Slowly, I dragged my eyes to her belly, then back to her face. From all I heard, pregnancy made women hormonal and cranky, not crazy. Right?

I opened my mouth to say something when I caught sight of Konstantin's expression. Subtly, he shook his head and I closed my mouth. The oddest fucking thing ever. Was the Pakhan appeasing his wife?

Tatiana chatted through the entire goddamn dinner and the topics were all over the place. From the latest fashion show in Paris and Nico Morrelli's twins breaking into their father's safe, to something happening in Europe that she was desperate to attend. The abrupt changes of topic gave me whiplash until I finally stopped listening.

Instead, I tuned her out and planned my next move on finding the fuckers who'd hurt Juliette. Tomorrow, I'd kill them.

Then I'd go back home to my wife.

Tatiana wiped her mouth with a napkin, her eyes darting to the clock before she stood.

"Yikes, I've got to call Isla," she announced, standing up. She gave Konstantin a pointed look. "Don't eavesdrop. Understood?"

"Would I ever?"

She shook her head. "In a heartbeat."

As she passed me, Tatiana offered a smile. "Nice seeing you."

When I turned back to Konstantin, his eyes were still on his wife. "Some might call you whipped," I remarked dryly.

He didn't seem offended at all, his smile widening. "I'd put all my money on the fact you're familiar with the feeling." My annoyance ratcheted up at his observation. "Don't worry. I'm in too good of a mood to give you a hard time about it."

"Thanks," I said.

His phone buzzed and he picked it up. "Aha, right on time."

I gave him a curious look. "What is?"

He flicked a gaze my way, typing on his phone. "I got you information on the two names."

Surprise washed over me. "Why would you care?"

A sardonic breath left him. "Believe it or not, I don't tolerate men that touch women, girls—anyone—without their consent. The previous senator found an early death because of it. It's disappointing that his son didn't learn his lesson."

I slid my phone open, my eyes skimming over the information. "Dead?" I muttered.

"Within the last year," Konstantin remarked casually. "Peculiar timing, huh?"

Indeed.

I locked eyes with the Pakhan. My gut warned me there was something he wasn't telling me.

"Spit it out, Illias."

"The deaths of both men happened to take place on the days that your wife met them." He dropped the bomb, the insinuation clear in his voice. "And no, I'm not stalking your wife. I had one of my men dig up a list of any individuals that these men came in contact with over the last two years. Your wife's name was the only one that was common to both men. She met Brandon Dole in New York. That same night, he was murdered. The same thing happened with the other."

A memory flickered in my mind. That day I watched her through the window of a cafe in Central Park having lunch with Brandon Dole. Did she kill him the same night?

"Did her brother meet them too?" I demanded to know.

"No. She met them both alone."

A secured file came through to my phone and I opened it. Gruesome images flooded my phone. Flesh skinned. Limbs cut. Blood painting every single inch of the surface and then an image caught my attention.

A drawing of a dick in blood on the single window of the makeshift torture chamber.

It was the same exact drawing Juliette had left on my grandfather's Hudson Convertible Coupe.

CHAPTER 35
Juliette

T he next day, I browsed the information that Kian had emailed me while seated comfortably in Dante's living room. Correction, our living room. It was our home. I texted Dante a few times asking whether it was okay if I used this or that but then he had reminded me it was *our* home.

"Do whatever you want to do in *our* home," he had texted back more than once.

So that was exactly what I was doing, relaxing in our living room. I'd earned some downtime. I sliced up the man I killed and he vanished without a trace. Burned to ashes. Poetic really, if you thought about it.

It was important to get rid of the evidence, although I had no doubt that Sofia Volkov would know her guy was gone. That woman was a mystery. It was impossible to get to her. I suspected that even when all the names on the list were eliminated, she'd still be out there somewhere.

Hiding. Living.

I reached for the remote and turned the television on. It defaulted to the last channel watched. The news channel. Just as I was about to switch it, *Breaking News* flashed on the bottom half of the screen. The newscaster went over the details of a gruesome body found. Tortured. Mutilated. Unrecognizable. A glimpse of a crime scene that turned even my stomach.

I looked away, hoping the body belonged to an evil person. I hated the idea of someone innocent experiencing something so brutal. I could stomach bad guys being tortured, but the good ones—it broke me every single time.

Letting the news play in the background, I returned my attention to my phone and reread Kian's email for the fifth time. It was business as usual. No inclination that we'd met. Which led me to believe he didn't know it was me back in Vegas.

That was the good news.

The bad news was that he didn't have the information on the rest of the men who caused my parents' untimely death.

I wasn't really sure why it was so important to me that I handled them all. Maybe I wanted to see justice served. It was hypocritical considering Liam, my adoptive father, was part of the underworld, but he didn't kill innocent women and children nor burn them alive.

Our parents died. My brother and I lived.

It fell on us to avenge them.

Since I'd learned of our history, sometimes I wondered if my brother's scars ran even deeper than I could fathom. He was good at keeping it all hidden. For the first twenty-one years, Killian hid all his demons so well that I never connected the dots. But now, I could see them.

The nightmares. His hatred of fire.

He didn't exactly fear fire, but it fucked with him. Kind of like having a man on top of me fucked with my head. It was a panic and terror that rendered you immobile.

I wondered how Killian handled his trauma. Duh, I knew. By keeping himself separated from everyone and everything. He hid it all under his cold exterior, but underneath it all, I knew the embers burned just as hot as the flames that killed our parents.

Beep. Beep.

The news pulled my attention back to the television. "The body has been identified," the blonde newscaster announced, her tone full of suspense. "It is none other than Travis Xander..."

I stared at the television in shock. And... happiness. It had to be Dante's doing. A feeling pinged off the walls of my chest, leaving me feeling raw. My chest grew full and the pressure eased, knowing the three men who hurt me were finally dead. *They are all dead.*

And soon, our parents' killers would be too. My brother deserved this feeling too. This freedom and revelation that the people who hurt you and the ones you love perished into the dust.

Just as I was about to call my brother, the doorbell rang.

Dropping the phone on the couch, I jumped to my feet and called out, "I'm getting the door!"

Dante had a cook and a cleaner roaming around here. It was actually great for company but not so great when they insisted on waiting on me hand and foot. I was at the door before the maid and grinned smugly.

"I got it," I assured her, but she remained glued to her spot.

As if she anticipated an attack, although what she would do if it was, I wasn't sure. I opened the door to find my brother standing there in a thick coat.

"Killian!"

"Hey, sis." He greeted me, then came in and hugged me, pressing a kiss on my forehead.

"What are you doing here?" I asked, flabbergasted to see him in Chicago.

He shrugged. "I had a man to find but turns out he's dead, so I decided to visit you."

"Dead?" I gasped. "Hopefully, he wasn't a close friend."

"No."

I quickly closed the door and glanced over my shoulder. The maid left, going back to whatever she was doing, and I returned my attention to Killian.

"Who is dead?" I questioned in a low voice.

"Nobody for you to worry about." His clipped answer had the hair on my neck rising. My sixth sense warned me that Killian was probably going after the same people as me. But if I enlightened him, he'd lock me up and throw away the key. He was too protective. So I let it go.

He slipped off his coat, his eyes studying me. "How are you?"

The worry in his voice and his eyes was unmistakable. "Great." I smiled.

His eyes narrowed, but he didn't pursue it. I led him into the living room where the news played and Killian's eyebrows rose.

"Watching the news?"

I shrugged, settling back on the same spot. "I can change it if you want," I offered.

He shook his head. "Don't. I'm just surprised you're watching it. I seem to remember you calling it garbage."

It was.

"I wasn't really paying attention to it," I admitted, lifting my phone. "I was playing on my phone."

He smiled. "Now that makes sense."

He took a spot next to me, his eyes traveling around the cozy living room. It was decorated tastefully and with comfort in mind. There was another formal living room in the house, but I preferred this one. I suspected that Dante did too, since I found traces of him all over this room.

His iPad. His watch. Even an empty gun magazine.

"So where is your husband?" Killian questioned.

I shrugged. "California."

"Why?"

My lips thinned. He didn't really think Dante would be reporting his business to me, did he? Reading the expression on my face, Killian decided to change the subject.

"I'm going to be gone for a bit," he said and my stomach tightened. I didn't like when he was gone "for a bit." It worried me to death that I'd never see him again.

"Where do you go when you're gone for a bit?" I questioned.

Sometimes I wondered what Killian had done and endured to survive in the underworld. The dark side of him often lurked around him like this black mist. It had always been like that, even when we were younger. It didn't bother me, but it made me worry for him.

Especially lately.

It seemed to almost swallow him.

"Here and there," he remarked vaguely.

"How are you handling the whole 'left at the altar' affair?" It had been an "avoid at all costs" subject for everyone and it was awkward as fuck, especially now that I was married. He didn't seem heartbroken, but it wasn't as if he'd break down and cry. In fact, I didn't think I'd ever seen my brother cry.

I, on the other hand, cried all the time.

"Just another day," he said, eyes still darting around the room.

"Not exactly," I protested softly, touching his arm. "I wish you'd let me in, Killian."

The way he looked at me sent warning bells blaring through my system. "The way you let me in, Jules?"

I stilled, unsure what he was hinting at. Maybe Kian had recognized me after all. Or maybe Killian learned something that was meant to be a secret.

I swallowed the lump in my throat. "What do you mean?"

The maid showed up with a tray of cookies and drinks. Good thing she knew how to welcome the guests. It never even crossed my mind to offer my brother any refreshments. I groaned inwardly. I'm going to be the worst wife, I swear. Maybe I should get a book on good housekeeping or something.

Killian picked up a cup of coffee, thanking the maid before she disappeared. He took a sip, contemplating his next words if his expression was any indication.

"I mean with stealing."

"Old news," I said hurriedly.

"The defense classes you've taken. Even learning to shoot." Fuck, how did he find that out? "You should have come to me, and I would have helped you."

"You're busy," I said, offering the lame excuse. I knew if I'd asked him, he'd have taught me. But there would also be questions that I would refuse to answer. Knowing Killian, he'd have a whole inquisition going.

My eyes met his soft blue ones and I feared he'd see something he wasn't meant to see. But I held his gaze, waiting. For what, I wasn't sure.

"You've changed, Jules." The sad tone in his voice hit me right in the chest. I didn't know why. "I've seen this darkness in you once before, but lately, it seems worse."

I blinked, my mouth suddenly dry. He'd seen my darkness. But how? I hid it so well. Didn't I?

Reaching for the glass of water, I turned my attention to the television.

"What do you mean?" I asked, keeping my tone light.

Killian shook his head. "I know you, Jules. You're my sister. A part of me." He wrapped his arm around my shoulder and pulled me into him. "You used to tell me everything. Even things I would have preferred not to know." I grinned, remembering those days. "Remember when you called me to announce you were a woman? All because you got your period."

I choked out a laugh. "I'm trying to forget."

"Or when you dragged me into a Victoria's Secret store so you could find me a girlfriend and help Aunt Aisling find a man with attractive lingerie?"

I chuckled softly. "That was a dumb plan." My mind flickered back to that day. It was funny. He remembered me dragging him to the Victoria's Secret store. I remembered him dragging me to Tiffany's. "Kill?"

"Yes?"

"How many men have you killed?" His expression said it all. Many. "Do you ever... regret it?"

His eyes locked with mine. Same shade of blue. I used to think they were Brennans' eyes. They weren't.

"Regret is pointless, Jules." His fingers tightened around me. "As long as we don't kill the innocent ones, I can live with it all."

"Really?"

"Better them than us."

I gasped. Not from shock but out of relief. Better them than us. I couldn't agree more.

"You want to know something, Kill?"

"Hmmm."

"I agree with you," I whispered. "Better them than us." I turned my face to him so he could see me. Really see me. "I'm not like Wynter. She's —" I searched for the right word, then finally settled for the simplest one. "She's good. Forgiving. I'm not like that. Not even close." My brother didn't interrupt, but his gaze told me he knew it already. "I feel that same darkness I see in you. That same hunger for revenge. It claws at me, demanding I do something about it."

One breath. Two breaths.

He nodded. "And that's okay. Don't ever be ashamed of it, Jules. Just promise me to be careful and not reckless."

I smiled. Always my brother—understanding and protective. "I promise." I leaned back into him. "I love you, brother."

"I love you too, Jules."

"Maybe we should go to Victoria's Secret again and I will find you the perfect girl," I mused, my eyes on the screen.

His chest vibrated as he tried to contain his laugh. "I'm afraid that trip will have to wait. Thank fuck."

For the next five minutes, the news flipped over all the bad things happening in this city and the world. The silence stretched, almost suffocating us both. I loved my brother. He loved me. But somehow the two of us had drifted apart. It could be the differences in our lifestyles or maybe Killian had too much shit weighing him down.

"Killian, you know that hot older guy you were talking to back in Vegas?" I asked, breaking the silence and keeping my eyes on the television.

"What older guy?"

I mean, how many hot older guys did he talk to in Vegas. Only one, if I had to guess.

"The old dude," I said, rolling my eyes. He gave me a blank stare. "Jesus, when I came up to you and you introduced him to me. Kian or something."

"Ah, yes. What about him?"

"How do you know him?"

Killian shrugged. "I don't. Not really."

I sighed, keeping my temper from getting the best of me. I'd have to tread lightly. It was obvious Killian already saw through some of my walls.

"You were talking to him," I pointed out.

"Yes."

Jesus Christ. Men could be so damn dense sometimes.

"What did you talk about?" I tried a different approach.

This time Killian narrowed his gaze on me, giving me a strange look. "Why?"

I held my breath. My brother was good at reading people and he was particularly good at reading me. After all, it seemed he was one of the only ones who noticed something had changed about me and we were rarely in the same city.

"Can't I be curious about someone?"

"You're married now," he grumbled, his jaw clenching. He still wasn't happy about my marriage to Dante. "You should limit your curiosity about men to your husband only."

It was my turn to narrow my eyes. "How sexist!"

"If Dante is anything like his cousin, he's over-the-top possessive and obsessive." That might be a mild understatement. "And let's just say if I see a single tear in your eyes, I'm going to murder the fucker."

Gosh, so much testosterone. I was quite capable of killing my husband myself. After all, I killed a man only yesterday, and if I might say so myself, I did a pretty good job. Although there was no need to point that out to my brother.

"Back to Kian." I steered the conversation to my original question. "Is he the same Kian that I heard rescued Autumn Ashford from Afghanistan." I feigned ignorance. "I assumed he was some kind of retired military guy, but then he wouldn't exactly associate with people like us. Would he?"

He shrugged. "He's a special case."

"How come?" I asked curiously.

"You're asking an awful lot of questions about him."

I groaned. "Because you're not answering my questions. Now tell me. Why is Kian a special case? And what does he do?"

My brother scratched his chin tiredly. "He went through U.S. Special Ops training but he's actually Brazilian. Brother to the head of the Brazilian cartel."

My eyes widened. "What?"

"He's the head—"

I waved my hand. "I heard you. But holy crap. Where does the security agency come into play?"

Jesus Christ. Had I been unknowingly working with the Brazilian cartel? I wasn't sure whether I should be impressed or not. Probably better that I wasn't impressed.

"I'd imagine it allows him to launder money through it," Killian said. "And don't think I won't figure out why you are so interested in someone I'd recommend staying away from," he added pointedly. "You don't need to be messing with someone like him, little sister."

After that, our conversation stayed in neutral territory.

CHAPTER 36
Dante

The clock said two a.m. when I pulled up in front of my home in Chicago.

I headed inside, striding through the foyer and then up the stairs. I was eager to see my wife. To sleep with her scent wrapped around me. Eager to share the news of Travis's death with her.

Maybe she'd trust me enough and tell me how she killed those men. Did she hire hitmen? If she had, I'd have to get their names and learn how trustworthy they were. I couldn't risk anything coming back on her.

I got to our bedroom and found her asleep, the soft glow of the moon streaked across her face. I studied that face, missing those blue eyes that stole my soul that day in the Royally Lucky Casino. It turned out the name was perfect, because I'd lucked out.

Fate brought her to me. And fuck it, I seized the opportunity and kept her with me. She was mine and let anyone try to take her away from me.

I dropped to my haunches next to her, watching her sleep. She slept on her side facing me, her knees pulled up to her chest. I lifted the covers and found her sleeping in my dress shirt and something about the sight had me grinning with satisfaction.

Maybe she missed me like I missed her.

Tracing my finger over her slightly parted lips, she let out a small sigh. I held my breath, waiting to see whether she'd open her eyes, but she didn't. She slept peacefully, her dark lashes fanning her cheeks. She looked peaceful and so fucking innocent that it had my throat tightening with fear of anyone hurting her again.

I just prayed it wouldn't be me.

CHAPTER 37
Juliette

I woke up to the faint scent of a forest and fresh rain and the heavy weight of a muscled arm draped over my waist. It made me feel protected, the strong, solid muscles comforting.

Dante's finally home, I thought happily. *Home.* It was amazing how quickly I'd started to think of this place as home.

He had been gone for almost a week. It seemed forever, although five days was hardly forever. We had exchanged a few texts, but we'd kept it short.

I didn't move, enjoying the moment instead. I let out a soft sigh of contentment and snuggled closer to him, listening to my husband's even breaths. Something about him made me feel protected. Safe.

And the news I saw flashing across the screen last night confirmed that.

Travis Xander was found dead. Evidence of torture.

My lips curved into a smile, and I kept my eyes closed, picturing how Dante made him suffer. I hoped the little bitch cried. Just like his accomplices. I made those two fuckers cry, especially Travis's best friend. Fucking Sam.

He begged like a bitch and a coward. They both did and the sadistic part of me hoped that Travis did too.

Ever since it had happened, I always avoided thinking about it. It brought on anger, self-disgust, panic. I knew it wouldn't go away overnight, but I couldn't help but feel relief that those boys were gone.

Nothing was left of them. Dead. Perished. Just like that.

What goes around comes around, motherfuckers! Karma's a bitch.

The sun shone through the windows, deceiving with its warm glow.

The ground was covered in a few feet of snow and no amount of sunshine would melt it today. I'd lain awake next to Dante for an hour, listening to him breathe.

Contentment filled my chest. I had arranged for an antique car repairman to fix what I'd destroyed. It would take a week or two, but he promised to make it a priority. After learning how much it meant to him, I couldn't not do anything.

Although, I had to wonder why he hadn't fixed it in the two years since I'd taken a bat to it and ruined the paint with my petty message left in lipstick. It actually still had that dick drawing on the window. Of course, I washed it before the guy came and picked it up.

I went to move but he pulled me back. I giggled, the mattress dipped, and Dante's body came down on mine. A choked grunt sounded foreign, almost as if someone else had made it. My ears buzzed. Images flashed through my mind. My heart raced so fast, I feared I'd pass out. Panic choked me and black spots swam in my vision. My body started to shake.

A muttered "fuck" sounded in the room.

"Juliette, open your eyes." A cold, commanding voice. The mattress shifted and my body rolled over, ending on the mounds of hard muscle. "I'm sorry." Dante's voice came through. It was compelling. The lifeline. "I was half asleep and my brain was too slow to catch up. I'd never hurt you. Open your eyes."

I did, looking down into dark, warm eyes. I was now on top of him, my body flat against his muscles and his hard length pushing against my thigh.

"You're safe," he assured softly, his arms roaming my back soothingly. Up and down. Up and down. Swallowing, I inhaled a deep breath, then exhaled while my heart still pounded hard against my chest. "You good?" he asked, although his tone was slightly strained.

I nodded, then buried my face in embarrassment. "That's not how I wanted your first day back home to start," I muttered into the crook of his neck.

Dante's hand wrapped gently around my nape and pulled my face away from him, locking his eyes with mine.

"Don't apologize," he murmured softly. "You're here with me. It's the best welcome home."

"Travis is dead," I rasped. "You made him pay."

He let out a quiet, tense breath. "I made him suffer," he said softly, vehemence showing through. "But it's still not enough."

My gaze drifted to the window where the sun rose up to the sky, promising a beautiful, cold day.

"It's enough." My words were quiet. It was more than I could have ever hoped for.

"Look at me, Juliette."

I did.

"I'd cut my dick off before I hurt you. And I love my dick." It wasn't exactly a declaration of love, but in my book, it meant more than any mushy words would have. It meant the world. Dante kept his eyes on me, his hand continuously roaming my back. "But you gotta face your demons."

My stomach clenched. He was right, of course. I'd allowed them to control my life for so long that it became part of me. And that was not who I was. I was stronger than that.

"Sh-should we try and switch positions?"

He shook his head. "No, stay where you are." His gaze dropped to my lips, his jaw pulsing. His eyes drifted back up to mine where possessive heat sizzled in his dark depths.

"Why?"

"You kicked me in the balls and they still hurt." We stared at each other. A heartbeat of awkward silence and he barked out a laugh. "Great reflexes, my wildling wife."

I tilted my head, trying to discern whether he was mocking me or being sincere. He must have read my expression, because he added, "I'm dead serious. The kick was on point."

My lips curved into a smile. "I guess so, if I kicked you in your balls."

He chuckled and the sound warmed my whole body.

"I have a gym in the basement. We could practice," he offered.

I scoffed softly, though there was no heat behind it. "You want to get your ass handed to you, huh? Or maybe your balls?"

His smile fucking dazzled and entered my chest, sending fireworks through my bloodstream. How could he go from someone I couldn't stand to someone who sent electricity through my veins in the span of a week?

It was as if he bewitched me.

He cupped my face and brought our noses together. "I want my wife to kick everyone's ass and balls. Even mine."

I should have known right then and there things were too good to be true.

CHAPTER 38
Juliette

After our breakfast, the two of us changed into our gym clothes. For me that was a sports bra and butt-hugging shorts. Dante opted for sweatpants that hung low on his hips and a plain white T-shirt. The abs that showed through that white T-shirt tempted and teased so much that I tripped over my own feet.

Dante's reflexes were better than mine because before I even knew I was falling, his fingers wrapped around my elbow, steadying me.

"Got to keep your eyes up, Wildling," he teased softly.

I met his dark eyes that burned with possessiveness and desire. He had no trouble staring at me and walking without tripping.

"Then why are you staring at me?" I mumbled, my cheeks burning already.

It had to be a permanent effect with this man. I never fucking blushed until he entered my life.

"Because I love your legs," he murmured. "And your ass. Your tits too." I shook my head, but damn it, I liked hearing him say he liked my body. I reached for the bottle of water and unscrewed the cap, taking a sip to cool off, when he continued, "But most of all I love the taste of your pussy."

I choked, almost spitting the water out. Instead, I swallowed and sent it down the wrong pipe, causing me to cough and my throat to burn. Immediately, Dante's hand came to my back and started patting it gently.

"Fuck, I'm sorry," he grumbled. "I thought you knew I'm in love with your pussy."

That's not helping, I wanted to say but couldn't find my voice.

Instead, I waved my hand and would have laughed if not for trying to clear my throat while tears burned in my eyes. Dante was fucking crazy, but it'd seem I kind of liked it.

"You trying to kill me?" I rasped, narrowing my eyes on him although there was no heat behind it.

"God, no." He tugged me along to the sparring mats. "I love your pussy too much."

Good Lord, this man would be the death of me.

"You haven't been in my p—" It was so dumb but I couldn't finish the word. I wasn't bashful by any means, yet around Dante my tongue got twisted.

"Your pussy?" he finished for me with a smug grin. "You're right, but I've tasted it."

Dante and I stepped onto the mats, the soft cushion under our tennis shoes. There was a table to the side and his eyes scanned it. There were different types of knives lying neatly there.

The killer in me kind of liked it.

"I want the one with the smooth, short blade," I told him.

He shot me a surprised look, but didn't question me. Reaching for it, he grabbed it and handed it to me, then positioned himself across from me. He looked completely relaxed, as if he knew he could overpower me with the slightest effort.

He was in for a surprise.

Keeping my own smugness at bay, I gripped the knife. I wasn't nervous. A part of me wanted to toy with him. Let him think I was clueless about fighting and then strike.

I dashed forward, Dante moved fast. Much faster than I did. He grabbed my wrist and whirled me around until my back collided with his chest. He might have won this round, but it gave me a chance to see how he moved.

"You win," I breathed, painfully aware of his hard chest against my back. His pelvis against my backside. And a bulge that did things to my inner thighs. I ignored my body's response and pushed away from him.

"Again," I said, locking my eyes on him. My heart raced as the adrenaline rushed through my veins. I wasn't sure if this got me pumping from fear or excitement.

He nodded.

I squatted my knees lightly, waiting for him to attack me. I should have known though that Dante always aimed to be a gentleman.

"Ladies first," he purred.

He seemed unaffected. Like we were just out for a stroll, while my heart thundered under my ribs. It was what my self-defense instructor called my weakness. He said I got too emotionally invested. Whatever the fuck that meant. I just wanted to win, otherwise I'd end up dead. So fucking sue me for wanting to live.

"Who says I'm a lady?" He should know better. I smiled darkly, ready to pounce on him.

"I do," he drawled lazily. "You're my lady."

Okay, that was sweet. I'd give him that. I still wouldn't go easy on him. So I launched to the left, then spun on my feet, sliding behind him. My hand came around his neck, my sharp blade pressing against his Adam's apple. I had to raise myself on tiptoes, since he was so tall.

Dante whistled and he sounded impressed.

"Not bad, Wildling." I grinned at his compliment, removing the blade from his throat. He turned around to face me, his eyes shining with pride. "I see I got the whole package with you. Beauty, brains, and a body that can kick ass."

I chuckled. "Don't go too far on brains. I have dyslexia, so reading is a pain."

He tilted his head to the side, watching me pensively. "I didn't know that."

I rolled my eyes, slightly embarrassed. I never liked pointing it out. "I worked hard to overcome it, but it's still there. Sometimes it's harder to get through some books than others."

He didn't say anything, just watched me with eyes that always saw too much. I wasn't sure how I felt about it.

"Regretting marrying your wildling?" I joked, yet something about the thought had my chest clenching uncomfortably. I didn't like it.

"I want every inch of you, Juliette." His voice was deep, his gaze burning with something I didn't dare to identify. "I want to know you inside and out—all your good, bad, ugly, sad, happy. I want it all."

A sharp intake of breath echoed through the air, and it had to be mine although I didn't feel it. Oxygen couldn't enter my lungs because my chest squeezed too painfully. I had learned to keep everyone out for so long that I wasn't sure how to let this man in. He seemed to have read my mind, because he said, "Let me in, Wildling, and I promise you, neither one of us are ever going to be the same."

Well, fuck me!

CHAPTER 39
Dante

I finished off my ham and cheese sandwich while waiting for my wife.
She warned me she couldn't cook but assured me she made
killer sandwiches. She wasn't wrong. Either that or I was hungry as
fuck. If only I could have her pussy for dessert.

My lips curved into a smug smile picturing how she'd blush if I told
her what I wanted for dessert. Her reactions were the highlight of my
fucking life. Seeing her blush was like another hit of heroin for a junkie.

"What are you grinning at?" Juliette's voice came from the entrance to
the kitchen. "Like you're contemplating taking over the world."

I chuckled. "Nah, just pussy," I remarked sweetly. "I haven't had
dessert since I ate your pussy. Nothing tastes as good as your—"

"Okay, okay." She cut me off, her cheeks turning crimson. "We get it,
my pussy."

My smile spread wider and I winked at her. "Not to worry, Wildling.
You're safe with me and skiing requires too many clothes for easy access to
your—"

"God!" she exclaimed, turning an even darker shade of red. "You really
like that word, huh?"

"Only with you," I admitted, then decided to give her a break. At least
for a little bit. "You ready?" I asked.

She looked ready. A pair of black leggings, the familiar yellow pullover, and yellow Uggs. Light blue snowsuit hanging over her forearm.

"I'm not putting this on until we get there." Juliette's eyes flashed with irritation. "I'll sweat my ass off." Her eyes flicked toward my sweatpants. "I see you dress casually for skiing too."

Something about the way she stared at a certain region had me smiling with smug satisfaction. Then as if she remembered her earlier argument, she returned her eyes to my face.

"I still don't understand why you chose that for our daily fun," she muttered. It turned out my competitive wife hated not being better than me at things. "I told you I'm not even a good skier. Everything snow, ice, or water turns into a disaster when I'm around."

I sighed. "Trust me, Wilding. If I can teach Priest, I can teach you. My little brother has two left feet."

She opened her mouth to respond but her phone rang at that moment. She pulled it out eagerly, then her brows furrowed. She didn't wait, answering it before it could ring again.

"Hello?" she said. I was close enough to hear that it was a man's voice and her face lit up with a broad smile. Jealousy shot through me like a lightning bolt, but I kept my shit together. I'd have to track that call and find out what fucker could put such a smile on her face. No one had that right. It was my job and my job only.

"Yeah, that won't be a problem at all," she purred. "I got the money."

She hung up and her eyes shone with mischief. I couldn't peel my gaze away from the way they glimmered. I had never seen her like this.

"By the way, thanks for the black Amex you left behind," she said, eyeing me as she reached for a banana muffin. It was her favorite fruit and apparently her go-to snack. When she ate, that was.

"I saw you went shopping," I remarked.

She shrugged. "I figured it's what you would have wanted me to do." She ripped off a piece of the pastry and popped it in her mouth. She made a small "mmm" sound that made all the heat rush to my groin. "Otherwise, why leave it?"

She had a point, although I never fathomed she could spend two hundred grand so fast without even buying jewelry. According to the transactions, fifty grand was spent at the retail stores. The rest was a cash advance.

Not that I cared. What was mine was hers and all that. For all I cared, she could blow it all. I made enough in a single day to support our lifestyle.

"Buy anything good?" I asked her.

She shrugged. "Yes."

"What?"

She smiled. "You'll see."

Then she flicked her eyes over toward the door. "Are we ready to go start this 'fun' you have planned for today?" she inquired, her fingers coming up to make air quotes.

There was a slight hint of sarcasm in her voice, but I chose to ignore it. She'd make her way down the slope if I had to put her on my skis to do it.

I rubbed a hand over my jaw, studying Juliette's posture.

She gripped the zipper of her jacket, playing with it while eyeing the skis I held for her like they carried a fatal disease. We drove up to Wilmot Mountain, the closest option to Chicago for traditional skiing. I didn't tell Juliette that while I succeeded in teaching Priest to ski, he hated it and preferred snowboarding. I could teach her skiing; I couldn't teach her snowboarding because only people with two left feet could snowboard and that is not me.

There was a class about twenty feet away with five-year-olds that showed more enthusiasm than Juliette.

I laughed. "Come on, you can do it. First, let's strap them on."

She didn't move, so I bent down and strapped her boots in. Then we got down to business and went over the basics. First, we tried to "glide" as she called it. Next, we ski-walked around the class being held for the little kids while they threw us curious glances.

"Okay, I'm ready for the real hill," Juliette announced.

"I don't think—"

"Dante, I'm ready for the real hill," she repeated, glaring at me.

I sighed. Stubbornness was Juliette's weakness. She let her emotions guide her too much. "I'm going to do it with you or without you," she added with a lift of her chin.

"Don't say I didn't warn you."

We walked to the top of the hill and Juliette positioned herself. Her eyes shone and her cheeks were red from the cold but there was clear excitement on her face.

I pointed to a spot. "Wait until I'm standing there, then ski down, controlling your speed. Use the poles the way I showed you."

She nodded eagerly, but my gut feeling warned me she wasn't listening. She was already picturing herself flying down the mountain.

"Juliette, are you paying attention?"

"Yes, yes. I'm waiting until you're standing there, then I'm going to ski down and use my poles the way you taught me. Piece of cake. Get your ass in gear."

I shook my head.

Making my way down the hill, I reached the spot and turned around to see Juliette already speeding down.

"What the fuck—" I hissed.

She was going too fast.

"Slow down, Juliette!" I shouted, waving my hands. She looked like she was daydreaming. The smile on her face was one of pure bliss, but it quickly turned into panic. She tried to stop, making an inverted V. All she did was tangle her feet and—*boom.*

She rolled down the hill and straight into me.

"Fuck!" she grunted as she crashed into me. Her breathing was hard and her eyes wide, but adrenaline must have still been pumping through her veins because she dusted herself off and announced, "I almost did it. Let's do it again."

I glanced around, wondering if maybe I wasn't seeing something right. She'd almost killed herself, not almost done it. The looks on passersby's faces told me I was right.

"No," I said firmly. She was only recently mine. I wouldn't risk losing her on some adrenaline rush.

"I was good," she claimed. "I just fucked up the whole inverted V but other than that—"

"Other than that, you could have broken your neck."

"But it was such a rush." She grinned, her eyes shooting back to the top of the hill. I was starting to wonder whether my wife was an adrenaline junkie. "I want to try it again," she begged.

I shook my head. "Please, Dante." She even fluttered her eyes. "One more time."

"No, Wildling. I want you alive, not dead."

She blew out a frustrated breath. "Fine. Then what can I do safely?"

I took in the five-year-olds and their little makeshift hill.

"That's a hump," she hissed. "It barely reaches my knees."

"When you can go over it without falling, then we can try the hill again."

She puffed out a breath, clouding the air in front of her. "Fine."

Her eyes burned with irritation as she pushed herself off me and got to her feet very ungracefully. I pushed myself up, my mouth curved up into a wide grin. My wife was adorable when she was pouting.

"Want me to help you?" I offered.

"It's a baby hill," she hissed. "I can manage."

I'd give Juliette one thing... she was definitely goal-oriented, putting all her determination into it. But it was clear after the twentieth time that she landed on her ass, skiing wasn't her thing. The kids had all vacated onto the bigger slopes or went back to warm up inside.

"This isn't working, Dante," she groaned softly, sprawled on the snow faceup, the front of her skis vertical in the air. Then, for dramatics, she even face-planted into the soft powder. "Oh fuck, that's cold," she yelped, lifting her face up and rolling over.

I chuckled. "You think?"

A teenage boy flew by us on a snowboard, almost running into Juliette and bypassing her by a thread.

"Watch it," I yelled after him. "You could have hurt my pregnant wife."

The kid's head whipped around and he lost his balance, tumbling over himself and down the hill. He landed on his ass, breathing heavily, although he had plenty of energy to flip us off.

"I guess I'm not the only one bad on snow," Juliette drawled. "And pregnant? Seriously?"

I watched as she tried—and ultimately failed—to stifle her laugh before breaking out in a full-fledged cackle, unfazed by the glares shot our way.

This was what I wanted from the moment I'd laid eyes on this woman.

CHAPTER 40
Juliette

The ride home was silent and I wondered what he was thinking. There was no telling with Dante. I debated asking him to share his thoughts, but then I wasn't quite sure that I wanted to know.

Somehow it felt like we were headed down the road that would be hard to turn back from. Not that I thought I'd had that choice. There was one thing that was certain in the Syndicate. Divorce wasn't an option. Not that I wanted it. I actually enjoyed getting to know him.

"Just so we're clear," I broke the silence, unable to keep quiet any longer, "I'm not having kids. Not yet anyhow." Dante shot me a look that didn't reveal much. "I'm not Wynter. I refuse to be knocked up."

"Okay."

I raised my eyebrow. "Is that all you have to say on the matter?"

He shrugged. "As long as you're happy. If you want kids, we'll have them. If you don't want them, we won't have them. I'm good with either, as long as you are here with me."

His words sent my heart flipping in my chest, and I had to stop myself from squealing with girlish delight. Nobody had ever been able to make me feel this with mere words.

"You'd seriously give up having children if that's what I wanted?" He nodded. "But what's your feeling on having children? Do you like them?"

He tilted his head, keeping his eyes on the road. For some reason, it felt so easy to talk to him. Whether it was because his attention was on the road or because it was him—I wasn't sure.

"I like them," he stated matter-of-factly. "My childhood wasn't the greatest. My mother was a shitty caretaker and hated us more than loved us." My eyes widened. "I think it's important we both want them. If we have kids, it's a commitment. To give them happiness, safety, love. Everything a child should have."

I swallowed. "Because you didn't have that?"

I turned my head and met his gaze. My heart stilled and I knew the answer before he opened his beautiful lips.

"No."

My hand flew to his and I squeezed it gently. "I'm sorry." I meant it, too. No child should feel unloved. "And you're right. It's a commitment and a promise. I know you'll be a great father one day."

He took my hand and held it for the remainder of the drive home. It was quiet. It was comfortable. It felt safe.

As soon as we got inside, Dante headed straight upstairs.

I followed.

And it frightened me. It terrified me that I actually liked him. Two years of fighting this attraction, and now, I was spiraling out of control and craving him.

My muscles protested with each step, but for some silly reason, I refused to admit it. He was already at the top of the stairs and must have noticed or heard my grunt as I took the first step because he halted and turned around.

One look at me and he was stalking over, scooping me up into his arms in one swift move. Bridal style.

"A warm bath will help your aching muscles."

"You are awfully fond of offering baths," I remarked dryly. "Are you insinuating something?" He chuckled but didn't answer, which had my eyes narrowing to slits. "Well, are you?"

I wanted to touch him, but I was too chicken to ask him. I hoped he'd offer to let me cuff him again so I could explore him. Every inch of him.

Kinky. Idiotic. Wrong.

It was all that, and yet, I still wanted it. With me in his arms, he climbed the stairs and headed through our bedroom and into the bathroom. My palm pressed on his chest, feeling for his strong heartbeat, but his breathing never changed. Like I weighed nothing.

Once in the bathroom, he gently lowered me to the edge of the bathtub, then started removing my shoes.

His focus was entirely on the task at hand. He removed my sock from one foot, then the other. Next my pullover followed, then my undershirt.

"Lift your butt," he instructed and I did as he asked. He shimmied my yoga pants down my legs. Then he reached for my bra and unclipped it. Goosebumps broke over my skin and a shudder rolled down my spine. My breathing hitched, and suddenly the ache of my muscles was the last thing on my mind. All I could focus on was the dull ache between my legs.

He let out a tired sigh. "I'm not going to take advantage of you."

He misread my body's reaction to him.

"Dante?"

"Hmmm."

His eyes remained focused on the task at hand as he helped me with my panties. But he made a point of not staring at my pussy. If he had, he'd notice the glistening arousal.

He reached over me and turned the tap on the slightest bit, testing the water on his wrist. Once he was satisfied it was the right temperature, he let it fill the tub.

He reached over my head for the bath products and retrieved one, leisurely pouring it into the water.

"Take a bath with me," I offered.

His eyes came to rest on my face, studying me. I squirmed under his scrutiny, feeling vulnerable completely naked while he was fully dressed. He watched me in silence, and just as I thought he'd deny me, he stood up and started shedding his clothes.

He pulled his shirt over his head, slowly and with utter confidence, then discarded it onto the floor right on top of my clothes. The firm chest with lean muscles I hadn't seen in almost a week came into full view and I couldn't help but shiver.

He was fit and well-built, but it was that predatory strength underneath his lean frame that appealed to me. He was sun-kissed, even in the middle of winter, and my fingers itched to trail over his body. His fingers worked on his belt next and my gaze was unapologetically glued to his masculine beauty.

I had never felt this desire with anyone before. Never felt this secure.

It should have alarmed me but it didn't. After all, no other man had ever offered to cuff himself for me.

He slid his sweatpants down firm thighs, leaving him standing in only black boxers. Pulling my bottom lip between my teeth, I waited with anticipation for his boxers to go. By the time he removed them, I quivered with need.

Holy. Fucking. Shit.

His cock was hard and thick, ready for me.

Arousal shot through me and my thighs clenched with anticipation.

"You still good with me taking a bath with you?" I couldn't answer, my eyes locked on his massive length. "I could grab the cuffs," he offered.

A choked laugh escaped me trying to envision that scenario. His cock twitched as if that little member liked the sound of my voice. It was the most ridiculous thought.

"Yes?"

I nodded, and when he went to move and I realized he thought I meant the cuffs, I quickly stopped him, saying, "Forget the cuffs."

My voice was breathless. Raspy.

I lifted my eyes up his body, locking with his twin pools of desire to ensure he knew I meant it. I shifted in the large tub so he'd have room to join me. Dante smiled and something in his dark gaze lit up. Lethally. Possessively.

"Any neutral zones in the tub I need to know about?" he asked, semi-seriously.

"No."

"That was so the answer I was going for," he drawled, his smile promising something deliciously naughty.

He joined me in the tub, his big body taking most of the space.

"Come here." He reached his hand to help me into the tub and settle me, then placed it around my waist to pull me into him. His arms were taut, steady, and strong around me as he lifted me and brought me to sit between his legs.

My back to his chest, his muscular legs spread on each side of me, it felt like a warm cocoon. His strong fingers came to my shoulders and rubbed long circles with tenderness. A sigh left my lips and my eyelids fluttered shut as I settled deeper into him.

"Your shoulders are tense."

My muscles loosened with every passing second and his touch was so soothing that I leaned forward, giving him better access to my back.

"That feels good," I admitted. "You definitely know how to use those expert fingers."

His dark chuckle filled the space. "Happy to be of service."

Every inch of my body was alight with a buzz that refused to go away. It heightened higher and higher, building in pressure. I leaned back, wanting his closeness. His warmth.

"Should I go lower?" Dante's voice was in my ear, his mouth brushing against my earlobe.

My legs opened of their own accord, although it wasn't what he was asking. I needed to feel his fingers on my sensitive core, to ease this throbbing.

"Yes, please," I breathed, rubbing my legs against his muscular inner thighs. I wanted to touch him. I needed him to touch me.

Dante's fingers seemed to be everywhere all at once as he inched lower, over my breasts, brushing over my nipple, pinching it until it was taut, then rolling it between his thumb and index finger. My moan echoed in the silence of the bathroom, vibrating against the tiled walls.

My head fell back against his shoulder.

"You're so fucking beautiful," he whispered in my ear, continuing his assault on my nipple. "I love seeing pleasure on your face." My core throbbed. My thighs were shaking. A burning sensation traveled through my veins. "I love seeing happiness on your face too."

Something about his admission had my chest swelling with some fluttering feelings. I had never craved anyone but this man. It felt good giving in to this need. I just hoped it wouldn't steer me wrong.

My hand lowered into the bathwater, inching closer to my sex. I needed to come. So desperately. My fingers brushed against my clit and another moan filled the air. Whimpering. Needy.

"I want to watch you finger yourself," Dante rasped in my ear, his big hands kneading my breasts. I could feel his hard cock pressing against my back, needy. Just like my pussy.

My cheeks turned crimson at the explicit images those words painted in my head.

"Me too," I whimpered, rubbing my fingers faster and harder against my clit.

He stilled. I did too. Like we were two bodies, driven by the same need.

"Now?" he asked, tentatively.

"Yes."

The words were barely out of my mouth when he stood up and lifted me into his arms.

His mouth never left mine as he strode into our bedroom, our bodies slick from water.

CHAPTER 41
Dante

My wife would be the death of me. In the best way possible.

The moment I'd set eyes on her, I'd known she'd be trouble. My trouble.

I hooked her legs around my waist and carried her into our bedroom. Thank fuck I'd had the brilliant idea to burn every goddamn bed in this house. I knew Juliette ordered another bedroom set for the guest room, but I bought out the manufacturer and then had them put a stop on her order. There'd be no other beds in this house.

I devoured her mouth like my life depended on it. Maybe it truly did. After all, it was only due to my devious plan that she was now here with me in *our* bed. If she ever learned of my schemes, I knew enough about Juliette to know she'd burn down the whole fucking city to get back at me.

Her curves fit perfectly in my hands, her soft skin like silk under my rough palms. Years of fantasizing about this wildling and it was even better than I had ever imagined it. Juliette's arms wrapped around my neck, tugging me closer to herself. She tasted like sugarplums—my favorite treat —and home. *My home.*

The kind that I never had but always dreamed of. I tightened my grip on her hair, our mouths colliding like we were starved for each other. Our kiss was hard, demanding and possessive, tension coiling in our bodies. Unlike any other woman, Juliette matched me inch for inch.

Her fingers wove through my hair, tugging on it as her tongue tangled with mine. And those moans. They were soft whimpers, and so fucking addictive, going straight to my cock.

I sat on the bed. Her wet body flush against mine, rubbing like a cat against me. Not wanting to scare her, I remained sitting, cradling her in my arms.

I pinched her nipple and she arched into my touch.

"More," she demanded on a groan. It wasn't surprising she was greedy, demanding. She never feigned modesty, and I fucking loved that about her.

Pulling an inch away from her, both of us breathing heavily.

"Look at me," I demanded. She peeled her eyes open and met my gaze, her mouth swollen from my kisses and parted in anticipation. "Are you okay if we lie on the bed?"

She nodded, her eyes fluttering shut as she leaned closer to me, demanding another kiss. I granted it, unable to resist her. If she only knew what I'd do for her. What I'd give up for her. I was so fucking smitten, it wasn't even funny.

Breaking away, I placed her on the bed and admired her beauty. Gleaming skin. Dark hair fanned over the white pillows. Face flushed with arousal. Eyes hazed with lust.

I wanted nothing more than to bury myself inside of her so deep she'd never forget me. So if she ever learned about how I manipulated her into this marriage, she'd remember how good we were together. How perfectly we fit.

"No going back after this, Juliette," I said, my words filled with gravel.

Confusion crossed her face. "What—"

"You're my wife and I'm your husband," I growled. "Until death do us part." I palmed her breast and swept my thumb over her nipple. I lowered my head and licked her nipple. A shudder rolled through her. "Understood?"

I might have been using her desire to my advantage. I didn't fucking care. I wanted her commitment. She wanted this as much as I did. Maybe she didn't love me as obsessively as I did her, but she cared, that I knew for certain.

"Understood?" I asked.

"Yes." She caved, pulling me onto the bed next to her. But not on top. She still feared missionary.

"You okay?" My balls ached but there was no fucking way I'd hurt her. Her needs were more important than mine.

Juliette arched her hips, grinding against my shaft. "Please don't stop."

I shifted off the bed, wanting to give her some space. Her terror would gut me and I didn't want to smother her.

I stood at the foot of the bed when a whimpering protest left her lips.

"I'm not going anywhere," I assured her, my eyes locked on her. Her tongue swept over her bottom lip and my dick twitched, picturing that tongue on my cock.

"Be a good girl and touch yourself," I ordered in a raspy voice. "Your breasts first. Show me what you like."

A small shiver rippled through her body. My eyes traveled over one and then the other, caressing every inch of them.

I watched Juliette's fingers tremble as she brought them up to her breasts, rolling her nipples between her fingers and then pinching them. Despite her blush, she didn't take her eyes off me. She moaned my name, and it was just about enough to make me come right then and there.

My gaze dragged from her heavy, full breasts, over her curves to the sweet pussy glistening with her wetness.

"Now spread your legs wider and touch your pussy," I rasped. "Show me how you get yourself off when you think about me."

A deep blush bloomed across her body and up her chest, coloring her cheeks. It had only been a handful of times that I'd seen the stubborn woman blush. It had become my life's purpose, seeing her ivory skin turn rosy.

I couldn't wait to trace every inch of her with my tongue. Mark her with my teeth, and more than anything, I couldn't wait to touch her. Claim her in every sense of the word so everyone knew who she belonged to.

Me.

One hand slid between her legs, her finger circling her clit, slowly at first but then faster and harder. Soon, she was whimpering with pleasure. Her blue eyes flooded with lust and locked on me, her mouth falling open and her breathing turning shallow as she rubbed her clit and brought her other hand across to finger her pussy.

My cock was so hard it hurt. I needed her like the fucking air in my lungs. My eyes locked on her.

Fierce. Ravenous. Destructive.

Together we'd be a volcano. No doubt about it.

"You thinking of me, Wildling?"

She watched me through heavy eyelids. "Yes," she moaned.

Fuck, the admission might have me spilling. I was so fucking close.

"Tell me what you're thinking," I growled.

Her tongue darted out, sweeping across her bottom lip. "I want you to tongue-fuck me."

Shit. Juliette liked the dirty talk. It made sense she was the girl of my dreams.

"You want to come all over my face?"

She moaned as her fingers worked faster, her knees still splayed apart as her arousal trickled down her inner thigh. It made my mouth water. Her thighs trembled from her ministrations, her pleasure building.

"Tell me," I growled.

"Yes," she whimpered. "I want to come all over your face."

Satisfaction filled me. Hot and needy.

"I'm going to lick every single inch of you. Your mouth. Your breasts. Your cunt."

Juliette's head tilted back and her eyes fluttered closed.

"Yes, please." The corners of my lips tugged up. It'd seem the only time my wife uttered that word was in the bedroom.

"You want me to fuck you?" Juliette shuddered at my question and her ocean gaze met mine. There was desire there but also a hint of worry. Maybe even fear. There'd be none of that between us. No fear. No hesitation.

"Whenever you want me to stop," I said firmly, holding her gaze. "You just say it. You're in control here. Got it?"

"Yes."

She was such a force to be reckoned with. I understood now that my

231

approach at securing our wedding would cause a horrible rift between us. So I'd prove to her that I would be good to her. Always. Nothing like my mother, who was cruel and hateful. Nothing like my father, who cheated.

But first, I'd have to ensure she never found out.

"Now tell me, who do you think about when you're finger-fucking your pussy?" I demanded in a hoarse voice as I stood up and stalked to the bed, grasping her chin in one hand and forcing her to drown in my gaze in the same way I was in hers.

"You."

"What. Am. I. Doing. To. You."

"Fucking me," she gasped.

I could smell her arousal, the slick sounds of her fingers sliding in and out of her pussy making obscene sounds.

"You want me in your cunt?" She nodded. "Your pussy wants to strangle my cock?" She swallowed, goosebumps breaking over her skin. Another nod. Not as sure. "Who's in control here, Juliette?" When she didn't answer, I pushed my hand into her thick auburn mane and gripped her hair. "Who?" I repeated.

"I am."

"Good girl." I would praise her until she started to believe it. "That's right. You're in control and we get to do only what you want." Her cheeks flushed a deeper red. "Now tell me, how am I going to fuck you?"

The slick sounds of her fingers sliding in and out of her cunt mixed with our labored breathing.

"While I'm bent over the bed," she answered, watching me under her thick lashes. "Or bathroom counter, so I can see you in the mirror, taking me from behind."

"Fuck." I'd blow my load if we continued with this. I released her hair and reached down, grabbing her wrist with my hand and forcing her to still. When she let out a protest, I chuckled. Darkly. "All your orgasms belong to me tonight."

I took her mouth in a hard, possessive kiss and moved down her neck, over her collarbone, shoulders. When I reached her breasts, I took her nipple in my mouth, sucked and licked until she was panting hard, her hips grinding against my thigh. I tugged gently on her nipple with my teeth, while my hands roamed every inch of her body. I couldn't resist making my way between her thighs, finding her slick with desire. I pushed one finger inside her.

"Fuck, you're tight." She was drenched, her insides clenching around my finger greedily.

"Please," she begged, her skin burning underneath me. "I need... Oh, I —I need—"

Her hips arched off the bed, grinding against me frantically. I knew exactly what she needed, so I kissed my way down her stomach until I reached her pussy.

"Is this what you need?" I growled against her, nipping at her clit. She thrashed back against the pillow, grinding against my face. I pushed my fingers deeper inside her before I dragged them out, only to thrust them in again. Enough to bring her to the edge, but not enough to tip her over.

"Yes, that's it," she moaned. "Please, Dante."

The sound of my name on her lips always did it for me. It was the most beautiful melody. The most perfect sound.

I lifted my head, and she stared back at me with a gaze full of lust and something else shining in those gorgeous blue eyes. It almost looked like adoration. Fuck, could it be love?

"You want to come?"

She nodded eagerly, panting, her mane sprawled around her head like a fan. "Please, Dante."

I lowered my head again and gently scraped my teeth over her clit before I sucked on it. A moan vibrated through the room, her hips bucked. She was dripping down her thighs and I eagerly lapped at every drop of it like I was starving. And all the while, I finger-fucked her, drowning in the adrenaline buzzing in my ears and her whimpering moans.

The taste of her was addictive. I knew it'd be something I'd do for the rest of our lives. Between her moans and her taste, there'd be no cure for me. She was my salvation. Juliette ground against my face, her movements frantic and desperate, and her pleading whines grew louder the longer I ate her out. I pressed my thumb against her clit and curled my fingers until they hit the spot. She arched off the bed with a sharp cry, shudders wracking her body.

She came so hard her body trembled, and I held her hips still so I could keep fucking her with my tongue. She was the altar to which I was always meant to worship.

My wife slumped back, lying in a boneless heap on the bed.

My balls ached and my cock was rock hard. Painfully so. I had to get to the bathroom and jerk off, or I'd get no fucking sleep tonight.

I moved to get off the bed, but Juliette stopped me, her fingers wrapping around my forearm. "Wait."

She stared at my cock. "Let me take care of you."

Her fingers brushed over my shaft and I sucked in a sharp breath.

"This was for you," I said, voice coarse as ever. "You're not ready for more."

As much as I wanted her to be ready for it all, we had time and there was no need to rush. We had our entire lives.

Juliette wouldn't have it though. Her nails dug into my thighs, her eyes locking on my cock that seemed to respond under her gaze. Precum glistened on the tip of it and the way she licked her lips had my dick throbbing.

"I want to make you feel good," she whispered.

"Juliette..."

The word died on my lips, morphing into a groan the second her hand wrapped around my cock. She shifted down my body, then leaned over and flicked her tongue over the head of my length, lapping up the beads of precum.

"Mmmm," she hummed, like she approved.

Fuck, that noise!

She took me fully in her mouth and all my reason ceased to exist. All I could concentrate on was her warm mouth around me. The sounds she made as she bobbed her head, back and forth. I was in heaven.

Nothing, fucking nothing, could feel better than this.

My blood shot through my veins like lava while my heart pumped hard with lust and love. It had to be love. She felt like home. Like a need that I couldn't live without.

I tangled my hands in Juliette's hair, her head bobbing up and down. She was so fucking beautiful. I loved her sassiness. Her spirit. And most of all, her soft side in those rare times she let me see it.

She attempted to fit all of me down her throat, but let out a small, frustrated sound. I pulled my cock out of her mouth, only the popping sound filling the space.

Her eyes snapped to me, flashing in defiance.

"I'm not done," she mumbled frustrated.

"Let's try a different—"

"Dante, I said, I'm not done," she hissed, cutting me off. Fuck, she was sassy and that made me even harder.

"Thank God," I rasped. "We're just going to swap positions, but you tell me if it gets to be too much. Okay?"

She nodded and I repositioned her on her back again. My body hovered over her. Instantly, she froze, her eyes filling with anguish.

"Okay, that won't work," I muttered, getting to my feet before she had a full-blown panic attack.

She jumped up from the bed. "Please don't go."

I cupped her cheek, the vulnerability in her eyes gutting me. If I could kill that fucking asshole all over again, I would.

"I'm not going anywhere," I assured her, both of us standing chest to chest. My thumb brushed over her lower lip gently and her tongue darted out, licking the pad of it, sucking it into her mouth.

She slowly lowered down to her knees. The queen didn't belong on her knees, but fuck, I wasn't a saint nor was I a man with morals. The image would forever be seared into my mind.

Her palms came to my hips, fingers curling into my skin.

"We can do it like this," she rasped softly. My heart raced against my ribs, ready to plunge my dick into her warm mouth, but I kept myself still. We'd do this at her pace.

"Tell me if it's too much," I reminded her.

At the nod of her head, I slid the tip of my cock across her lips before I nudged it into her mouth. She eagerly took me in, but I paused every few inches to let her acclimate to my size until I was finally, blissfully, buried all the way down her throat.

A growl vibrated in my throat. Juliette's eyes were locked on mine with her soft expression. Her gaze was dark and she was so brave. So fucking eager.

She sucked on my cock, her head bobbing back and forth. My head fell back, but I kept my eyes on her. My fingers gripped her hair as she kept taking me in and out. Her eyes welled with tears, and I stilled. "Too much?"

She shook her head and I pushed myself inside, deep into her throat. A groan vibrated in my chest and we worked up to a rhythm—starting slowly, then faster and harder. Juliette's small noises and moans sent tiny vibrations up my cock.

"Fuck, that's it, Wildling."

Sweat beaded on my skin as I drove in and out of her mouth. The pressure built up at the bottom of my spine. Her warm mouth took me eagerly, taking every thrust with a moan deep in her throat. I didn't last long. The silky warmth of her mouth, the sight of her breasts bouncing, and her eyes on me pushed me over the edge.

My orgasm slammed into me with the power of a hurricane. Fireworks exploded behind my eyes. I spurted deep into her throat, filling her. White cum trickled down her chin, but she ignored it as she swallowed every single drop.

I pulled out of her mouth, the buzzing still loud in my ears, my veins, and my head. I swept the cum off her chin and smeared it over her lip. Her tongue darted out, licking it clean, and I was hard again.

Just like that.

"Fuck, woman," I rasped.

She blinked, a hazy expression taking over. I cupped her face, helping her up onto her feet. "Are you okay?"

"That was... wow."

A sardonic breath left me. "I agree."

I gave her a quick kiss before I scooped her up and carried her back onto the bed. Exhaustion and satisfaction lined her face.

She hadn't complained about there being only one bed in the house since that first night. I interpreted it my way—she wanted to sleep with me too. Well, aside from the bed she ordered and I canceled but it was all semantics. She *wanted* to sleep with me. I was just ensuring she got what she wanted.

I tucked her beneath the covers, then slid in beside her, pulling her into me.

CHAPTER 42
Dante

The very next morning, my wife insisted we get out of bed early and get dressed.

"Why?" I grumbled. "It's only eight and it's the weekend."

Something soft hit the back of my head. A pillow. Instead of throwing it back, I grabbed it, rolled over onto my stomach and put it on top of my head.

"Dante, get up," Juliette insisted, nudging me back and forth. If I was a frail thing, I'd have whiplash.

"Shouldn't you be exhausted, wife?" I mumbled.

"Not even close." I could hear the smile in her voice. So I got rid of the pillow and turned onto my back. I loved her smiles. I wanted her smiles, her laughter, her everything. I stared at her for a moment, my eyes lingering on her face.

Juliette was breathtakingly beautiful, and when she smiled like this, she could bring the entire world down. Her eyes twinkled and my heart skipped a fucking beat.

I was so fucking in love with my wife, but deep in my black heart, I wondered if she'd ever feel a fraction of what I felt.

She hovered over me, her face close and I couldn't resist cupping it, bringing her closer. The distance between us disappeared and I pressed my mouth to hers.

"We could stay in bed," I suggested, breaking the kiss. "All day."

Her smile widened, but she shook her head. "Get up or I swear, I'm gonna sleep on the couch." Her threat would never come to fruition because I'd get rid of every couch in this house if need be. She wrapped her slim fingers around my bicep and pulled me up. "Now let's get dressed."

Ten minutes later, we left the bedroom. Me wearing a three-piece suit and Juliette wearing her signature jeans with her yellow sweater.

Juliette dragged me through the house. When I attempted to shift our path to the kitchen, she shook her head.

"No time."

I grinned at her excitement. "Time for what?"

"You're going to ruin the surprise," she scolded.

"I'm scared of your surprises, Wildling," I admitted. "Usually they end up in smashed windshields or shut-down casinos."

She smiled gleefully. "I promise nothing bad this time."

My wife looked so damn beautiful and happy, it made my heart flutter in my chest. Yes, this woman made a fucking wimp out of me. I wondered if she'd laugh in my face if I got down on one knee and proposed to her properly.

I wanted to slide a ring on her finger because she said "yes" and not because I tricked her into it. But that would mean I'd have to admit to her my wrongdoings, and I feared that would take us two steps backward instead of forward.

"Come on," she urged, tugging me along. "We'll be just outside for a bit."

"Do we need jackets?" She was dressed warm, but the temperatures were in the single digits. A jacket was definitely a must.

She waved her hand. "I'm so pumped up, I'm breaking a sweat. If your fragile body—" She cut herself off, eyes hazed over and traveling over my body. She licked her lips and my dick instantly responded. "Get a jacket if you want it," she rasped, breathlessly.

Amusement ignited in my chest. "We could go back upstairs."

She swallowed, her cheeks flushing. "We can't. He's waiting for us."

I shot to attention instantly. "Who?"

238

She rolled her eyes, a smile playing around her mouth. "So many questions."

I shook my head. "One second."

There was one rule I always followed. Never leave the house without a .45. You never knew where and when the enemy would strike. I had no intention of being caught with my pants down, so to speak, especially now that I had my wife to protect.

Heading to the nearby cabinet, I reached inside a secret compartment. I had those installed all throughout the house and worked only on my fingerprints. I had seen Juliette handle a gun when Sofia attacked us. It was obvious she could handle one, but I wanted to ensure she could handle other weapons before I gave her access to all of it.

I tucked the gun into the back of the waistband of my pants. She tilted her head and I cocked an eyebrow, challenging her to say something. Juliette was never too shy to express her opinion.

"I want you to have them work on my fingerprint too," she finally said. "Or I'll start breaking them all."

I had no doubt she meant it. She already smashed through the one in our walk-in closet.

It was still the last thing I'd expected her to say. By the expression on her face, she wasn't joking either.

"First, we'll ensure you can handle a gun safely."

She smiled knowingly, obviously confident about her shooting skills. "I can handle it. You saw me handle it when shooting at Sofia Volkov."

I tilted my head, ignoring her reminder. Honestly, it fucking terrified me to think of anyone pointing a gun at my wife. I wanted to put her in a bubble and keep her protected.

"We shall see," I said calmly. "Hopefully they're better than your thieving skills."

Her eyes narrowed on me, lightning flashing in her gaze. "You're going to eat those words."

The moment we stepped out the door, my steps faltered. My grandfather's 1934 Hudson Convertible Coupe was parked fifteen feet away. It looked like my grandfather's convertible, but it couldn't be. That one still sat in my collection garage, with Juliette's artwork on the windows. It had to be a replica.

"Where did you find the same model?" I asked. "Even the same color."

She smiled sheepishly, and despite the cold, her cheeks were red, matching her lips. Her eyes shone in excitement as she tugged me further down the driveway.

"It's the same car," Juliette announced triumphantly.

I blinked, my brain too slow. "How?"

She straightened up, a proud expression flashing in her eyes. "I did some research and found an expert in the restoration of antique cars."

As if on cue, an old man stepped out of my grandfather's car. He looked to be in his sixties, his silver hair a mess.

"Juliette." He waved my wife over and she skipped over to him, excited.

"It looks so good, John." She beamed. "You did an amazing job."

He chuckled, revealing a few missing teeth. "I was able to find the original parts on the same model cars. Same color too."

Juliette clapped her hands, then whirled around as she reached him. "So ta-da!" she exclaimed, grinning from ear to ear. "What do you think?"

I was still glued to my spot, staring at her and the car. I blinked, almost expecting the light to play tricks on me.

John laughed. "I think your husband is speechless."

She waved her hand. "Trust me, John. Dante is never speechless." Juliette shot me a triumphant look. "He probably can't believe I was able to pull it off."

I finally made my way to the car, studying it with a critical eye. I couldn't find a single fault. Not that I wanted to find one. The thought alone spoke volumes. Especially coming from Juliette.

"I'm sorry I damaged it," Juliette remarked softly. "I know how much it meant to you."

It meant a lot to me. But she meant even more. Which made this even worse. Guilt was a fucked-up thing.

"Do you like it?" she asked, insecurity lacing her voice.

I looked up at my wife's hopeful face and prowled over to her. My hands came to her slim hips, and I lifted her into the air, squeezing her into my chest. She squealed playfully, her eyes glimmering.

"I fucking love it," I rasped, emotion swelling inside me.

The day this girl set foot in my casino was the luckiest day of my life.

Royally lucky, through and through. Or maybe it was the day in the alley when my life turned the corner and headed in the right direction. It slowly brought me back to her. Who could have ever known that the little girl who'd offered me her pink scrunchie would one day become the very reason for my existence?

"Do you forgive me?" she asked, cupping my face. "If I knew what it meant, I would have never done that stuff to it."

John was chuckling next to me, but I couldn't peel my gaze from my wife. Maybe I was fooling myself, but I thought I detected love and tenderness in her sapphire gaze.

"I'd forgive you anything, Wildling," I admitted hoarsely. It was the truth. "But this..." I shook my head. "This means so fucking much."

It was so fucking worth waiting two years. For her. For my grandfather's car to be repaired.

I had often been tempted to get the car repaired but something always held me back. Now I knew what it was. *This.*

Juliette leaned forward, pressing her lips to mine.

If only we could have stayed here, in this moment, forever.

CHAPTER 43
Juliette

After John was gone, Dante decided to take us out to lunch in his grandfather's car. We even put the top down despite the cold. I merely suggested it and he then insisted.

"Your wish is my command," he said and I grinned like an idiot while my pulse fluttered.

The cold breeze froze my cheeks, but I didn't care. I smiled happily, tilting my face up to bask in the sun. Dante looked in my direction, a spark passing through his eyes.

He remained silent as we drove, taking all the back roads into the heart of the city so I wouldn't freeze. His thoughtfulness did some weird things to my insides, but I couldn't exactly say I hated the feeling.

City noise surrounded us. The sound of the engine purred lazily. And my husband threw glances my way every so often, the heat in them enough to warm me from the inside as my pulse drifted between my thighs.

"Does it drive the same way?" I asked, because for some crazy reason I wanted to hear his voice. I wanted to know everything there was about him.

He flicked a gaze to me, smiling. Darkness glinted behind his eyes along with a feeling I didn't dare label.

"Even better," he drawled. "Now, the car is part of my grandfather and you."

His words sparked something inside my chest and fireworks of emotions exploded through me. It was so easy to fall for him. I'd fought it and fought it for two years, only to end up here. In his car. In his city.

And I fucking loved it.

Hand on the wheel, he drove the speed limit and obeyed all the traffic laws. There was something humorous about it considering his line of work. I was a terrible driver. I cruised slowly through stop signs and always went over the speed limit. It was the reason I'd managed to total one too many cars.

"Did I thank you yet?" His question pulled me out of my thoughts.

I smiled. "You have."

He drove the car like it was an extension of him and I knew—I just knew—it was the right thing having it restored. I'd done right by him.

"Were you and your grandfather close?" I asked, although I knew the answer. If he cared about his grandpa's car so much, he had to care about the man.

Dante nodded. "Very. Priest and he were close too." A dark expression crossed his eyes, but it quickly evaporated. "Our dad was often too busy and Mother was..." He paused, as if searching for the right word, but couldn't quite find it. "Anyhow, he was a good man. He'd bring Priest and me over to his place, then we'd work on cars. Or his garden. And the whole time, he'd tell us stories about Grandma."

I chuckled, trying to imagine Dante working in a garden and failing.

"You and the garden are hard to imagine," I said softly. His head tilted to the side, catching my gaze and holding it for a moment, before he returned his attention back to the road.

"Your grandpa sounds like a great guy," I added. "Mine, well, Wynter's grandpa really, he just likes to play chess and card games. I hate those, but Wyn is good at them."

"Does that bother you?"

I shot him a curious look. "What?"

"That he's not your real grandpa," he clarified.

I pulled my bottom lip between my teeth, trying to think of how to respond. I never really thought that much about it. Usually I was glad

Wyn would entertain him so he wouldn't put me through the pains of playing games.

"No, not really," I finally answered. "He was always good to us, treating both Killian and me like we were family." I thought back to the one time I heard his protest about Killian inheriting the Brennans' business. Back then, I didn't know we weren't really Brennans. "I understand now why Grandpa didn't want Killian to inherit the Brennan empire."

"That's shitty," Dante noted wryly. "Liam raised you as his own. Killian should inherit. After all, he was raised as a Brennan."

I shrugged. "Dad wants him to, but I think Killian is refusing. Especially now that Dad has a true son." He nodded in understanding, but I could tell by the expression on his face he still didn't agree.

"Was it a shock to learn that Priest was your half brother?" I questioned.

He shook his head as we came to a stoplight, then cast a glance my way.

"Yes and no." When I raised a brow, he continued, "My mother was a bitch. She treated both of us poorly, but Priest more so than me."

I swallowed, something about his tone warning me it wasn't a good story.

"What did she do?"

Dante remained silent for a long time. The light turned green and the car drifted forward. Just when I thought he wouldn't answer, his voice came through.

"Priest's story is his to tell." The darkness and vehemence behind those words sent a shudder through me.

"And yours?" I pushed, although I wasn't sure why. It wasn't fair to demand his story when I wasn't quite ready to share mine.

"Let's just say my mother liked to get back at our father by lashing out at us."

His words sent shock rolling through me. Something pounded in my chest, clawing for revenge. For punishment at anyone who'd hurt my Dante.

My brows furrowed. *My Dante.*

When did I start thinking of him as mine?

Dante's admission hung in the air as we ate our lunch.

His expression was darker than I'd ever seen it, and something about it didn't sit well with me. I wanted to make him feel better.

We made our way back to his car parked in a private alley and he opened my door before I sunk into the leather seats. The roof was back on, and as he got behind the wheel, he put the key in the ignition and reached for the button to lower the roof back down.

"Don't," I rasped.

His eyes flitted my way curiously. Dark. Hot. So fucking inviting.

Something pounded in my chest, threatening to steal my breath away. Or my courage. So I acted.

He tracked my every movement as I leaned over to him and kissed him. My lips touched his to an old Italian song by Dean Martin. "That's Amore."

I wondered whether it was love that I was feeling, but I couldn't think about it right now. Instead, I let his scent soak through my skin. His warm, soft lips devoured me just as hungrily as I devoured him.

A moan climbed up my throat, and before I knew what I was doing, I left my seat to straddle him.

Our faces were inches apart, our breaths mixing as our hearts danced.

Love, I thought again as I traced my index finger along his bottom lip.

Those lips that always seemed to have a smirk on them when looking at me. Before, it annoyed me. Now, it excited me because it represented *him*. I couldn't imagine my husband without that sexy smirk.

He parted his mouth and caught my finger between his teeth, nipping it.

I shook my head. "Ouch."

It didn't really hurt, but for some reason I liked giving him a hard time. Almost like foreplay. Maybe that was what the past two years were for us. Foreplay.

He hid his demons and I hid mine, but in the end, maybe our demons had brought us back together.

"Seats go all the way back," I uttered softly.

Dante raised his brow in surprise. "And how do you know?"

I grinned. "I inspected your car before I let John take it. To ensure it came back in the same shape—minus the damage."

Reaching to the side of the seat, I pulled the lever and the seat fell back in one loud thump, us with it. I pushed my face into his throat, inhaling him deeply, my thighs throbbing.

"Dante," I whispered, grinding myself against his growing erection. "I want—"

"I don't have any cuffs on me, Wildling," he ground through clenched teeth. But even as he uttered those words, his hands found their way under my sweater. He pinched my nipple through the thin material of my bra and my head fell back.

"Are you wet for me?" he grunted as my hips rolled against his erection. The friction was so good, but not enough.

"Yes," I admitted, nipping his throat. My hips rocked, my butt brushing his cock and each time a whimper vibrated in my throat. "I want —" What did I want?

"You want my cock?" he rumbled and a sharp sigh left my lips. It was exactly what I wanted. "How do you want my cock? In your pussy or your mouth?"

White-hot lust ignited through my veins like waves crashing against the shoreline.

"In my pussy," I rasped, grinding my hips against his pelvis. He was hard, his length pushing eagerly against my entrance. Except our damn clothes were in the way.

His hands cupped my face and forced me to lock eyes with him. "Are you sure? This isn't exactly the time or place."

My need for him grew until it felt close to bursting. "Says who?"

His thumb brushed across my lips and down my chin. "I do. Our first time shouldn't be a tumble in a car."

His dick thought otherwise. He was so hard, I couldn't resist grinding against it. He let out a grunt and a smug smile curved my mouth.

"Your cock disagrees," I murmured, brushing my nose against his. "My pussy too."

My cheeks heated at my words, but I refused to be embarrassed. I wanted him. He wanted me.

The buzz of the city was a distant noise. A soft melody came from the car speakers, although I couldn't identify the song. The noise of the heater turned up, blowing hot air around us. All I could hear, feel, and smell was this man. My husband.

"Please, Dante," I whined. "It'd make today perfect."

It seemed it was all he needed to hear. "Get your clothes off," he demanded, his voice full of gravel.

I didn't hesitate. I fumbled and twisted, he helped as I got rid of the sweater, my shoes, then my jeans. I reached to unbuckle my bra but Dante's hand came to mine.

"Leave that on," he growled.

"But I want your mouth."

His lips curved into a smile that made my insides clench. "You'll have it, but there's no fucking way you'll be naked if someone passes by."

I opened my mouth to argue, but he grasped me by the throat and swallowed my next breath in his mouth. He won, but so did I. The growl that vibrated in his chest told me his control was slipping.

His kiss was so intense that it sent fire blazing through my veins. My blood sizzled. My body tingled with so much need, I feared my orgasm would be imminent.

I brought my palms up to his chest, feeling his hard muscles underneath. As I clawed through his three-piece suit, he nipped at my bottom lip, then licked it, soothing the sharp sting with his tongue.

"Mine," he hissed, his hands on my body. That first touch, first feel of his rough palms against my skin felt like a touch of fire against freezing cold skin. It burned, in the best way possible.

A moan traveled up my throat. The cold temperature turned into a balmy summer heat. At least in the small space of his car. His shirt unbuttoned, I scraped my nails down his chest, marveling at the strength I felt there.

He hissed against my lips, then slid his tongue inside my mouth. I ached so bad, I trembled. His palm slid over my hips and to the curve of my ass, pressing me harder against him. Between his gentle yet firm grasp on my throat and his palm pulling me into him, I was lost to this feeling.

My body melted against his. I ground my hot entrance onto his cloth-covered cock while needy sounds vibrated through me. The heat of his body was an addiction, and it had nothing to do with the cold outside. It stole my breath away.

His mouth found my nipple, biting it gently through the material of my bra. It sent a shiver down my spine as I pushed my breasts into him.

His hand left my throat and pushed up into my hair, grabbing a fistful and tilting my head back.

"Look at me, Juliette." His voice was thick. Rough. Commanding.

I forced my eyelids open, meeting his dark gaze that once upon a time, I thought nightmares were made of. I was so fucking wrong. His gaze was heaven. Temptation. Salvation.

His hands roamed over my body, touching every inch that was accessible to him. His gaze followed everywhere he touched me, as if needing to memorize me. I did the same. I wanted to remember his hands on my skin. Forever.

The soft sounds of our harsh breathing filled the closed space. I leaned forward and kissed his neck, then licked his skin. My insides liquefied and a low moan traveled up my throat. He tasted so good.

"Mine," I murmured softly.

"Yours."

A simple word and it had so much power. His touch moved lower, reaching the wet material between my thighs and every nerve in my body trembled in anticipation. Desperate need clawed at me, burning and demanding.

"Touch me there," I breathed. I wanted him so badly, I trembled. But so did he. "Please."

I brought my hands to his belt and fumbled with it. He let me, watching me with so much reverence, I thought I'd burst into flames. The sound of the zipper sent an echo through the car, announcing the point of no return. Not that I wanted to.

I lowered my gaze and surprise washed over me. "No boxers?"

Fuck, why did I find that so erotic?

"Does it bother you?"

I shook my head, my gaze fixated on his cock so close to my hot entrance. It hadn't even touched my pussy, and I was panting. Forgetting his earlier request, his fingers curled over the hem of my panties and a ripping sound followed.

I was soaking wet, the slickness of my arousal trailing a path down my inner thighs as he dragged the material up through my center.

Deliriously, I stared down between us, his cock right at my throbbing entrance. My heart thundered under my rib cage and fire burned through me, watching his hard shaft at my folds. His fingers reached for my clit, circling it. The pressure built, sending a shudder through me.

I watched us through heavy eyelids, both of us focused on our nearly joined bodies.

"Are you sure?" Dante's voice penetrated the lustful fog. I rolled my hips again, letting the tip of his cock slide inside my entrance. The sight was erotic. So fucking hot that I could orgasm just from it. "Juliette, look at me."

Tearing my gaze from our joined bodies, I sought out his face. Those dark eyes that shimmered like night skies pulling me into their darkness, a place I now knew I'd been all along.

My tongue darted out, wetting my lips. "Yes, I'm sure."

He observed me for a moment, as if trying to decipher whether it was a good idea or not. The truth was that I had wanted him from the moment I spotted him in his casino. It spooked me because it was an unfamiliar reaction. I never wanted any man, yet with him, my body went into overdrive. Like it had been asleep for decades, waiting for him.

He expected panic to kick in, but it was nowhere to be found. As if he killed it when he ended Travis's life. His fingers traveled north to cup my butt and a soft moan vibrated between us.

"I don't want any more ghosts between us," I murmured, leaning over and brushing the tip of my nose against his. "All in."

Something flickered across his expression, but it was gone before my next heartbeat. I held my breath, waiting for his response. I didn't want to hide behind that dark period of my life anymore.

I wanted what Davina had with my dad. I wanted what Wynter had with that unhinged Basilio. He might be slightly psychotic but he had Wynter's back. All the DiLustros—Dante, Basilio, Priest, and Emory—had each other's back. And the way Basilio watched Wynter with so much longing and vehemence could set the world on fire.

When it came to Dante DiLustro, I was the subject of that look. He watched me with something so raw and intense that it made me want to curl into him and let him protect me.

He killed Travis for me.

His eyes lowered and I followed his gaze. His grip tightened on my hips while my fingers clutched his shoulders.

Slowly, I sank down on his length. He was so hard, so big, and *so* hot. The heat was overwhelming.

He groaned. I panted.

"You still good?" he grunted. The tenderness in his voice drifted through the air and hit me right in the chest.

"Yes."

One of his hands left my hip and slipped between our bodies until he found my pulsing clit. I moaned as he circled it, hard and fast. He lowered his head, his mouth licking and biting my nipple through the material. I slid further down on his length taking all of him, and both of us hissed.

"Fuck, Wildling," he gritted. "You're so tight."

Tension radiated through him while hot lava burned through me. Both of us watched our joined bodies, our desire pulled taut. My body trembled at feeling him inside me, and I leaned forward, pressing my face into his neck.

He gripped my hips, rocking me against him. Slowly at first, then gradually faster and faster. My clit ground against him, sending shudders through me.

His hands moved over my back, down my chest, around my neck, only to end back on my thighs. And all the while, I ground on him.

"You feel so good." His words pressed against my ear, heavy with need and awe. "You have no idea how long I've been dreaming about this."

Dante was shaking, his control hanging by a thread. He kissed my throat, nipped my bottom lip. I felt him everywhere.

"You're so wet," he rasped, nipping at my earlobe. He gripped my hips, both of us chest to chest, and bounced me up and down on his erection. Hard. Rough. So fucking right. The fire inside me built and built.

My moans and whimpers echoed in the small space. My fingers clung to him like he was my life raft.

"Oh... Oh, God. Oh my God."

I could feel him deep inside me, hitting my G-spot. With each thrust up, his pelvis ground against my clit, and another moan filled the space. He swallowed the noise in his mouth as my climax shot through me. Bright spots swam behind my eyes. The fire inside me burst, spreading through my body down to my toes.

With a last thrust, he followed me, chasing his own orgasm. He shuddered and finished inside me, his hands gripping me tightly.

His mouth softly skimmed over my neck, and I relished in the sensations that I had been denying myself for so long. Our heavy breaths filled the silence.

Content. Heavy. Full of bliss.

I should have known it wouldn't last. Nothing in life ever did.

CHAPTER 44
Dante

Another week had gone by.

Juliette and I fell into a routine. We'd have breakfast together, then I'd go to work. Sometimes she'd meet me for lunch in the city. Other days, she'd work on her St. Jean d'Arc School building project—a facility to provide education for future heathens of mayhem—in collaboration with the girls. And then we'd end the day by having dinner together. Sometimes we'd eat out, other days in.

Priest joined us today for dinner at our place.

After dinner, we made our way into the pool room and I watched Juliette attempt to play against my brother. I offered to help Juliette, but she refused it. It was her against Christian.

"Christian, just remember—" Juliette loved to taunt. "You lose and we'll put some Irish gangster portraits around your house." My brother gave her a dry look and she smiled sweetly. "It's the first and last time I'm calling you by your first name. I just wanted to see how it sounded."

"Actually, with Wynter around, I hear that name more than I have in all my life." It was true. We'd called him Priest for so long, we rarely ever used his given name. But now, it has circulated more and more. "It doesn't bother me."

My wife wedged her tongue between her teeth as she positioned herself. She was fucking adorable.

"It's a nice name." We both glanced her way, trying to determine whether she was joking or not. She must have felt our eyes on her because she turned her head and smiled softly. "Seriously, it's a nice name. Priest is kind of scary. But Christian... well, it's perfect."

"Woman, you're married to me," I reminded her in a growl.

Juliette grinned. "Your name is perfect too, hubs." Hubs? It was the first time she'd call me that, and fuck, I loved it. She returned her attention to the pool table. "But your brother has to tell me what's bothering him if not me calling him by his name." It didn't surprise me she picked up on it. "I... Well, I don't want to repeat it. We're family now and I only agitate family a certain way." She rolled her eyes playfully. "Just ask my brother."

I didn't think my brother would answer her. I certainly wouldn't divulge his aversion to the Irish. It was his story to tell, not mine.

"Come on, Wildling." I put my hands over hers, my chest to her back. It had my groin brushing against her backside and I had to stifle a groan. Way to get hard while we had company. "Let me help you get this game finished. Or my brother will be here all night."

And while I loved my brother, I'd rather be alone with my wife. "Hubs, your brother is always welcome. Of course he can stay all night."

I scoffed. There was nothing on this earth that would make my brother stay tonight.

"Irish gangsters." Priest's voice shattered the air. "I don't like Irish gangsters. Or the Irish in general."

Silence stretched. The pool game forgotten, Juliette let the pool stick fall to the table and she straightened up. I wrapped my arms around her, keeping her close. I didn't think she'd do anything and Priest would never hurt her, but it was hard to overcome the instinct.

"I'm Irish," Juliette reminded him softly.

Priest's lips tugged up. "Not anymore. Now you're one of us. You're a DiLustro."

She tilted her head, studying him. "Okay, but my parents were Irish." I knew what would come next and so did Priest. Yet, he didn't try to stop her. "So is your mom. At least partly." My brother's jaw clenched and his eyes turned a few shades darker. "My dad—Liam—told me something that stayed with me. Take it or leave it, although I hope you'll at least think about it."

Priest's gaze locked on my wife. It was probably the first time he saw her without her barriers up and constant snarky comments.

"What's that, Jules?"

It was right then and there, I knew. She was part of us—our family. Nothing and nobody would ever change that.

"He said it didn't matter what nationality, race, background you were. There are rotten eggs everywhere, but they don't make the whole batch rotten. Of course, the first time he passed on that little piece of wisdom, we happened to be on an actual farm where I was hunting for actual eggs. The farmer wasn't happy."

Laughter followed. Ghosts still lingered—more so around my brother than me—but the promise of the future shone brighter.

Most of the nights that followed, we found ourselves in the bedroom exploring each other's bodies. I fucking loved that Juliette was so curious —handcuffs or no. I didn't mind. She was curious about everything. Sex. My body. Even my work.

Toward the end of the week, we stayed in. My father and Juliette's aunt came for dinner. Although now that we were all seated around the dining room table, I wished we'd gone to a restaurant.

It was easier to limit the length of the visit when you were in a public place.

My father looked good. Happy. So did Juliette's aunt, Aisling. It had taken them decades to get to this point. I just hoped it wouldn't take Juliette and me decades to get to our happily ever after. We were close, I thought. Although, neither one of us had spoken those three little words.

I love you.

I'd loved her for so long, it was part of my every heartbeat. Juliette was a different story though. She kept herself guarded. I could understand it now that I knew what happened to her. She dealt with it on her own, building her walls, and it'd take a while to break them down.

"You look good." My father sat next to me, smiling. "I'm happy for you."

I loved him. I really did. But I resented him. It was hard not to. I resented that he was so distant during our life that he never noticed Mother taking her anger out on my little brother. I resented that more than anything. If she wanted to beat the crap out of me—fine. But she'd put Priest through hell and my father had been completely oblivious.

I wasn't even sure that he'd understand if I told him. Not that I ever would. I'd given my little brother my word.

Juliette must have sensed my tension because her hand came to rest on my thigh, squeezing it gently. She understood. I knew deep down—even without spoken words—that she understood it.

"Thanks."

"So what have you two been up to?" Aisling asked.

"Just stuff," Juliette answered, smiling. "We're just trying to get some kind of routine going."

"Good, good," Father said. "Routine is good for the kids."

My wife froze.

"It's too soon to talk about children," I stated calmly. "We just got married and want to have time for us before we decide on kids."

Tension left Juliette's shoulders and she sighed a relieved breath.

Aisling chimed in with a wide smile. "You're right," she agreed. "Wynter says you're busy with the school project. I am so excited to see how it turns out. St. Jean d'Arc will be something unique for sure."

Juliette met my gaze, then returned her attention back to her aunt. "I'm excited too. It will be a huge accomplishment."

"We'll all be there for the opening," I told her playfully. "Just think of all the troublemakers like you and your friends stirring up trouble. I can't wait to watch the four of you scold them."

The dinner concluded without any disasters. No reminders of past wrongdoings or ghosts.

After our guests left, Juliette changed into a tiny pair of silk shorts and a matching tank top. She preferred to sleep in as little as possible. I preferred her sleeping naked and usually, by the time the sun came up in the morning, that's exactly what she was, in my arms where she belonged, no less.

It was hard to keep my gaze away from her. She sat next to me, her bare legs folded and scrolling through her phone.

We moved into the small living room. It was her favorite room in the house. The signs of her were slowly overtaking the house. Her scrunchie in the key bowl. Lotion on the nightstand. Her ChapSticks. She seemed to have one in every room.

"Let's play pool tonight," she uttered out of the blue. I cocked my eyebrow at the unexpected announcement. "I need to work on my skills and you are an expert. Your brother said you won every pool game except for one. Who better to teach me?" My lips tugged up. She had an amazing memory and cataloged everything anyone ever told her. At least it seemed that way. "Unless you prefer I find another teach—"

I didn't let her finish. "I'm the only one allowed to teach you anything," I growled.

"So let's play," she remarked. "We have nothing better to do."

"I certainly have better things in mind," I said in a low voice. "I thought you said you don't care for playing pool."

She shrugged. "Correction, I don't care for playing pool with others. You might be an exception."

An amused breath left me, picturing Juliette reading rules on shooting pool.

"So, yes?" she asked, her eyes glimmering with hope.

"As if I could ever refuse you."

She swung her legs and jumped to her feet, squealing in delight. She pressed a kiss to my mouth, grabbed my hand, then dragged me toward the other side of the house where the pool room was.

We entered the billiard lounge and Juliette's eyes darted left, right, then back to the left.

"I really like this room," she remarked. "Every time I step inside, I feel like I'm in a bar."

"I know you've seen plenty of those," I retorted, tapping her lightly on the ass. "After all, it was where I first spotted you."

She gave me one of those carefree smiles and my heart skipped a beat. It only happened around my wife whenever she smiled or laughed.

"I didn't see you," she commented as she took the room in. There were four armchairs, a fully stocked minibar and of course, the professional pool table. The walls were decorated with movie posters in frames from movies that were filmed in the States. *Scarface. The Untouchables. The Godfather.*

"I meant to tell you when your brother was here. This decor is very original," she said, her gaze lingering on the famous mobsters.

I grinned. "I knew you'd like it."

"I can't help but notice they are all Italian." She sauntered through the room to the pool cue. "If I win against you, you have to put up a poster for *Gangs of New York*."

I barked out a laugh. "You got it, Wildling."

She was a quick study. Twenty minutes of instruction later, a bit of practice, and she was ready. Not to beat me in a game of pool, but to at least play against me.

Juliette bent over the table, holding the pool stick, trying to hit the nine ball. Her tongue was wedged between her lips in concentration as her eyes narrowed on the ball. She missed the first one. It was my turn next. I sent the ball into the pocket.

She moved and I flicked a curious glance her way. "What? It's my turn," she remarked, then seeing my expression, she added hesitantly, "Right? The rules are kind of confusing."

I didn't have the heart to tell her she wouldn't get a turn until I missed getting the ball into the pocket. So I straightened up and let her take a turn.

She positioned herself again, bending over the table.

"Want me to help you?" I offered.

She threw me a glance over her shoulder. "You trying to make me lose?"

I grinned. "Never."

"Okay, then help me," she caved. I came up behind her and leaned over her, my chest pressing up against her back. She hadn't been successful sending any of the balls into the pockets so far. My hand guided Juliette's as we sent her ball flying into the pocket.

For a second, Juliette's eyes widened and she stared at the table as if she expected the ball to reappear. Then she squealed enthusiastically, turning her head and pressing a kiss to my cheek.

257

"Did you see that?" she gushed, glancing back at the pool table. "The ball went in."

I smiled at her enthusiasm. "I did. Great job."

"Okay, so now it's your turn." I nodded. "Do you want me to help you?"

I chuckled. "I'm okay."

Positioning the cue tip of the pool stick on the table, I decided this game was best played if I saw a smile on my wife's face. So I shot and missed. It was her turn again and I helped her. Needless to say, when we came to the end, my wife won.

"It seems I'll be hanging up a movie poster from *Gangs of New York*," I concluded, watching her wide smile and her sparkling eyes. She shifted her body around so she could face me and my gaze glided down her body slowly.

Her nipples pushed through the thin material of her silky camisole. Her bare legs tempted me to touch them and leave marks.

And I stared at those blue eyes that reminded me of the Ionian Sea, feeling peace wash over me.

For the first time in such a long time, I was happy.

CHAPTER 45
Juliette

"T was the night before Christmas," I rhymed as I swung my bag, back and forth, "when all through the house, not a creature was stirring, not even a mouse."

The words of the poem kept repeating in my head, over and over again.

Christmas was my favorite time of the year. Usually it was about the only time that we resembled a family. I had two bags of gifts, Killian trailing alongside me while handling something on the phone. He was in his first year of college, and suddenly he was very important. At least he thought so.

I rolled my eyes; he was more annoying than anything. At the tender age of thirteen, I thought myself to be the most important girl in the world. After all, I'd be going to high school soon.

"Wait here, Jules," he ordered, stopping by Tiffany's.

"Are you buying a gift from Tiffany's for Wynter and me?" I squealed excitedly.

"Stay here," he ordered. In typical brotherly fashion, he ignored me and entered the store. Curious and a bit nosy, I pressed my face against the cold glass, but couldn't see anything apart from Killian's broad shoulders.

The cold wind swept through, sending a chill through my bones. Winters

259

in New York were frigid. I couldn't wait until Killian, Dad, and I flew back to California.

Warm weather. Palm trees. That was heaven.

Glancing around, I took cover in the alley where I hoped the wind wouldn't whip against my legs as badly. I felt the chill even through my jeans and heavy coat. It was just impossible to warm up, so I started jumping up and down, my ponytail whipping back and forth.

"Hurry up. Hurry up," I muttered impatiently, my teeth chattering.

A kicked can echoed through the alley, startling me. Another kick and I mustered up the courage to turn around, only to come face-to-face with a man. A stranger. His features were obscured by a hoodie but his hands weren't. Glinting in the light of the streetlamp, I could see he was holding a knife.

"What are you doing, little girl?" he drawled in a thick New York accent.

"N-nothing," I stuttered, my eyes darting over his shoulder to the store-front where I should have been waiting for Killian.

He took a step forward, and I instinctively took one back. Except now, it put me even deeper into the dark alley. I knew I'd made a mistake. My little heart pounded against my chest, threatening to crack it open.

Another step toward me. Another mirrored step backward.

My heart continued to drum under my rib cage, but still I tried to be brave. Smart. That was what Dad always said. Be smart. So I attempted to scare him off. "M-my brother's with me."

He chuckled. "Then I'll slice his throat too."

My eyes widened, then darted around in horror. I opened my mouth, readying to scream when another voice interrupted.

"Take another step toward her, and I'll shoot you."

My eyes snapped in the direction of the voice. A tall boy stood there, about Killian's age. Tall. Strong. He flicked a gaze my way, then returned his attention back to the man with the knife.

"Last warning," he said. "Get lost or I will end you."

"I know you," the old man hissed.

"No, you don't know me," the boy-slash-man with eyes as dark as midnight claimed. "If you did, you'd be running for your life."

The man must have decided to live and that I wasn't worth it, because he scurried away. No, he bolted. I watched him disappear while I held my breath, and it wasn't until he was out of my sight that I was able to release it.

"You okay?" the boy asked softly.

I swallowed, extending my hand with the bags. "H-here, you can take it all," I offered. I felt disoriented, worried that maybe this boy saved me from the other thug, only to rob me himself. It wasn't worth dying over. It would seem shopping right before Christmas was a bad idea, after all.

He smiled, pushing the bags gently back. "You keep the bags."

My eyes darted between him and the bags. "You... you don't want them?"

He chuckled. "What am I going to do with Victoria's Secret bags?" he mused as the smell of rain and damp forest mixed with the crispy winter air, filling my senses.

My cheeks heated when I realized what I was holding in my hands.

"It's for my aunt." Wynter and I wanted her to find someone, and this could be the first step. At least, that was what Cosmopolitan *magazine had told us. "I'm buying for my dad next, but I have money," I mumbled, embarrassed. "I don't have anything else to give you." I drowned in his dark gaze. I had never seen such dark eyes. They were like the obsidian pools of night.*

"What makes you think I want something?" he asked curiously.

"Don't all muggers want something?" I retorted.

He smiled, his dark eyes shining like the midnight sky. He was beautiful.

"All right, then," he agreed, amusement sparking his gaze. "How about..." He appeared to think as I held my breath. What could he possibly want? "Your hair scrunchie."

I reached up to touch my ponytail. "My scrunchie?" I repeated, confused.

He grinned this time. "Yes. That way when I find you again and you're older, you'll remember that you owe me."

"And if I don't recognize you?" I wondered.

He smirked confidently. "Don't worry, I'll recognize you."

This time, I smiled too. "So you'll be like my shadow prince, stalker, or something?"

He nodded. "Or something," he confirmed.

I pulled my hair band out, my mahogany strands cascading down my shoulders. He extended his hand and I dropped my hot-pink scrunchie into it, the bright color looking silly in his large palm.

"Thank you," I murmured, offering him a big smile. "For saving me. One day, maybe I'll be the one to save you."

As he walked away, sadness lingered in my chest when I realized I had no way of knowing whether I'd ever see him again. I could only hold out hope.

My eyes opened, the memory of the boy and what he did for me still vivid in my mind as I looked around the dark room. I hadn't thought about that night in so long. I had never quite forgotten it, but I didn't think of it—and that boy—as often as I did in the beginning. It happened when I was thirteen, Christmas shopping with Killian during my visit to New York. Aunt Aisling never came to visit the East Coast, and that time, Wynter remained behind with her.

My face pressed against the pillow and a heavy arm hung around me, the images from that night flashing through my mind. The boy. His smile. Those eyes. I stared at the darkness around me, remembering the boy who saved me. He smelled like forest and rain. And when he smiled, something in his eyes lit up. Warm and comforting. Like home. Or belonging.

It reminded me of—

"Go back to sleep, Wildling," my husband rumbled against my head, spooning me. The dream dissipated into a distant memory the moment his teeth grazed over my neck, nipping on my skin, before sucking harshly.

I inhaled deeply, letting his scent into my lungs. It was so familiar from the moment I met him. My memory nudged at my sleepy brain, but the moment his hard erection pressed against my ass, it was game over.

Pleasure shot through me. Hot and needy. The memory forgotten, I said the first thing that came to my mind.

"Then why are you turning me on," I moaned as his hands roamed over my body. He pushed the straps of my silky pajama top off my shoulders and cool air brushed against my heated skin.

I rolled my ass back against his hard length. His groan sounded in his chest and he grabbed my hip, grinding me harder against him. Heat drifted between us. Need drifted south, throbbing between my legs.

The rustle of sheets and Dante turned me in his arms, then rolled onto his back, pulling me on top of him. It'd become our go-to position. He didn't trust my panic not to kick in.

I leaned forward and pressed my lips against his. "I want you on top of me."

He watched me through his half-lidded eyes. Possessive darkness lurked there.

For me.

He must have seen something in my gaze that assured him of my request. In one swift move, he flipped me so that I lay under him. His gaze traveled over my exposed breasts and a soft growl escaped his lips as he took one nipple into his mouth.

His teeth grazed against the sensitive peaks, sucking steadily while one hand traveled further south and slipped into my pajama bottoms. His middle finger brushed over my clit and a moan slipped through my lips.

"Dante."

A satisfied growl vibrated through his chest.

His fingers moved down from my clit and slipped inside me. I gasped, arching my back. His lips brushed against my ear and whispered, "I love my name on your lips." His fingers moved in and out of me, while his teeth bit down on my earlobe. "You'll scream it, Wildling."

I frantically nodded my head in agreement. I'd do anything. As long as he kept doing this. His fingers pumped in and out of me ruthlessly, drawing whimpers and moans from my throat. My silky top slid down my body, bundled up around my waist.

Dante's mouth left my earlobe, then traveled down my neck, over my breasts and stomach until it came between my thighs. His fingers wrapped around my top and pajama bottoms, then dragged them down my legs.

His eyes glimmered like black skies as he stared at my sprawled body, my parted legs.

"Look at that glistening pussy," Dante grunted. "Are you hungry for my mouth or my cock?"

"Both," I whimpered.

Parting my legs wider, he hooked them over his shoulders and latched on to my sex. I moaned into the pillow, my hips bucking at the sensation as he dragged his tongue over my folds.

Dante's tongue circled around my clit, over and over again, and I arched my back, grinding against his mouth.

"Please," I moaned, rolling my hips, needing his mouth on my clit.

He chuckled darkly. "Here?" he taunted softly, nipping softly at my clit.

"Yes!" I cried out, my pussy throbbing. His fingers, still deep inside me, stroked my G-spot, while his tongue laved at me. I thrust my hips up, grinding against his face. Dante flicked his tongue over my clit hard, over and over again.

"Dante... Dante... oh, God." My cries became screams. My moans louder and louder.

My hips bucked under his expert tongue. My muscles clenched around his fingers. The orgasm exploded through me, violent like a category-five hurricane.

As my body shuddered under his assault, Dante showered me with praise. "Good girl," he murmured, kissing the inside of my thighs. "Such a good girl."

I was throbbing. Pleasure just wracked my body and I was already greedy for more. As he came to rest his forearms by my head, his cock brushed against my throbbing pussy.

"Dante," I whimpered, arching against him.

"Do you want my cock?"

"Yes, yes," I moaned. "Please, Dante. Fuck me. Fuck, I need you so much."

He pushed the tip of his cock, dripping with precum, into my pussy. "Please. *Please.*"

He slammed all the way into me, and we both moaned. My head fell back and my eyes rolled back in my head, my spine arching off the bed.

His hands grabbed my hips as he pulled out, only to slam back in again.

"Are you mine?" He thrust into me again. *Hard.* "Who does this pussy belong to?"

"Yours," I moaned. "I'm all yours."

He pulled almost all the way out, only to thrust back into me deeply. Roughly. Then he increased his pace and intensity, taking me fast and hard.

He was right. I screamed his name that night.

I woke up the next morning later than usual.

To an empty bed and not a husband in sight. Glancing at the clock, nine a.m. stared back at me in glowing green. It was later than usual. Dante kept me up until five a.m., running his hands and mouth all over my body. He drew so many orgasms out of me that I had to beg him for a reprieve or risk passing out.

My lips curved into a smile as I thought of all the ways he'd made me come. This thing with him was raw and so intense and I feared it'd burn out.

I shook my head, chasing the thoughts away. I slid out of bed, my muscles achy.

"A shower will help," I murmured to myself.

It helped. Ten minutes later, I was dressed in black leggings and a three-quarter-sleeved off-the-shoulder shirt, the color of the bluest skies. Not bothering with shoes or socks, I padded through the house in search of my husband.

I knew he wouldn't have left the house without us having breakfast first. He insisted it would be our tradition. To have breakfast together every morning and dinner together every night. Unless he was traveling.

As I reached the bottom step of the ground floor, I heard his voice coming from the office. My feet were soundless against the white marble as I made my way through the foyer to the opposite side of the house.

Slick furniture and expensive framed paintings greeted me. That was one thing nobody could take away from this house—it was decorated to the nines with slick modern furniture mixed with a certain old elegance.

I was almost by Dante's office when I heard multiple voices and my steps faltered. The tense words exchanged inside the office had my stomach twisting in knots.

"She'll have your balls when she finds out," Basilio stated, his voice coming through a speaker.

"We should tell Juliette," Emory chimed in.

My heart picked up pace, each beat like a whip against my ribs. Something about her tone sent dread through me.

"No." Dante's voice was low. Dark. Deadly. "And none of you will ever mention it again."

My brows furrowed, wondering what it was that Emory wanted to tell me. Maybe something happened? Worry shot through me and my hand reached for the door handle, pausing in midair when Priest's words came through.

"If anyone finds out we drugged Juliette to marry you, there'll be hell to pay. And war to wage. And we can't afford it right now. Not with Sofia Volkov attacking us."

"She's bound to find out you slipped the drug into her drink," Emory tried again.

I froze at hearing the words. Did he just say that Dante slipped a drug into my drink?

Drugged me? Dante drugged me. Oh my God, Dante drugged me.

Old ghosts came knocking. My throat squeezed. Images haunted.

"Technically it was Priest," I thought I heard Basilio's voice say; I couldn't tell. My pulse thundered in my eardrums so loud, drowning out the rest of their conversation.

I blinked my eyes, the burning liquified and blurred my vision. My ears buzzed.

He lied to me. He betrayed me.

My chest cracked. The pressure on my heart built and an ache so deep it was hard to breathe spread through me. The rawness of it made it feel like I was bleeding out.

My gaze lowered and I expected to see my crimson blood on the pristine white marble beneath my feet. Yet, there was nothing. The white marble hid the black heart.

A hollowness formed in my chest. That ache grew dull and expanded over me, leaving a dark hole in my chest.

As a tear rolled down my cheek, I steeled my spine, shoving the pain somewhere deep. Glancing around, I spotted one of Dante's easy-to-reach weapon spots. In a daze, I walked to it, then brushed my fingerprint over the code.

The safe opened and I studied its contents. Gun. Swiss knife. A blade.

I reached for the gun, but images of a dead Dante didn't sit well with me, and I didn't trust myself not to shoot him. Not right now.

My fingers wrapped around the blade.

As I made my way back to Dante's office, blood roared in my ears. Fury surged through my veins. And red crept through my vision.

I let the anger take over. My heart pounded, shattering with each passing beat.

I shoved the door open and Dante's eyes snapped my way.

"Let's have a conversation, husband," I said softly, calmly even. But emotion scratched at my throat and burned in my eyes.

Dante watched me with those eyes, the colors of midnight skies.

I grasped for the anger. For the rage that he deserved. I wanted to scream. I wanted to lash out. Instead, I let the coldness wash over me and steal some of the pain away.

Otherwise, I feared it'd tear me apart.

Dante had set me free, only to rip my heart out. Everything with him had been a lie.

I never took my eyes off him, letting the walls build higher and higher, and this time, nobody would penetrate them.

My husband didn't care about me. He took what he wanted, had even resorted to drugging me. We'd been married for weeks, and he had had plenty of chances to come clean. He didn't.

"Hang up, Dante," I said calmly. "Or I'll blow up this city's network and leave it in the dark as I leave town."

"Fuck." Multiple voices came through the line. "Juliette—"

Dante ended the call, cutting off his brother.

Silence, heavy and damning, crept through the room like a venomous snake. Dante stood up from his spot, circled his desk and leaned against it, casually slipping his hands into pockets. His eyes that usually burned with heat were now cold and hard. He ran his gaze over my face, then to my hand clutching the knife.

His eyes came back up, holding my stare.

"Let me explain, Wildling." His voice was so fragile, as though all of him might break. But I couldn't feel sorry for him. I wouldn't. He broke *me*. He shattered *my* heart to pieces.

Anger, red hot, seared through me, and instantly the coldness was gone, leaving in its wake burning lava. Before I even realized I'd moved, I held the blade to my husband's throat, the sharp piece grazing his skin.

"Shut the fuck up before I shove this knife up your ass," I hissed, my voice shaking with anger. He didn't flinch. He didn't move. "Or down your throat. And don't think I won't. In fact, I'll enjoy it very much."

I remained still, anger urging me to slice his throat. To make him pay for making a fool out of me. For betraying me. For lying to me. And worst of all, for hurting me and making me believe any of it was real.

I didn't dare move any further, the blade dangerously close to ending his life.

CHAPTER 46
Dante

The look of betrayal she wore sliced through me.

Looking at her hurt. Hearing the tremors in her voice hurt. It tore at my chest; it suffocated. My jaw clenched as I stared at her. The sight of her glimmering blue eyes staring at me with so much pain that it suffocated me.

I stood up, putting my hands into my pockets. They shook with the fear of losing her.

Fucking Christ.

I had to get a grip. Studying her face, I searched for words. I couldn't find any. Maybe I could start at the beginning.

"Let me explain, Wildling."

She was on me in the next breath. I fought my instinct to block her. I wouldn't be able to live with myself if I hurt her, so I forced my every muscle to remain still while she held a blade to my throat. And by the look on her face, she wanted to slice it.

"Shut the fuck up before I shove this knife up your ass," she gritted on a hiss, blue lightning flashing in her eyes. "Or down your throat. And don't think I won't," she threatened, although she really didn't have to. I fucking believed her. "In fact, I'll enjoy it very much."

Jesus H. Christ.

I'd worried about Sasha Nikolaev's unhinged ass at my wedding. No wonder he smirked, the fucker probably knew Juliette was just as nuts as he was.

But then I knew that. Didn't I?

The evidence was right in front of my face all along. Stealing. Kicking me in the balls. Destroying Grandfather's car.

But then she repaired it, too, my reason whispered. My rationale made no fucking sense. Bottom line was that Juliette was slightly unhinged. Wild. Deadly, even.

Although in this instance I couldn't blame her. I'd hurt her. I'd betrayed her.

A buzz of trepidation crawled up my spine and snaked into my veins. My little brother was right. I should have told her and begged for forgiveness. She shouldn't have found out this way.

Fuck, fuck, fuck! *Fuck!*

A thousand icy needles pierced my skin and into my heart at the hate in her eyes. My heartbeat spiked with a panic I hadn't felt in so long it stole my fucking breath from me.

"So what now?" Roughness edged my tone, my heart pounding hard enough to bruise me. "That's it? We're not going to talk it through?"

She glared at me, then smiled. Darkly. "Talk about what?" she hissed. "How you drugged me?" The vein in her neck pulsed, her hand holding the knife slightly trembled. "Did you grope me while I was all compliant and under the influence?" She sneered. "You must have realized it was the only way you could get me to bed, huh? You're just like them."

Them. There was my confirmation. Secrets she kept close to her heart. Comparison to them felt like a bullet to my heart. Fury and tension knifed through my gut. Getting stabbed hurt less than this.

"I didn't touch you," I gritted. My jaw clenched so hard it shot pain to my temples. "Not even when you tried to grope *me* and rip my clothes off."

"You fucking lied to me," she roared, her bottom lip trembling. The sharp blade of her knife pressed harder against my skin. Warm liquid trickled down my throat and I guessed she cut the skin.

I could taste her anger on my tongue. It simmered and simmered, until it exploded. Like a volcano.

"Did it ever occur to you to ask *me* to marry you?" she roared. "Or to ask *me* out on a date?" The pain on her face was like a punch in the gut. "No, you didn't even bother to ask me what I wanted. You went to my father. Why? Because you wanted to force my hand?"

"That wasn't my intention."

It didn't matter. I'd shattered her heart. Maybe I deserved her wrath.

Except, I loved her. I couldn't live without her. It took every ounce of effort to swallow past the lump in my throat.

"I love you, Wildling," I said, my voice low. It might not have been the best time to profess my love but here it was. I was putting it all out there. "I've loved you for so fucking long. I waited for you to come around. To give us a chance. But you're so goddamn stubborn."

The expression on her face told me clearly she didn't care about my justification—nor my love—but I kept talking anyhow. I still held on to the hope that she'd see the reasoning behind my actions.

"Let me fix it," I begged. The words burned my throat like alcohol against a raw wound. "Let me prove to you that I'm worthy of your love."

Her lip curved into a snicker, disgust crossing her expression.

"Love," she snickered. "I don't fucking love you. I could never love someone so fucking manipulative."

She might as well have sliced my throat because those words were a stab to my cold black heart. It hurt like a motherfucker. But I kept my expression detached while the wheels in my brain turned.

A lengthy silence filled the space between us, strangling my lungs. I wished, just like when I was a little boy, that I could turn back time and make it alright. Fix it before it all went to hell.

The air crackled with tension and a thousand needles pricked my skin. My gaze fixed on my wife, I tasted her hate. Her bitterness. Her pain.

"I'm leaving you," she said, her voice full of unrestrained loathing. "And you won't be coming after me."

I leaned forward, letting the cold blade press harder against my skin. "I'll always follow you, Wildling." I couldn't let her go. I'd never let her go. "Besides, you made a promise," I reminded her, "never to run."

"That was before I knew what a pig you were." Her eyes turned a shade lighter, as if her pain were bleeding into them. "You are fucking crazy if you think I'll ever forgive you, Dante," she hissed. "I can't even stand to look at you."

Okay, that fucking hurt.

A sardonic breath left me, hiding my own pain and focusing on hers. "You are so fucking stubborn. You're attracted to me. You can feel it. Yet you'd rather cling to your hate and choose to end something that could be good for both of us."

She scoffed. "Excuse me for not just falling down to my knees for you. You got some fucking nerve. You drugged me. Married me without my consent. And now you just want me to overlook it and pretend it never happened. Is that it?"

It sounded worse when spoken aloud, but she knew I never touched her. We were bound to end up together. She knew it. Deep down, I knew she did.

"I was fucking wrong, yes," I said, letting out a bitter laugh. "But I'd been patient for goddamn months. Years."

"So you decided it was time to drug me," she noted calmly. Dangerously.

"It was the wrong thing to do," I repeated, my jaw clenching so tight that it made my ears buzz. "I didn't touch you that night. I just rumpled the sheets and slept next to you. Even when you tried to strip my clothes off, I made sure they remained on." Her cheeks burned, but not from arousal. This time it was from her fury.

"You broke my trust," she finally said, and it tore me apart. "This is over."

"Far from over. There's no divorce in our world," I snapped. "You know that as well as I do. It was the reason my father couldn't marry your aunt."

Our gazes clashed and so did our wills. I should have known she wasn't the forgiving type.

"Then we'll be married, but we won't live together."

She whirled around, leaving the faint scent of sugarplums behind. Every fiber in me urged me to go after her, but I knew it wasn't the right time.

"Don't leave town or I'll go to war with your family," I warned softly, but the vehemence showed through. It had the desired effect. Juliette stilled by the door, her posture stiff and her hand gripping the knife, prob-ably contemplating throwing it across the room and lodging it into my heart. "I'll tear this world apart for you," I vowed.

She didn't say anything else. She didn't even acknowledge my words.

My throat worked with a hard swallow past the lump lodged there while a horrible ache in my chest swelled. The tension barely held me upright and I folded over, hands on my knees. The pressure inside me strangled my heart and my lungs, making me suffocate from the inside out.

Slam.

The mansion shook and the house of cards started crumbling.

Then there was silence. Empty and hollow. Just like me.

CHAPTER 47
Juliette

My control was slipping.

If I didn't get out of here now, I feared I'd use the knife on him, then set this whole fucking house on fire. That was how fucking mad I was.

But even stronger than the fury was this bloodcurdling pain clawing at my chest. My heart hurt so fucking bad that I thought it would shatter for good.

I'd adapt to it. I knew it firsthand. It would hover in my chest until it became part of my every breath and every heartbeat. Or until death came knocking on my door.

Tears blurred my vision, cascading down my face as I made my way out of the house. Luckily my purse was right at the door, next to Dante's keys and my flats I kicked off last night. I slid them on, then headed outside, slamming the door behind me so hard it felt like the entire house shook.

Ironically, the first signs of spring danced through the air, mocking my dark mood. I drove around the city that suddenly felt dark and unwelcoming for hours.

His words echoed in my brain and screams bubbled in my throat with the need to drown it all out. Coming to a red light, I pressed my forehead against the wheel. A tornado of emotions swirled through me and I had no way to get them out. I needed an outlet.

My control finally snapped. "Fuuuuck!" I screamed at the top of my burning lungs. "Fuck, fuck, fuck!"

I banged my forehead against the wheel like a crazy person. There was a high-pitched ringing in my ears. I wasn't dying but fuck it felt like it. This was the type of pain that tore at your insides.

Beep. Beep.

A honk of a car penetrated through my hysterical screaming. I stilled, my voice frozen in my throat. I straightened up in my seat and blinked. Then took a deep breath and exhaled. The world slowly came back into focus.

The intensity of my emotions slowly faded and numbness settled in. Empty and cold.

I resumed driving, circling the city. When I drove by the street where The Library at Gilt Bar was, a brief pang in my chest was the only reaction. The numbness had started to take over.

But still as I drove by, I couldn't tear my gaze from the door that led to the memory.

Bang.

I slammed the brakes, my head whipped around.

"Are you fucking kidding me?" I groaned. Dante's side mirror hung, half torn off. I glanced behind me. "God, not today," I muttered.

Of all the fucking days to hit another car, today was not it. Putting the car in park, I got out and went around to assess the damage. My hands shook as I pushed them into my hair.

Why did I have this incredible urge to grab a baseball bat and start smashing vehicles? I took calming breaths. One. Two. Three.

"Beating cars with baseball bats is bad," I murmured to myself. My pulse slowed, the adrenaline that wanted to rush through my veins and take over the rage receded. "Thou shall not damage others' property." Then, remembering what Dante had done, I added, "Except your husband's."

"That doesn't sound very good for your husband."

A deep voice came from behind me and I whirled around, coming face-to-face with Kian. What in the fuck was he doing here?

"I'm actually here for you," he answered my unspoken question. Unless I actually said it out loud.

"How did you know where I was?" I asked suspiciously.

He gave me an exasperated look. "I knew your identity all along, Juliette. I was actually on my way to your home."

My brows furrowed.

"Why?" I asked suspiciously. Now that I knew who he really was, wariness was at the forefront of my mind. "I mean, you probably have better things to do than stalk me. And I already have a stalker."

His lips curved up. That silver-gray scruff on his face gave him that hot daddy look.

"Your husband, I presume," he noted. His voice was deep and raspy. I could almost picture how women swooned over his looks and grunts he'd produce when he—

I shook my head. Why in the fuck was I even thinking about that? I didn't give a shit about Kian. Some Brazilian drug lord. I was done with all men in the underworld.

Liar, I thought. To which the sensible part of my brain yelled, *Shut up!*

"I didn't say anything," he remarked dryly. Lovely, now I was losing my mind too.

"Not you," I said through a tired sigh. "I was talking to myself." His brow rose but he didn't say anything.

"Is this your car I banged into?" I asked.

"Rental."

"Well, send the bill to Dante DiLustro," I uttered, my husband's name on my lips tasting bitter. "Feel free to mark it up."

"So generous of you." He was mocking me, no doubt. It wasn't as if the guy needed the money.

"Back to the original question," I said, taking a small step back. You could never be too cautious with drug lords. Well, Kian was the brother of a drug lord. But whatever—tomato, tomahto. The point was, just look at the one I married. He was certainly no Boy Scout. "Why are you here for me?"

He watched me wordlessly and I found myself fidgeting, my fingers gripping the material of my shirt. Correspondence via email or text was easier to handle—it let you hide behind an unknown, cryptic number. Or maybe not, considering he'd learned my identity.

"I have one more name for you," he declared and I stiffened. I hoped he didn't know, but somehow he wouldn't be a very good criminal if he didn't bother to trace his clients.

"You knew all along it was me?" I questioned and his reply was a curt nod. "Why do you run your security-slash-background agency?"

"What else should I do?" he questioned.

I shrugged my shoulders. "Your brother's cartel. Considering you're a drug lord and all."

A sardonic breath left him. "I've never been called that before."

I rolled my eyes. "Probably not to your face."

He tilted his head. "Probably," he agreed. "Maybe I got out of the cartel," he remarked casually. "Maybe I passed that on to someone younger. Or maybe I haven't gotten into it like my brother."

I scoffed. "Right." His dark eyes flashed with something, although I couldn't read the expression. Not that I cared right now. "So, the name," I said. "Might as well give it to me. Although next time, please don't bother with a personal delivery."

"See, that makes me want to deliver it that way from now on."

"I swear, you men are annoying the shit out of me today," I said through gritted teeth. "Just give me the name and be on your way."

"You won't like it."

I swallowed. "Why?"

He didn't answer, just handed me an envelope. I took it.

"Reevaluate your priorities, Juliette."

That was all he said, and before I could utter another word, he left me standing in the middle of the street. He didn't get into the truck I banged up. Instead he went to the sidewalk full of pedestrians.

I blinked and the man was gone.

As the sun set, I finally made my way to a hotel.

I pulled up at the first one I spotted. Luckily for me it was The Ritz-Carlton.

Parking Dante's Rover out front, I grabbed my purse and let the valet park it, heading for the reception desk.

"May I help you?"

The receptionist greeted me with a bright smile. It made me feel even worse.

"I need a room," I stated, lowering my eyes and digging through my purse. Dante's black Amex was still with me, so I just gave her that. Her eyes flickered to the card, then the name on it. "Indefinitely," I added.

I wouldn't risk war between our families. Until I could get my shit together and think of something, I'd stay here.

The receptionist took it after a brief moment of hesitation. "May I see your ID?"

Annoyance flared in my chest. I was tired, emotionally drained. I just wanted to go into a room and sleep. I hadn't done a single productive thing today, and yet, I felt like I'd been run over by a bus.

No, just my husband's lies, I thought wryly.

I dug inside my wallet for my license and handed it to the receptionist. She disappeared into the back office—no doubt to validate my identity and the fact I held DiLustro's black Amex—while I turned my attention to my phone.

There were two dozen messages and a handful of missed calls. All from my friends. One from Dad and one from Aunt Aisling.

I felt eyes on me and looked up to find the receptionist back with an even brighter smile that almost blinded me.

"All good." She beamed. "Your husband confirmed you have unlimited spending."

My first inclination was to snap at her for calling Dante my husband, but then I took a different approach. I smiled sweetly with a fuck-you edge to it. The receptionist's smile dimmed although it wasn't aimed at her.

"That's so lovely," I told her, smiling sweetly. "In that case, I insist that you ask your chef to be prepared to cook all your best dishes for the next month. On my husband. And please send someone to the nearest shelter and ask what they need. A night at the hotel, a day at the spa, anything and everything. It's on him." Then, just in case she questioned it, I added, "It's on us. My wedding gift."

278

Her eyes widened, almost popping out of their sockets. "Everyone at the shelter? Everything?" she stuttered.

I gave another try at my sweet smile. An honest one this time. "Yes. Make sure all their charges go on that black card. Got it?"

Twenty minutes later, there was a five-hundred-thousand-dollar charge on Dante's black Amex. It didn't make me feel better.

I entered the impersonal hotel room and the welcome was as expected. *Cold.*

Locking the door behind me, I made my way deeper into the penthouse suite and sank onto the couch. My eyes traveled over the sleek furniture. Something about this room made me feel alone. Not just alone, but lonely.

The gaping, hollow feeling in my chest slowly spread, allowing all the feelings I'd been trying hard to keep at bay to pour in. Each breath splintered into a painful throb. The pressure built, my heart ached. I blinked away the burning behind my eyes. *Unsuccessfully.*

A lone tear rolled down my face, and it cracked the dam. Tears poured down my cheeks like a damn waterfall. I hated it. I wished there was a way to harden myself and not feel a damn thing.

Every breath squeezed. I couldn't drag enough air into my lungs, the buzzing in my ears increasing with each passing second.

Not bothering to strip off my clothes, I crawled under the cool, high-thread-count sheets. Curling into a fetal position, I shut my eyes, hoping that sleep would find me. It didn't. Instead, images of Dante taunted me.

His smile. His stories. The way he kissed me. How he let me cuff him.

It was the latter that broke me.

The pressure behind my eyes exploded and the sobs crawled up my throat, wracking my body. Tears trickled down into my ear, onto the pillow, their saltiness staining my lips.

And just like that day almost a decade ago, my sobs remained unheard. They were quiet sounds trapped in the cold hotel room, suffocating me once more. Something inside me broke.

I felt utterly alone. Just like that night ten years ago.

CHAPTER 48
Dante

Pain wrapped around my throat and refused to let go.

I'd had some shitty moments in my life. Even my childhood didn't come close to this pain.

The skin on my back itched at the memories. *Whack.*

The way the belt would swish through the air before it slashed across my back. The cold air against the raw skin.

"You're just like your papà," Mamma hissed, her eyes hateful and full of anger. At me. At Christian. "Confess your sins. Both of you are children of the devil."

Then she made us go to Sunday mass again, but afterward, she made us repent. For what, I didn't know.

She grabbed my shoulders and shook me so hard, it gave me whiplash. The world blurred and my teeth rattled.

All the while I clutched the little toy car my grandpa gave me. He was Mamma's papà, but he was good. Kind. Nothing like Mamma. But I shouldn't have brought it along. I knew better. Even my little brother knew. He warned me to leave it at home.

Except I loved it so much, I wanted to keep it with me.

Mamma snatched the toy out of my hands and threw it across the sanctuary. It hit the wall and pieces flew into the air, skidding across the floor.

Then Mamma shoved me back onto my knees. Pain shot through my thighs and I whimpered. Whether in pain or for the toy, I didn't know.

Whack.

Another slash across my back and my eyes blurred. I refused to cry, but a tear made its way down my cheek. I felt Christian's sad blue eyes on me. He bit his lip so hard, blood trickled down his chin.

He knew his turn was coming, but I wanted to spare him. I wanted to keep Mamma away from him. She always hit him harder and his back was still raw from the last whipping.

It was my job to protect him. He was younger than me.

She turned her attention his way and I reacted without thinking.

"I'm going to tell Grandpa you broke the car he gave me," I blurted out, my voice shaking. "He'll put you in time-out."

My body twisted, and I saw it coming. I didn't cower nor did I try to block it. She backhanded me so hard that I saw stars. The next hit I didn't expect. My head slammed against the corner of the altar and everything went back.

Yeah, our mother—correction, my mother—loved her church time. But she loved her belt even more.

I shook my head, chasing the memories away. She didn't deserve my memories. She'd taken enough from Priest and me.

But still, I couldn't help but compare the ache in my chest to the beatings Mamma used to put us through. That was a fucking fairy tale compared to this agony.

She hates me. The knowledge punched me in the chest and connected with my ribs. It was so violent that I swore a crack sounded in the room. *I love her and she fucking hates me.* I'd beg for forgiveness on my knees, but she'd probably laugh in my fucking face.

My phone rang and I answered it without looking. "DiLustro."

"What in the fuck happened?" It was my brother. Fuck, I should have looked at caller ID.

"Yes, what happened?" Basilio chimed in. "We thought she fucking shot you."

I pinched the bridge of my nose. I was certain that Juliette had wanted to shoot me. I wondered what held her back from slicing my throat.

"No such luck." I laughed bitterly. Truth of the matter was that she might as well have killed me. I couldn't live without her.

"Where is she?" Basilio asked.

"Unless she gave my Rover to someone else, she's driving around Chicago." It was quite possible she'd ask someone to get in my car and drive around while she ran. I never knew what to expect from my wife. "I told her if she leaves the city, I'd start a war."

"Jesus Christ," Priest grumbled. "I told you it was a bad idea."

"Agreed. We fucking told you," Basilio said.

Of course, my brother and cousins couldn't wait to taunt me with those four words. *I told you so.*

"If Juliette calls Wynter, my wife will go ballistic," Basilio added. "She'll demand your balls or she'll have mine."

"Then give her your balls," I remarked dryly. "And please, spare me your shit," I said.

My words tasted bitter and I hadn't even started drinking. I was too busy refreshing that fucking tracking app, ensuring she stayed within the city limits. One step outside Chicago and all hell would break loose. She was mine and the only air she would breathe was in my city.

"I don't understand why you're so hung up on her," Basilio mumbled. "The girl barely spares you a glance and you're chasing her like she's your salvation."

I gritted my teeth. "Maybe she is."

"If she's your salvation, we're all fucked," Basilio noted.

"You are not helpful at all. Why don't you fuck off and call someone else for your three-way conference call."

"She's actually fun," Priest came to her defense, making me smile. Juliette had inched her way into his heart. "She hides her kindness and fierce convictions under thorns."

"Well, that sounds familiar," Basilio retorted dryly. After all, we—DiLustros—were experts at it. "Then I am happy to have her in our family."

"You better, cousin, because she's not going anywhere."

I ended the call, then stood there for several minutes, stunned by the silence and emptiness that remained behind. I always knew Juliette would turn me into a pussy-whipped wimp without even trying.

Everyone thought it was her refusal that made me want more.

It wasn't.

It was her fire. Her strength that she hid under her reckless behavior. Her fucking glowing smiles. And then her vulnerability. It made an appearance when she thought nobody was looking.

I saw it in the little girl I saved ten years ago. I saw it in the same girl, now grown. My wife.

Juliette didn't realize it but every time we were together, despite her glaring displeasure at seeing me, she'd helped me heal. Maybe it was the masochist in me but being around her helped me heal from things she didn't break.

Things that both my brother and I hid from the world.

"Mr. DiLustro."

The maid's voice pulled me out of my thoughts. "Yes."

"You have a visitor. Is it okay to bring him here?"

I frowned. Who would be visiting unannounced? The only people who ever did that were my cousins and my brother. And they never waited for the maid to answer the door.

"Yes." I unbuttoned my jacket to ensure I had easy access to my gun. Footsteps sounded, approaching closer. The door opened and surprise washed over me. "Kian?"

Of all the potential visitors I could have had, he was the last one I expected. We barely exchanged a few words back in Las Vegas. I usually kept to the Syndicate when it came to business dealings. Once in a while I ventured outside of it like I had with Alessio. But that business relationship made sense. I had my shipments coming from the north through his territory. Correction, no longer his territory, since he'd gotten out of the mafia business.

"I hope you don't mind the visit," he said, taking my extended hand.

"Just surprised is more like it." It wasn't the best time but I kept that one to myself. "To what do I owe this visit?"

He pulled out a yellow envelope and handed it to me. My eyebrows scrunched.

"What is this?" I questioned.

"Insurance that your wife gets out alive," he answered. When I gave him a blank look, he shook his head. "I shouldn't be surprised she hides her extracurricular activities from you."

Dread pooled in my stomach.

"Explain."

He smiled coldly. "Your wife has been hunting." When I gave him a confused look, he continued, "She's been searching for the killers of her birth parents and picking them off, one by one."

"What?" It couldn't be. Juliette had a temper but she wasn't a killer. The image of the dick painted in blood flashed through my mind. Maybe—

I shook my head. "How would she even connect with you?"

I hated the jealousy in my voice. If Juliette wanted to kill and hunt her parents' killers, she should have come to me.

"About a year ago, she reached out to my agency. I assume the reference came from our mutual friend."

"Who is...?" I questioned.

"Branka Nikolaev or her friend, Autumn. They are sisters-in-law now."

The jealousy still didn't go away. Fuck!

I opened the envelope and started reading the report. With each passing second, worry grew. "Juliette's family—birth family—helped the old-man Brennan get Sofia Volkov's daughter?"

Kian nodded. "To say Sofia has it out for Juliette is probably an understatement."

I continued reading and the piece of information I saw next sent an even bigger shock through me. "Does Juliette know about this?"

Kian stood up, and headed to the door. He stopped with a hand on the knob and turned to me, his gaze locking with mine.

"About her grandfather, I'm not sure, but about her friend... if she doesn't yet, she will soon."

He left, but the dread stayed behind. It felt heavy and tasted like copper.

My cell phone rang again but I ignored it. The moment the ringing died off, it resumed and I glanced exasperatedly at the caller ID expecting my annoying family.

It wasn't. It was a local Chicago number.

My brows furrowed as I picked it up. "Yeah?"

"Mr. DiLustro?"

"Yes."

"Hello, this is Alissa from The Ritz-Carlton. Your wife is here—" Everything after that was fuzzy. I authorized whatever charges Juliette ran, barking for them to keep her in their best suite. Still on the phone, I jumped into my Bugatti and sped through the city.

I probably violated every single traffic law, but I didn't give a shit.

There was no doubt in my mind that she didn't want to see me. But I *had* to see her. Just a glimpse. To ensure she was okay. I'd get a room next to her or sleep in the car. It didn't matter.

As long as I was close to her.

Entering the lavish lobby, I was immediately recognized. Not bothering to check in, I headed for the elevators. I instructed the personnel on the phone to provide the best suite, so that would be the Presidential Suite.

"Mr. DiLustro," came a female voice from behind me as I pushed the elevator button. I didn't bother acknowledging the woman. I pressed the button again, over and over. Patience wasn't my virtue. Not unless Juliette was involved. "Mr. DiLustro, I just need to tell you something."

"Then say it," I grumbled.

"Your wife instructed us to feed a homeless shelter for a month. Put all their charges on your card. Clothes. Night at the hotel if they need it. Spa. Anything, she said."

I stilled. "How much?"

She swallowed, panic crossing her expression. "Little over five hundred thousand. But your wife insisted."

A sardonic breath escaped me. I guess I should be grateful the damage was this minimal.

"I-is that okay?"

The elevator door opened and I entered it.

"Whatever my wife wants, you give it to her," I instructed as the elevator door shut. My nerves twisted as the soft whirring sounds of the engine pulled me closer to the woman I love.

Ding.

The elevator slid open and I stepped into the hallway.

My nerves pulled tighter as I made my way to the door of the Presidential Suite. My hand trembled as I lifted it to knock on the door. It froze midair as I heard a soft noise. I held my breath, listening for it. Nothing.

I pressed my ear to the door and I heard it again. A muffled noise that sounded almost like... sobbing.

"Wildling," I called through the door.

Silence followed. No answer.

"Juliette, answer me," I demanded softly. My heart clenched in my chest as I worried about her. The idea of her crying made me want to tear the door down. Good God, my wife was making a wuss out of me. Even worse, I didn't give a shit.

Without her and her happiness, this life wasn't worth living.

"Go away." Her voice was clear. Strong. Yet there was a hint of a tremor in it.

"Open this door."

"Didn't you hear me?" she snapped. "Go away."

I took a deep breath before slowly exhaling. "I don't want to argue. I just want to see that you're alright, then I'll leave."

Silence. No movement. No other words. Nothing, like I wasn't even here. So typical of Juliette to ignore me.

"Wildling, I'll give you ten seconds to open this door before I break it down."

"Go away, Dante," she hissed. "I don't want to see you. I'm fine, but I'd be better if you were nowhere to be seen or heard."

Goddamn it! Why was she so fucking stubborn?

"One, two, three—" I started counting. If the silence on the other side of the door was any indication, she hadn't moved. "—nine, ten. I'm coming in."

"Don't you dare—"

Her sentence was cut off when I kicked the door open.

CHAPTER 49
Juliette

I had always known Dante DiLustro was fucking crazy.

My tears forgotten, I jumped out of bed, still dressed in the same clothes, shoes included, and strode to my husband.

"Are you fucking nuts?" I shouted, my palms against his chest and shoving at him. He was all hard muscle and towering over me. I didn't let that deter me. "Did I stutter when I said go away?"

His eyes glinted with something dark.

"When I'm checking on you, you open the fucking door," he said, his voice deep and angry. "Understood?"

I glared at him. "Fuck you, Dante. Don't think for a second you get to show up here after the shit you've done and I'll be all welcoming." I pushed against his chest. "Get. The. Fuck. Out."

"Not until you tell me why you were crying."

"I wasn't," I said defensively. "I was sleeping. At least I was trying to, until your crazy ass slammed through the door."

He raised his hand and I flinched, but all he did was run a thumb over my cheek, smearing the wet tears. He cupped my face gently, forcing our gazes to lock. His shimmering like a night sky and mine a teary one.

I couldn't handle this shit right now. I couldn't stand his touch, so I shoved his hand away. "Don't."

287

This time *he* flinched. Raw pain slashed across his beautiful face and speared me through the chest. I ignored it, telling myself I didn't give two fucks.

He'd broken my trust. He betrayed me.

He took a step back, stuffing his hands in the pockets of that signature three-piece suit. His brows were drawn tight over those dark, tired eyes. Stubble shadowed his cheeks and jaw. It must have been there this morning, but I was so pissed off, I'd failed to notice it. He didn't shave.

"Can we talk? I want to—" He paused, his throat flexing with a hard swallow. "I don't have an excuse, but at least I can explain what happened that night."

A raspy laugh tore from my throat. "You want to explain? A bit late, don't you think?"

I hated to admit that his betrayal slashed me deep. It was worse because I had started to trust him. To like him. To lo—

I shook my head. No! That was going a step too far.

"Yes, I should have told you sooner," he stated calmly, his jaw ticking. His eyes grew darker, into unnerving obsidian. "Please let me explain."

I sighed. I was tired. I didn't want to argue, and truthfully, I wanted to know what occurred that night, if only to fill in the gaps from my memory. But I wouldn't forgive.

"Okay." Relief washed over his face and he tilted his chin toward the couch. "We should sit down."

My eyes flickered to the door that hung off the hinge. "First have that damn door fixed," I told him. "I'm not spending a night in this suite with the door wide open."

He pulled the phone out of his pocket and typed a message. "Someone will fix it tonight."

We walked deeper into the suite and I sat down on the couch. He took a seat on the chair.

"I love you, Juliette." The dark timbre of his voice sent shivers rippling down my spine. I didn't want to hear those words. They didn't fix his betrayal. "I wanted you from the moment I saw you on top of that bar in that ridiculous orange dress. Then you bumped into me in Chicago and our lives became intertwined." His breathing was sharp and his scent wrapped around me. "The more you fought me, the harder I fell."

His words sent me spiraling. All of it was ridiculous. "So it's my fault. I wouldn't fall into your arms so you... what? Took matters into your own hands?"

"No. I waited, Juliette. I fucking waited." He reached inside his suit and pulled out a stack of letters. They were neatly wrapped with a band. He handed them to me. "I waited for you to come around. For you to see that we were meant to be. Otherwise, why would destiny keep bringing us back together? First, that little girl with the ridiculous Victoria's Secret bags."

My heart drummed against my ribs. He remembered. He recognized me! Paralyzed by shock, my images of that night in the alley scattered through my mind.

They flashed like a camera. *Click. Click. Click.*

My dream—memory—came back to me and pain slashed through me. The same scent. The same dark eyes. How did I not see it sooner? The boy who saved me a decade ago. The boy who I promised I'd save.

He was Dante. Dante was him.

"It was you," I murmured.

He nodded. "Why would we keep crossing paths? It had to mean something."

"It's a small world," I stated, my voice slightly cracking. He'd saved me. I promised him that day that I'd save him. I hadn't.

"I fucked up. But after waiting two years for you to see me—actually see me—I started to lose hope." His breaths were heavy with regret. "I had my heart set on you since I met you as a grown woman. Yes, I made a mistake, and I am sorry. For betraying your trust. For not doing the right thing. For not waiting another two years."

A dull ache formed behind my temples, refusing to recede.

I met his obsidian gaze and I knew he saw my decision because he closed his eyes for a brief moment. When he opened them, there was raw pain in them.

"I would have forgiven you anything, Dante." My voice broke. "Anything but this."

Dante exhaled a shuddering breath, his face taut with emotion. Vulnerability. For some stupid reason, I hated seeing the hurt on his face. He reached out, offering me the stack of letters.

"Read them," he said, exhaling one final shuddering breath. "I'll wait for you." His raw whisper clawed at my heart, fresh wounds bleeding out. "I'll wait for as long as it takes, Wildling. But I'm not letting go."

He turned to leave, making his way out of the hotel suite he'd paid for. Once by the doorframe, he leaned against it and folded his arms.

He added softly, "I'll never let go, Juliette. You're mine. You've been mine your whole life."

Then he leaned back against the doorframe and closed his eyes. I waited and waited, but eventually his breathing evened out and it looked like he'd fallen asleep.

"What are you doing?" I asked, frowning.

He never opened his eyes. "Guarding your door."

Flabbergasted, I stared at him, almost expecting him to give me that smirk and tell me he was just joking. It never came.

"Go to sleep, Wildling," he said, never opening his eyes.

I lay back down, closing my eyes and gripping the letters he had given me. They burned in the palm of my hand, but I refused to open them. I wanted to wait until I was alone.

The events of the day flashed through my mind, mixing with those images from ten years ago. The ones I tried so desperately to forget. They both started with a dance and ended—

I cut off the direction those thoughts were heading. I couldn't deal with it.

Not tonight. Not ever.

Squeezing my eyelids tightly, I tried to focus on my breathing. In and out. In and out.

I must have dozed off because my mind wandered off into forbidden territory.

"Something is wrong with this bitch," Travis said, laughing at my body that refused to move. I wanted to scream, thrash, and claw. But my muscles failed me. I lay there, wishing I were unconscious.

"What?" Brandon asked. I didn't even know him, but he'd get to know me really well one day, when I killed him.

"She's not crying or begging," Travis hissed, then slapped me across the cheek. "Why isn't she screaming?"

Not a single sound left my lips, although a solitary tear rolled down my cheek.

They didn't even bother to restrain me, knowing whatever drug they slipped me would render me immobile.

Travis straddled me and I tried to retreat into my mind where I couldn't hear their voices. Where I couldn't feel them touching me.

"Hold this bitch down," Travis ordered.

"Why? She's not even fighting," Sam questioned.

It didn't matter, because Sam ended up doing whatever his despicable friend ordered him to do. He was weak like that.

Then Travis lay on top of me, his heavy body suffocating me.

He laughed. They laughed. My screams rattled around in my head—I couldn't breathe. Darkness swallowed me, a vise around my chest preventing air from entering my lungs.

I jerked violently awake, a cold sweat slicking my skin and beading across my brow. My body shook. My lips trembled. I raised my hand, noting a bad tremor as I wiped my palm over my eyes.

My eyes darted around the room until they landed on Dante studying me with a clenched jaw and a frown. His muscles bulged as if fighting his instinct to prowl through the room and toward me.

Before he could do that, I lay back down and turned my back to him.

The nightmares were back.

The next morning, I woke up to an awful grinding noise.

Glancing at the clock, six a.m. stared back at me. I shifted on the bed, burying my head under my pillow. I needed to mute all these sounds so early in the morning.

Footsteps sounded against the floor. Firm. Heavy. *Familiar.*

"You're awake." Dante's deep voice came from somewhere near.

"And you're still here," I grumbled. "What the fuck? It's six in the morning."

"The door's getting fixed."

I couldn't believe the man stayed here all night. I slept restlessly without his heat around me, and each time I woke up, I couldn't keep my eyes from darting toward the door. Dante was still there, in the same position. It was kind of eerie that he hadn't moved.

But I didn't offer to let him sleep in the bed with me. Instead, the letters he gave me lay next to me.

"I got you some coffee," he added, his voice a warm timbre, clouding my senses. I ignored it. "It's the way you like it."

I groaned. I didn't want him to be nice or thoughtful. He fucking drugged me. I wanted to murder him, not drink the coffee he bought me.

Rising into a sitting position, I begrudgingly took the offered coffee. A travel cup with a Starbucks sleeve around it so I wouldn't burn my fingers.

"You went to Starbucks?" I questioned, narrowing my eyes on him. The two men struggled on the other end of the suite to set the door on its hinges. The accusation was clear. He left me alone with two strangers.

"No, I called them to bring it up here."

"Oh."

Okay, I couldn't hold that against him. I took a sip of the coffee and my eyes fluttered shut. The liquid warmed my insides as it traveled down my throat. There was nothing like that first cup of coffee in the morning. And considering all the shit that happened, I'd take what I could get.

"Once they are done, you can go," I told him, my fingers wrapped around the sleeve of my cup.

"No."

My eyes snapped to him, locking with that dark gaze.

"It's not your call to make," I remarked coldly.

My chest felt like it was in a vise each time I thought about what he had done to me. He might have set me free, but he had also set me back.

Maybe that was the reason I kept fighting him at every turn for the past two years. My sixth sense warned me.

Only to end up here. I sighed heavily.

What he had done was too close to what I went through ten years ago. I fought a shiver that threatened to wrack my body. I refused to be that weak, vulnerable girl again. I was stronger now.

"You can be mad at me," he stated calmly. "You have every right to be." A soft snort left me. *Nice to have his permission*, I thought sarcastically. "But you're my wife and I'm going to follow you around and keep you safe."

My eyebrow rose. "Don't you have work to do? A syndicate to run and all that."

He ignored my tone and sarcasm. "I'll handle everything remotely. And I have people that work for me. They'll take care of any in-person stuff."

My phone buzzed at that moment and I reached for it. My brows furrowed. It was a text from Wynter.

I'm coming to Chicago later this morning. Lunch?

I groaned. She'd try to play peacemaker. I didn't want that right now.

Hoping she'd go into labor any minute, then realizing it likely wouldn't happen since she was months away from her due date, I typed a reluctant reply. ***Sure.***

She was sure to see my eagerness through this text.

Putting my phone away, I met my husband's eyes and glared at him. "You, your brother, and your cousins are like a bunch of old gossiping women."

I must have caught him by surprise because he was speechless for a moment.

Then he got his wits together and replied, "I didn't tell them. I was on the phone with them and they heard your tone. Knowing you, they assumed you had gone ballistic."

"I don't go ballistic. You DiLustros do." Narrowing my eyes on him, I curled my lip. "You know what the worst part is?" I didn't let him answer, instead I continued, "The signs were there all along. I know I can handle my alcohol. Yet, I let you convince me I was so drunk that I blacked out."

In all my years, my friends and I drank some hardcore stuff. I had never blacked out. Fucking ever! I should have known something was off when I couldn't remember a single damn thing from the night that Dante and I had our drive-through wedding.

Our gazes clashed, accusations in mine loud and clear.

"Were you even drunk?" I blurted out. "Or did you drug me, then drag me to the drive-through chapel?"

He didn't miss a beat. "I wasn't as hammered as you, but yes, I was drunk."

"Where was everyone?" I asked icily. "Somebody should have stopped you." My question and unspoken accusation hung in the air. Silence stretched until it suffocated. "Unless they were in on it all along?"

I had my suspicions.

"Your family left well before the two of us started dancing," he explained. "Then you and I started drinking and dancing."

"That doesn't answer my question." My anger simmered beneath my skin. Even the buzzing in my ears increased a notch.

Dante's eyes shone with something dark and unapologetic. "I'd be lying if I said I regret our marriage, Juliette."

I shook my head in disbelief. "Do you not see how wrong that is?" I gritted. "What you've done."

A hard smile cut across his beautiful face, but his eyes burned into mine. Relentless. Demanding.

"The only thing I'm sorry about is that I hurt you," he admitted, his voice cracking. "I didn't know about what happened to you. If I had, I wouldn't have taken that approach."

"But you'd have still done something," I accused.

I stood my ground, but the electricity buzzed through the air and in my veins. It didn't matter. I couldn't forgive. I *wouldn't* forgive. And I certainly wouldn't forget.

A forbidding silence licked at my skin. It was so loud that it hurt my ears with words and feelings that were left unsaid.

He reached into his pocket and pulled something out, opening his palm. My eyes widened. The hot-pink scrunchie I owned once upon a time lay in his hand, staring back at me. He kept it. All these years and he kept it.

"This is my last resort, then," he murmured softly, tension suffocating the space between us. Somehow it didn't shock me that he remembered. He must have known all along. Although, it surprised me that he kept my hot-pink scrunchie. A whole decade and he still had it. "I'm here to collect the debt." I held my breath as I waited for him to drop the bomb. "Be my wife."

I couldn't keep a strangled gasp from escaping. "No," I whispered. "No, no, no."

He lied to me. He drugged me. How could I ever move past it?

"What are you afraid of, Juliette?" he rasped, fatigue lingering behind his eyes. "That you might like me? You'd rather throw away our chance at happiness than leave your stubbornness behind."

An invisible thread snapped. "I did like you." I heard the too-loud pitch in my tone and cringed. "I was fully prepared to deal with the consequences of our wild night." My hands make air quotations around "wild." "I let you in and it was all a lie."

His fingers wrapped around my wrist and brought my hand to his chest. Hard muscle. Warmth. A steady, strong heartbeat.

"It wasn't a fucking lie," he rasped. "None of it was a lie. Not for me."

CHAPTER 50
Dante

"Why in the fuck are you here?" I snapped at my cousin. Basilio didn't miss a beat. He shrugged, glancing over toward the table where his wife sat with Juliette. The two of us had taken a spot at the bar and kept watch over them.

"My wife wanted to see her cousin. I like to make her happy."

My goddamn cousins and brother had an annoying way of getting in my business. Did I nag Basilio when he was killing everyone in search of Wynter? No, I let him do his thing. Why, then, for fuck's sake, could he not let me do mine in peace?

It had been twenty-four hours since Juliette overheard our conversation. Of course, Basilio told Wynter and the latter insisted on coming to ensure my wife was okay. My. Wife. So here they were. They should all let me handle this shit and fuck off.

Soft laughter traveled through the air and my gaze pulled back to my wife. She had her mask on, her happy smile and relaxed posture. Like she had not a care in the world. Before Vegas, I wouldn't have been able to spot the signs, but now, I could see them.

The way she shook her head. Or the way she gripped her drink. And she was antsy. Her eyes kept darting around the room, but she purposely ignored the bar section where Basilio and I were seated.

We were back at The Library at Gilt Bar.

A part of me was pissed off that she decided to bring her cousin here. This was *our* fucking place. Our first lunch. Our first date.

Fucking Basilio. "I really wish you hadn't come," I gritted, reaching for my glass of scotch.

He chuckled. "My heart warms at how much you care." I flipped him off, but he didn't seem deterred from seeking answers. "Okay, so how pissed off is she?" he asked, flicking a glance toward my wife. "What did she damage?"

"She banged up the Rover but it was an accident." Basilio's lips twitched and the look in his eyes clearly said he didn't believe me. It didn't matter. Juliette said it was an accident and I believed her. She never bothered concealing the destruction of my property before.

"She's too reckless. Impulsive, too," Basilio stated for the hundredth time. It pissed me off every fucking time. "Those attributes mixed with our genes are a recipe for disaster. I just wonder if maybe you shouldn't just let her be."

I shot him a glare. "Like you let Wynter be?" My cousin searched for Wynter day and night—relentless and crazed.

"What do you see in her?" he questioned, further agitating me.

"Frankly, I didn't know what you saw in your wife," I hissed. "Did you hear me questioning you on it? Fuck no. So please, for the love of God, just accept her. Because Juliette isn't going anywhere." At least, I hoped.

In typical Basilio fashion, he didn't let my outburst bother him. If I'd said something like this while he was searching high and low for Wynter, he'd have probably put a gun to my head. But as it was, Wynter calmed his crazy.

"Are you sure about that?" Basilio asked. "She just doesn't seem like a woman that would stay put just because you told her to."

I gritted my teeth. "She'll stay."

"And why is that?" When I narrowed my eyes on him, he added, "Just humor me," when he knew I wasn't going to answer him.

"I threatened war against her father." Okay, it wasn't my proudest moment, but family was one of the rare things that Juliette would protect. So I made it work for me. For us.

Both of us glanced back to the table where the girls were sitting.

"Jesus, you're really aiming for an early death," he muttered.

As if Juliette heard him, her eyes flitted our way only to glare at us, flip us off, then return her attention to Wynter.

My cousin let out a heavy sigh. "I have nothing against her, but I think maybe you should tell her what you like about her. What you love—" He gave me a pointed look. "Yes, we all know you love her. Trust me, a crazy DiLustro is usually an in-love DiLustro."

And with that, he changed the subject, leaving me pondering on it.

CHAPTER 51
Juliette

Dante had been sitting at the bar for the past two hours, his gaze burning into the back of my head. Goose bumps rose on my skin, running down my arms. I didn't need to turn around to see that he was staring. I could feel the intensity of his laser-focused stare as if he were touching me, electrifying me.

I forced myself to avert my eyes. His attention might have been exclusively on me, but I refused to give him my own, so I made a point to appear aloof and take in my surroundings instead. Honestly, I worried his burning gaze would weaken my resolve.

"So how long will this last?" Wynter asked. I shrugged my shoulders, taking a sip of my water. "Have you talked to him since—" Wynter's voice trailed off, noting my glare.

"Talk to him about what?" I hissed under my breath. "The fact that he drugged me? That he forced me to marry him?" Wynter's gaze drifted away from me uncomfortably. "Please don't tell me that I should forgive him," I uttered exasperatedly.

Wynter could be too sweet sometimes. We both grew up in a similar environment, but where she was always calm and collected, I was rash. Or maybe I'd become rash somewhere along the way because I had to deal with my anger issues on my own.

"I didn't say that. It's just that... well, you seemed to be happy and you've been raving about how sweet he is. Then just like that, you shut him out? Maybe you should talk it out."

I narrowed my eyes on her. "So you think I should forgive him?"

Wynter just shrugged, her curls bouncing. With her pregnancy, I swore she had even more hair. Her face glowed, and every time I saw Basilio with her, his hand was on her belly like it was a crystal ball. It was annoying as fuck.

"Well, I don't think you should just end it," Wynter replied diplomatically.

"Of course you don't," I remarked wryly. "You were fine with your husband kidnapping you, instead of kicking him in the balls."

I was being a bitch, I knew it. But wasn't it time that we stood up for ourselves? These men, mafia or not, couldn't just do whatever the fuck they felt like and expect us to fall in line. How would they like it if we drugged them? Kidnapped them?

An idea flickered to life—so deliciously wicked—but I quickly pushed it away. Except, it remained lingering in the dark, fucked-up corner of my mind. To give back what he had given me. Except, I didn't think I could do it. It was a violation of my free will. If I did it to him, it'd be a violation of his free will and it didn't sit well with me.

"Why don't you tell me why you are really upset?" Wynter asked calmly. "Yes, I admit, it was wrong of him to do that. But he didn't hurt you." The old panic suffocated my throat, slithered through my veins. It took only one night to make a different person out of me. It changed me forever. "Jules, talk to me. Please."

A shudder rolled down my spine as I met my cousin's eyes. Everything about Wynter made you want to smile. I didn't see that same light in myself. Only darkness. And heavy secrets that dragged me down for far too long.

"Remember when—" I swallowed, my gulp audible. "First year of high school, I went to a school party hosted by one of the families without you." Wynter waited, watching me. "There was no alcohol. Just dancing. Some boys and girls. I don't know." I pushed my trembling hand through my hair, then got mad at myself for being weak. Too sensitive. "Three boys slipped something into my drink. Then dragged me into a bedroom."

It was as far as I could go. She'd get the picture.

My cousin's hand came to mine and she squeezed it. "Oh my gosh, Jules." She shook her head, squeezing my hand so hard, it turned purple. "Why didn't you tell me?"

I swept my tongue across my bottom lip. "I was ashamed. Scared. Maybe even in denial. I couldn't believe it happened to me."

"Who did it?" she hissed. "Basilio and Dante will—"

"They're dead," I told her calmly. "I killed two of them. Dante killed the third."

Surprise washed over her expression and she blinked in confusion. "Dante knows?" I nodded. "He knew about the drugs and he drugged you?"

I shook my head. "No, he learned... afterwards." *When I couldn't sleep with him.* I kept that piece of information to myself. "Don't tell Dad. Or your mom." She shook her head, her curls bouncing. "Don't tell anyone about any of this," I added.

I didn't want anyone going after Dante. That was reserved only for me. And it turned out, I didn't have the stomach to torture him. *You don't have the stomach or the heart to torture him?* my mind asked, mockingly.

Silence stretched.

"Well, there are two options as I see them," Wynter answered, inter-rupting the silence. "You can work it out with him and set some bound-aries. Or you can live a separate life and never have a relationship with another man." When my eyebrows shot up to my hairline, she chuckled softly. "He'll never allow you to have another man. You realize that, right?"

I grumbled. "Well, then he can suffer and not have another woman." I knew I was proving my stubbornness but I was past caring.

"Okay, whatever you say, Jules."

She didn't believe it. By the look on my cousin's face, I could tell she thought eventually Dante would get another woman. A mistress.

My jaw clenched so tight, it made my temples throb. "Well, if he gets a woman, I'll show him exactly how I operate," I hissed.

And I meant it. This was a two-way street, motherfucker.

301

As if the universe heard my vengeful thoughts, from the corner of my eye, a vibrant red dress caught my attention.

As if in a daze, I watched a gorgeous blonde saunter her way through the bar and straight to Dante and Basilio. Neither man turned until the woman said something.

Slowly, like they were synchronized, the two men glanced over their shoulders. Basilio's eyes lingered on the woman for a fraction of a second, before he turned back to his bourbon or whatever he was drinking.

I held my breath watching Dante. Whatever the woman said had him shaking his head. But she wasn't leaving. Instead she leaned forward, giving my husband a glimpse of her generous cleavage. To Dante's credit, he didn't lower his gaze to it.

One point to Dante DiLustro, I thought wryly.

But then her hand came to his forearm, the red-painted nail skimming over his suit jacket

Oh, no she didn't! Not my fucking husband.

A buzzing rang in my ears, high-pitched and piercing. A red mist coated the room, and before I realized what I was doing, I was by the bar, violating every personal-space rule imaginable.

My hand wrapped around her hair and pulled. Gasps traveled through the room but I ignored them. All my attention was on this bimbo hitting on my husband.

"Do you see his hand?" I asked in a hiss.

"What the fuck?" she screamed, trying to yank herself away from me. It only hurt her more, because I tightened my grip.

Her eyes darted to Dante, pleading for help. He didn't move, that familiar smirk playing around his lips. Basilio, on the other hand, looked almost impressed. Instead of ignoring the bimbo, his attention was now fully on her and me.

"I asked you a question," I hissed, yanking on her hair harder. Wearing a red Valentino dress, I looked plain next to her which pissed me off even more.

"W-what?" she whimpered.

"Do you see his fucking left hand?" I gritted.

"Yes."

"What do you see?"

"Who is this fucking crazy bitch?" she cried.

"Watch it," Dante warned, his tone quiet and dangerous. "That's my wife you're talking to."

Her expression shattered. I didn't care. Something about the way Dante said "my wife" had my chest warming up in an unreasonable way.

"Focus on me, bitch," I drawled, still gripping her hair. "What do you see on his hand?"

Her eyes studied Dante's hands frantically. "A-a ring?"

My lips curved into a sarcastic smile. "That's right. A ring. Which means he's married." Her eyes darted to Basilio and I yanked her attention back my way once again. "He's married too." I leaned closer to her, our faces so close I could see her pores. "If I see your filthy fucking fingers anywhere near my husband again, I'm gonna cut them clean off, then shove them up your ass."

I released her without warning and straightened up. I fought the urge to shove her, but instead I stood between her and Dante. Wynter would have to protect her own husband from greedy, unwelcome hands.

Her eyes darted to my husband and that made me want to smash her face against the bar. But I didn't. Maybe because I had a better handle on my temper than I thought. Or maybe because Dante's hand came to my ass, and strangely enough, I found it calming.

The woman wobbled away, her face pale and her eyes frantic.

I turned to look at my devious husband and found him grinning like a little boy on Christmas morning. The man acted like I had just given him the best gift ever.

"Don't get too full of yourself," I snapped at him, wiping that grin off of his face. "Just because I don't want you anymore doesn't mean you get to play with anyone else."

And I walked away from him, terrified of the green monster he unleashed within me.

CHAPTER 52
Juliette

As we'd strolled down the streets of Chicago back to the hotel, it didn't escape me how tense Basilio and Dante were. First, I thought it had something to do with the incident back at the bar. But the moment two of Dante's men pulled up and joined behind our husbands, I knew that wasn't it.

"What is that about?" I asked my cousin as we entered The Ritz Carlton.

Wynter just shrugged, avoiding my eyes.

"Wynter," I warned. "You know something."

She shook her head, but still avoided my eyes. I gritted my teeth but didn't push. I'd do that when we were alone.

"Juliette," Dante had called out and I glanced over my shoulder. "I've got to take care of something. You and your cousin stay in the suite." My eyebrows shot up at his order. "*Please* stay in the suite."

I didn't answer but Wynter did. "We will. You two be careful."

And there was my confirmation that she knew what was going on. With the two bodyguards glued to us, we took the elevator up to the top floor to the Presidential Suite.

The moment the door of my hotel room closed, I leaned against it, let out a breath, then kicked off my shoes. Dante, being Dante, had someone bring a bag full of my clothes when he came knocking—correction, smashing—down the door.

Alone now with Wynter, I said, "Spill it."

She blinked her eyes, giving me an innocent look. "I don't know what you mean."

"Spare me. I won't drop it until you spill it." She knew me well enough to know that was the truth. "What's going on?"

She sighed, pulling me to the other side of the suite and making me sit on the bed. My eyes flickered to the stack of letters and the envelope Kian had given me yesterday on the nightstand. I had yet to open any of them. I wasn't even sure what held me back. Maybe it was the warning Kian gave me when we parted ways.

Wynter sat next to me and I waited for her to say something. When she didn't, I couldn't hold it anymore.

"Well?" I urged. "Don't make me die of old age here before you start talking."

"They got a tip," she said, uncertain. She played with the hem of her shirt. "Sofia Volkov might be in the city."

I straightened, my attention fully on her. "What? Really? Where?"

She shook her head, chewing on her bottom lip nervously. Two years ago, Sofia Volkov almost killed Basilio. Wynter's crazy great-grandma was a bit on the psycho side.

Rubbing her stomach, Wynter leaned back against the pillows. For an Olympic ice-skater, she had gotten awfully lazy.

"I don't know," she muttered. "I wish I did. Maybe I could go there and talk to her."

I scoffed, shaking my head. "You and I both know there's no talking to that woman. She's batshit crazy."

She rolled her eyes. "Yeah, there's that."

"Do you have Basilio on the Find My iPhone app?" I asked her. Wynter's light green eyes narrowed on me suspiciously.

"Well, if he's moving, then we know he's okay," I reasoned, my tone slightly defensive. I didn't have Dante on my app; otherwise I would have looked it up myself.

She tilted her head. "That's actually a good idea."

She pulled out her phone to open the app and we both leaned over it.

And sure as hell, it showed Basilio's flashing dot moving.

"Are they going out of town?" I asked, frowning. "It looks like they're leaving the city limits."

"My guess is they'll stay close by," Wynter stated. "Neither one of them would want to be far from us with the rumor that Sofia Volkov is around this area."

I nodded. She was right. Basilio wouldn't risk it for sure. He knew the old woman still wanted Wynter in her clutches.

The little dot on her screen moved, then came to a stop. "Hey, what's that?" I asked, pointing to it. "A hospital?"

She tapped on it lightly and a name came up. "Tinley Park State Mental Hospital," she murmured. "Built in 1959, it's an abandoned asylum in Chicago. It's massive. You can get trapped in it with no way out."

I shook my head and scoffed.

"It says that all there in the app?"

Wynter rolled her eyes. "No, but I tapped on it and expanded the research. Damn smart-ass."

Then a soft groan left Wynter's lips. "Don't tell me you're turning so soft that calling me a smart-ass makes you feel guilty?" I asked dryly.

"Nope, not that."

I sought out her face, but she was shifting off the bed already. She almost looked like a little pill bug—I called them roly-poly bugs—on its back, trying to get up.

My lips curved up and I shifted off the bed, helping her to stand. "You're big as a boat," I remarked.

She shot me a glare. "I'll remember to return the compliment when you get knocked up." It was my turn to roll my eyes. She'd be waiting a long time. Kids were not my thing. She sighed. "I swear, I spend more time in the bathroom than anywhere else."

I raised my eyebrow.

"Need to pee?" She nodded and I saw my window of opportunity. I tilted my chin toward the door in the far corner. "Bathroom is there."

She wobbled her way there and I wasted no time. I was dressed well enough to fight. I dug through my purse for my phone and the knife I'd kept from yesterday. As I pulled it out, a red stain caught my eye. It was

Dante's blood from when I'd cut the skin on his throat. Guilt flickered in my chest, but I ignored it.

No time to dwell on it now. I slid the blade in the back pocket of my jeans. Grabbing my pair of Chucks, I quickly slipped them on before rushing to the door.

Resorting to my acting skills, I slipped a panicked mask on and opened the door.

"Wynter's water broke," I hissed, my voice pure panic. "Can you two carry her and take us to the hospital?"

The two men barely waited for me to finish the sentence, rushing past me. What a bunch of suckers!

The second I flew out the door, I dialed up the secured line that Kian gave me. The elevator door pinged open as if waiting for me. Destiny was on my side—at least for the moment.

"Juliette," he greeted. The fucker probably knew since day one who I was, even though I insisted on giving him only my first initial.

"Where are you?" I asked as I entered the elevator.

"This isn't a good time." I could hear in his tone he really meant it. There was tension and something else I couldn't quite pinpoint lingering.

"I don't give a crap," I hissed, focusing more on my needs. I wanted Sofia Volkov dead. For what she had done. If nothing else was going right in my life, that part would. Damn it! "I need you to do a fast track on Dante DiLustro. I need his exact location." I knew where Basilio was. I just needed confirmation that Dante was still with him. I needed to get to the Volkov bitch before Dante did. She was my kill, not his.

He let out an amused breath. "Well, that's easy," he mused. "He's actually meeting me in a few minutes."

I frowned. Did he work for Dante too?

"I guess you're collecting on all ends, aren't you?" I scoffed. "Where are you meeting him?"

"At an abandoned mental hospital." How fucking appropriate.

"I know exactly where you are, then. Thanks." I hung up just as the elevator opened. I rushed through the crowded lobby and exited onto the sidewalk of the busy Chicago street.

"Taxi!" A businessman flagged a cab that came to a screeching stop and I rushed to it.

"I'm so sorry, but I have to steal your cab." I shot him an apologetic look. "I have to get to a mental hospital or there'll be hell to pay." Then I smiled sweetly and added, "You're more than welcome to join."

The look he gave me was clear. He'd rather walk to the ends of the earth than share a cab with me. I shrugged and slid into the cab.

"Tinley Park State Mental Hospital," I said to the cab driver. His gaze flickered to the rearview mirror, probably ready to tell me to get out of his car.

"It's closed."

"I know. But I need to get there. Fast. I'll pay you triple."

That got him going. The problem? I didn't have any money on me. Nor a credit card.

Shit!

"Do you take Apple pay?" I asked casually as I scrolled through my phone.

"No."

Okay, Dante would pay the man once we got to the asylum. Or Basilio.

Worst came to worst, I'd ask Kian to front me some money.

CHAPTER 53

Dante

"An abandoned mental asylum," I muttered, thinking how fucking appropriate it was.

And creepy.

We left the city limits about twenty minutes or so ago and followed Kian's directions. I started to wonder whether he fucked up. There were abandoned and boarded-up houses along the road to get to this building.

We pulled up into an open area. A water fountain stood crooked in front of the entrance, hanging on for dear life. Kian was already there waiting for us.

"I guess he came with reinforcements," Basilio noted. "Who is he?"

I studied the guy next to Kian. They were both about the same height, but they looked nothing alike.

"Maybe he works for Kian," I remarked. "Although he looks familiar."

I was good with faces and I was certain I had seen this guy's face before. Then it hit me. "BlackHawk SF," I declared.

Basilio raised his eyebrow. "I don't think the military would take you. Our track record isn't desirable for clean-cut military guys."

"Kian's guy," I said, ignoring his comment. "He's one of the three guys that run BlackHawk SF Security."

Basilio's gaze shifted critically over Kian's right-hand man. "Are you sure?" He sounded dubious. "The name suggests ex-military and this guy... That hair isn't exactly a military cut. Did you ask him what's up with it?"

I scoffed. "Maybe he got tired of buzz cuts and decided to grow out his hair." Although he had a point. Most veterans kept their hair military-style even after they finished their service. "Why in the fuck would I ask him about his haircut preferences?"

Sometimes my cousin was a dick. Priest was more of the quiet guy, and at this moment, I wished he were here instead.

I parked next to Kian and his guy before jumping out of the car. Unbuttoning my suit jacket, I checked my gun, ensuring it was accessible.

"Kian," I said in greeting. Sometimes I wondered what his endgame was. It was hard to tell. He never divulged any information about himself.

"This is Astor," Kian stated coldly. "Darius and River are watching us through their sniper rifles and tracking the movements in the building through body heat cameras."

Basilio and I nodded.

"Anyone inside?" I asked, tilting my head to the building.

"Someone's definitely inside," he stated matter-of-factly.

"And we're standing in the middle of an open space... why? I'm not in the mood to be a target right now."

"Darius and River have eyes on every window of this building," Kian's right-hand man answered. He started moving, and for someone so large, he did so with surprising stealth. The intelligence behind his gaze assured us he wouldn't be a burden but rather an asset. Good, because we'd need all the help we could get if the crazy bitch was inside.

He extended his hand, two small devices lying there. Earpieces. "It will allow us all to know what's going on at all times."

Basilio and I slid the device into our ear and headed inside.

We climbed up the cracked stairs, all four of us entering the building. An open area greeted us, knocked-down chairs, wet floor, gray walls... ceilings caving in. It was a mess. We made our way through dark hallways, all the while hearing faint voices traveling through the vents.

The four of us shared looks. We didn't speak, not wanting our voices to carry through the empty hallways.

"There are no security cameras." A voice came through our

earpiece. "There are no movements on the upper floors. But there was movement on the first floor. Two bodies. Hard to tell whether there's a female. They've disappeared, so they must have gone into the basement."

The body heat cameras—at least those he had—couldn't track them in the basement.

My lips stretched into a thin line. I just wanted this shit with Sofia Volkov to be done. The information Kian had shared with me yesterday revealed that psycho bitch had it out for my wife.

Because of the part her birth family played in Sofia Volkov's madness. Because of Juliette's bloodthirsty path to revenge. *Not that I blamed her.*

I spotted the door to the side and the direction above it showed it led directly into the basement. I whistled softly and everyone's eyes turned my way. I pointed to it.

There was tension building in the air and inside me. It crawled through my veins and pricked my skin.

Astor opened the door that led to a winding staircase. There were cobwebs hanging off the ceiling, but it appeared they'd been prowled through recently, shifting as though someone had recently come through.

We must have all had the same thought, because Kian mouthed, "Someone's down there."

There was an eerie silence as we took the staircase that was getting more use today than it had in decades. Once we were all in the basement, we scanned the area. There were only two ways out of here. Back up the stairs or down a long, dark tunnel that led *somewhere.* And possibly to someone.

We stood still for a moment and then I honed in on the sound. It was very faint but I could hear it, and by the expression on everyone's faces, so could they. The sound of footsteps.

One. Two.

Two sets of footsteps. Just like the snipers claimed. But then static came through the headset.

Mumbled words. Incoherent sounds. Then a single word. *Trap.*

That word I understood. The door above us opened and bullets started flying.

"Fuck," the four of us said at the same time, drawing our weapons and breaking into a run, chasing the two ghosts ahead while being chased by others.

My hands wrapped around my blades tucked in the back of my pants and I sent them flying through the air, landing in their chests. Unfortunately, it wasn't enough. There were more of them coming.

Fuck, I wished I'd dressed in jeans. Three-piece suits were a pain to fight in.

Four men came from behind us. Another four running toward us. We were trapped. Fucked through and through. Basilio and I aimed at the ones chasing us, shooting them down one by one. Kian and Astor fired their guns at the men in front of them.

We were running out of ammunition. Without alternatives, we grabbed the guns from the fallen men and kept shooting.

The circle was closing in on us and there was nowhere to go.

CHAPTER 54
Juliette

The cab pulled up to a creepy abandoned building and the first thing that registered was the sound of guns firing.

Without waiting for the driver to stop, I jumped out of the car and started running toward the entrance, hearing the cabbie yelling at me as I went.

My steps halted as I came face-to-face with two guys pointing guns at me. My eyes locked on them, two fucking gorgeous men that would steal any woman's breath way.

"Juliette," one of them called out. I blinked, sure I'd never met them before. You didn't forget a body like that. And that hair. Subconsciously, I pushed my hand through my own hair, hoping it at least looked decent. Then I groaned. What was wrong with me? It was not the time to be vain.

"How do you know my name?" I barked.

"Kian," he stated flatly. "He warned us that you'd probably show up," he continued with a snort of exasperation while shoving an AK-47 into my hands along with several ammo clips which I shoved into the back pockets of my jeans. I'd fired one only once, during my training. I didn't think it was time to admit that though, so I went along. "I'm Darius. This is River. There's been an ambush."

A flash of concern washed over me. For Dante. Even for Basilio.

"By whom?" Although I was fairly certain I knew. "Sofia Volkov?"

They nodded, their expressions darkened, full of rage and hate. Gosh, that woman had more haters than anyone I'd ever met.

"Okay, so what's the plan?"

Darius slid off his Kevlar vest and handed it to me. "Put this on," he ordered. Without arguing, I quickly did as was commanded. It was obvious these two knew what they were doing. I only sliced and diced people. But these two—they were born killers. "You stand between us, two steps behind. I don't want anything happening to you."

"What a gentleman," I snickered, although my chest slightly warmed at the thought. They were strangers, and yet, they were protecting me.

After they explained what we were going to do—more specifically what I needed to do which, frankly, wasn't much—we rushed inside. It took us no time to find about ten men, flocking like a bunch of geese at an entrance leading to a stairwell.

A shared look and the magic started happening.

I never even got to raise my fancy weapon because in the time it took me to register what was happening, they'd killed every single one of them.

"You gotta teach me how to do that," I muttered, impressed.

"You got it, killer." River winked, grinning.

Leaving behind a trail of dead bodies, we made our way down the wobbly staircase, iron bars rattling with our weight. Then we continued down a small, dark hallway. There were sounds of bullets and fighting, but we couldn't see anything.

Pushing our way through the darkness, we found them. "There they are," Darius hissed, pointing ahead of us.

I followed his gaze and my heart froze at the sight.

Dante, Basilio, and Kian were fighting against about ten men. Armed men. Dangerous men.

A sudden noise had one of my bodyguards pushing me onto the ground. They followed, huddling on top of me while something flew above our heads and hit the back of the tunnel, rattling the stairs and exploding against the rock wall. But that wasn't what froze me. It was the two bodies suffocating me.

Tremors rolled through me. My heart drummed so hard, it must have bruised my ribs. Fear wrapped around my throat and cut off my breath. I attempted to breathe, but it was impossible. Instead, my lungs iced over and refused to work.

"A fucking RPG!" River hissed while my ears buzzed. Not from whatever the hell just zipped past us but from the panic that clawed at my chest. "Fucking lunatics. They used a rocket launcher down here! They'll bring the building down."

My heart clenched. My breathing heaved. But there was one feeling that pushed through the fear and panic. Concern for my husband. I wanted to lift my head up and make sure Dante was alright. Did he hear that thing and duck too? He did me wrong, but I didn't want him dead. I just wanted to torture him a bit. Drug him as a payback, maybe. Not have him die in this place.

The ground shook again and I closed my eyes, breathing in smoke and cursing Sofia Volkov to hell. This fucking panic that enveloped me made me useless.

Darius tapped River on his shoulder, his big hand on top of mine. I rolled my eyes. I fucking hated having anyone on top of me, in any capacity.

"Can you please not suffocate me?" I grumbled, a bead of sweat forming on my forehead. It was the absolute worst time to have a panic attack. "Give me some space."

Darius gave me a peculiar look but he said nothing. Thankfully, he scooted an inch away and the grip on my lungs eased slightly.

"Thanks," I mumbled, embarrassed. He didn't pay me any attention, his eyes on the stone ceiling.

"Over there," Darius whispered, pointing to the ceiling. I followed his gaze and saw it. There was a camera in here.

"How in the fuck did we miss it?" River hissed.

Buzz. Buzz. The camera moved.

"Shoot it," I said, keeping my voice low. "That sick bitch is probably watching us and laughing right now."

A cackle came from the speakers we couldn't see.

"Right you are, Juliette Ava Cullen." It was the first time I had heard my birth name spoken out loud. It felt wrong because nobody ever referred to me like that. I was no longer a Cullen. "I'm going to end your whole bloodline."

315

"Why?" I choked out, although I didn't expect an answer.

"Because your family cost me mine," she spat, bitterness clear even over the speakers.

"Man, she holds grudges," I grumbled before continuing loud enough for her to hear. "Although I'm not sure how I could be guilty of my grand-father's sins." My birth parents got caught in her hatred and now she aimed it at Killian and me.

She cackled. Laughed and laughed, the sound reminding me of a witch's cackle on Halloween.

"Your birth grandfather helped the Brennans take my baby from me. Now, my life goal is to wipe out your bloodline."

I stilled, frozen as my eyes darted around. She was answering my questions. How could she hear us unless she had this whole place wired?

Putting my forehead on the dirty ground, I turned my face slightly to look at River. "She can hear us," I mouthed.

He nodded. It wasn't a surprise they came to the same conclusion. "We find the panel and blow it to pieces."

A terse nod. "Blow her to kingdom come," I stated in a hushed tone. "At least her men, because I don't think she's here."

"Judgment day has come, Cullen scum," she announced.

It was then that it hit me. It wasn't that nobody had ever referred to me as a Cullen. It was that I'd already begun to think of myself as Juliette DiLustro.

"Come and get us." I didn't know which one of them said it, but he didn't have to repeat it. All three of us were on our feet within the same second.

Suddenly, we were surrounded by more men. *Where the fuck were they all coming from?* All at once we were in the same trouble as Dante, Basilio, and Kian were. Fear wrapped around my throat and my eyes darted around. There were way too many of them.

"Use that AK-47," River barked and I didn't think, just acted on instinct.

Taking it off my shoulder, I raised and pointed the gun at the enemy and pulled the trigger. Bullets started flying in every direction. River and Darius fought in tandem, working as one. River wrenched the gun from one guy, tossing it aside. Darius had his hand wrapped around the throat of another guy while I kept shooting at the never-ending mass of targets.

My heart thundered, each beat cracking my ribs. I gasped for air, my lungs squeezing. My body shook, but I refused to stop. It was a matter of life and death. And the whole time, I kept my finger on the trigger.

River barked some orders, but I couldn't hear them. My teeth chattered from the impact of the staccato motion of the semi-automatic rifle. Shots rang out but I could no longer hear them. My hearing must have been damaged from the incessant rapid-firing *bang, bang, bang*.

One of the men had his gun pointed at Dante, his finger on the trigger. I was afraid I'd hit Dante if I tried to shoot the guy, so I reached for my knife in the back of my jeans, unsheathed it, and threw it at my target. I held my breath as it sliced through the air. *Swish. Swish.*

It landed in his chest. One man down. Many more to go.

Dante's gaze met mine and the promise I gave him a decade ago rushed to my mind.

"One day, I'll save you too." My lips moved, but I couldn't hear my voice.

CHAPTER 55

Dante

"One day, I'll save you too." She mouthed the same words she'd said to me ten years ago.

I had a feeling we'd all need saving to get out of here in anything but a body bag. Why the hell was she here? She should have been safely tucked away in that goddamned hotel room with Wynter. Fear gripped my throat as I saw the danger surrounding Juliette as she stood sandwiched between two of the men I could only hope to hell were Kian's.

My pulse roared in my ears. Blood thumped through my veins.

I started moving, barreling through the men that separated me from her. I was prepared to destroy them all. Adrenaline coursed through my veins, fueling me to push forward. My fists wreaked havoc on every one of Sophia's puppets who tried to get in my way.

I needed to get to her.

Plowing forward, I grabbed a hold of one man's neck and twisted it until I heard the telltale *crack*. I watched his body slump onto the ground before moving on to the next one. Bullets rang. Kian and Basilio fought alongside me as we waded through the enemy—hitting, smashing, and destroying.

Blood coated my hands. My suit. My shoes.

Yelps and screams. Bones snapped. Necks broken. I was like a madman, fueled by sheer fear.

Until I reached Juliette.

The moment she was within my grasp, my heavy breathing eased, inhaling her sugarplum scent.

"Get in the circle," Kian barked. "And shoot them all."

"You good?" She nodded. "Give me your gun." She shoved it at me along with a new ammo clip.

I didn't hesitate. I shoved Juliette behind me as we circled her, our bodies creating a barrier that I could only hope would be enough to protect her. The shooting began, and while it felt like it went on for a long time, it couldn't have been more than five minutes.

Bodies piled up. Blood soaked the ground and the walls. Men started fleeing. Basilio was wounded. Kian sported a few bruises. River's breathing was irregular, but he remained calm. Darius took a bullet to his shoulder, his left sleeve soaked in blood. He must have given his Kevlar vest to Juliette. I'd owe him for life.

In one fluid motion, Juliette pushed her small body between me and Basilio, and before I could blink, she gave chase.

"Juliette!" I shouted, going after her as the rest of the crew shuffled behind, exhaustion and injury slowing them down.

My feet thundered against the ground, more footsteps behind me. Curses and grunts filled the air. I didn't need to turn around to know it was Basilio, Kian, and his men right behind us. A heavy steel door in front of us was ajar and Juliette shoved through it.

Why in the fuck was she chasing after them?

The door shut behind her and I cursed. I didn't like having her out of my sight. I shoved through just in time to see her lunge for the last man, the one who moved the slowest.

"You motherfucker," she hissed as she tackled him onto the ground. Jesus, she'd hit him like a linebacker. I watched as her fingers traveled down the man's body, lower and lower until it wrapped around the cold steel of the gun and she wrenched it free from his trousers.

Other men aimed their guns at her, but before they could move, bullets sounded. From my gun. Basilio's. All of ours. Men fell to the ground. But Juliette hadn't pulled her trigger. She had it aimed against the back of the guy's head, panting.

I let the other men keep an eye out for potential threats as I made my way to her. She didn't look away from the man on the ground.

"You fucking bastard." Her body was shaking but her hands were steady.

"Juliette," I called out softly. She didn't respond. What was it about this man that had her so worked up? I couldn't see his face. The only thing I could see from the back of his head was that he was older. "Wildling, look at me."

She didn't. I put my hand on her shoulder and it was only then that she raised her eyes. They were glazed. Fury and pain staring back at me. It hit me right in the chest. It fucking hurt. Worse than any beating I got from my mother. Worse than seeing my little brother in pain. Worse than anything else.

I tugged on her and pulled her to her feet. "Move and I'll make your death agonizingly long and painful," I told the man on the ground. Juliette stood slowly, as if her limbs were too heavy. Once on her feet, I pulled her back a couple of feet and said to the man on the ground, "Now turn around and get up."

He did, and the moment he was on his back, I recognized him. My gaze shifted to my wife who kept her gun trained on him.

"Edward Murphy," I stated in surprise. "Why are you working with Sophia Volkov?"

Ivy's father betrayed the Cullens. Her best friend's father. It was the information Kian had given her, although I wished he hadn't. He should have given it to me to take care of it. I should have sheltered her from this pain. Protected her.

"Who else?" Juliette asked, her voice calm. Too calm. The old man didn't answer and a shot pierced through the air. A bullet lodged itself into his knee. I didn't stop her. She needed this. "Who fucking else?" she hissed.

The old man's eyes locked on Juliette. Resigned. Tired. Old. "Just me."

Juliette's eyes darted to Kian. "His was the name in the envelope."

A terse nod. She turned back to Ivy's father. *Bang*.

Another shot. "Liar." Her voice was cold. Her expression even colder. Hate consumed her now. She believed her friend betrayed her. "Fucking liar. I'm going to end your line, just like you wanted to end the Cullens."

"Juliette," I spoke softly.

I cupped her face and made her look at me. Tears glimmered in her gaze. "Don't jump to conclusions."

"My wife lost her life because of her," Murphy stated, all the fighting seeming to have left him. "I had to protect my children."

"What do you mean?" Jerking herself out of my grip, she shifted her focus on the old Murphy and got into his face. "You have sons. You are powerful. They are feared and ruthless. The Irish kings. And you are scared of Sofia Volkov?"

"You mean the Irish pricks," I thought I heard Basilio mutter.

I ignored him, waiting for Murphy's answer. A heartbeat passed. Heavy. Traitorous.

"I had to protect my family. Just like your family protected you."

"What do you mean?" I demanded to know. "Your daughter lived with the Brennans while you schemed. You need to come clean or this won't end well. For anyone."

Edward growled, his eyes flashing with fury. "Don't you dare touch them. They are innocent. Liana especially."

I stilled. I thought the old Murphy only had one daughter. Glancing at Juliette, it was obvious she had the same thought.

"Who is Liana?" Juliette asked him eerily. When he made no move to answer, she got into his face. "Who. Is. Liana?"

"My other daughter." Murphy's tone was resigned. Tired. He knew his road had come to an end. "My illegitimate daughter."

Well, fuck me. Goddamn secrets all around us.

Juliette shook her head, anger crossing her expression. "Does Ivy know?"

He gulped. "She doesn't."

"You could have asked for help," she hissed, her breathing harsh. "You could have said something!"

"Aye, I could have," he admitted. "But I didn't."

Juliette swallowed and raised her hand. "You're only getting a fast death for Ivy's sake."

Then she pulled the trigger.

CHAPTER 56
Juliette

We made it out alive. Barely.

Back at the hotel room, I stared at my reflection in the bathroom. My hair was a matted mess. My face was covered in blood splatters. My clothes stained crimson. I was glad Dante was able to get us in through a back entrance. We would have never made it two feet into the lobby without all hell breaking loose.

I'd killed men before. Tortured them, even. Blood stained my hands, but it never felt like this before. I looked the same—more or less—but I didn't feel it.

I'd killed Ivy's father. My chest twisted, something ugly spreading through my veins.

Hate. Bitterness. *Regret?*

I didn't know. All I knew was that it felt heavy. It made it hard to breathe. Did Ivy know? Or was she truly clueless about who her father really was?

I placed my forehead against the mirror, leaving red smudges on it, and let the coolness of it soothe. But it didn't calm me, didn't make me feel better.

There were too many revelations. Too many thoughts swirling in my head.

Wynter and Basilio left shortly after we got back. Wynter was frantic when she saw us, and it took everything Basilio had to calm her down. Dante refused to leave me alone. He was stubborn, but so was I. I just couldn't bear anyone's company right now.

All the death, killings, the torturing—none of it bothered me. The revenge was sweet. But killing Ivy's father hit me all wrong. There was nothing sweet about it.

"Juliette."

Dante's voice came from behind me. I hadn't even heard him enter the bathroom over the ringing I still felt in my ears from the gunshots.

"Yes." My voice was distant. Resigned.

I didn't bother moving, the fatigue heavy in my bones and in my soul.

"Want me to start the shower for you?"

"Sure."

Truthfully, I wanted to crawl under the covers and fall into oblivion. A dreamless sleep. I wanted to forget. My thoughts were all over the place. The innocent girl I'd once been was now a killer. A sadistic killer.

God, I'm so tired. So fucking tired.

I wanted to be that little girl again who had no cares—no troubles—in the world and was thankful to a boy who saved her. A simple token of gratitude—a pink scrunchie.

He moved around the bathroom, his footsteps firm against the tile. The sound of plumbing and the rush of water. A shudder rolled down my spine. Cold and biting.

"Are you cold?"

"Yes. No. I don't know." I closed my eyes. I didn't think there was anything to warm me up from this. The chill had seeped deep into my bones.

His hands came to my shoulders and I tensed, my spine stiffening. "It's okay. I'm going to help you undress and then you can get in the shower." Another shiver. "Nothing else," he promised softly.

The backs of my eyes burned. Why did he have to be nice to me? It made my emotions bounce all over the place.

He carefully peeled my clothes off, piece by piece, his touch tender. My throat squeezed and so did my chest. Maybe all the killings, starting with Brandon Dole and ending with Ivy's father, had finally caught up to me. Although I still didn't feel an ounce of guilt over killing Brandon nor Sam. In fact, I felt no remorse over killing anyone. But Ivy's father...

"Okay, it's on the warmer side." He pulled me away from the mirror and led me to the shower. "If it's too hot, let me know and I can adjust it."

I stepped under the spray and felt... nothing.

A heavy sigh filled the bathroom. It was Dante's. He kicked off his shoes, then his ruined suit coat. Still fully clothed, he stepped into the shower and started washing me. First my hair. Then my body. His movements were methodical. His eyes were sharp on me, ensuring I wouldn't lose my shit and fall into a full-blown panic attack.

But I didn't. There was nothing left. I was just empty. Hollow.

Ten minutes later, I was clean. He dried me off and dressed me in pajamas like I was a child.

"Right leg," he instructed. I did what he said, slipping my foot into the soft material. "Left leg." I repeated the motion. "Hands up."

I sighed and put them up so he could slide a shirt down my body. Then he reached for a glass of water and two little white pills.

When I sought out his gaze, he said, "Ibuprofen."

I nodded, placing them on my tongue and downing the entire glass.

"Okay, now to bed."

He didn't have to say it twice. I crawled under the covers and he tucked them around me. Kind of like Liam used to do when I was a little girl.

When I was innocent.

I squeezed my eyelids shut. "I'm not going to sleep with you," I rasped, my voice barely above a whisper.

"I'll be on the couch," he stated matter-of-factly. Like him sleeping on the couch was the most natural thing in the world. "Get some sleep. I'm going to take a shower."

I didn't answer. It took too much effort. My body was too fatigued. My mind too clouded.

The blackness threatened to swallow me whole.

Images flashed through my mind. Some that I'd lived through and others that my imagination conjured up. The thug in the alley. Dante saving me. The rape. Dante, there again. My parents as they burned. Dad as he saved me.

I awoke with a start, the sheets stuck to my sweaty skin. Catching my breath, I slowly opened my eyes to find Dante sleeping on the couch. The moon dusted its glow over his beautiful face, and I found myself wishing I could see his dark eyes shimmering like the sky that currently ruled the night. His arms were folded over his chest and he had his feet up on the coffee table, right next to his handgun.

Guilt pinched my chest, but I ignored it. I wasn't prepared to forgive and forget.

Shifting on the hotel bed, my eyes caught on the letters Dante had given me. They sat waiting on the nightstand, right next to the envelope from Kian, unopened. It was a moot point to open Kian's envelope, but it wasn't too late for Dante's.

I reached over and took them. Keeping my movements soft, I slowly unfolded the first letter. To my surprise, it was addressed to me.

Juliette Brennan.

The little girl who said she'd save me one day. It should have been funny, except that it wasn't. She didn't know she was saving me from the moment she handed me that ridiculous scrunchie.

In the days that were dark, it kept me sane. That vibrant, happy color. I kept it in a safe place and only dug it out when I needed the reminder.

I still have your pink scrunchie, Juliette.

The moment I saw you again—first dancing on top of the bar in The Eastside and then in my casino—I knew you were the one for me. Your mouth. Your smile. And your eyes... they are my heaven and hell. My happiness and torment. My desire and emptiness.

If I have to move heaven and hell, Juliette, one day you'll be mine.

And I'll be yours.

I stared at the letters, glowing under the light of the full moon. My eyes flickered to Dante's sleeping face, then back to the words that opened something within me I couldn't quite distinguish.

Was it forgiveness? I shook my head. No, it couldn't be. Was it love? I didn't know. But it was strong and feral. Consuming. It terrified me with its intensity. The boy who saved me. I promised to save him too, and all I had done was give him a hard time. Maybe it was time to start afresh—for both of our sakes.

Taking a lungful of air, I breathed out as I unfolded the next letter and started reading. And then more letters followed. They spoke of his most secret thoughts, admissions about his feelings that I doubted he would ever voice out loud. Then there was the one about his mother and I wanted to cry for the little boy who had suffered so much. It explained a lot about who he was, and why he did the things that he did.

It wasn't until the first rays of dawn flickered through the window that I finished reading the last of them.

Unfolding it slowly my eyes skimmed the pages.

To my wildling wife.

I finally have you.

It feels like heaven but also hell. I fear our time will be limited and you will hate me once you learn what I have done. I hope you never will, but I learned a long time ago "hope" wasn't for the likes of me.

You're the one thing I can't bear to lose. The one thing I've clung to for all these years.

You see, I'm fucked up. Whether I was born this way or my mother made me this way, I'll never know. In my life, there were rare things and a few special people I got attached to. My grandfather's gifts were some of those things. My brother was one of those people. And my mother took enjoyment in torturing me by destroying those things, especially the people I loved.

The girl with a pink scrunchie saved me. She gave me strength as she handed me that little pink piece of cloth and elastic. If a girl could promise to save me, I could surely save my brother and myself too. From the ghosts of the past to the terrors of the present. It was your simple strength that gave me mine to do something I should have done a long time ago. I made sure that my mother could never hurt us again. I killed her for all the wrongs she had done.

To my little brother. To me.

But certain wounds were too deep. Christian has been dealing in his own way. And I... well, you were my way of dealing. You became my obsession but also my love. It started as a fond kind of affection for a little girl. But then, it matured into a deep love, slowly but surely, as our paths kept crossing, like fate was making sure we'd find each other again.

This will be my last letter. I want to enjoy every second of you. I'll enjoy this taste of heaven for as long as I can, so I'll remember it through the days of hell that I know are bound to come. Some things are inevitable—like the truth.

I hope at least part of you will know that I never intended to hurt you. You're my most cherished possession even though I can never own such a magnificently independent woman. But know this, you own my heart.

I love you. Remember that when the times are hard.

Your Dante.

P.S. That bedroom furniture will never arrive. I bought out the company and canceled your order.

I swallowed, then folded the letter back up—carefully—like it was the heart of a fragile little boy. Maybe it was. My eyes traveled to my husband and saw an entirely different man sleeping on the couch. He looked the same. He smelled the same. But there was something fundamentally different.

Not something. Someone. *Me.*

I slid out of the bed and padded barefoot across the room toward him. The closer I got, the stronger his scent was. Calming. Soothing. I leaned over and put my hand on his shoulder and he jerked, reaching for his weapon.

"It's me," I murmured softly.

He blinked, sleep still heavy in his eyes. "Is everything okay?"

I nodded. "The bed is big enough for both of us." I tugged on him, his eyes suspicious as he looked at me. Maybe he thought I'd kill him. We'd probably end up killing each other in the end, so he probably had reason to eye me warily. "I haven't forgiven you for drugging me. I haven't forgotten that you asked my father rather than me for my hand in marriage." I tilted my head pensively. "It would have been nice to just date for a while. But we'll deal with that tomorrow. Or the day after." I pulled on his arm again. "For now, let's just get some sleep."

It was the least I could do.

CHAPTER 57
Juliette

A heavy floral scent lingered in the air.

It smelled nice but not as good as the rain and forest one that I had grown accustomed to. I blinked against the sunlight pouring through the windows and slowly the hotel room came into focus.

"What the—"

Yellow daisies filled my hotel room on every conceivable surface. It felt like the sun had crawled into this space and just decided to shine in here. I inhaled deeply, my eyes fluttering shut. It used to be my favorite scent until I ran into Dante. Now I longed for the green, herbaceous scent that lingered on his skin.

"Are we ready for breakfast?" came a familiar voice.

My eyes shot open to find Dante leaning against the wall, his hands in his pockets, watching me with that glimmering gaze I had grown accustomed to.

The boy who'd kept my hot-pink scrunchie. The boy who saved me.

But also a boy who drugged you, my mind warned.

My brows furrowed. I didn't want to think about that right now. I wanted to enjoy the gesture.

"Did you do all this?" I asked instead.

He nodded. "Your favorite flower."

"Stalker," I murmured, but I couldn't keep the smile from my face.

He grinned. "You know it." Then his expression turned serious. "It's the first day." When I raised my eyebrow in question, he continued to explain, "It's the first day of the rest of our lives. I'll court you." I couldn't hold back a soft chuckle to which he rolled his eyes. "I'll wine and dine you. We'll take it slow, and I'll show you that we fit. You and me, we were meant to be. You belong to me and I belong to you. Like cacti belong in the desert. Like flowers belong to spring. Inevitable."

I pulled my knees to my chest and studied him. The silence filled the yellow space and set my nerve endings on edge. His words resonated deep inside me. When I was with him, I felt at peace. He was home. Longing and belonging wrapped in my heart, my soul, and my life. So why did I not say anything?

"So, hungry?" he asked again and I nodded. It took three minutes for him to have a cart full of food rolled into the room, along with orange juice, cranberry juice, and apple juice.

When the waiter left, I couldn't help but tease, "That drink assortment is for children. We should have gotten mimosas."

"You won't find me drinking mimosas," he remarked dryly, making a plate. "Besides, you gave up alcohol. Remember?"

Unintentionally, he brought something up that now filled the air with tension, stretching the oxygen thin. But I couldn't let it ruin *us*.

My brows furrowed. It was the first time that I truly thought about us as an item. All our secrets were out in the open. Most of our ghosts had been laid to rest.

He handed me a plate full of my favorite foods. Parfait. Eggs Benedict. Mixed fruit cup.

"You're going to eat with me too, right?" I didn't want to eat alone.

"If you want me to." I nodded and he made himself a plate. It was one thing I'd learned. Dante always had an appetite. The two of us started eating in a weirdly comfortable silence. It was still tense, but it was pleasant.

I peered under my lashes at him. He was uncharacteristically quiet, seeming lost in his thoughts.

"I read your letters," I said softly.

Dante's shoulders tensed and he stilled before he drew his eyes up to meet mine. Something lifted the darkness behind his gaze. Something volatile. Raw.

Oh. He was letting me see his vulnerability.

It was something I wasn't accustomed to seeing on him. He always hid behind his smirk and layers upon layers of arrogance. Seeing this side of him put me on edge.

"So where do we go from here?" I asked, since he remained silent.

A sad smile curved his lips. "You tell me, Wildling."

I swallowed, pain hollow in my chest. When I didn't say anything, unable to find my voice, he asked, "Do you want to end this?"

A shudder rippled down my spine. An invisible blade lodged itself between my ribs and refused to budge.

"What if I said yes?" I croaked.

Dante's usual mask slipped for a flicker of a second before it was back on, hiding even a hint of whatever emotion my answer created.

"Please, Wildling, give us a chance," he said softly. His throat was flexing with a hard swallow. His eyes flickered with longing as they searched my face for something I wanted to give. I really did, but I couldn't get past the fact that he drugged me.

Drugged me!

"I can't," I rasped, wrapping my arms around myself, chilled to the bone. My pulse roared through my veins. Pain slashed through my body. "Everything is so fucked up. I have more people to find and kill. And I'm just—"

Tired. Disheartened. Alone.

"I'll help you." My eyes found his, nothing but sincerity there. "You want to kill those motherfuckers? I'll help you find every single one of those men and tear them to pieces."

Staring at him, I felt like I'd lived a hundred lifetimes, and I hadn't even lived a quarter of a century. Maybe Wynter was right. I kept too many things unsaid. And it wasn't helping anyone, including myself.

"You stole my free will," I rasped. "When you drugged me, you stole *me*. You took my right to consent, to function, to defend myself. Just like those—" My voice cracked. The comparison didn't feel right despite everything that had happened. Dante never forced himself physically. "I can forgive a lot, but drugging me... It's hard for me to forgive it. I killed those boys who drugged me."

And Dante killed Travis. For me. He made him suffer. He tortured him. For me.

"Do you want to kill me, Juliette?" The tone of his voice indicated he'd let me kill him if it meant my peace and well-being. Except, it wouldn't bring me peace. It'd hurt just as much. No, scratch that. It'd hurt even more.

"No, I don't want to kill you." He became too important to me. I didn't know when or how, but he found his way so deep inside my head and my soul, it'd be impossible to live without him. "There's been too much killing." I swallowed, the admission suffocating me. "I killed my best friend's father," I whispered.

Dante exhaled a heavy breath, his brows drawn tight over his eyes. "And I killed my mother."

I opened my mouth, then closed it, unable to find words. Although in my humble opinion, she seemed to deserve it.

"Is it because she hurt you and Priest?" I asked eventually, my heart squeezing for the two little boys I'd met in those letters. He nodded. "Why didn't your father help?"

He stared out the window, his face stony. "He was busy running the Syndicate and Chicago. He was rarely around, and when he was, he was absent. It's the DiLustro curse. Obsessing over women we cannot have."

Bitterness laced his voice.

My appetite gone, I pushed my plate aside.

"You drugged me," I breathed. "I just can't—" Move past it. Forgive. Forget.

Dante flinched. "I wish I could turn back time and change what I did," he said hoarsely. "I never meant to hurt you." My chest ached. For him. For me. It made it hard to breathe. Determination crossed his face. "But I'm not giving you up."

"What if we're just not meant to be?"

Dante's chest heaved like he couldn't get enough air into his lungs. "We *are* meant to be. You and me. Why would fate keep throwing us at each other?" I shook my head, unsure. Hesitantly. "You saved me,

Wildling. Just like you said you would. But not from the bullet. You saved me from the darkness."

His eyes met mine, his face full of determination. He stood up and made his way to the door.

Without looking back, he called over his shoulder at me. "I have men watching the hotel. You'll hear from me, wife. I'll make it up to you." He turned to face me. "I'll wait until you trust me again."

And with that, he left me.

CHAPTER 58

Juliette

Three boys who started my nightmare. A single man who ended it
—my husband.

~~Brandon Dole~~

~~Sam Dallas~~

~~Travis Xander~~

The Russians who destroyed my birth family.

~~Petar Soroko~~

~~Raslan Rugoff~~

~~Igor Bogomolov~~

~~Yan Yablochkov~~

~~Vlad Ketrov~~

~~Nikola Chekov~~

~~Jovanov Plotnick~~

~~Edward Murphy~~

Sofia Volkov—not yet dead, but will be very soon. One last name
remained an enigma.

Dante lived up to his promise.

And it was a promise, not a threat. It had been over a month since I left his mansion and came to stay at the hotel. A month since I'd killed my best friend's father.

Dante, Kian, and his team kept the news from spreading but I knew, deep down in my gut, I knew Sofia Volkov probably watched the entire thing. And one day, she'd use it. Against me. Against our family.

I knew it was something that shouldn't be kept from Ivy. Yet I did. She called me to tell me her father was dead and she cried. She fucking cried and I said nothing. I was the worst friend. The worst fucking person on this planet.

A knock sounded on my door and I jumped off the bed, running to it.

I swung the door open, coming face-to-face with my husband. "Now you're knocking, huh?"

He grinned. "Anything for my bride."

A bouquet of yellow roses and a gift.

For the past month, he came over every day armed with flowers and gifts, twice a day. He was over for breakfast and for dinner, following the routine we had when we moved in with each other after the wedding. And he always brought different yellow flowers and a gift that reminded me of something.

A full bowl of pink scrunchies wrapped with a pink bow. The deed to his casino, which I refused to accept and he refused to take back. Jewelry. A brand-new knife.

"It's sharper and easier to use," he stated, then offered to practice with me.

Then he gifted me a pink crystal-covered handgun of all things, then took me to a gun range where we practiced shooting.

I set the flowers into the vase that I already had waiting for them. He'd spoiled me now. If he ever showed up without flowers, I'd think something was wrong and he no longer loved me. It'd kill me.

My movements froze.

Holy fuck! It'd kill me. I needed his love, but he also needed mine. Slowly, I turned around meeting his eyes and the flowers were forgotten.

He loves me and I love him.

Those words whispered over and over again. *He loves me.* The words I never wanted him to retract. The words I never acknowledged. More importantly, I loved him. So fucking much that it blinded me.

He handed me the gift. "Don't buy me any more gifts," I scolded him for the millionth time. I didn't care about the expensive gifts. The small ones hit me in the chest. I tore the wrapping off the box and a small gasp tore from my lips.

It was a toy. A toy car that mirrored the one I smashed—and had repaired—but instead of it being empty, there were two little figures sitting in it.

"You and I," he rasped. "Driving into the sunset."

My resolve weakened. It evaporated into the atmosphere. Our gazes met and so many emotions flickered in his that my chest squeezed until I thought it would burst.

I struggled to forgive him for drugging me, but I suffered right alongside him. I wanted so badly to trust him. To never doubt him. My reason said he wouldn't do something like that again, but my heart feared. It barricaded itself so he wouldn't disappoint me.

"What if you don't get something you want from me again?" I blurted out my worries. "How can I be sure you won't force it on me?" I needed to know. "Like, what about babies? Will you switch my birth control if I say I don't want them?"

"Juliette." Dante's voice cracked. He fell down onto his knees and his big hands came to my hips, pulling me to him. The hope in his eyes cracked my heart. "The only thing I want is you. Just you. I will never—fucking ever—do anything to hurt you again."

There was such raw emotion in his voice that goose bumps rose on my skin. He bared his soul, letting me see it in his eyes. Every single fragile piece.

I might be a fool, but I believed him. I fell down to my knees, putting my gift next to us, and wrapped my arms around him, burying my face in the crook of his neck. His scent drove shudders of desire and so much love through me that I thought I'd burst.

I love him. I loved him so fucking much that it hurt. Maybe I fell for him when he killed Travis for me. Or maybe when I was a little girl and he was a tall, handsome boy who rescued me. I didn't know. I didn't care.

All I knew was that I couldn't live without him. He felt right. He drove me nuts, but he also made me feel safe.

I didn't care how long I'd loved him, I just knew that I did. My nights were lonely without him. The bed was too cold.

"You're a jackass for drugging me, but you're nothing like the ones that hurt me," I murmured, cupping his face.

His face hardened and the darkness that plagued all the men of the underworld flickered across his expression. Unforgiving and hard.

"I'd kill them all over again," he rasped, and I knew he would. That was who Dante was. Relentless and stubborn, almost to a fault. "I just want to make you happy."

My pulse accelerated as we drowned in each other's gazes. A tear rolled down my cheek, then another one.

"I love you," I whispered. There were so many feelings dancing in my lungs, bouncing off the walls. "So fucking much that it scares me."

He froze, his eyes glimmering like black diamonds. "What?"

The rasp of his voice sent shivers down my back.

"I love you, Dante." I inched closer to him, inhaling his scent deep into the marrow of my bones. "I don't know when it happened or how it happened. But I know that living without you would kill me. You love me at my worst. I hope you'll love me at my best. At least as my better self."

Another tear rolled down my cheek. The weight lifted from my chest with my admission. My stubbornness and hate had made me blind. I should have seen it long ago. I fell for him hard.

"Do you know how long I've waited to hear you say that?" A sob tore from my throat. It was silly to be so shaken up about it, yet here I was. It felt like I'd come to an earth-shattering revelation. "Jesus, I love you so much that being without you physically hurts. It hurts." Another sob wrecked me. Concern was etched between his brows, he watched me worriedly. He brought our faces close together, the tip of our noses brushing together. "Why are you crying, Wildling?"

I sank into him, wrapping my arms around him and gripping him to me for dear life.

"I don't know." I buried my face in his chest and inhaled his scent deep into my lungs. He smelled so good. So warm. *So mine.* His embrace made me feel safe. "I missed you. I might be becoming a wimp."

We must have looked ridiculous. He was dressed in his typical three-piece suit. I was wearing a casual midi dress in his favorite color. Blue.

"I missed you, Wildling."

I'd seen him every day for the past month, but it wasn't the same. We didn't touch. We didn't kiss. We talked. He took me out on dates. We were getting to know each other. I was with him, but it wasn't the same as *being* with him.

"We've seen each other every day," I pointed out, sniffling.

All this time, I'd been afraid to let him into my heart. But truthfully, I'd hurt myself in the process too. I'd believed myself too vulnerable to love, but what I failed to see was that letting myself experience it could also make me stronger.

"It's not enough." Dante pulled away an inch and tilted my chin up, his eyes boring into mine. "I want you with me every day, all day. All night. I want to burn with you."

I swallowed hard. It was time.

I was ready for him.

"I want to go home."

CHAPTER 59
Dante

She loves me.

Nothing and nobody mattered but those three little words. From her. My little wildling wife.

Trouble and happiness became one and the same for me. The devil in disguise. A fallen angel with broken wings. The two of us—ruined, untamed, and desperate for each other.

It was who Juliette DiLustro was. And she was mine. I broke every single traffic rule speeding from the hotel across town back to our home, holding her hand in mine. When I had to shift the gears in my grandfather's car, I put her palm on my thigh, and to my fucking delight, she left it there.

I scooped her up into my arms the moment we jumped out of the car. She giggled, the soft melodious sounds warming my chest. It was the only thing I wanted and cared about.

My wife's happiness and contentment. That made me happy.

"I feel like a bride," she remarked, smiling. Her face was buried in the crook of my neck, her lips skimming across my skin.

We barely made it through our bedroom door when I couldn't hold back anymore. I slammed it behind me with my foot, then crushed my lips to hers. She moaned. I grunted. A shudder rolled through me. The kiss was deep, fierce and consuming. Desperate.

She dragged a hand down my body and fisted the hem of my shirt in her grip. Pulling slightly away, her blue eyes met mine, shining brightly like stars in a clear night sky. Her lips were swollen and slightly parted.

"W-what?" she questioned, her lips back on my neck and moving as she murmured, "Please don't tell me you want to take it slow now. I might burst."

A choked laugh escaped me. She was the only one who could make me laugh. I wrapped my hand around her long hair and pulled her back so I could see her eyes. Her expression. Our faces were so close I could see her dilated pupils and the blush warming her cheeks.

"Do you need to take it slow?" I grunted. "We have all the time in the world."

Beneath my fingers, her body quivered. My hard cock strained against the zipper of my pants. And my heart... Jesus Christ... it thumped erratically in my chest. Needing this. Needing *her*. That organ had been beating in my chest only for her for as long as I could remember.

She shook her head. "No, I don't need to take it slow," she whispered, leaning into my touch as I grazed my thumb down the length of her throat before sweeping it back up, caressing her.

"Do you want to cuff me?" I offered. Her breath hitched and satisfaction curled through me, a pleasure wrought from the darkest depths of hell until it felt like heaven. In my entire life, I had never been cuffed until she came into my world. I feared if I ever got arrested, I'd get a boner because it would remind me of her.

"No cuffs," she murmured, her grip on the fabric tightening. "Let's see what you can do with your hands, husband."

I hissed out a breath at the coy flirtation. God, this woman! She was brave, strong, loyal. Everything I needed.

I sat down on the bed, Juliette on my lap.

"If you change your mind, you tell me." When she blinked her lustful eyes in confusion, I added, "About cuffing me."

Then I captured her mouth again, stealing her breath away. Just the way she stole my heart. I wanted to own her. Possess all her moans and shudders.

My free hand traveled down her back, sinking south to the base of her spine. I squeezed her ass and then twisted her around, yanking her blue dress over her head. She took initiative and did the same with her tights, yanking them off. It left her in a bra and panties, looking like temptation.

My wife.

"Your clothes," she murmured. "Off." She didn't have to say it twice. Shifting her onto our bed, she watched me, kneeling and waiting. The sight was so fucking submissive, it made my balls ache. I had never stripped off so fast in my entire life. A small smile played around her lips, and when I raised my eyebrow, she said, "I have never seen anyone strip so efficiently."

I leaned forward and nipped her bottom lip, my hands coming around her back and unclipping her bra. "That's me, Wildling. Efficient. Now, get rid of your panties."

She shifted on the bed and took her panties off. On her hands and knees, I couldn't resist tapping her ass with the palm of my hand. Not hard, but strong enough to leave a mark on her pale skin.

Her moan shattered the silence in the room. She didn't jump to her feet. Didn't hide her ass from me. Instead, I watched in amazement as her ass pinkened, pushing back into my touch.

She turned her head, meeting my gaze over her shoulder. "Again."

"What?" I husked in surprise. Her shoulders trembled when I leaned forward, draping my front over her spine. Her mouth curved into a smirk. The dare burned in her blue eyes. *Kiss me. Ruin me. Love me.*

"Don't make me repeat myself," she said, her tone husky. Tempting. Her ass thrust back into the palm of my hand. "Again."

The temptation was like liquid heat in my veins. The skin tightened across my back and my cock throbbed with the raw need. Precum glistened on the tip of my shaft, ready for her tight pussy. I feared my control would snap.

I spanked her round, rosy ass again. Another moan. I could come, just from this. Her sounds and the visual of my handprint on it.

She glanced over her shoulder, her gaze trailing down my body and lingering on my cock. Her blue eyes darkened.

"I love you, Dante. I want to burn with you. Feel you. Talk to you. Sleep with you. Just you." Fuck. With my head pounding—both of them

—I slipped my hand, fingers spread wide, over her throat. I angled her head to the left and then trailed my mouth over the sensitive skin behind her ear. A shudder tore through her, and her head fell forward with a moan.

"I love you, Wildling. It's always been you."

My cock pressed against her ass and she ground against it while I tugged her earlobe between my teeth, then lower, a bite to the juncture of her throat and shoulder. A shuddering moan slipped from her lips and her hips rocked backward against my hand. Needy and wanting.

For me. Just for me.

"Don't move," I ordered.

But, Juliette being Juliette, she flipped her hair over one shoulder and the fire in her eyes challenged me. Taunted me.

"Or what?"

I wrapped my fist around her strands, tugging her so close that her lips parted beneath mine.

"Or I'll stop." Although truthfully, I didn't think I could.

Her lips curved in a dazzling smile. The kind she never fucking gave me.

"You said you'll make me happy," she drawled, her tone breathless. "If you stop, that won't make me happy."

Deliberately, I lingered for a few heartbeats, baiting her, tempting her, torturing us both, before growling, "I'm going to bend you over and turn your ass red."

Her cheeks flushed bright red. "Promises, promises." She wiggled her ass, then shifted around. "Want me to get in position and wait?"

My mouth dried as I watched her climb onto the pillows and push her ass up in the air. Tinted pink. Her glistening pussy in my full view. It was mine for the taking. She was mine.

"Burn with me, Dante," she begged, licking her lips. Fuck. I couldn't resist her. I'd burn with her at the expense of the entire world. Nothing and nobody mattered to me—just her. She asked me to burn with her and I'd do just that.

My hands on her hips, I admired the beautiful view. My handprint on her ass. Her graceful back arched. The view called to the raw part of me that wanted only her. She belonged only to me.

Mine to pleasure, mine to take, and mine to ruin.

Keeping my legs spread, I dragged her ass backward and a small gasp tore from her lips when her ass brushed against my rock-hard erection. Sweeping my hands down the length of her smooth legs. Then I brought them around, hungry to feel every single inch of her body under my palms.

She was breathing heavily. My mouth against her ear, I whispered my praise. "You're so beautiful, Wildling. And all mine." She whimpered. "I'm going to touch every inch of you." I brought my fingers around and took her peaked nipple between them, pinching the sensitive nub. She moaned, low and throaty. "You will tell me if you get scared. Understood?"

Her answering whimper shattered through me. It wasn't fear. It was pure, raw lust.

Flicking her nipple one last time, I flattened my hand and skimmed the length of her stomach. She had a beautiful body, made for fucking. My hands trailed over her abdominal muscles, then the curves of her waist. Her desperate gasp when I bypassed her pussy and trailed my fingers down her inner thigh was her only complaint.

It surprised me because patience and Juliette didn't belong in the same room. If my balls didn't ache so badly, I'd laugh. There was something so raw about Juliette trusting me to reward her.

I traced my fingers back up, up, up, so close to where we both wanted them, before veering south all over again. A frustrated noise vibrated in her throat but no other words came.

"What do you want?" I murmured. I brushed my mouth over her hot skin, the back of her neck, then her spine. She whimpered and moaned, grinding against me, but she didn't answer.

"Cat got your tongue?" I moved my hand from her thigh and slapped her lightly against her aching pussy. Right above her clit. She screamed my name. "Tell me," I demanded.

Her entire body shuddered. "Your hand... on my pussy," she whimpered.

I cupped her core, easing the burn. She was drenching my fingers. I could feel her throbbing for my cock. I dipped my fingers through her wetness, feeling her walls clench around them.

"P-please," she said, her head falling back.

I pulled out my fingers and brought them to her plump lips. "Taste yourself."

She obeyed immediately, her lips parting and her tongue flicking against them as she wrapped her mouth around my fingers and sucked them deep.

A groan reverberated through my chest. I fucking wanted her mouth on my cock, but I wouldn't last. I wanted her pleasure first. She ground down, her ass circling over my crotch. Pulling my fingers out of her mouth, I reached down for her pussy again. My wet fingers found her clit, applying pressure, circling it faster and harder.

Then I plunged two fingers deep inside her. "Dante," she moaned. "Oh... my... God."

I curled my fingers within her. Pressed my thumb down on her clit. A cry wrestled from her throat and I knew it'd be my end.

"Please, Dante," she pleaded. "I want you inside me."

I pulled my fingers away, then flipped her over on her back and lined her pussy up with my cock. I slid myself against her drenched folds, her heat tempting me. Her hips arched, dipping the tip of it into her greedy pussy.

She held my gaze. No traces of panic. No ghosts. Just her and I.

Her nod was all the assurance I needed. Her hands around me, her fingernails at my back, I thrust inside her, filling her to the hilt. My groan. Her moan. Our tortured souls.

"Fuck, you feel so good," I grunted. Her eyes were still on me, half-lidded and full of lust. "Ready?"

"Please, yes," she whimpered and I was lost.

I gripped her throat and started moving. I pulled out, only to slam into her again. The only sound filling the space was flesh against flesh, both of us lost in each other and speechless. She felt like heaven, the closest I'd ever get to God. I fucked her so hard, I feared I'd break her.

I watched in amazement as Juliette shuddered beneath me, her pleasure-glazed eyes on me, urging me to go faster and deeper.

Until I fell apart right alongside my wife.

Because the two of us... we belonged together. The two of us, we fit perfectly.

Epilogue

JULIETTE - FIVE YEARS LATER

St. Jean d'Arc School opening.

Happiness was family. But most of all, my husband and our own little world that revolved around the two of us and our son.

Unlike Wynter who went on to have three children, Dante and I agreed on one. There were rare occasions where we'd wish for another, but then Dante and I would visit Wynter and that wish quickly dissipated. Our two-year-old, Romeo, had plenty of cousins to play with, so he certainly didn't feel lonely.

The sound of the music and laughter floated through the air. The breeze blew through my hair, and I took in the scene around me. The large school grounds were filled with visitors and interested parties.

Next to me, our son was high on my husband's shoulders, the spitting image of his father. Big dark eyes. Dark brown hair. Smart as a whip and already slightly arrogant. It was in the DiLustro genes apparently; it just couldn't be helped. I watched as Romeo reached down with his chubby hands and pulled on his father's hair.

Dante winced and it made me grin.

Romeo was the apple of our eye. Dante adored our baby boy and he loved me. Even when I was annoying, stubborn, blind to see the obvious, he always loved me. And true to his vow, he had never gone behind my back again.

When he wanted a baby, we talked about it. When I wanted to kill someone, we talked about it. Life wasn't just good. It was fucking amazing.

Dante's eyes met mine and a soft smile curved his lips. He bent his head and kissed me softly, taking my hand in his. That sexy smirk I used to hate, now I couldn't live without it.

"I'm so damn happy," he said softly. "You causing trouble at my casino was the best day of my life."

I chuckled softly. It was a crazy road, but somehow it all worked out. For the best.

"You and Romeo are the best part of my life," I murmured softly against his cheek.

"I love you," we both uttered at the same time.

He never let me go a day without hearing those three sweet little words. And I ensured I did the same.

After all, I made him wait two years, and wait he did.

What's Next?

Thank you so much for reading **Devious Kingpin**! If you liked it, please leave a review. Your support means the world to me.

If you're thirsty for more discussions with other readers of the series, you can join the Facebook group, Eva's Soulmates group (https://bit.ly/3gHEe0e).

About the Author

Curious about Eva's other books? You can check them out here. Eva Winners' Books https://bit.ly/3SMMsrN

Eva Winners writes anything and everything romance, from enemies to lovers to books with all the feels. Her heroes are sometimes villains because they need love too. Right? Her books are sprinkled with a touch of suspense, mystery, a healthy dose of angst, a hint of violence and darkness, and lots of steamy passion.

When she's not working and writing, she spends her days either in Croatia or Maryland daydreaming about the next story.

Find Eva below:

Visit www.evawinners.com and subscribe to my newsletter.
FB group: https://bit.ly/3gHEe0e
FB page: https://bit.ly/30DzP8Q
Insta: http://Instagram.com/evawinners
BookBub: https://www.bookbub.com/authors/eva-winners
Amazon: http://amazon.com/author/evawinners
Goodreads: http://goodreads.com/evawinners
Tiktok: https://vm.tiktok.com/ZMeETK7pq/

Made in United States
North Haven, CT
13 January 2025

64389857R00219